Invitation from a Mobster

Jiří Ovečka

Clink
Street

Published by Clink Street Publishing 2022

Copyright © 2022

First edition.

From the original Czech language "Pozvánka od mafiána" translated by
Veronika Šuranská and Joshua Jones

Illustrations inside the book by Pavel Cupák

ISBNs:
978-1-914498-43-5 Paperback
978-1-914498-44-2 Ebook

I dedicate this novel to my Eva, without whom I would have never written this tale. I hope she will forgive me for all my crazy antics, this novel being the peak of it all, in which I even kill her.

Preface
Dream of the Chinese Empire
and its glorious rebirth

Beijing, the Year of the Serpent – 2001. An insignificant day, an insignificant month, yet a significant event. One member of the Central Military Committee lay dead at home in his bathtub. The bathroom door and window were both locked from the inside.

Information for the general public: heart failure.

Reality: either suicide with an unknown motive, or an inexplicable murder. The face and body were covered in slashes from a razor and the eyes had been gouged out. The commissioner's facial expression was one filled with terror and suffering, the mirror covered in blood, as if running the suicide itself on repeat. His hands being covered in gore with the doors locked from the inside, suggested that he really had to have done this alone. The act was never explained. According to the official report, nothing had been stolen, nothing had disappeared, and nothing had been overlooked.

The following day, four people – three members of the Central Military Commission, along with Major Li C'cheng, met in Beijing at dusk on a strictly confidential address under strict safety measures. They called themselves "the Supremes". No names. They came together in the dark, soberly, with all cell phones turned off and all reception-interference devices turned on.

Major Li C'cheng was drumming his fingers on the table nervously. He was upset. Completely disgusted and annoyed. Why did it have to come to this? He had given them several warnings.

The first Supreme: "Were you able to unlock the safe?"

The second Supreme: "Yes, it's not there. I looked through it myself. The decree has disappeared."

A long silence.

The first Supreme: "The situation is beyond awful. What is to be done? Is anyone at least aware of the exact wording?"

The fourth Supreme – Major Li C'cheng: "I am aware of it, but not word-for-word. By heart, I will try to write it down, but it will not be an exact transcription, certainly not."

More silence followed. Then the Major promptly spoke, all of his disgust pouring out like an eruption: "You fucked up. Why didn't you destroy the decree? And since you didn't destroy it, why didn't you at least make a copy of it?"

The third Supreme: "Yes, we screwed up. Screwed up. But I'm asking you, who would have guessed that it would come to this? Now, we have to try and fix it, as quickly and as effectively as possible. Otherwise, we are putting the future of the entire Middle Empire at risk."

"After all, the Edict of Emperor Guangxu clearly said that it will occur in the year of the Serpent – why didn't you pay attention to this information?" said Major Li C'cheng, persisting in his objections. He was aware of how daring this statement was. His position was lower than anyone else present. While the others were the highest ranked officials of the Chinese People's Liberation Army, he was actually no more than an insignificant major. But together, the fates of hundreds of millions of people rested in their hands. From one angle, he had them in the palm of his hand, he was the only one who could fix the situation – but even so, he was simply furious. They were the ones who had killed his child. He was the one, who had discovered the Edict. He was the one who had uncovered everything. He had warned them of all the pitfalls and risks. And were they doing? Nothing. They were simply sitting on their fat behinds, doing nothing at all. Then they had the nerve to be worried sick that they would lose everything. Not only the chairs they were sitting on but everything. Worse still, they would destroy the whole Middle Kingdom. Rooting through the hardly-seen archives of the Forbidden City, Major Li C'cheng had something of an advantage – he was also a genealogist, even though it was only a hobby to him. Hobby or no, this little practice gave him access to almost anything. Anything!

A sort of burning anger and aggression emanated from his unnaturally long face, more powerful still given his stern attitude – or at least seating position – of a soldier. He had very little hair despite being only thirty-nine years old, but this didn't seem to bother him. He could care less. This, combined with the look in his captivating eyes, made it clear that their hands were full with an incredibly hard headed, merciless, and self-centred individual, who always needed clearly defined targets ahead and he was then willing to sacrifice everything, even his life, for these targets. If he abandoned a target, it was only because he had already achieved it. Despite this, C'cheng needed to have another task in sight, lest his life wind into complete chaos, hopelessness and nothingness.

His special position as an exploratory officer allowed him, as a soldier, to move unusually freely throughout the People's Republic of China. On top of this, whatever he needed, he got, wherever he may have been. No problem for him to have a motorised unit or even heavy machinery at his disposal. He only had to justify his actions to one member of the Central Military Commission in the Southern Chinese province of Jiangxi – the leader of the entire Chinese Army. Code name Wu Kuang was the only means Li C'cheng had of contacting him directly, possibly in front of the whole committee, though only in theory. This had never happened before. Every member of the Committee had done everything in their power to avoid Li receiving any stamp of approval. Even so, no General could reprimand Li C'cheng. No one could release their anger towards him. Each week, he gave surprisingly confidential reports to Wu Kuang. Using the most secretive encryption programs, he writes seemingly innocent messages about whether or not fruit is ripe, whether it's too dry and whether its harvest time. After deciphering, even then the message would hold almost no meaning to the person who had deciphered it. Only the intended recipient could understand the true meaning of the message. If a personal meeting was inevitable, this meeting would be held in secluded areas of Beijing. Personal meetings always showed that something was wrong, that some crucial event was about to take place. C'cheng tried to avoid any and all formal meetings. Freedom of choice and discreet behaviour – he loved his freedoms. To have to stand on a stage in front of a militarised zone, where eager crowds expected everything of him was the utmost torture. Not from embarrassment, not in the least. His hate was simple. He loved manipulation from behind the scenes.

Li C'cheng had been enjoying his absolutely and exceptionally privileged position for barely two years. And he had worked truly hard for it. Thanks to his genealogical research, he was deserving enough. At first glance, such research would have nothing to do with military activities, but not in this case. Ever since he was a little boy, Li C'cheng had enjoyed genealogy. A psychologist would probably have a relatively simple explanation for this. A complex. A complex he had acquired as a result of feeling humiliated by his parents. Poor peasants from the Eastern province of Shandong, they were guilty of raising their own pig. Despite outcry from the insulted community, especially the figurehead, C'cheng's parents still did not dispose of this symbol of capitalism, this seed of regression that stole time and labour from progressive work in the cooperative. The culmination of this conflict took place during a break from the fields, when Li's father went home to feed the pig unlike everyone else, who listened analytically to the thoughts of Mao Zedong – ideas that were to lead to better results in the growing of wheat. This defiance upset the figure head of the cooperative enough that after consulting his supervisor in the Cadre Brigade, the Red Guard invaded the home of Li's parents. They discovered Confucius' dialogues and a volume of Tu Fu's ancient poems in their cottage during their heroic fight against the "Four Elders".[1] Long forgotten about, the books had been tucked away behind a wardrobe by Li's parents.

Since Li's parents owned these books, they were considered intellectuals, intellectuals who were fated to be exterminated for their hindrance to society and their haughty selfishness. The fact that they were illiterate peasants, unable to even read any of these books did not do them much justice. The infamous and perfectly elaborate process of thamzing[2] followed: a public denouncement, an utter degradation of the human personality. A sign was hung on his mother's and father's necks, reading – "An enemy to humankind" before

---

1   The motto for the fight against "reactionism" during the Cultural Revolution in China – old ideas, old culture, old customs and old habits.

2   An assembly of public criticism and self-criticism, where victims were humiliated. It took place on a mass scale with crowds of spectators. In Tibet, after China's occupation, it was the cruellest form of rape, dishonour and torture, which usually resulted in death.

they were fastened so tightly to a goat that their hands and shoulders were dislocated. At the age of six, Li witnessed his parents laying on the ground facing each other, tears of agony streaming down their faces, scolding one another for their terrible behaviour. They had each long known that the thoughts of the other were treacherous, inhumane, that they had been keeping their immoral selfish behaviour a secret at the expense of others and by looking down on others they had betrayed all moral values – all of this took place under the spiteful echo of the surrounding crowd.

By the end of their suffering, they were still able to impel their son to believe he had been poorly raised, that the only righteous thing to do was disown them as his parents. This is what little Li was then encouraged to do by the villagers in the crowd. All of this under the supervision of the Red Guard. After Li uttered the childish words, "… you are evil, mean and I am disowning you as my parents, I never want to see you again…" they took him to his sister, who lived in the city and took care of him. In the end, it was this that saved him, later even leading him to serve in the People's Army. Never speaking of this incident, he had never again seen his parents.

It's hard to say what went on in Li's little soul after these events unfolded. He had never confided in anyone about anything that had happened, not even the best friend he had actually never had at all. Nothing like this had ever happened. He was drawing a blank. This event had been erased from his mind, his mind had erased it. But perhaps not – the result of a few unspeakable days at the age of six, his feverish genealogical efforts explained this morbid internal desire for social acceptance, for a satisfactory ranking in the Chinese system, into which he would proudly rise up and with a confident smile, look around at his neighbours, who he could obviously outperform in many ways. He wouldn't have to vent it out loud and no one would have to pat him on the back. Even so, he would have to see that he had become irreplaceable and grand. C'cheng was looking for anything that could help him reach such prestige. He was proud to be living in today's province of Shandong – in the former state of Lu, the birthplace of the insurmount-able father, Confucius. He was eagerly searching for his past and adored rummaging through the old archives. In those years, he had even signed up to be a member of the Youth Association, so that he could gain more opportunities. He wasn't interested in Communism as such, even though he could obviously never say such a thing. Both the Youth Association and later the Army guaranteed him a certain order. Everything would have its place. Everything was cre-ated according to precise developments. But assigning any-thing, especially an object, any special value or power, with the possibility to influence events is nonsense. Therefore, to him, even the historic Imperial Seals, which he personally had the privilege of viewing, were merely three pieces of interconnected rubble, if artistically crafted. He couldn't understand the concerned looks he received from histori-ans, who could hardly believe their eyes. Whoever got to know him more closely, was continually taken aback by his obviously split character. On the one hand, Li was a history buff, digging through the venerable archives, and on the other, he was a grounded barbarian, shunning friendship and holding his ancestral legacy in utter indifference.

There was an accident while he was investigating the history of one of the branches of his family tree. Many of the genealogical documents had been stolen or destroyed when considerable damage had been inflicted during the revolutionary shift, from the volatile times of the Republic through to the invasion of the Japanese, then the Soviets, right up to the initiation of the Communist Party and Mao

Zedong's seizure of power. During the Cultural Revolution, the archives had suffered the most damage. An embargo issued on foreign researchers prevented any long-forgotten and potentially compromising material regarding the representatives of the people from resurfacing, further preventing any important events from being presented in the wrong light. It was necessary for the society of the New People to decide on the actual course of history, the good and the bad. To this day, there are still numerous sealed boxes waiting to be discovered. Li had gone to great lengths to demand special consent to freely study the deposited historical material from the military committee. He had even dug up the confidential Edict of Emperor Guangxu, which no one had even known to exist.

The Edict, determining new orders and norms for both heaven and earth could be dated back to September 19th, 1898 – the second-to-last day of the so-called One-Hundred-Day-Reform, during which the young Emperor Guangxu made one of his last desperate attempts to change an Empire that was headed nowhere.

There are several theories, interpretations and opinions justifying the absence of any kind of motivation, a driving force, which would have propelled the Chinese Empire onward and upward, just like in European and American cultures. Simple reasons like ossification aside, inner awareness of oneself and the limitations of the imperial court, its blind-sidedness, its attempts to maintain the status quo are others alongside possible philosophical, pacifist and peaceful reasons. This, for example, could be related to the Buddhist spurning of ambition for career prestige and hegemony – everything is in vain and everything will pass. The imperial court was also tasked with projecting the never-changing Confucian order into its understanding, together with its clearly defined ethical and moral relationships to rules and obedience, which prohibits resistance against a higher power. It is futile to search for a key to understanding all these relationships, which are subject to scientific research. In truth, the most tragic development at the end of the Chinese Empire was primarily influenced by the activity or rather inactivity of Empress Dowager Cixi, who reigned from 1861 until her death in 1908. Her reign was something of a tradition for Chinese women, who couldn't directly rule their country by means of regency. Instead, she herself chose the imperial successor, who was a puppet on her strings. Her choice was for a child ruler, placing her as deputy to the throne.

The same was true for Emperor Guangxu, also a nominal leader, but prudently aware of the direction in which the Empire was headed thanks to his youthful idealism, and decided to alter the course. He and his reformers lived a hectic and fast-paced life in the time of the One-Hundred-Day Reform in 1898. Even so, they were enthusiastic and hopeful of China's beautiful future. The young, imperial leader was captivated by this never-ending euphoria of thoughts, ideas and desires. He visited fortune tellers more than ever before in an attempt to find some peace of mind. This led him to a fundamental prophecy, which should have altered the path of Chinese history. No one is able to testify the exact words of the soothsayer to the Emperor, any witness long having taken their words to the grave. There is no documented proof of these sessions. Therefore, all elements are subject to speculation.

However, Emperor Guangxu released an Edict that is undoubtedly inspired by these prophecies. Unknown to anyone, the Edict could not be revoked by Empress Dowager Cixi. The Emperor released it in the final days of the reform, before the regent dismissed the protestors, trampling the new ideas.

In the 1990s, Major Li C'cheng discovered the Edict hidden in an unopened archive. The Edict spoke of the establishment of a new Dynasty of the Chinese Empire. In truth, the document was so strange that it was almost laughable, if not astounding in its total ambiguity. If it weren't for certain formal symbols, such as the description of the Empire and its three Imperial Seals, a person would have doubted the document's authenticity or at least treated it with the sober common sense of the Heavenly son. The yellowing and dignified-looking document, rolled into a tube, was relatively long, written in vermilion ink. Primarily, it described the constellations of stars and their expected movement. The Emperor was clearly strongly influenced by astrological and alchemistic tendencies to prophesise, like some psychic sorcerer, implying the state of China in the upcoming century. His Edict ordered the subsequent adoption of the new dynasty. Through various symbolic allusions and figurative expressions, he implied that the next fifty years would be a time of blood, chaos, re-birth and desperate searching. This would all terminate in red darkness, which would literally, "bind the Central Empire and pull it down deeper and deeper into spiritual hell."

But the most mysterious part of the Edict was still to come. "… all around, no matter where thou looketh, there will be only dotage, thou shall come across only spiritual skeletons and e'en the gold-plated world that surrounds shall swarm variously with ravens and vultures; yea, the Earth shall lose reason to spin and therein shall there be no need to count of years; then shall Heaven give birth to a DREAM – in the year of the Serpent. Behold: in this DREAM shall there be the daughter of the Heavens. In the Edict, the current son of the Heavens ordered the entirety of the Empire and the insignificant world around it to adopt this DREAM as a representation of the new imperial dynasty. Only then would spiritual revival come. It would exterminate the ravens, cleanse the goblets of human sin, make bells rejoice, make the dizi[3] play, correct the people's thoughts and open their eyes.

All the edicts and orders as well as all the successions of the Heaven's mandates are only blowing in the wind afterwards. There will be no trace of it once the storm blows over. What is not has never been, until the DREAM arrives. The DREAM will put everything back in order and it will take care of all the damage the wind had caused…"

The interpretation of this prophecy may be so different that neither the ones who have read it nor the ones who have merely heard of it, could interpret it accurately. Neither of the representatives of the Central Military Commission dared publish it. On the contrary, those, who knew what it was about or even knew that the Edict existed, agreed to not spread its word, otherwise they would be sentenced to death. Therefore, for the longest time, only seven prominent people had known of it.

However, what about its content? Five Supremes, people, who knew of the Edict's content and existence, including Major Li C'cheng, agreed that this Edict posed no threat to the People's Republic of China. It shouldn't have even posed a threat to the long-founded and progressive establishment in the power of the people after its possible release. Even though none of the participants wanted to speak of the prophecy's meaning, deep down in the bottom of their souls, they were all worried. The word "DREAM" can either mean nothing or everything. Was it the Emperor's literary fiction or divine inspiration? The Emperor had no idea of the present motto, which was to be China's future driving force. "The dream of China's magnificent rebirth." This is the motto repeated over and over again in the minds

3   Dizi – a traditional Chinese bamboo flute

of every Chinese citizen. However, what does the word "dream" mean, as interpreted by Emperor Guangxu? Is it the same? Is it not the same?

The five Supremes feared the ethical impact this motto could have on the development of China. The Political Bureau was already forced to accept several measures since Hong Kong had been back in the hands of an Empire. Huge amounts of work were needed with elements that had gotten a feel for American and European free-thinking. The Supremes had agreed on the fact that no one could even imagine the monstrous symbolism and anti-humanist revolt that such a moral spear could be. They could not risk the nostalgic desire for a beautiful, fairytale past, with its alluring rituals. Moreover, it was possible to speculate on the accuracy of the prophecies of the twentieth century, forming bizarre links and interconnections between the Red Darkness, the domination of the people under the symbol of the red flag, the motive of the dream and so on. After long discussion over whether or not to directly burn the Edict or to keep it, the Supremes agreed that one of the members of the Central Military Commission would keep it in his safe. There was to be no other copy of it and everyone would forget the whole thing had ever occurred.

And yet, when interpreting the delicate meanings of the words and expressions in the Edict, the Supremes failed to realise one fundamental thing, or to deem it important. This part of the Edict described the uselessness of adding up the calendar years, mentioning the year of the Serpent somewhat subtly, remaining inconspicuous. Li C'cheng discovered the Edict in 1986 and according to the Chinese zodiac, 1989 and 2001 were both years of the Serpent. There is always a twelve-year interval between them. With a bit of imagination, the expression of uselessly adding years could mean entering a new millennium, where the first year of the Serpent is 2001. While the Emperor wrote of a time of dotage and annihilation, when looking around, it is worth admitting that the world, especially Western civilisation, had never before gone through such hopelessness, as defined in the Edict. This was written at a time when there was doubt over whether the development of abilities, strength and power was proportional to moral growth.

But four of the Supremes were late in discovering these speculations. They came at a time when the fifth Supreme, the bearer of the Edict in question, was found dead in his locked bathroom in 2001, the year of the Serpent. Nothing could officially go missing from his safe after it was opened because no one, except the five Supremes, knew of the secret Edict of Emperor Guangxu.

What now? There was still no reason to sound an alarm. The opposite: there was a far greater reason to keep everything a secret. The result of the confidential discussion was accordingly to give Major Li C'cheng special authorisation to locate and destroy the Edict and then to take care of anyone who had come into contact with this document. Major Li could have anything he needed available to him. The only person he was to confide to was a member of the Central Military Commission, one of the four (living) Supremes. The chairman of the Central Military Commission and the future president, Xi Jinping was added to this list later on. Not until September 2012, that is, around the time of increasing global media speculations, leading to Xi Jinping's mysterious and brief disappearance.

– – –

Five years have passed since that mysterious death. Major Li C'cheng is sitting with his head down in his room, reciting the Edict word for word, as he had memorised it. The year is

2006. For five years Someone, He, or possibly She, a potential threat to the whole Order has freely roamed the planet. And he, Major Li C'cheng, the one who had first discovered the Edict, knows no more than he knew five years ago, after receiving authorisation from the Central Military Commission to deal with confidential duties. Something has to happen and some progress has to finally be made. Li must be extremely receptive in order not to overlook any hint that could lead him in the right direction. But there is the question: where should he start? Angrily he glares at the monitor, replaying only the news. Sing Tao's page. He clicks on it. He scrolls down in disgust until he comes across an ad. And there it is. His jaw swings wide. Finally, he has found a thread in his search.

BOOK I

1.
Out of Europe

For over an hour now (or it feels like over an hour), Vitas has been sitting patiently on a chair in a small, smoky office of the Czech Public Television station listening to a series of intellectual analyses, critical remarks and pejorative reviews on his film documentaries. It's like being in a small chicken coop. Fluorescent bulbs are unpleasantly flashing despite the beaming light of day, intensifying the bird's feeling of despair, all while sitting on the twelfth floor of a factory, by the window, waiting for a verdict, only to automatically hang the bird on a hook.

He is sitting on a perch, observing the whole situation unfolding on his camera, which is right behind him above his head. He is zooming in slowly and smoothly across the table of crumpled papers, down into a close-up of Elza's head, who is sputtering out the outbursts of a diva. Thanks to her sharp, youthful-looking face, her short hair, the jangling of her bracelets, her plain clothes and above all, her expression of sovereignty, Vitas classified her among the more experienced of people, among the very successful, celebrated artists, who permanently have a green light, destined to a great career.

Since childhood, Vitas has had a very strange ability, or rather a game, or better yet a fetish. As a little boy, whenever he walked past someone, he took a snapshot of them in his mind's-eye. It was as if he made a freeze frame, he memorised all the details of his victim and then played with it. He zoomed-in on their face, as if it were taken in high-definition, enlarged it and analysed the details: the eyelashes, the pupils, the teeth. Often, it was only his fantasy that led him to notice drops of sweat or wrinkles. It usually had something to do with his relationship to the person in question. Therefore, Elza's head was full of warts, with strands of hair sticking out among them and a volcano-like formation in the middle of her head, spewing lava at irregular intervals.

But what did he do with the models that he thought up in his head? In general, he assigned them their original character, but in a far more concentrated, redundant form, also including their positive and negative physical dispositions. The details of a real picture of a person he liked (which often changed from day to day) were shaped into kind, almost fairytale-like, imagined figures. He included the characters in various situations and created the most absurd tales. He registered them at some moment in time, in feelings of astonishment, despair, anger, happiness and fake adult smiles. He played with them like with puppets. He made the sad puppets happy and made up different plots for them. While walking down the street, he would simply – snap, snap – be able to take up to twenty pictures of passers-by, who had no clue of the game they would soon take part in, the many things they would go through. True, it once backfired on him. One day, when he was eight years old, he was coming home from a mandatory visit to his aunt's house. His aunt gave him a very fake, sour smile and three acidic kisses, like sulphuric spit. All the way home he was enraged. The steam from his raging mouth rose swiftly. His repulsive aunt had put him in a vengeful mood. He pictured her slicing an onion, a large drop bursting in her eye, her whole face twitching into a tiny, wrinkled grimace. Layers of the ochre body began peeling off and her narrow maroon lips puckering into black. Submerged in this metamorphosis, he didn't notice the mailbox outside his house, which was at the level of his head. When the doctors woke him up from his state, after diagnosing him with a mild concussion, they asked him repeatedly if he had had a fight with a friend, or if someone had attacked him. No one could believe that he had just been walking along a straight sidewalk on a bright, sunny day and bumped into a mailbox for no other reason than that his unbearable aunt had smothered him with her repulsive lipstick.

"… the exhibition is so degenerate that you really have nothing else to build on anymore. And you deploy your conclusions straight away as a lifeline. The straight A student, who feels he's happy not so much from the many research objectives completed or the awards he received but from the journey he had to take to achieve his goal… Basically hell or high water…" Elza is throwing her arms around, rubbing her fingers together as if she had disgusting slime between them. She is shouting these words involuntarily to the rhythm of the blows coming from the next office. The editor-in-chief of the journal has a map of the world in the room with a group of reporters playing darts with blindfolds, aiming anywhere at mother Earth. The location with the greatest number of shots then wins and becomes the subject of the next documentary, where a few prominent reporters will go. It doesn't matter that they don't know the language, or that they don't know what to film once there. You're sure to find the eager hands of a child in a country divided by war… They know how to pull at the viewer's heartstrings, get them to feel. So, a perfect "PHT". Vitas doesn't even remember who, from his circle of close friends, came up this ingenious, yet subtly ironic expression. PHT

– profoundly humane tale. The meaning is outwardly respectable, but completely pejorative. It all has to do with how many tears you can get the audience to shed.

A dull dart shot into the drywall, comically ridiculing Elza's enthusiasm. "What exactly are we trying to achieve here?" pondered Vitas. Although Elza was well aware of the shots' significance, she acted as if she was oblivious to it. She kept throwing her hands up energetically, spitting all over the room. Snap! Vitas saved this shot into his mind, took a deep breath in, exhaled and very slowly yet clearly articulated: "… and you, go to hell!"

Calmly, slowly, as if he had thought long and hard about this statement and all its possible alternative consequences, he got up and left the room, leaving the astonished Elza with her mouth wide open. He could care less if there'd been some truth to what the diva was saying. He didn't care that his attitude could close doors to his work. He didn't care at all. He was even pleased by it. Some weight had been lifted off his shoulders and he felt a lot freer.

He got lost in his thoughts while walking through a maze of television station corridors until he almost fell into a bucket of mortar. A bricklayer was putting a wall up, where a door to one of the offices used to be. He was smearing grey matter on a brick like honey on bread. He was doing it with such love and care, like a sculptor immersed in his almost finished masterpiece. If possible, a chap could maybe even lick the extra substance dripping down the edges. Vitas didn't notice the bricklayer until he encountered his shadow. Under normal circumstances, Vitas would start some small talk with him. The bricklayer's profession was interesting – he took care of some VIP offices, such as the chief-of-news' offices, the journalism, production offices, and those of other TV positions. There was so much employee turnover on these privileged positions that for years, this bricklayer's only job description was to constantly put drywall where drywall used to be and tear down walls and doors that were already torn down before. The bricklayer had to meet the demands of the media moguls. All of them had been convinced that they were irreplaceable in their positions, that their positions were stable and their demands on their offices reflected it. After years of working there, everyone got used to the bricklayer. The immortal bricklayer with his immortal work was as much a part of the corridors as the walls, doors, windows and the dead flower on the window sill.

While clinging to the service pole of the tram and mindlessly staring out of a dark window, watching the blurry "something" of his reflection alternate with some quick-changing express lanes beyond, he realised that it wasn't even poor Elza's fault. He is the one at the crossroads of his life – at the height of all his problems – and now he has to figure out what to do next. Elza had just been the final straw in his existence. He had reached a point where there was no other way he could react. This straw had been dipped in etching acid, the traces of which can no longer be edited out. It would leave a hole in the clothes, a hole in the bowl… a hole. The cup is flowing over, the acid is unstoppable.

Incoming text messages or calls can be heard at almost every stop, when the PA announcement sounds. He can hear Elza's angry voice, warning him against these irreversible steps in his life. Lengthy and haunting text messages follow: "… you used to be a great publicist but you're a much worse documentary filmmaker… Do you even understand the difference between being a publicist and a documentary filmmaker…?"

Coming home, his eyes drill the clock into the wall. A two-storey building on the outskirts of Prague. The middle of no-place. The serenity he once enjoyed is now killing him. His eyes focus on the wall. He is staring at a painting of the first Czech president, Tomas G. Masaryk. It is a black, very dark painting, which forces Vitas to dig through the dark cliffs of hard-to-identify lines to the depth of his eyes, just to have his eyes retrace back to see the whole picture, like a helium-filled balloon. His eyes keep airily navigating this painting like a hamster spinning on a wheel. The nostalgia of the painting only intensifies Vitas' gloomy mood. His life is flashing before his eyes like a fast-paced movie. The same pace with which he keeps looking into Masaryk's eyes… Vitas realises that he cannot go on like this. He bursts out in frantic, painful emotions. He knows he has to overcome this self-deprecating mood, no matter what it takes. Some way. Any way.

He gets up. He is packed and ready to go in half an hour. He knows he only needs a change of clothes and cash. He is standing on a sewer in front of his home, aware of the symbolic nature of this moment, which is borderline theatrical, slowly opening his cell phone to see several missed calls and unread messages. He skilfully removes the SIM card and holds it between two fingers for a moment. In his emotional state, the SIM card represents his ID card, his living identity, a specific person containing his entire past. Everything, including his heartbeat is recorded on this small piece of plastic. He slowly lets go of the small piece of plastic and watches it disappear into the darkness of the sewer. To him, this is like a sharp and deadly blade slitting his throat without drawing a single drop of blood.

He throws the rest of the device into the trash and then takes it right back out again. He realises that someone could interpret such evidence, once someone goes looking for him. Well, let's be honest, if anyone ever does go looking for him.

He looks at his house hidden behind a large linden tree

one last time. He had remembered this tree as a small, malnourished rod that had fought long and hard to survive on the rocky ground. This linden had been witness to his and Eva's lives for many years. He feels shivers down his spine but his lips are tenaciously clenched. He has already made one step forward, turning around, thinking he'd get one last glimpse, one last snap on his virtual camera, when he notices the translucent colour in his mailbox. He had never been used to opening it because it was always Eva, who used to do that. He wasn't even capable of sending a letter during the email era. Reluctantly he opens the mailbox – it has gotten in the way of his sentimental, theatrical situation somewhat. It is as if the head of a frustrated director were about to pop up over the fence, shout "cut!" and thereby interrupt a suspenseful but cheap movie scene. "A dark cloud got in the way and ruined the scene. We've got no choice but to resume shooting once the dark cloud clears off." That's when all the invisible crew members will climb out of their holes, all chatting nicely, the tension melting in the same way that soldiers feel when a colonel tells them to stand at ease.

He is staring confoundedly at the envelope. There is no sender, though it bears a collection of Indian and Chinese stamps. Despite all reluctance to stay there another second, he tears open the envelope. It has been a long time since he last saw a handwritten letter. His eyes jump straight to the signature – Kromen.

He takes a deep breath. To him, the name Kromen represents a gangster, a murderer, but even so, a nobleman, renowned as one of the biggest Czech mobsters of the 90s – the era of the Wild West Gold Rush. Vitas himself however has a fairly ambivalent relationship with Kromen. He admires and despises him at the same time. Though both men had become famous in their turn, they had each represented a significant shift in life and a certain symbiosis for one another. Their relationship was similar to that of an alligator allowing a bird to peck out the remnants of food from his gaping mouth.

Dear editor,

I hope I can still call you that, even though you haven't been one for some time. To me, you'll always be the nosy paparazzi you once were. Please don't take it the wrong way, you understand me I'm sure.

Well, let's get right down to it. You no doubt notice this letter comes to you from the Far East. And don't be surprised by the abundance of stamps. It was simply to ensure the letter reached its destination – who knows what post offices it's gone through.

So, there's a reason for this letter. I am at a very interesting point in my life, but I can't go into much detail now. I can only hope that if you hear and see these words, you believe that I'm serious. These aren't just words blowing in the wind. This situation is not only imperative for me alone, it could be important for the whole world. I apologise in advance. I don't want to come across big-mouthed or conceited. I'd prefer you to see for yourself. So I'd like to invite you to my current home – Tibet, near the Indian border. The only detail I can give is that the reason I'm inviting you has to do with your own past and present. At least I hope you weren't lying to me when you said you were a Christian... I can say no more. I'd rather this letter wasn't the subject of tomorrow's headlines. I know you still have close ties with the media. That being said, in our case, such a thing would be the end of you and me. I hope all our old disagreements have long been forgotten. I still think the two of us are destined to share our fates, for better or worse. Believe me when I say that this time it's not a bad thing.

There's no doubt that this is a very delicate and important matter. It should be enough proof that there's a paid plane ticket in your name leaving from the Ruzyne Airport, Prague. You'll be flying via Frankfurt – Delhi to the Jolly Grant Airport, where someone will collect you and transport you from there.

Excuse the tone, but at this point, there's no room for any doubt, unneeded complications, or dawdling. Since you don't understand the big picture yet, take it as a paid trip to a place that you've only dreamed of in the past.

More in person. Have a nice day,
Sincerely
Kromen

2.
Out of America

Aviel is tapping away at the keyboard, glaring at the monitor, as if a drama is unfolding before his eyes. His fingers are trembling as they lie spread out on the keys exactly the way the *Beginners Guide to Typing* had specified. He gently strokes the keys to an irregular rhythm, never pushing them all the way down, just vibrating over them like the chaos of flashing light bulbs. As an experienced IT expert for a renowned banking firm, his mind is able to understand the drama unfolding on his monitor in JavaScript. But the letters merge into strangely different conclusions. The Java hieroglyphics form various, mostly pejorative word combinations like some cryptic scene in a thriller movie. He sees his wife with her plain, slicked back, blonde hair and a perfect mask, as if flawless. What he once saw as a perk now comes across as dull, boring and lifeless. He'd give anything to find a flaw that would make her human. He feels empty next to her and this emptiness spreads far and wide into the fog. He feels nothing and sees intrusive, cold boredom in her presence. Anger, resentment and the frustrations of a simple life boil inside him. The only topic of conversation is money. Circular, paper… matter. The world of elves running around copper-plated highways among transistors and resistors is no longer enough. He has also parted with the thought of running away to Central Park. He needs to run along a forest trail until completely collapsing.

But this is only the precipice of his problems. He married her despite his family's objections. He wasn't Catholic. A Rabbi once took him into a synagogue to discuss disinheritance. Explaining that the Lord is still his Lord to the Rabbi was all in vain. No one believed him anyways, a lost cause because who had committed the deadliest sin. But he couldn't help himself. Even the reformed didn't seem changed enough to him, or perhaps this fixation was only in his mind. It didn't matter. He feels restless, divided and disgusted by his own being. Maybe the world all around is pure and it is actually him alone who is guilty of sin… "Oh, Lord, where and how will I find the purpose of life…?"

No matter where he looks, he sees the same signs, reading "rotten soul, rotten man" everywhere. This tears him apart even if no one can tell it's happening. He has long stopped wearing a kippah, not to mention sideburns. He must have lost his mind twenty years ago when he hooked up with her. Today, he is disgusted by the thought of going to work, coming home or attending parties. That is if anyone even wanted him anymore, after all, he has become known as a grouch, a chronic party-pooper.

Aviel closes the whole program of illegible words and starts googling. But again he goes rigid, his vision blurred, his thoughts wandering. Where has he heard of it? Who told him? Apparently, if a couple breaks up, it's never the other's fault. It's a matter of two. Filled with unbalanced chaos, the creeping awareness of his exploitation, he has been listening to the constant attacks surrounding him for months, maybe years. Often they only have to be perceived as attacks to be decisive for him, even if they're quite innocent.

Only now does he realise that he hasn't spent much time working. But work hasn't fulfilled him for years. It's not that it has become boring, though after years of working in the virtual world, he realises that the constant shifts and advancements in technology will simply be replaced by further progressions. Whatever he has been working towards or has invented himself will immediately be replaced with some new thing and it all seems so meaningless to him. Futile. Vain.

His desk is a mess. There are various graphics-cards, fragments of green, fibreglass-plated motherboards lying around... Since he became the head of the IT department, he has had more freedom, the mess on his table seen as one of the eccentric and peculiar habits that computer nerds have. And worse still, his sanity reflects his results at work and has been closely monitored and evaluated by his colleagues. This isn't by far the most important bank in New York, but every person in every position is always being watched, if only by his competitors. Where he operates or what he does is irrelevant. Big Brother is constantly looking, judging, with another twenty candidates waiting to take his post. And if a fall on the career ladder seems like a ticket to an easier job, think again. Even if at the bottom rung, among the homeless, that spot on the park bench will still have to be fought for, just as for that post in the IT position. This is what he hears and this is how it seems. These words are engraved in his mind like words engraved on a tombstone.

He glances down from the monitor at the small screws from a computer case lying on the table and notices something that doesn't typically belong. A letter with exotic stamps. He can't imagine when the secretary could have put it there. How long has it been lying around? He rips open the envelope and is shocked to read the signature – Kromen. How dare he write to him? He crumples the letter between his enclosed flyers in disgust and launches it into the trash can without even reading it. His JavaScript no longer means anything. It just vaguely and meaninglessly appears on the screen. He remembers the time, perhaps two years ago, when he had first met this unhinged businessman from the former Communist Europe. The mysterious Kromen had been burdened by an equally mysterious problem. He had been going on about some treasure buried somewhere south of Prague. Considering that he had wanted him to commit gross fraud in the accounts, the treasure couldn't have been all that valuable. It sure was a great idea though. The simplicity of it was genius. All you needed were a few good IT moves, his speciality. This being said, even the most flawless fraud has its "buts" though Aviel could care less about "buts". That's why they hadn't parted on good terms.

Perhaps not to regret anything later on, he quickly takes the crumpled letter from the trash can and begins reading:

Dear Aviel,

I hope you're doing better than last time we were introduced and that you aren't so afraid of me nowadays… – HA – only a joke, friend! I wouldn't want to embarrass or upset you at all. Quite the contrary, I'd like to offer you something unforgettable, an exceptional experience that will neither deprive you of anything nor leave you without becoming rich. It has something to do with what we talked about some time ago, that fortune hidden not far out of Prague.

Unfortunately, I'm not in a position to go into much detail. Enclosed, you will find a plane ticket. Please don't hesitate, the itinerary is easy to follow. This is a very delicate matter. It is plainly impossible to give you any detailed information at this juncture. Your non-arrival could transpire to be a significant tragedy, but I'm afraid I can't elaborate on the fine print. This is my oath, in the name of Moses (you said you were a Jew). Board the flight and follow the instructions.

More in person, I'm sure.

Best regards

Kromen

3.
A Trip to the Top of the World

Vitas and Aviel. They each have a 120-mile car ride ahead of them from the Jolly Grant Airport. Their first meeting took place in this very cab. Prearranged, just as Kromen had promised.

"So, any idea where we're going? What's this all about?" Aviel asked eagerly after only several minutes of sitting in the cab.

Vitas' English isn't all that great. He knows a lot of words, but since he doesn't speak often, he sometimes finds himself helpless. Either way, he had no answer to the question, so he just gestured with his outstretched hand and cluelessly shrugged his shoulders.

They both fell silent before saying another word. Deep in thought they realised they were at an age when they no longer have to entertain anyone. Both of them are over fifty and Vitas is about two years older than Aviel.

Side by side, each seems like the opposite. Aviel has hair black as a coalmine. He tries to tame the occasional curl into a perfectly mathematical shape. He has a short part in his hairline, which is slowly receding the longer he stays out East. Vitas' hairdo is like an untamed, wild shrub. The word comb lacks all meaning to him. Some grey hair seeps through his brown tangles. Aviel has a gaunt face with a fine, grey patina. Vitas' massive yet short nose dominates his wider, pinkish cheek bones. Vitas' nose is half that of Aviel's long, scrawny one. Vitas is 71 inches tall and as a result of the mental hardships of his recent months, he has become almost as thin as Aviel, who is almost four inches taller. The true difference between them, at first glance, should be their religious beliefs, although neither of them really perceives this difference at all. Both consider themselves very passive believers, who are only aware of their religion's spiritual dimension, and even then they feel a little lost even in that sphere. Between them they realise there is something more than just the periodic table of elements, but that this something is completely intangible, unpredictable. They have been searching for a way through the possible meanings like an out-of-control airplane flying through a milky cloud once the pilot has lost all sense of direction.

– – –

They are driving uphill in the last part of their journey and civilisation is slowly fading. The countryside is also changing from the jungle of deciduous and coniferous trees to alpine junipers, birches and firs tended by nature with far greater deliberation than by man, as if each plant valued its habitat more than the other.

The air pressure also begins dropping slowly and the wind cuts deeper into the throat. They are approaching the top of the world. The Himalayas. It is as if they were standing on the ocean shore before high tide and the white, foamy, curved top of the wave is eagerly gushing towards them.

They are driving along a bumpy road to one of the last orchards. It could still be called a village – Taknaur Renge. But their journey is interrupted. There is a caravan with fourteen yaks, a heavy load, dozens of horses and six bald

Asian monks wearing chupas[4] with red cassocks underneath, waiting for them at the turn in the road a few miles before the village. Most of the monks have a large, round earring in their left ear. Even from afar they could be heard: "Jingzhi! Jingzhi!"[5] Originally, this word had only referred to the English peoples, but later on, it began to include all members of Western civilisation.

One of the monks steps forward, saying "Welcome, welcome." The pride he felt at his knowledge of a foreign language no doubt makes him feel slightly superior to the other monks, who are far more sincere. His suspicious eyes circle around like pool balls, ready to pop out of his head, while he examines the faces, clothes, belt buckles and everything that Aviel and Vitas are wearing. "I'm Lao Pu-wei – this way, please."

This was a bit of a stumbling block. Vitas had only ever sat on horseback once some thirty years ago and Aviel had never ridden a horse at all. They both feel like they are standing on a ladder balancing on the seat of a carousel ride. All the monks begin to laugh, all except for Lao Pu-wei. They give Vitas and Aviel a few minutes to get used to it and then slowly set off. The other monks, though far more earnest, speak no English, instead simply smiling at their guests. There is always someone getting in their way and each monk openly observes them like a child checking out a new toy. And all continue to laugh. Once they die down, they pick up the pace, keeping up with the leader of the pack, Lao Pu-wei. Aviel tries to start a conversation with him, in order to break the ice. To be polite, he asks where they are going and how long it will take.

---

4   Chupa – a traditional wide and long coat usually made of black or white wool, lined with a colourfully woven or tie-die stripe of sewn fabric.

5   Jingzhi – (tib.) literally means "Englishman", generally refers to a "man from the West".

"I am only fulfilling the wishes of the honourable Lama Rinpoche," Lao bluntly replies. "If it were up to me, I wouldn't start anything new," he adds sternly, ending the conversation. Aviel and Vitas look at each other with an understanding of the difficulty of things to come.

It becomes clear that they still have a long road ahead. Vitas is galloping along on a horse that he has finally gotten used to after twenty minutes. Aviel has no such experience at all. The whole journey, he struggles. After half an hour riding, Vitas settles into a monotone beat, freeing himself of the challenging journey to the top of the world and embarking on a long train of thought…

4.

Kromen – An Enemy of the State

Vitas became an investigative journalist in Cheb, a little city close to the border with Germany, at the beginning of the 90s, during the Wild West Gold Rush era in Czechia. This was the period after socialism, which was still called Communism, was abolished. It was a time of change. Thieves were learning to steal, the police, though a little late in the game, were slowly learning to catch them and Vitas was learning to become a journalist, just like all other journalists. Without warning, everyone jumped on their case like wild teenagers. Like bees in heat, flying from flower to flower once the sun finally emerges following a downpour, making up for lost time. The sudden feeling of unexpected possibilities and unsuspected power came over them. I can do anything! And in reality, this wasn't all that true. It was difficult to take over responsibility. It took people years to comprehend and this was something many others were not destined to achieve.

The fact is that Vitas had the courage, frantic stubbornness and the literary ability to create a story. He'd do anything for his case. He'd sacrifice his sleep, flirt with insanity, or get locked up in prison. He soon found an ally in a photographer for the Cheb newspaper. Since the photographer was bald, he was nicknamed Barehead. Together, they were able to climb over the barbwire fence of the former barracks that belonged to the city. Beyond, a company, which had close ties to the mayor, illegally parked its trucks in this space. Together, they came up with the term: "quick shot". Anyone, who has ever read Winnetou, knows what this means.

Winnetou and Old Shutterhand are sitting by the fire in the prairie night and Winnetou notices two glowing dots in a nearby bush. They are being followed by an enemy. Winnetou starts playing with his rifle, checking the breech and barrel... Old Shatterhand is an experienced prairie hound, who knows what this means. He immediately notices two eyes glaring among the bushes. Winnetou is carefully examining the rifle's breech, barrel and silver-plated gunstock, when suddenly "Boom! Boom!" Two precisely aimed shots hit the hateful enemy right between the eyes, killing him dead...

Vitas and Barehead sometimes sat in a restaurant simply to take a picture of a certain individual, either a con artist, a mafia member or even an honest person for the sake of documentation or future trouble. All they needed to say was: "quick shot" and both prairie hunters knew what to do. Barehead took his camera out and showed it to Vitas. Vitas shook his head and asked what to do with this gadget and this wheel and this trigger. They kept on playing this game and only an insider would notice the "Snap! Snap!" The person in question is turned into an eternal picture without even realising it. The quick shot.

Later, when Vitas found himself on thin ice as a result of his endeavours in Cheb, a large German media company promptly bought the newspaper, putting an end to their shenanigans. The real business began here. There were only a few people to get all the work done, leaving no more time for snooping around. Vitas began to feel a certain nostalgia

– Chebness – a term that, to him, expressed the gloom of a dreary autumn day, when depression, melancholy, longing and homesickness begin … In that vanished era, whenever Vitas found himself at some pub or other, he knew exactly who'd be there and what he'd say. But this new time became one for high-speeds and looking for the nearest concrete pole…

Barehead and Vitas had prepared a scam as their leaving gift. It was January, twenty below zero, all things layered with ice. Barehead came across a dead dog. A mutt, a crossbreed with something from every animal on the street, including the cats and the rats. As a puppy, the dog may well have had white fur and brown spots, but by that time he was long since grey. It's impossible not to feed such a dog out in the street, but if it tries to lick your hand, it's better to run away, fearing rabies. In essence, a dead, frozen dirtbag.

Barehead could think of nothing better than to throw the mutt into a dead-end alleyway bin overflowing with trash, placing the lid on top carefully, just so that the frozen dog's body, feet and head would protrude slightly, then to snap a picture. And very inconspicuously, Vitas put the picture to press with a headline that read "Cheb Dog Found at Dead-End". Representatives of the German corporation didn't quite catch the punchline. They couldn't grasp the typicality of such Czech humour. But if the outraged reactions were anything to judge by, many Cheb readers also missed the joke.

Ladislav Frank, however, an employee of the Cheb Cadastral Office, came to see Vitas during this epoch of investigative paradise, before the newspaper was taken over by the German corporation, at the peak of the major cases, which Vitas was later to label as a wild prairie hunt for helpless, hungry bison, wanting to steal a bit of the forbidden fruit. The editorial staff were located in a former convent, so there was an ancient, noble spirit lurking over the frantic economic and political cases local to the place… Any editor or visitor had to go through a spiritual purgatory before they even got into the office – his spiritual hardships awakening his hopes, leaving him begging to be caressed, pleading for a cure and to sleep between the centuries-old brick and mortar that had long been drenched in blood, tears and faith. Years later, once restitution restored the convent to the Church, the spiritual haze radically dispersed into open-plan offices, constructed by the German corporation in a newer building in the centre of the city. There were seven editors sitting in one office, yelling on their phones. All individuality, intimacy and nobility were lost.

"I don't care what's going on around you or what cases you're solving right now Mr Editor," said a thin, wrinkled man: Ladislav Frank. He had a slightly sad but stubborn look in his eyes, which could pierce the tip of Vitas' nose. He didn't even blink. He was wearing a business suit, the kind that many older men continually wear. An all-purpose suit used as overalls, office clothes and for evening functions. He put his faded diplomatic briefcase on the floor next to the table. "I'm sixty-five years old. Not much surprises me anymore. Since I've retired, I help out at the Cadastral Office and there are things happening there that I just can't ignore. There's access there to unbelievable sources… Interested?"

It was as if Vitas was waking up from a dream. He was already used to filtering through the overflow of important cases. Not wanting to offend the elder man, he quickly replied, "Of course I am. Anything specific in mind?"

"Obviously, otherwise I wouldn't be here." Frank, although a bit insulted, pulled out some official documents from his briefcase and put them on Vitas' table.

"It has to do with the former middle school – the Rudolfinum building."

Vitas nodded to show he knew what building Frank was talking about. Although he wasn't a local, there was no way he could have been ignorant of the Rudolfinum. An ancient building, built quite literally during the time of Rudolph II and in the spirit of the time as well. It had become renowned as a dilapidated block in the centre of Cheb for years now. It was a middle school for generations, but several years before, the Building Office had decided that the school could no longer continue in its activities, unless the building underwent major renovations. The building's stability had been compromised during a bombing in the Second World War. Peculiar that it could serve educational purposes for the next forty Communistic years and then suddenly close down.

"The city owned the Rudolfinum 'til 1991," explained Frank, presenting a handful of documents as proof for his claims, pointing his index finger to some numbers and words, like a woodpecker pecking away at the beloved lichen-eater under the tree bark. "The city sold this property to two individuals for three and a half million in March 1991, based on a purchase agreement, even though the building was valued at five million crowns. Six months later, these two individuals sell the building to Vesna, owned by Kromen, for four and a half million. Everything's fine up 'til then. Nothing out of the ordinary. You look at it now, the building's valued at ninety million. Now, the building is valued at twenty times the original price!"

"And what about the property?" interrupted Vitas, who was missing the point.

"Nothing. Vesna owns it."

A moment of silence followed, the two men looking at each other, each waiting for the other to speak. Ladislav Frank couldn't wait, he spoke first: "Could you just explain this please? Only three months pass between individual estimates and no modifications are done to the property in that whole time. You can go see for yourself. Fungus is the only thing that grows there. Well, go ahead and write a piece on fungus multiplying estate value to the nth degree… How's that sound?"

Vitas gulped and nodded in agreement: "Sounds like an extremely valuable fungus." He couldn't stand it anymore and said, "What's behind all of this? What's really going on?"

"I don't know. I really don't know. I've one explanation – perfect money laundering. Kromen and his gang legalised a lot of money."

Vitas shook his head in disapproval. Doubtful, as for years after the revolution, there had been no reason to launder money in Czechia. No one had questioned anyone on the origin of money and gossip had never put anyone behind bars. On the contrary, it was believed that a decent, legal theft only deserved recognition. But as for the real reason? Even more doubtful that Kromen would clarify…

Neither Frank nor Vitas had any idea that they had gotten their hands on a unique theft that hadn't even reached completion. They had no idea that a Lien Agreement would be drawn up at an investment bank and that thirty million crowns would be taken out in a loan on this property. And that Vesna, beyond the foreclosed property, would be transferred to Karabinikov from the Ukraine, disappearing somewhere out East. They had no idea that Vesna had or would have about fifteen such properties and five such companies operating in Czechia. Thanks to this idea, Czech banks would lose about three billion Czech crowns, there would be a number of mysterious deaths surrounding the case and dozens of police officers involved, none of them successful in their efforts… But given Kromen's influence, no one would really know which police officer worked for Kromen and which for the best interest of the state. Over the years, Kromen would become a concept (and Vitas would have a lot to do with it). A name that stands for illegal money, a thief and a supreme mobster, one with immense influence over politicians.

Neither Frank nor Vitas could have known any of this when they were sitting together in a gloomy convent room of the Cheb Editorial Office in 1993. This is why an inconspicuous, soon-to-be-forgotten article about how fungus multiplied the value of the ruins of a once-famous building to twenty times its worth was written. There was however a miraculous increase in the number of orders for this one particular, completely insignificant, provincial issue.

5.
On Top of the World

The sun is at its peak and although at a high position, it's so warm that it forces the monks to take off their heavy chupas and skilfully tie them to the saddle. Their eyes slowly become used to the changing scenery. The grass is still cheerfully growing on both sides of the wild Jadhang River, cutting into the Tibetan alpine plateau. Patches of green grasses, rhododendrons, asters and sage-bush are struggling for survival on the surrounding barren hills. A juniper dominates over the wooden flora, the birches and the firs. The river rustles along the left side of the riverbank a few feet below. The gushing white water splashes on the sharp rock edges, forming a glaze over the flat surface. The path leads along a narrow gorge, surrounded by sharply rising mountains and rock formations up to four or sixteen thousand feet.

The change in air pressure is a lot more noticeable now. The view is wider. The hill on the right side is fading away and a widespread surface appears in front of them. The monks get off their horses and call out, "Lha Gyal-lo!" They pass one long stone wall, known as a mänthang.[6] There are several ropes with colourful, triangular-shaped prayer flags hanging on them and sacred inscriptions are carved

---

6   Mänthang – (tib. sman-thang) Walls dozens or hundreds of yards long that divide a road. They are usually covered with sacred inscriptions.

sporadically in the wall. Vitas cannot identify any of the inscriptions. They all walk clockwise around the wall, so that the wall is on the right-hand side. Aviel and Vitas look at each other. They realise that they have arrived at a significant point.

This is no-man's land. A trapezoid-shaped area about 700 miles squared showing little information about its owner on the map. Some even see it as a separate, nameless territory. This territory doesn't belong to any country. India considers it a part of the Uttarkashi district and actually takes care of it. However, since China seized control of Tibet in 1952, it has considered this tiny yet highly mountainous area as its own, demanding possession of it. According to the Chinese government, it is part of the Zandi area, which is part of Ngari, the western most part of Tibet.

This tension is the result of a short Chinese–Indian war in 1962. A sequence of skirmishes in mountainous borderlands had been initiated by the Chinese military offensive, in which almost 2000 soldiers died. Although the Chinese later surrendered due to other internal and external issues, many territories remained under dispute, yet to be resolved.

Today the reality is that the inhospitable land and the low population in this region make international conflict impractical for the gain of a few small and desolate hills. Hardly worth a dispute of any benefit to anyone, both sides are playing possum (at least for now).

The easiest way to this destination is the one that the caravan is on. The mountainous Western border of Tibet makes it very difficult to cross, although the first distinct traces of Tibetan civilisation, the Guge territory, are a mere sixty miles to the east. Monuments historic sites – ruins of the formerly renowned Guge Kingdom, are part of the archaeology of the region, hardly-explored relics to the present day. Their traces date back to the tenth century, when

King Yeshe-Ö ruled over the Western part of Tibet. This King contributed to the great Buddhist renaissance in Tibet.

Lao Pu-wei picks up the pace. Leading his horse, he rushes along two yaks carrying huge loads, as everyone else follows. They are approaching one of several low-rise buildings. Vitas and Aviel stand aside, the monk talking to an old herdsman. Soon the herdsman disappears, returning almost at once with butter tea and tsampa,[7] a traditional Tibetan dish.

Neither the tsampa nor the tea can warm them as much as the words that follow: "Fourteen more miles and we're there." What they don't realise is just what fourteen miles means.

After seven miles, they take another break in Naga. A nameless stream flows into this settlement from the right and its springs spread all the way to the Gangotri National Park, not far from mountains 20,000 feet tall.

The expedition carries on along the Jadhang River, which branches off after two miles. The regular path leads along the central stream.

Instead they turn left, upstream to the Jadhang. The dense and indisputable elements with their sharp sprays of foam grasp madly at boulders. Far and wide it seems this is the only form of life. A bare artery cut open, giving life to the whole body by means of its insane cascades.

Sometimes they are on horseback and sometimes they walk the terrain, which surprisingly can be tread on with relative ease. It is a hard, rocky surface. However, fatigue from numerous hours on horseback, walking at high altitudes and the thinness of the air has taken its toll. Every step becomes agonising. Their shirts, although drenched in sticky, salty sweat, pleasantly cool their tired muscles.

---

7   Tsampa – Tibetan national dish – roasted barley with barley butter, with various other ingredients if possible.

It is getting dark and Aviel and Vitas are trying to muster up their last bit of strength. As the sun sets it becomes colder, the mountains surrounding them casting long, mysterious shadows. A valley with a lake suddenly appears before them. A tributary of the Jadhang, its spring dozens of yards away, flows into it. The lake resembles an oasis in the desert. Dozens of yaks, horses, sheep and goats fight to devour the grass that grows around the water. Monks wearing brown cassocks are tending to the animals, while curiously checking out the newcomers from afar. The small, wooden buildings that stand near the river do not serve dwelling purposes. They seem almost industrial and not until later will our Jingzhi discover that this is the place where monks had once extracted gold. Apparently, there is an abundance of the mineral all around Tibet. Traditional Tibetans cannot mine gold by digging for it because to them this means pulling out the roots of their holy ground. Intervening into the natural structure awakens the spirits and goblins of air, earth and the underworld. Legends have it that these spirits and goblins are then able to take their revenge. But panning for gold is another story...

Although full-grown, strong trees are rare, a huge, 160-foot tall fir tree stood at the foot of the hill, where they had first turned away from the flow of the river. According to ritual, everyone must walk around it in a clockwise direction, just like they walked around the several mänthangs that they had passed along the way. The tree is surely over 100 years old. Although beautiful, it doesn't seem to fit in here. It stands a few yards from a rocky precipice. At the foot of the cliff, there is a large, smooth rock, about a half yard wide and tall, with some Tibetan inscription written on it. It is obvious that the inscriptions are almost ancient. The hands of time, wind and rain have almost levelled them with their surroundings. The inscriptions are in the shape of verses, one on top of the other, perhaps poems. Our pilgrims don't know if it is a tombstone, a memorial plaque or some liturgical text. Apparently, they have reached their destination. The monks take the horses to the stables by the pastures. The yaks with the loads, some monks and our guests begin to mount the steep hill. The caravan sets off along the tough, rocky path around the now-curved, now-pointy, various-shaped protrusions, menacingly scattered before them. They offer shelter to anyone who would shine a light on a newcomer. Even so, to ask the monks the name of the mountain that they are ascending, the almost 13,000-foot high peak towering over their heads, they will say: Jadhang. At the source of the Jadhang River, everything around is Jadhang.

A plateau surrounded by several caves, perhaps only drilled rocks forming a semicircle of solid wall, opens up before them. But this is an optical illusion. There are in fact several different cuts along the whole wall with narrow passageways leading to more gorges and corridors.

It is as if the whole wall has several other floors. A parallel path or terrace leads along various levelled holes about 40 feet above the ground. Monks, wearing red cassocks, are running in and out of these holes. Like busy worker-bees, running all around at their tasks.

Snap! Vitas has to immortalise this picture. It too, is forever engraved in his memory. The unit resembles an enormous anthill, yet everything appears natural, inconspicuous, as if by divine spit, leaving behind a formation of miniature beetles in a cauliflower-head looking mushroom. Thanks to the massive rock, it is also very difficult to see life on this hidden island of air. Any life is hardly visible even by satellite or high-flying planes.

There are walls built in the openings where the monks are running in and out. These walls are built according to the sizes of the holes and have variously shaped, dense doors. There are Buddhist symbols displayed above these entrances. These symbols are either simple ornaments or intricate, colourful masterpieces of the Buddha sitting in the shape of a lotus flower. The mills of the circle of life stand symmetrically overhead and every monk that passes spins the wheels, so they rarely ever stop. The symbol of life, of samsara, of constant rebirth, constant return, a sign of evanescence… It is as if colourful prayer flags are gushing from the earth and whispering spiritual messages into the wind.

The Jingzhi are standing in front of the wall in something resembling a giant courtyard. There is a massive, imposing chorten, symbol of the awakened mind, in the middle of this courtyard. In India and the rest of the world, it is better known as the stupa, but here, its meaning is broader, more mysterious. The base of this stone formation is thirteen feet long on all sides with a roughly-milled sphere on it. There is a cone with several rings that sits forty feet atop this sphere and the tip is shaped like a small inverted umbrella. The individual parts symbolise the elements of life – water, fire, air, earth. There are several inscriptions, sacred messages, perhaps even those same verses written one on top of the other, almost identical to the verses seen down at the pastures at the foot of the rock next to the tall fir tree, engraved along the perimeter of the stone.

A box for victims, eroded by the passing of time, which has long lost its purpose as a reliquary gives Vitas the same feeling as would the fountain of a Medieval European castle, witness to feasts, grief, invasions, plagues, the tales of kings and ordinary people long blown away by time. Unquestionably, it is an object to respect and honour, as one cannot contest a thing superior to reason.

There are small, narrow doors in the chortens from the

side of the lamasery, where the remains, often no more than dust and whiteness, of the most important monks used to lay after the funeral rituals. Unlike common chortens, put on display for the admiration of tourists, this one is not painted or decorated. So, with its ochre, sandstone colour, typical to this region, and with its raw cracked surface, it blends into the countryside until the moment the whole formation is ahead, leaving the wanderer numb with the spiritual vibrations that exhort him to bow at its foot.

The shade of another mountain seems to cut the anthill in two. The shadow moves right before the eyes along with the vanishing sun. It becomes colder. It is as if the chortens, which once radiated so much energy, have turned into sleeping yet menacing goliaths at the wave of a wand.

The monks remove the loads from the yaks in the courtyard and busy as ants, take it apart and carry it into the passages according to the rules known to them. The yaks are then led back down to the pasture. Lao Pu-wei abandons the caravan and accompanies the two foreigners into one of the holes in the rock. The other monks stop, watching them curiously and amused, they sometimes whisper: "Jingzhi…" Vitas and Aviel are accommodated in a spacious room, with pillows and fuzzy blankets on the floor…

Aviel, at the very edge of sleep, looks up in a daze and slowly, begins to say in a tired voice: "If there truly is a God, then this is the exact place where he fell flat onto his nose…"

6.
Meeting the Enemy of the State

Vitas is desperately avoiding puddles, mud and asphalt holes. He feels like a bird bouncing around among tossed seeds. He passes an old Volkswagen Beetle and judging by the flat tires and rust, it's clear that its days of road racing are long gone. Nothing but a corpse.

The destination is in sight. Compassion Street, building no. 3. The whole subdivision on the outskirts of Prague looks like a warzone. The homes look worn-down, but you get the feeling that very affluent owners live there because there are satellite dishes and security cameras all around. Moreover, judging by the small details, like brass doorknobs, even though they're fixed to worm-infested, peeling doors, not to mention the curtains and chandeliers visible in some windows, you can tell that this is a well-off neighbourhood. The current period has taken its toll – 1994, in the wake of the Velvet Revolution and after the fall of Communism. People are getting used to far greater possibilities and external appearances are beginning to matter. Over the past few years, many homes got a new face life. The first signs of these new possibilities often manifest themselves in tacky fads, which are more of a sight for sore eyes.

There's only one word on the doorbell: Kromen.

Two years have passed since that innocent article came

out in the Cheb newspaper and Vitas has lost a lot of sleep over this case. Through his other interesting reports, he has worked his way up from the regional journal to the national newspaper, *The Way*. On top of this, he also published a number of successful cases for this national paper. He has the ability to pinpoint the essence of the case and present it to the reader in such a provocative way that the reader feels as if they were at the centre of the problem in the piece. He also added irony and humour to an article, whenever possible. He isn't afraid of taking on any case. Whether a picture of a group of pickpockets at work just three feet away, or cases of political or economic criminals, he isn't afraid. He has become familiar with all genres, including news reports. However, since they are short, he is careful not to put too much of his heart into them. He feels a lot more at home with journalism and investigative news.

But now is the time for something substantial, as he is applying to be a reporter for Czech TV, and good impressions are paramount for him. He has been preparing both the Rudolfinum case and an investigative newspaper article for the television station. He is certain that this is a good case because after reinvestigating the Cadastral Office, he found out that the fraud was complete – the Investment Bank had lost thirty million. While a real topic, he still has no idea that it is only a desperate fraction of the real case. He thinks he's taking a small bite out of a big fish. However, what he can't see is that it's only a chicken wing.

He raises his finger to the doorbell.

The slamming of a car door and the dead weight of bodies force him to immediately turn around. A young man with a beard and army pants is quickly making his way towards him.

'How didn't I notice the people in the car? Bad senses!' Vitas scolds. The man in army pants stands six feet in front of him. His hands in his bulging pockets, ready for action. It's like a scene from a Western, staring at him with his dark, narrowed eyes …

Meanwhile, Vitas' index finger is pointing at the doorbell. He feels that if he pushes it, he will set off a bomb. "I just want to ring the doorbell here…" says Vitas vaguely.

"Well, of course," mumbles the man calmly. It is as if this is the most commonplace thing to do and they were standing in line in the centre of Prague, waiting for ice cream.

So, Vitas rings the doorbell and ignores the man because the door is what's most important to him.

Still nothing. Vitas looks at the man, who seems (by his appearance) to have a question.

Suddenly, the window opens and out peeks a very handsome yet desolate, thirty-five-year-old shaggy head. The man's hair is as thick and brown as tree bark. Strands of his hair fly around him in all directions and even slap his face when he makes rapid gestures. But it is his eyes that are the most prominent. Even at such a distance, they cast quick and unpleasant glances. Wearing a dark t-shirt with the inexplicable logo of some rock band or another, he wields a TV remote, almost trying to turn Vitas off if he decides he doesn't like him.

"What do you waaant!!?" he bellows (emphasis on the "aaa…")

SNAP! Vitas can't resist but immortalise him in his mental photobook. He has no idea that this will become one of the "most touched and yellowish" pictures he has ever taken.

"Hello – Mr Kromen. Are you Mr Kromen?" Answerless, he accepted and continued. "I'm Vitas from *The Way* journal. You were formerly the owner of Vesna. Did you take out any loans…?"

"Go to hell," he interrupts Vitas, waving his hand as if to

get rid of a fly. "I haven't owned it for a long time now. Go see the current owner or executive."

"But wait, Vesna took out a thirty million crown loan from the Investment Bank when you were there," snaps Vitas quickly, so that Kromen doesn't close the window.

"Maybe, but I've transferred the whole company, liabilities and everything, all onward, totally a legitimate step, and I'm not interested in what's going on with it now. Go…"

"… I know, but where's the money – is the Rudolfinum going to become a ruin…?"

Kromen's smile takes Vitas by surprise. He realises that by playing dumb (a game, which usually works), he is actually making himself look dumb.

The dishevelled man closes the window and pulls the curtains shut. Although he had been smiling, you could see that it got him thinking.

Vitas turns his head to the man in the army pants, who has witnessed the whole conversation. This man has now moved his hands from the 'always ready!' position behind his back. Rocking back and forth gently, he disappointedly shouts: "Well, that went well, didn't it?"

Vitas, dejected, returned to the newsroom. He had his own office right on Wenceslas Square. It was a small but cosy office, hidden in a dark maze of corridors in an ancient building. He even had a bed. Before he moved his family to Prague, he would commute back and forth from Cheb. When the editor-in-chief wanted Vitas to change offices and to be with the other editors, Vitas blatantly told him that in that case, he'd have to resign. He had no intention of blackmailing the editor-in-chief. He was merely stating a fact. Even so, it worked. They didn't want to lose Vitas. His cases made headline news every week. He was working on one case after the other.

When he got back to the office from Kromen's house,

he found a letter on his desk. It was a regular letter with a Vaclav Havel stamp on it and a stretched out, smudged seal going across the left shoulder, neck, chin and right eye from the Prague Central Post Office. Vitas' name and newsroom address were under the stamp. Nothing else – no sender. He ripped the envelope open the way he always does, ripping one side with his index finger and thumb, peeling off a part of the text. Just enough, so that he could stick his finger into the envelope and slide it across to the other end, ruthlessly tearing the whole envelope, like an icebreaker crushing through ice, leaving only snow, a rough scar and crushed, greyish matter. The envelope falling lifelessly into the trash can, its grave, and Vitas holding a clean, white sheet of paper with two words written on it: DESIST NOW! He turns the paper over helplessly, hoping to find something else written on it, possibly in the same font, though he'd have to heat the paper or drizzle lemon on it in order to decipher the letters. Nothing. The words had been written in regular blue pen, clearly using stencils because they were all the same but unevenly spaced out and at different heights. There was even some engraved, colourful calligraphy at the end. What is he supposed to stop doing? Is it a threat? Or just a recession? It's likely connected to a case. Which one? He's working on many. Kromen? Nonsense. He just got back from there. What can this be? Maya? Nonsense.

Maya – a beautiful name with a dark past. Maya the hated. Maya the beloved. Maya pure as snow. Maya the criminal… The source of glances, emotions, insidiousness, sadness.

The Velvet Revolution in then-Czechoslovakia was the cork. A cork that burst out of the bottle, followed by many magnificent bubbles, as well as dirt and ruin – all the deformed and crushed matter boiling up under the pressure, looking out into the world through a thick, green bottle. As communism in Western Europe fell, the Western world, now a bit bored and annoyed by its consumerism, was anticipating a newfound breath of fresh air stemming from this freedom. New hope. A new philosophy. It was looking forward to being caressed, for the slavery of communism had to plant a seed of hope in order to escape this vicious wheel of consumerism, devouring everything in sight just to preserve its existence. Instead of a warm caress or a clear, philosophical idea, it was covered in dirt from the bottle and quickly followed suit to the Eastern model, learning to scam people and frown on the passers-by, knowing that even though it's a beautiful day today, it will be cloudy and gloomy tomorrow.

Maya was the wife of a famous singer, a dissident, who had doors open to the world. The doors suddenly opened for everyone, except some people had to unlock these doors, some people had to force the doors open and some people only scratched them, but were unable to get them to open. People got a sense of freedom, much of which was helpless. Some took full advantage of it and only a fraction grabbed it by the horns and followed their hearts and minds. But Maya opened her eyes just like everyone else and saw blue collar labourers turn into members or parliament, if not government officials and Vaclav criminally becoming president… Changes were bubbling all around, shouting, hoping… and what about her? What piece of the pie would she bite off?

Maya's hands were trembling when she grabbed the paper with the Government of the Czech Republic heading. The vice prime minister is hereby authorising her to search property of the Church and the Youth Socialist union. It was as if she got the golden ticket to enter the Land Registry Book located at the Fruit Market in Prague. This Institute had lost its significance over the years of Communism. Its archives range from the times of the Empress Marie Teresa to the Communist Revolt in 1948. The land registry records every transfer and ownership of property. Sometimes, it even mentions tangible property related to the land. At first, it had to do with aristocratic property. Property owned by the Church and municipal property was added later on. A so-called geodesy was established during Communism in the 1960s. The Land Registry Book had lost its purpose because property could suddenly be recorded anywhere into the geodesy, at national committees and nothing was out of the question, it all depended on who had the higher card – the date or importance of the People's Office. After all, all property was either in the hands of the state or nationalised, meaning nothing really mattered. Everything had to serve the people, so anything could be confiscated as needed, on behalf of the people, the people themselves included.

Very few people knew how the Land Registry system worked. It wasn't until the 1990s that even its employees started discovering unbelievable structures and interconnections, jointly interwoven with other records.

Anna had long been an employee of the Land Registry and an avid right-wing supporter. She looked a lot older than she actually was as a result of her tiny, hunched appearance and wrinkled face. But she was that much more energetic and passionate about everything she did. She herself was perhaps a part of the archives, which were huddled together on long shelves, sleeping under a layer of dust, when she was questioning Vitas.

What brings you here? What's going on? Why here and why now...? Once she believed that he was there because he truly wanted to uncover the whole truth about miraculous Maya, she enthusiastically broke out in an avalanche of emotions and mutually intertwined facts: "I stared at her, mouth wide open, Mr Editor, when she talked about riding on a scooter with Vaclav at the Prague Castle, how everything was so free-spirited there, how they're getting rid of the old Bolshevik order and how all the awful Communists are angrily stepping down from their comfortable positions. Well silly me, I believed every word she said. I would have granted her every wish. She had anything she wanted before she had to even ask. Any document, anything. She made herself right at home here, snooping around everywhere, looking at anything she wanted... She even brought a scanner with her! And then this! That was the shock of a lifetime for me!"

Although dear Maya neither found Church or Youth Socialist Union property, as the government had authorised her to do, she did find out that she was the owner of a large building, in the heart of Prague, on one of the most lucrative locations in the heart of Europe, opposite the Ministry of International Affairs. She pulled the old papers out of the Land Registry Book, which bore the name of her ancestors. Everyone gazed at her and patted her on the shoulders. "Well, Maya, you are very rich." Since one of her friends worked at the housing cooperative, the ownership was transferred in her name at the blink of an eye. The tenants of this large building were less amused by this fact, but it surprised no one. They were only envious. They had wanted to establish a cooperative and take care of the building, but those plans were spoiled. Counterfeits? No, Maya would never do such a thing... – a fundamental and irrefutable argument that was gladly accepted by all her friends.

Everything would probably stay that way. Maya would own beautiful property, leaving her swimming in a sea of gold coins. She'd have everything. But, even so, that wasn't enough. Maya spoke out in public, astonished at this truly unexpected turn of events. She couldn't believe her eyes, but she was holding documents from the Land Registry in her trembling hands, entitling her to claim a large part of the Strahov Monastery, a gem, possibly even dominating over the Prague Castle, in the heart of Prague. And she did it. She presented her entitlement to the Premonstratensian Order that had owned this gem since the twelfth century. Later, realising she may have bitten off more than she could chew, she became a little worried, removing a fragment to imply that she revoked ever making such a request, but choked helplessly, it was already too late. The whole ordeal was underway. Maya had crossed a certain and sensitive line, which could either leave her drowning in a pot of gold or burn her to ashes. Nothing in between.

The Premonstratensian Order had its librarian. This is nothing unusual, especially when the Monastery is home to one of the world's most famous and magnificent libraries. However, with this librarian, it seemed that time stood still. Not only still, but began to turn back centuries. When Vitas first visited, he was afraid that he had stepped into a time capsule to the beginning of the Medieval Ages. This librarian was the exact archetype of an antique monk, limping, cross-eyed through the glasses on his nose. To speak with him is to be embarrassed not to know where he's looking and to want to avoid all offense. But Vit the librarian grabbed Vitas by the shoulders and with great inner tension, spewed out one argument after the other: "The documents are covered in meaningless stamps. These stamps shouldn't even be on these papers! This stamp didn't even exist at the time – 1939. Adolf Schwarzenberg's signature, including the stamp, is the exact forty-first percent enlarged copy of his signature from the Schwarzenberg Dynasty publication from 1936." Vit the librarian was providing fact after fact and everything he said was accompanied by indisputable evidence.

Vitas staggered out of the Monastery. Is it even possible for the Premonstratensian Order, so opulent prior to the war, to be selling a piece of the Strahov Monastery to poor Maya's grandfather, who, incidentally, had grown up in an orphanage? And that this grandfather reached the height of his career as a painter? Where would he get the money from? Vitas addressed the nuncio from Prague, the envoy from the Vatican, with specific questions. A very polite answer meant very impolite content, which isn't fit for the representative of such an Institute to say. "Any sale of this kind is and has been completely ruled out..."

The Land Registry supported the article he published in the paper and apart from the miraculous findings discovered by Maya, there were no other documents proving her claims. On the contrary, new evidence appeared in related organisations (the Real Estate Office, the District Court in Prague 3), showing ties to completely different owners, none of them painters, such as Maya's grandfather.

The article received an overwhelming response. Dissident and right-wing public officials told the media that Vitas had conspiratorial ways, was an undercover Communist spy and a Communist servant... Vitas smiled, knowing he was under the magnifying glass now more than anyone ever. Some particular political dissidents, formerly exposed, had lists of special undercover Communist spies that had never been published before. These people were now restlessly denying everything. Vitas knew that no one would find him anywhere. On the contrary, his signature could only be found on anti-Communist manifestos at the end of the Communist era, including the request for Vaclav Havel to be released from prison. Vitas later saw the irony in this in relation to the case.

All truthful and false lists were being scrutinized and the truth is that very few former undercover Communist spies were discovered among the huge number of investigators, public prosecutors (later state representatives) and lawyers.

This was music to the ears of Maya and her friends, who opposed handing over millions in property to the most honest person in the world, seeing it as a conspiracy of undercover Communist spies, envious and inhumane, vile hyenas.

While Vitas was diligently studying all the material on Maya and thought about how many personalities she could control, he attributed an interesting ability to her – a spider, with almighty charisma, a journalist and later senator, one of the biggest advocates during the course of extensive court proceedings defending herself, the investigators and the public officials from their opponents. It was not until a few years afterwards that a major reorientation occurred, proving she was guilty and professing her a master of black magic.

Even so, there is no way that Maya can be the author of the mysterious letter that Vitas is holding in his hands. And why should he even attach any meaning to these letters? It doesn't matter, it's meaningless to him. It changes nothing.

Little did he know that this mysterious person would become his shadow.

7.
The Awakening

Vitas felt as if he was standing in a whirlwind. He was immersed in a suffocating nebula, spinning rapidly in circles, trying hard to avoid this strange spin and rinse cycle. His eardrums almost popped because of the loud trumpet noise. He stopped waving his hands, covered his ears and let the wind blow him farther and farther away...

"Come on, sir, it's time, it's time..." Kromen nudged Vitas. Vitas finally opened his eyes and woke up. Hot, black vortices spiralled into him from two endless tunnels – Kromen's eyes. In the distance, all that could be seen were these miniature dots. He was nodding his head ironically, but in good faith. His perfect, cared-for skin and slicked, partly greyish, perfectly parted hair, as if straight from a fashion magazine, seemed to contrast with his ruthless, devilish eyes. This all gave the impression that Vitas had woken up at the Prague Hilton. The rest of Kromen's body, hidden behind a brown cassock, brought him back to reality.

Vitas laughed with mixed emotions. "I do have a good sense of imagination but I had no idea," watching the mobster's absurd transformation into a holy pilgrim on an eternal journey. "Well, I haven't seen you in a long time... so, I didn't expect you'd have your own hairdresser, your own makeup artist here – a whole team of people taking care of your image," he said ironically as he was stretching.

"Don't choke, snoopy," said Kromen defensively, though his face was glowing. "Welcome to Jadhang. I am glad you came." Kromen had to speak up because several rag-dungs, thirteen feet long trumpets held by two monks, the third blowing into it, made long, hoarse, tenor notes, summoning the monks to morning prayer.

"Enough of this, get yourself up quickly and let's go partake in their rituals," said Kromen still smiling, tossing his head somewhere into the rocky maze.

"First of all, how about you tell me what's going on here? Why am I here, what am I supposed to do here?" asked Vitas clearly, but Kromen interrupted him sternly: "Not now, we'll have more time to talk about everything later." Kromen wryly grinned. "Yes, a lot more time. Let's go, let's go..."

Morning prayer was held in the dukang,[8] a large room filled with pillows, in a cave. A monk was banging into a large brass gong at the front of the room. Over a hundred monks had already gathered inside and more were coming in. Kromen, Vitas and Aviel sat down on pillows near the wall. The wall was engraved with various ornaments and Buddhist frescoes. The opposite wall was covered with bright-red, stripped, large carpets. The whole dukang wasn't all that bright, lit up by dozens of yak butter candles. Gold-plated, Tibetan text, illegible to Vitas, was engraved on the spaces on the wall. A series of mantras, the holiest of which dominated the front of the altar in gold letters read: – OM MANI PADME HUM. There are six sacred syllables representing six worlds, which contain fire and water, passion and eternal peace. All human senses are awakened by the sound and intense announcement. In the eyes of true believers, the spoken words transform into reality and energy. This

---

8   Dukang – a ceremonial hall for religious rituals and monk gatherings

specific mantra formula has numerous interpretations but all have one thing in common – to say them with honesty, is to have said everything. Nothing more would remain.

Lama Thorpe Tandzin was sitting at the bottom of the altar, under the mantra, in the lotus leaf position, his back to everyone – an abbot of the local lamasery – a man wearing a yellow, silk robe and a tetreng, a magical rosary with over one hundred different human skull bones, around his neck. Sitting in his meditative position, his right hand twists into an unnatural position, his abdomen resting on his knee as he slowly turns a dordje,[9] a golden eight-spoke thunderbolt, seeming to focus all his energy into it. At first glance, it resembles a small dumbbell, but rather than weights at the end of the bar, there are eight spokes in a circle with one in the middle, forming a ball. Given the Lama's intense concentration, it seems that he is drawing a lot of energy from this ritual object, or at least this is what he believes and how it inadvertently comes across.

– – –

The room suddenly falls silent and all the monks stop playing the loud instruments. Lama Thorpe sharply glances over the audience and focuses his attention on Kromen, before instantly shifting his gaze to Aviel, who is sitting next to him. He looks at him closely for a moment and then looks at Vitas. The wrinkles on his round, Asian face make him look more strict and wise. You can see every bone there and the exposed parts of his body. This wrinkled face is proof of great inner strength and tenacity. The distance between them is taking away the intensity of the glare. If

---

9 Dordje / dorje / vajra / thunderbolt – originally from Sanskrit, often translated as "diamond". In fact, it means "indestructible". A ritual object often used in tantric rituals. It is one of the most important Buddhist symbols.

they were closer, Vitas wouldn't resist. Snap! Vitas put this face, hidden behind candle light into his album.

The Lama closes his eyes sharply. His tense hand holding the dordje, stopped still, the star object facing the ground as if he was using the dordje for support, as if the dordje were held up by an invisible rod, perhaps even levitating his whole body. The long silence is unbearable. First, there is a quiet hmmmm. The other monks follow and it gets louder. The mouth begins opening and the "hmmmm" gradually becomes one "hmmmmoooaaaoooohmmmm," followed by a much faster and thoroughly articulated "mani padme" and then again "oooooooooohmmmmm…" ending somewhere in indefinite silence…

Then, the monks fervently sing a few sacred psalms. Our two visitors are watching the ritual in astonishment. Kromen doesn't partake in the singing, he could care less. Instead, he was examining the two new guests, with an ironic smile. The look in his eyes said it all: "It's nothing, just some boyish horsing around." However, Vitas and Aviel feel very relaxed, as if a great burden were lifted off their shoulders and they are surrounded by tranquillity.

The Lama began speaking after about half an hour of singing, psalms and chanting holy words. Unfortunately, neither Vitas nor Aviel understood any of it because it was in Tibetan, so they only let the sound of the words leave an impression on them. However, according to Kromen's facial expression, it was clear that he wasn't much better off.

"All knowledge and experience can be summarised by one word, distress, pain, anxiety and tears alternating with health, happiness, joy and laughter. It has all been here before and everything will come back again, just as we will enter a new dimension. It's not in vain that we have been suffering, distressed and dying for years. Change is coming, good fortune is on its way and the supreme truth will come.

It will only be a breeze that we brothers have to be prepared for. We cannot miss it. We cannot let it get away. If we want to enter a higher dimension in the next life, we must act. So, brothers, let us pray, meditate, practise the Buddhist arupa-jhan, study the words of Buddha, the Supreme, enlightened Buddha, the Siddhartha Gautama. Let's open our eyes, practice our will, our body and let us not resist what is meant to be. No one knows if it is frost or heat, sweet or salty, or whether it will come in the form of a vulture, a fish or a human being, lava-rock or snow. We will have to recognise this SOMETHING and devote our lives to it. If we grasp it the way we're supposed to, it will bring us joy, happiness, love, laughter, a higher dimension and new life."

A long pause was interrupted by "Oooohmmmm, MANI PADME Hhuuuuuummmm," and all the monks joined in again. Commotion then broke out. Some monks were banging on drums, others on gongs and all rag-dungs and shells were making noise... It didn't take long and the ceremony was over. Several monks stormed into the dukang, passing out tea with butter and tsampa.

Our trio turned to face each other, holding the pillows in their hands and sipping tea. You could hear the soft murmurs of monks talking to one another throughout the whole room.

"Well, I don't understand Tibetan, so it made not much sense to me, but was nice to listen. And what's this here?" asked Vitas in broken English, so that Aviel would also understand. He keeps asking himself if he has made a mistake in accepting Kromen's offer. Should he put an abrupt end to their relationship? He can do that whenever. Now he's interested in seeing what today and tomorrow bring...

"Well, where should I start...?" asked Kromen, scratching his ear.

"With the truth, the truth," urges Aviel.

"Gentlemen, I have a pretty special relationship with both of you and I know, or at least I think that I can trust you. But it's not that simple. I've been here for four months now, I've fully adapted to the way things work, but I'd like to go back home at some point. My family and children are there. So I have one matter that I have to take care of and I have to take care of it quickly. We have about two weeks to take care of it and then go back. It'll be so cold here in a month that we won't even consider going back until next spring. Is that clear?"

"And what is it that we have to take care of?" asks Aviel.

"I'll tell you, when the time is right."

"Are you kidding? You bring us all this way here and don't say a word? We're all in this together now!" Aviel and Vitas were both shouting over one another.

"Sorry, but I didn't make any promises," said Kromen in his defence. "It was your own decision to come here. Neither of you would be here unless you wanted to! And what did it take for you to get here? Not much! Nothing!"

"It took time and work," lied Vitas. "Is that not enough?"

"Blah, blah, blah! I even paid for the trip. Others would give anything to go on such a trip…" Kromen suddenly lowered his voice because a monk in a red robe came, hands folded and bowing, was looking at everyone kind-heartedly with his ingenuous smile. "So, are these your friends, Kushok Kromen?[10] It's very nice to meet you. May you find peace and truth here and god-willing, your awakening."

"Yes, yes, Kushok Tungjur, this is them. Lama Rinpoche will be very pleased. They can give us what we are all expecting of them."

"And may we know what is expected of us?" asked Aviel, well aware of the fact that he is embarrassing Kromen.

"I will fill you in on everything," said Kromen

---

10 Kushok – A title of respect applied to those who are ordained.

ostentatiously so that monk Tungjur could hear. He then got up just so that he wouldn't remain seated next to a highly-ranked monk. Kromen took him aside and conspiratorially asked: "Do you think the honourable Rinpoche would accept me? I would like to discuss these important matters with him."

"I'll see. I think he would also like to talk to you. I will let you know. Will you take care of their accommodations and whatever else they need? They have to be happy."

"You know you can depend on me. I've kept all my promises. I hope the holy Lama Rinpoche also stays true to his word."

"I cannot speak on his behalf, but if he gave you his word, he'll follow through with it. However, he also has to make sure that everything is as it's supposed to be."

"No doubt about it," concluded Kromen with a confident smile, bowed and parted ways.

"Let's go," he said abruptly to the ones sitting down. "Let me first show you around."

The trio stepped out of the dukang. The morning sun was shining brightly, so despite the high altitude and brisk air, it was warm. Kromen shows his friends the monumental rock formation, which is used as refuge for the lamasery. In essence, it is a plateau on a plateau, the top of the world. The hills and slopes with their caves and cliffs all at different heights make this part of the world an isolated kingdom. It's almost as wide as it is high. There are monks drumming to a different beat all around. It looks like most of them are obviously going to work, leading yaks and goats out to better pastures, some monks meditating, discussing with one another, mumbling sutras and mantras aloud...

"The lamasery is one of the biggest and most secret monasteries in Tibet or in India, to be exact," Kromen explains to his kind. "The Indian territory of Ladakh lies a couple seventy miles to the north. Ladakh is commonly known in the world as Little Tibet, recognised as the largest Buddhist refuge. However, only a few insiders know about this place here. There are about 130 monks of various specialisations here. The Gelugpa School[11] is most widespread here. I don't know much about it and that's not even my intention. However, only about thirty monks are truly devoted to intensive spiritual activity and less than ten monks make up a so-called Kashag, the former Tibetan Government, so here, they call it little Kashag or just Kashag, Everyone knows what you are referring to. Lama Thorpe Tandzin rules over the Kashag."

"And what about the remaining majority?" asks Vitas, as he observes the hustle and bustle all around.

"These are all sorts of people, who fled from China either for political reasons or just because they were hungry. Or they come from different places. Some are mental misfits, some are just happy to be working, so they have something to eat. It's a bit of everything. Every community has a crazy guy, a brainer, a poet, a thief and a rat. This place is no exception. The world is as such. The majority are Buddhists, or at least that's what they act like. A few of them are Hindi and we even had a couple of Muslims and Bönist in residence until recently. Bönism was a religion that preceded Buddhism. As a religion it left behind some shamanistic nonsense, bad habits. Yes and now we even have two Buddhist hermits walled up…"

"Walled up?" exclaimed Aviel.

"Yeees," chuckles Kromen, as he pulls both of them down a rocky path to a completely separate and isolated rock formation on the far side of the lamasery. First they

---

11 Gelugpa – ("The way of the virtuous order" or the "School of exemplary virtue"). The last of four Tibetan Buddhist schools. It is also known as the "Yellow School" or the "Yellow-Cap"

must walk along the rocky path around the rock and then climb up another one just to see a white-capped, ochre-covered part of the wild mountains stretching out north-east, in the same direction as the ancient city of Guge.

"One is a Tibetan monk, who formerly fought as a partisan against the Chinese and the second pilgrim to come here in the spring, one week before me. He is a Buddhist, from somewhere in China. He liked it so much here that he decided this would quite literally be the end of his journey. The Lama agreed and they walled him up in that rock over there," showing them the massive rock formation in front of him.

"Wung Pien, their guardian, doesn't bring them more than a bowl of tsampa, tea and water once a day. He hands it to them through a small hole and then closes the hole up with stone, leaving them just a few seconds to see the light of day. No one can speak to them, so that they can fully concentrate on their meditation. As the Buddhists say, so that they can release their spiritual, astral body from its useless physical body."

Kromen is pointing to a manmade, secluded niche. It is closer to an unnoticeable bulge avoiding most attention. "That's where the mad man is…"

"How long will he be there?" asked Aviel.

Kromen chuckled, "Well, for a few years or perhaps until he dies, until the time of enlightenment. Once he dies, they will tear him and the site down, and leave his body as prey for vultures, according to local custom. And that's where the other mad man is. He's some old Khampa, allegedly fought with the Chinese during the invasion of Tibet," pointing to another bulge about 200 yards away.

Annoyed, Vitas burst out: "Why are you ridiculing it? You can't laugh at something that is fulfilling to others…?"

"I understand that we're all different, but why should

someone die in this dark hole, alone, without having anyone to talk to? Being alone in a dungeon is the worst kind of punishment!" Kromen's voice was gradually getting louder and louder. "Not even the worst criminal in Europe is punished for the most perverted murders in this way!"

"He knows why he's there. One cannot deny the centuries-old tradition that this culture has gone through. Native people of the Amazon would laugh at your ways and the things you're saying."

Kromen threw his hands up in annoyance. "Ok, so I get why the Lama wanted you here. How could he have known that you'd be so tolerant? How could he have known that you'd play the role of the all-knowing, enlightened being…?"

"He wanted me, personally?" Vitas interrupted him in shock.

"Well, you should know if you're so smart." An angry Kromen, who unexpectedly switched to Czech, threw his hands up in surrender, turned back towards the lamasery and stepped down alone. His companions followed a few steps behind but then gave up. "You always were the clever one," he yelled out angrily in Czech, as he was running down the rocky path, waving his hands. "And how far did this intelligence get you? Nowhere! How much did you make? Nothing! Are you happy, did you achieve what you wanted in life? No! No! You only yelled at others and deprived them of their illusions!" called Kromen as he was walking away.

"Well, hold on! Why don't you at least tell us what's going on?" called Vitas. Although Aviel didn't understand Czech, he sensed the nature of the conflict, put his hand on his shoulder and calmed him down.

"Leave him alone, he'll get over it. Let's go for a walk and look around."

They watched Kromen waving his hands around a bit longer, until he disappeared between the rocky lamasery. Both Jingzhi decided to explore this inhabited rock maze.

8.

The Rudolfinum

"I don't understand," says Rokos, the producer and moderator to Vitas, shaking his bald head with a heart-felt smile. "Explain it to me one more time. How did the scam actually go down?"

"Simple," says Vitas a little nervously because it's his first interview with a producer and this could change his future. Becoming a reporter for the renowned *Bad Penny Journal* would mean a significant shift in his career. He had been a journalist for years now and he felt like he needed a change. He enjoyed creating a story out of every case. He was tickled by the musical, verbal and image synthesis of components. The information is sometimes relayed by picture and sometimes by sound. Sometimes they complement each other and sometimes they oppose one another. It's amazing to be able to use the art of counterpoint, when the respondent is enthusiastically testifying or explaining Exhibit A, but Exhibit B pops up on the screen, thereby degrading his version without even saying a word. Irritating the public by constantly shifting the solution of a dramatic situation, intertwining seriousness with humour, throwing your audience off and fumbling your way to revealing the truth… Only very few people know how to play with words, image and sound. The majority of reporters and editors only use tunnel vision – he stole one million, so they hunt him down like wild game! This is a simple, preconceived equation, where one sees the outcome beforehand.

"It's common to take out a loan on real estate or use it as a lien. However, then you can't do anything with it because the bank has bound the property with a lien. If you do it like a natural person, a foreclosure officer would come after you. You have to pay the loan off otherwise you will lose the property. However, if the property is owned by a legal person, a company that obviously has owners, these owners can transfer the company even with the mortgaged property. This is completely legitimate. No one can say a word. And if you transfer the company to someone in the Ukraine, who disappears somewhere out east, you only pay something to the White Horse, or nothing at all if you show him the bottom of the dam and in the end, take the whole loan. Have the bank go after someone they will never find. Who cares if the property is a ruin that doesn't have the value of the loan? That's not your problem. No one can do anything because according to the law, you have nothing to do with it," added Vitas rapidly.

Rokos briefly looks into Vitas' eyes and then points his index finger at him. "And are you sure, do you have proof?"

Rokos is the show's screenwriter and moderator, and although it isn't visible on-screen, he is rather short and clearly suffering from a Napoleon complex. Secretly, he wore high-heeled shoes, always had his chest out, nose high, giving the impression of a curved bow. His fat belly pierced the air in front of him, his head thrust back with his heels. The ones that sometimes bent him more, sometimes less, made his moderating stunts more suspenseful, especially when it came to the TyTy public opinion polls, in which he fought for top positions. On the outside, Rokos acted as if such a stupid poll for the most popular TV personality, intended for has-beens, meant nothing to him. However, when Vitas once barged into his office, he found Rokos drooling over the results of the TyTy public opinion poll. He quickly switched the channel, but even so it was obvious. However, Vitas was most annoyed when they were out in public together. People would bow in front of Rokos when they saw the two either walking down the street, on their way to lunch or just discussing something, saying, "Mr. Rokos, you are doing a wonderful job. You have such amazing reports..."

Vitas always felt like shouting, "You idiot, he does nothing but criticise and stick his face on camera. He has never put together any report!" Always, he would only wave his hand with pride, acting as if on top of it all, that he could care less, though, in truth, it did matter to him.

But it was Rokos' side job as a media trainer that soothed his Napoleonic ego the most. Companies, especially entrepreneurs dealing with a touchy subject in business, hired him and he, being the media guru he was, would teach them how to act in front of the camera and what to avoid doing. His side job earned him some decent change. Rokos took it to such perfect lengths that he even brought tapes of his reporters' reports to the media training to show them what mistakes these reporters were making. He and his organisational business partner, Bozik laughed, because he actually sold the report twice, once to the public and the second time to improve the level of Czech entrepreneurship. He even managed to pull off the following stunt, but only once. One of his reporters had humiliated a not-so-decent businessman in a report, and he was able to convince this furious businessman, who was determined to file a lawsuit, to not only withdraw the case, but also to pay thousands more for it in the form of media training. The motto was simple: to defend himself against slanderous reports in the future. "I saved the station from a lawsuit," he and Bozik laughed, his chest pushed out proudly like a bow.

"Everything is secured. I have records from the Land Registry Office, lien right, everything," says Vitas to a tense Rokos.

"Ok. I want to see the script. You have three days to film. If you have no experience filming, I'll give you a highly experienced independent cameraman and sound guy. Go for it!"

A script? A script it would be. When he presented Rokos with said script, Rokos only mumbled something and ran off to the next office, where other reporters were either talking on the phone or chatting to each other.

"So, darlings, this is the first time I have ever seen a script in my life. Shame on you and start reading!" Vitas was smiling shyly. He didn't know if this was a show of admiration or irony. The latter would leave him broken. The script evoked laughter. Colleague Budil grabbed him by the shoulders and said: "Don't be silly, you'd never film anything if you wrote everything in such detail. And how can you know in advance that someone will ask you this exact word and this exact word? You can do it in a feature doc, but not some investigative report, when you have no idea what anyone will say. Everyone will run away anyway and no one will want to talk to you. Don't be ridiculous. And besides," stretching his face to look like a strict teacher, "you're fucking up our standards!"

Vitas himself had no idea how it happened, but he managed to shoot the report exactly according to the script, including the part where he couldn't find Kromen. He wasn't at home, and neither did Vitas meet the man in the army pants, he wasn't at the company. He was nowhere to be found. He had no idea that Kromen knew his every step, having read the whole script before shooting started.

The report caused uproar at the TV station. Many colleagues congratulated him on his grand entrance. This very clever scam-non-scam dealing with the transfer of an indebted company received such feedback that six other police units wanted to interview him. The Foreign Police on the fight against organised crime, the Unit on the fight against economic crime, members of the Security Information Service, and so on. But the meetings were to be confidential, off the police or media radar. At the time, Vitas had no idea that some of these people worked for Kromen himself, who desperately needed to know what Vitas knew of.

"Hello, is this editor Vitas?" asked a voice on the phone, coming from Vitas' office at the Czech TV station. His transition from a newspaper journalist to the renowned, investigative show, *Bad Penny* was quick.

"Speaking. How can I help you?"

"I'm Inspector Adam Petrovsky of the Economic Crime Unit. I have to say that I found your report on the Rudolfinum in Cheb very interesting. Would you have time to stop by our Office on Bartholomew Street to talk about it?"

"Why? Will it be of any significance?" asked Vitas calmly. He was getting bored by meaningless meetings with different police units. And it doesn't hurt to bluff a little…

"No doubt about it. I think we have the same goal in mind."

"I'm afraid we may have very different goals in mind, but anyway. One condition – the meeting is mutual and you also tell *me* something."

"Why not?" We'll talk. How about three o'clock, day after tomorrow?"

"Deal."

— — —

When the guards brought Vitas into the office, two men, out-of-uniform, were waiting for him.

"Hello, editor," one of them shook his hand with a guilty smile, which he immediately explained. "Unfortunately, Inspector Adam Petrovsky had to go out into the field to cover a story, so the three of us will have to make do. I am…"

"… I'm sorry, but this wasn't our agreement," reacted Vitas angrily. "You could've at least called me…"

"If only we had a number. I tried calling you but I couldn't reach you," a difficult to dispute argument. Cell phones were not commonplace at the time.

Vitas accepted the situation, despite great resistance, but limited himself to less substantial data. He kept the most important information to himself. Whatever he did say was very simple. The police officers wrote on typewriters so slowly that Vitas would have rather written it for them.

"Sign here and if you think of anything else, call us."

"Tell Inspector Petrovsky that I may think of something else, but he'd have to come see me personally, with some gift of his own…"

The police officers only responded by raising their eyebrows, refraining to comment. Vitas left the renowned historical Crime Unit on Bartholomew Street, disgusted. Success-driven, he was expecting a lot more than to be sucked of valuable, hard-earned reportage. He didn't realise until a lot later that this was common practice – squeeze everything from a lemon and then throw it away, whether police officer, or journalist.

— — —

"YOU'RE SCARING DECENT PEOPLE!" read Vitas repeatedly with a grim face. Four words written on white paper. This letter was delivered to his *Bad Penny* office. He received anonymous letters at *The Way* newspaper every month. These letters read, "YOU'RE KIDDING!" "YOU'RE INSTIGATING!" But this is the first letter of this kind at the TV station. There's no point dealing with it. What should he do? He sees no solution. But even so, every time he reads these few words, those faint shivers run down his spine...

– – –

Judge Brodek's hair was so red that you'd mistake his curls for flames if you were sitting around a bonfire with him at night. He had dark brown eyes, which seemed to be obscured by a light haze, yet were extremely lively. He had felt like an outcast to society his whole life, but as soon as he had become a teenager, he had fit the position of an isolated individualist. Even so, the cause and effect was unclear, whether his physiognomy affected his character, or vice versa. The most feasible explanation is that both reflected his development, the development of an intellectual, who forever focuses only on studying. Interested only in regular life as long as it helps him to understand the law. For him, the law, the constitution and the legal code have always been, and will continue to be more than the word of God. It will always be more than any moral value because fulfilling the law is of the greatest moral value to him. For him, the greatest authority in life isn't the Father, or God, but the law, which among other things replaced these dimensions – both the Father and God. This view of the world, despite being as narrow as the view of a tank operator seeing reality through a small window, enabled him to successfully overcome all obstacles and follow his target, not distracted by any unnecessary feelings or whims of personal life. A very promising career was taking shape in front of the relatively young, barely forty-year-old judge. Law and order paved a straight and glittering path in front of him, making it perfectly clear as to when and under which conditions the next stop will come.

This was Judge Brodek in the eyes of Vitas. He didn't even budge in the largest Prague courtroom, as Maya pounded false accusations towards the Communist undercover spies, with prejudice and bias against everything human. Brodek always heard her out with a dead and motionless face. His decision was always completely based on the cold, legal formula. The horrible acoustics in the courtroom forced the audience to lean forward while sitting in order to eliminate the echo resonating from every word, which sounded like the irritating hum of bees. The judge's terse, curt reactions were like a dam chaotically squashed with bees. All the more annoyingly they then flew out into the dark echo of the vast audience, which was primarily made up of the former dissident underground. They tried forming an attack swarm to reinvade this archenemy.

Vitas was also under strict supervision in the courthouse. Maya's supporters were angrily taking pictures of him, pointing at him and whispering with furrowed looks on their faces. Their anger with Vitas was primarily based on the helplessness of finding any connection Vitas may have with the undercover world of Communist spies. The right-sided Vitas was obviously very amused by this helplessness. Not the real Vitas. Vitas was grateful for the revolution. He was also enthusiastically rattling his keys on Wenceslas Square, yelling "It's here!"

Of course it's possible to incriminate anyone, including Vitas himself. And he was well aware of it. Obviously the fact that he came from a very religious background could be used to discredit him. The believer in him "protects the property of his spiritual brotherhood!" Ugh.

His uncle was a Jesuit, a famous editor-in-chief for the Vatican in Rome, where he fought Communism via radio and newspaper. Another one of his great uncles was beaten by Communists because he was a famous mystic and philologist.

And as for Vitas? A believer, unable to personify God in any precise way. The Communist period in then-Czechoslovakia had been liquidating the Church and this obviously influenced his upbringing, for the better and for the worse. During the Communist period, his parents permitted forbidden worlds only to the extent that they wouldn't harm him. Vitas regretted it over time, but he couldn't blame them for anything. Parents generally want the best for their children, even if it hurts them, or even kills them.

He recalls an event at school when he was eight years old, as if it happened yesterday. It was 1968, and Czechoslovakia had been invaded by Warsaw Pact forces. At the same time it was also a time of inner tolerance and cohesion. Religion was one of the most volatile subjects, which was later completely abolished by the Communists. It was an evening on a school night and his father was standing three feet from his homeroom teacher, sweating badly. Little Vitas was looking up at the two adults and… SNAP! Everything had stuck in his memory till this day. Although he didn't understand, he felt great tension in the words and the atmosphere alone. His father quietly told the teacher that he would like for his son to attend religious studies, but only if it weren't recorded in his personal file. Comrade teacher was equally tremulous. She didn't know where to look. She was thoughtlessly stroking Vitas on the head as if she were trying to smear old paint off the doors. She probably had no idea that she was even stroking his head at all. With a lot of effort, she blurted out: "I'm sorry but I really can't do that. He will either attend and it will be recorded or he won't attend and it won't be recorded. But I have to record it correctly."

There was a long, embarrassing pause and everyone was looking somewhere else. Comrade teacher had obviously long wanted to leave and disappear, while my father wanted to persuade her, but nothing was coming out of his partially opened mouth. It was as if the words were stuck inside like some kind of clogged valve...

Little Vitas was only staring up at the two heavily breathing heads, not understanding what the problem was. At the time, he had no idea that recording such a marginality would fundamentally influence his destiny. All the other schools would remain closed to him. Older, after realising this, he never blamed his father. This example perfectly depicts the atmosphere he grew up in. His clearly negative attitude towards Communism wasn't to arrive until much later.

His approach to God was influenced by his young environment. Although he believed in God, the older he got, the more that going to mass every Sunday became very unpleasant for him. A strict Catholic environment in a Communist enclosure and the presentation of decimated Church leaders evoked feelings of distrust wrapped in airtight, suffocating black velvet. He perceived everything with feelings bordering on phobia. When he walked into the Church, something gripped his chest like a vice and little Vitas secretly began wondering what the difference between God and the Devil was. Originally, he thought that God was supposed to be like his older and wiser brother, who would help him in desperate situations and situations that he couldn't tell his parents about, all while being a funny and happy companion. Unfortunately, this wasn't how it worked. Even so, there was still no doubt in his mind that God liked to play jokes. He had to laugh, watching the people on Earth.

— — —

There were various ways that Maya fought against the accusation of tampering with and falsifying official documents. She couldn't rely on facts because those were clearly against her. Court proceedings were frequently postponed due to illness and investigations into higher instances regarding any possible bias, which were always rejected. Every now and then, poor Maya had to go into custody, due to the enormous number of falsified documents. She and her supporters immediately reacted by saying that poor Maya's health was deteriorating, custody being a risk to her life. Ample speculation of Maya's health forced Vitas to address the prison doctor.

"There's no way I can tell you anything about anyone's condition, let alone someone in custody. Are you crazy?" yelled the doctor over the phone. But Vitas presented all the possible and impossible arguments against him, including that, in Maya's words, they were hurting her in custody, until he managed to upset the doctor to the point that he began to shout: "What were you thinking? That this is a walk through the rose garden or what? It's certainly mentally challenging, anyone here can get stomach ulcers…"

"Stomach ulcers, you say…?" Vitas quickly recited him word for word.

"Of course. Every other person here."

"She was supposed to be on her deathbed…?"

"Bullshit. She's as fit as a fiddle. She's definitely healthy enough to insult people…"

After much hesitation and consultation, Vitas didn't end up using the information from the interview. He knew that no matter how ridiculous it was with regard to the given circumstances negotiated in court, publishing the diagnosis could be a very vulnerable step. Even so, he continued working intensively on the case. He attended a dozen court trials, where he studied Maya and Judge Brodek's behaviour. He admired the way Brodek accepted the insults and dishonesty of the defendant and her supporters with an attitude of paramount reserve.

9.

The Lamasery

It may be overly elaborate to call it a rock maze, but the two men continue on their inquisitive walk around the rocky paths, not far from the monastery.

"You must have some idea why we're here?" asks Vitas. This question has been gnawing away at both of them.

"Because we wanted to get away from civilisation," Aviel laughs bitterly but immediately adds: "Obviously I don't know exactly why, but I assume it's got something to do with me being a Jew and you a Christian. But I have no idea what's expected – I'm not even a practicing Jew."

"My Christianity's a bit off, too," adds Vitas. He barely finishes his sentence when an older monk with incredibly striking facial expressions comes towards them. His cheek, neck and seemingly all the tendons of his head constantly surge and shift as if an electrical current were moving them. A traditionally bald head emphasised by untamed muscles.

"Jingzhi!" he calls while holding his left earlobe. Without waiting for their responses, he yells at both of them in city-school English. "Be so kind and tell me what came first: Buddhist or Hindi tantra?" His hands shoot up in the air, both index fingers seemingly poking into each of them.

Vitas and Aviel look at each other awkwardly and

evasively, Aviel answers: "I've got to admit, I have an issue with the concept of tantra, let alone know which one came first."

"No wonder," laughs the Hindi scholar. "Atheist Jingzhi know nothing about basic history. My name is Mhosai Mangcug. Hindi tantra obviously came first. Buddhism followed and took it by the... Well, best not speak about that here or they'll stone you to death," he chuckles, grabbing his belly.

Aviel and Vitas don't get the joke and fidget uncertainly. He was speaking a foreign language.

"How do you like it here? What did you think of mass?" he asked curiously.

"I don't know. We don't understand it much," Vitas embarrassingly tried avoiding a clear answer. "We don't speak Tibetan either, but it was soothing for the soul."

"Absolutely. However, the masses are different in other lamaseries. The Tibetan proverb says: like every region has its dialect, every lamasery has its own doctrine. Have you seen our library yet?" he asked, suddenly changing the topic, while poking them with his index finger again. "You haven't? Follow me." He immediately shot towards the rocky walls pierced with caves. "It was built by our enlightened Lama Rinpoche. Over the years, he has ensured that the world's greatest wisdom is gathered here. I think you will be in awe."

They snuck into one of the many caves in the lamasery's maze of rocky corridors. They were in the library, which was an intertwining of expanding corridors and rooms with relatively low and rounded ceilings. There were hundreds and thousands of books on the shelves lining the walls. People were sitting sporadically on the many blankets and pillows spread out on the floor and studying old manuscripts.

Mhosai led Aviel by the shoulder as they walked quickly

through the individual rooms of the library. Vitas followed them in agony. He could barely keep pace.

"Kushok Akhum, here they are…" he said mysteriously to the elder monk with piercing eyes. He looked at them curiously, as if everyone in the lamasery knew everything about this new couple, while smiling at the fact that the couple was ignorant of their important, yet completely unknown role.

After introducing themselves, the elder Akhum took Aviel to the side and guided him into the cave, where Aviel realised that he was in the Jewish literature section of the library, noticing the Star of David on the spines of a few books. He was staring at the manuscripts of Kabbalah, the writings of Moses, and the Talmud…

Vitas found himself in the Christian chamber and was equally amazed. He withdrew an ancient edition of the *Spiritual Exercises* of Ignacio de Loyola, the founder of the Society of Jesus, reading through the travel logs of Ippolito Desideri, who was one of the first Jesuits to travel through Tibet at the beginning of the eighteenth century.[12] He even found a few volumes of eulogies about the Jesuits' thoughts on the lives of species that have passed on. He had to smile at this localised concentration of clergymen. He himself anarchically proclaimed that his greatest personal bible in life was John Kennedy Toole's novel, *A Confederacy of Dunces*. But he accepted he would never find any such book here. Bitterly, he admitted to himself that his interest in books didn't mean he was well-read. He went through the various stages of his life. He had read Dostoevsky even when it was hardly possible, under his school desk. He was desperate

---

12 Missions in Tibet began with the Portuguese Jesuit, António de Andrade (1580–1634). However, the first European to ever visit Tibet is said to be Odorico da Pordenone an Italian Franciscan of Czech descent, also known as Odoricus of Friuli. He visited Tibet in the fourteenth century.

when he had a good book open, his eyes skimming over the words, lines and sentences as if he were reading, but his mind somewhere in the clouds. Not understanding the meaning of the symbols, he read the same words over and over again. Another thought would just blast off into a completely different one when he kept trying to read a word, or new actions than the ones written would tangle in black symbols on this white backdrop. Names were the biggest disaster. Bernie is Margaret's cousin... If this piece of information wasn't repeated at least twice in some form or another to him, Bernie was only a man in a mask, who evoked merely chaos and horror. And then there's Sofia. He had absolutely no idea how, when, why and where she came from. He even tried it with detective stories, full of suspense, but the result was only slightly better.

Vitas was stuck around a pile of books. He was flipping through the work of Ignacio de Loyola and this time, his thoughts surprisingly, did not stop him from reading.

10.
On Chickens

One year had passed since the Rudolfinum case. Vitas definitely wasn't bored at the TV station. He had shot numerous documentaries, earning him a decent living, but in the meantime, he was still waiting for the big one. He realised that the Rudolfinum in Cheb was nothing compared to a big case. He might have got a lot of contacts thanks to this case, to police officers maybe, and people were approaching him from regions where real estate was being refinanced or falling into ruin.

These were large buildings, like chateaus and estates. But they always ended up dilapidated either because Communism took its toll on the property, or there was a lack of interest in the property, or even the property was the subject of restitution. Then, it was easy for experts to overestimate the value of the property multi-fold its actual price, only after Kromen had already bought the property in question, however. To be more exact, after one of his White Horses bought it, as his name no longer officially appeared in any such cases.

Bohemia Bank had once lost twenty million crowns on a glassworks company that Vitas discovered in Jenštejn, and once the smaller Hana Bank lost another 400 million on the same company, forcing it to go out of business, and at that point he decided it was time to go clean. The historic glassworks company had been the lifeblood of several villages located in the Bohemian-Moravian highland regions since the beginning of the nineteenth century. The traditional glassworks craft was to be trampled over by several financial speculations.

The first case he intended on introducing after the Rudolfinum case was the farm in Neprevazka, where the Czech Savings Bank lost ninety million on chickens. He had thoroughly surveyed the terrain, the locals were his witnesses, and the new owner spoke on camera because of his eloquence. Above all, he ridiculed all the drummed-up plans which Kromen's people used as justification before applying for a loan. The ridiculous amount that they needed for chickens would make anyone imagine that ten chickens required their own TV and bathroom.

Vitas was so fascinated by the chicken case that he bought a chicken coop for his home. This may suggest a certain diagnosis, but he had got so caught up in what was going on at work, that this fixation had no choice but to manifest itself in his personal life. He lived with Eva and their two children on the secluded outskirts of Prague. He had to make up for the mentally demanding burden of his cases somehow. Eva also saw this and even offered him some alternatives. Since he talked so nicely about the chickens when the bank had lost tens of millions, she convinced him that returning to nature was the only way to save his life and not end up in a madhouse or morgue from a heart attack.

However, they were both city people and village life was well beyond their comprehension. So, after speaking with the locals, they bought a flock of village-bred hens, as they still had their maternal instincts, still able to take care of their potential young, as opposed to "factory-bred" ones. Vitas and Eva renovated their broken down shed in order to make an independently standing, fenced, spacious enclosure. Where necessary, Vitas covered any hole with a board or piece of whatever he could find. They then quite grandiosely called this building a chicken coop.

And, so, they were looking forward to their first egg. But the family of weasels were looking forward to it a lot more. The weasels whipped-out the entire chicken coop, one after the other. The price of one egg went up to sixty-five crowns, which was very high given that the regular price was two crowns. Vitas tried covering up every hole and opening and even ended up guarding the coop, constantly checking it himself. Useless. Carnage. The weasels wouldn't eat one hen, they slaughtered everything in sight and blood was splattered all around. The weasels didn't disappear completely until Vitas built a better fence around the coop.

Even so, this wasn't enough for Vitas, and he went to his neighbour who probably owned one of every domestic animal, to pick out a young, white rooster. Vitas named the rooster Stalin. He was handsome and his beak stuck up. He swayed majestically from side to side like a big, yet ridiculous and timid boss.

Since then, the chickens were much better off, until the rooster suddenly disappeared. Vitas later found out that he ran over the hill to tell his friends how good he had it at his new owner's house. The next day, when Vitas was returning home from his investigative meeting, he saw a bunch of roosters making their way over to Stalin's kingdom. They ate all his grains and took care of all the chickens. Stalin observed helplessly. Vitas tried shooing them away, as if he were Stalin's bodyguard, protecting his girls from these frisky invaders.

Despite all his breeding failures, Vitas enjoyed the solitude. His cases, the gangsters and the dead bodies, were outweighed by nature itself, the soothing flow of greenery and silence, or at least for the moment.

– – –

The White Horse in the chicken case was Blikotka, who had also appeared in a number of other cases. But the companies didn't end up in his hands. He remained merely the White Horse. From him, the company was transferred to a Ukrainian man, one Karabinikov.

"It looks great," nods producer Rokos contently, as he continues reading the script. After Vitas' last experience, this one is much shorter than the Rudolfinum script. Rokos inadvertently stretches like a bow, obviously thinking this report will be a success.

"I hope this is accurate…"

"No doubt. I'm working on five more cases."

"Wait, wait – where is this Kromen, exactly? How come he's not speaking anywhere?" sputtered Rokos.

"I've tried endless times, but he just doesn't communicate…"

"Well, but this has to be included! You have to address him and if he gives you the cold shoulder, it has to be on camera. We cannot make a mistake here."

"Fine, no problem. But I already know what he'll say," said Vitas confidently. Vitas had already become the show's script editor and the producer trusted him.

The *Bad Penny* exclusively used external crew members, who were hired by a company with an unusual name: NBM. This company seemed to create the reports, although only for TV. NBM was owned by Rokos' friend, Franta Bozik and it sure must have been a good business, though Vitas could care less, not wanting to stick his nose where it didn't belong.

"So guys, count on Kromen giving us the cold shoulder," said Vitas to the cameraman and the sound guy near the office phone-line. "If it's not on camera you'll learn first-hand what bullying is," The tension in the room relaxed slightly. He was so nervous that drops of sweat ran down his back, but this was no different from usual for the cameraman and sound guy.

"Kromen," says the voice on the phone.

"Hello, Mr. Kromen, it's Vitas from the Czech TV station, *Bad Penny*," he adds quickly because he needs to have everything on camera, including himself earnestly introducing himself to the person on the other line. It was as if he were also warning him that everything he may say may be used against him in future. But this is how it should come across to the audience, although the victim on the other end rarely suspects it. This is common, everyday practice. If rejected, it leaves a good impression on the viewer. But something completely different happened here.

"Well, hello, I remember you, editor," said a heart-warming voice on the other end. "It's very nice to hear from you."

Vitas was startled, trying to come up with his next line, while staying focused on the camera. "I would like to talk to you, Mr. Kromen, sir. Would that be possible, in front of the camera of course…"

"Of course, no problem. You have no idea how happy I'll be to see you and to have the opportunity to explain everything. Can I invite you to my place, in Slapy? I'm sure you already know that I've rented out the whole former premises of the Communist Party on the bank of the Slapy reservoir." Kromen fell silent for a moment. It was clear that he was flipping through his diary.

"Sure, no problem. We just have to schedule the camera crew," Vitas, making room for negotiations, distinctly signals the cameraman to cut the film.

"Well, I'll admit I'm busy for at least the next ten days, but not after that, say in ten days' time, on Wednesday, ten o'clock. How does that work with you? Plenty of time to arrive and we'll have unlimited time for each other," explained Kromen.

"Fine, deal."

"I'll be expecting you."

Vitas was prepared for anything, but such a heartfelt invite had thrown him off. What should he do for the next ten days? How would he survive? No doubt about his nerves, the constant *what if… what if…*

What if Maya hadn't received pardon from President Havel?

Maya's trial has been going on for almost a year now, seeing that she has constantly delayed and suspended it. Judge Brodek had persistently deflected one attack after another, all in vain. There were always different investigators and different state representatives. The newspapers fabricated stories, denunciations and accusation of denunciations.

The President's pardon was unprecedented given that the case was unresolved and judgment had not yet been made. What were Havel's reasons? "… Serious health problems, who knows if she'll live to hear the verdict … it's been going on for so long …"

For Maya, this meant she couldn't be punished. If she didn't accept the pardon, the trial would continue, but only to determine if she was guilty or innocent, and that's that. There would be no punishment.

Judge Brodek's world was crumbling down. At once, all law and order had completely lost its purpose. He was walking on broken glass that cut into him, but he didn't have the strength to clean it up. There was no one to clean it up. God had died and there would be no rebirth. Thousands of hours or work, thousands of documents… Telling him that everything he had ever lived for, everything he had ever done was a big mistake. He cannot accept it either as mistake or wrongdoing. There is no value, no life, only death. He found it in himself to make a statement for the media, simply saying the case was unfair. This was music to Maya's ears. He was immediately and successfully under attack for partiality in the case. He was dismissed. For almost a year afterwards, he was unable to take part in any case. Piles of papers just flowed into the smog of mist. He couldn't get to the bottom of anything, day in, day out. One year after being dismissed, he had to face disciplinary proceedings for lack of productivity. The Czech Republic became saturated with court cases, all being suspended for one reason or another, while he dared to take on one case in six months about some layabout or freeloader. People began resenting the un-change. They resented the fact that society wasn't developing the way they had expected. Suddenly a little grey mouse appeared, causing families to break up, the stock market to crash and a war to break out in the Persian Gulf. Everyone went at it with sticks, beating it until blood squirted everywhere and pieces of hair remained on its crushed bones. It was a feast for the media, a bright and negative example of the Czech judiciary system, the lazy judges in their incompetence, Judge Brodek held up as an example. Who would kick him when he was down? How would he be punished? Would the punishment not be small!?

— — —

As for Vitas? Alternating stages of anger, disappointment and disillusionment... even regret for signing a petition to free Vaclav Havel from prison during the Communist era. Even if Havel were to be declared a saint in a hundred years' time, he would still remain human. It took Vitas years to come to terms with this. Not that he could completely forgive him, but at least he could admit that Havel's legacy was remarkable enough that this pardon was only marginal, the blindness of a great man, defeated by his angry friends.

Yes, Maya received a pardon, but Stalin did not. Early the next day, Vitas took an axe in the haze and frozen Chebness of the morning and killed Stalin along with all of his promiscuous hens.

Maya didn't accept the pardon and the trial was adopted by a new judge. Everything started from the beginning, including Maya's constant delays and complications regarding the trial. Everything went back to how it was.

– – –

One white sheet read: "YOU SNOOP! ARE YOU GOING TO KEEP POUNDING OUR HEADS??"

11.
The Dalai Lama's Fortune

"What's wrong, smart-aleck, something got you thinking?" Kromen, with his sarcastic but sympathetic voice, interrupted Vitas, who was sitting among the pile of books. Sometimes, it's hardly possible to tell the difference between humour and irony in such mutual discussions.

"I think you'll have plenty of time to discover the long-uncovered wisdom here. I would like..." Kromen paused for a moment, his gesture froze, as if hesitating whether to say it or not, "... to tell you one more thing, to take you to my place, to give you the local cassock, so that you're not so conspicuous and can blend in a little with this comradely group..." His eyes were playing merrily, as he even added an apology along with an explanation in proud defence: "... And so on."

Aviel was already waiting for them in front of the library and they went into the lower parts of the lamasery together, where there was something of a productive background. The sheep stables, bharal[13] goats and other local animals were all the way at the bottom, glued to the rock by the pastures near the pond and the Jadhang Gad stream. A massive

---

13 Bharal – a more technical term for blue sheep, also called a nahur. Zoologists can't agree on whether it's a sheep or a goat because it has many features from both animals.

yak and dzo[14] also had their place down at the pasture, but they seemed to enjoy being outside. Thanks to their thick fur, they were never cold. Of course, there was also poultry. The hens were happily eating grains under the supervision of a majestic rooster. Vitas was overcome with Chebness, only the soft breeze of it, the air of the past that continued to return...

There were several sheds and a few small industrial buildings and workshops for panning gold near the stables. The main area of industry was at the bottom part of the top of the lamasery. The workshops led directly to the courtyard with the chorten. These workshops were used for the lamasery's technical operations. There was also a very primitive but otherwise practical and fully functional lavatory. There was only a trickle of water that was pumped from the small reservoir by means of a sophisticated ram pump mechanism running from a pond into a rapidly flowing stream, slowly going up the hollow tree trunks to the top of the lamasery. This meant a constant supply of water. The whole apparatus was hundreds of yards long. It had to have been incredibly difficult to build. Embarrassing as it might be, it's worth admitting that hygiene isn't a top priority for monks, meaning that even with only the little water supply at the top reservoir, it had never run out.

The solution for warmth was equally clever. Something that could be described as central heating was installed in the area of industry below, and distributed hot air. It was true that the middle of the lamasery barely warmed up during any harsh winter weather and the surrounding rooms had to have their own heating in the chambers. Traditional pebbles were formed into bowls and containers used to heat wooden coal or whatever else was available. Traditionally, yak droppings and juniper were then burned

---

14 Dzo – a cross between a yak and domestic cattle.

in the central boiler. Other wood was too valuable, so it was only used rarely for this purpose.

Kromen took his guests straight into the bathrooms. They had to take their clothes off and shower… Vitas felt like he was back in the times of socialism, a soldier in the 80s.

And just like Aviel, once the ritual purge was over, he got a brown cassock. No one said anything about the change.

Kromen took them into his kingdom. It was a smaller room, quite far from the centre. But it gave a sweeping view of the whole lamasery from the opening of the cave door, and since it was so high up, he also had a good view of the surroundings.

There was a bed, a table and one relatively primitive chair in the room itself. "Since I've only got one chair," he gestured his head towards it, "sit here." He pointed to the blanket and pillows in the dark corner of the room.

He lit a few candles with a nasty scent. "No time to be fussy. The candles are made from the fat of dead yaks. You'll get used to it. I've got some batteries here, too, but I'm saving those. I'm not going to waste them on our conversation. Now, I'm going to offer something I've never offered anyone before, because it's never made sense," he exclaimed importantly, while withdrawing a full paper bag.

"Coffee!" he said proudly and began brewing it. "You'll get ample good tea here, but only Kromen has our good coffee," he laughed merrily, turning on the gas burner.

"Where'd you get the gas lighters from?" asked Vitas curiously. The answer was a loud chuckle. "You know how things were during the Bolshevik era – if a soldier takes care of something, he shall have it." This was a well-known phrase commonly used during military service. Paradoxically, it was the same phrase that Vitas was just thinking about. It obviously meant nothing to Aviel, he merely looked on, uncomprehending, but it was clear that he was about having a cup.

"From here, we set off on expeditions into civilisation, if you can call it that. We go there to buy things that can neither be made nor grown here. And of course, how else..." Kromen stood smiling proudly before them, holding the coffee kettle in one hand and three cups in the other, "... I am obviously the general manager, the commissioned offer, the public relations spokesperson, the operations manager, and whatever else you want to call it here."

Vitas burst out laughing. "Of course, no one far and wide would be a better bootlegger than you. You've obviously expanded your expertise to the untouched local regions, too..."

"Is that supposed to be funny?" said Kromen bluntly. "You really don't know the boundaries, do you? You think I'll put up with your insults forever?"

"I'm sorry," Vitas repented, surprised. "But you're setting yourself up for it. It all seems so absurd to me here. You and I are both like aliens in this environment. I still can't seem to come to terms with it. I still feel like I'm dreaming, that it's not real." Vitas was trying to make sense of his confused feelings. He still didn't know if he had made a good or bad decision in coming to a place to be constantly aware of this figure of his past – Kromen, the one responsible for his failures in life. A life-giving fire that burns everything in its path. He resented him, but also felt very hopeful to finally overcome the tragic breaking point. A kind of Stockholm syndrome, with the hostage emotionally dependent on his kidnapper. Kromen had torn his whole life down and Vitas now wanted him to rebuild everything, while wanting to remain at a safe distance from Kromen's inner world. What was he expecting? But he hadn't known what else to do at home in Europe. The ground under his feet was burning, he couldn't sit, stand still or lay down, so what were his choices? How could he have tamed his mind? But he certainly didn't want to discuss the topic of Europe, or anything related to the idea, with Kromen.

"You'll come to terms with it," Kormen reassured him amicably. "But don't get me wrong, I wasn't a bootlegger, only a businessman during a time when it was prohibited, during a time when virtually nothing was possible. And you know it because you also don't like Bolsheviks. It was Bolshevik himself who gave the word bootlegger such a bad name. Why get so worked up about it?" Kromen waved his hand, suddenly switching to a more peaceful mood.

"Look, gentlemen, you'll probably be here a long time or at least until the spring. It's now the beginning of fall, which means it will be impossible to go down the local roads in a few days. We are cut off from the rest of the world here. And I don't know about you, but I'm definitely counting on returning back to civilisation and family, but that's not going to be possible until at least April next year. So, until then, we're brothers and sisters, here for one another. Questions?"

"Not sure about my partner," Vitas pointed to Aviel, "but I'm only interested in tomorrow." Aviel nodded in agreement.

"Well that's not too demanding. I've been here since the spring and I'd like to get out, I just need to take care of one thing."

"What's that?" they both asked in unison.

"I'll tell you." He jumped off his blanket, digging around in the boxes under the table. He came back with a map and laid it out in front of them. It was relatively old, black and white and long-creased. "This is Tibet in the year of Iron and the Tiger, around 1950. What happened this year? As a young boy, the Dalai Lama fled from Lhasa to India to get away from the Chinese. He comes back one last time only to run away for good in 1959. But!" Kromen theatrically pointed his index finger to add an artifice of drama, but coming across rather silly.

"At the time, whether you know it or not, the famous Mr Khyenrab Tenzin was the economic administrator of Lhasa, the capital city of Tibet. If you were taken aback by hearing this name, good. Any resemblance to our famous Rinpoche – abbot – Lama Thorpe Tenzin is not all that coincidental. Simply said, our abbot is that caretaker's son. This caretaker had great foresight. He'd uncovered a fair fortune in gold and silver from Potala, the Dalia Lama's Palace, and many other keepsakes before the Dalai Lama first made off. He sent several caravans to Sikkim, a small princedom not far from here..." Kromen tapped on the map and circled the place with his finger, but neither Vitas nor Aviel could've told if he were speaking about France or South America.

"So?" Aviel urged Kromen, impatient to continue.

"Now, it's a federal state, a part of India. The territory is under Tibetan rule, so today it's China, then Nepal, Bhutan and of course India. And that's where most of this fortune is deposited. It wasn't exchanged for money until much later. This money then went to charity, helping the Tibetan government-in-exile, Tibetan refugees and so on."

"Since they feared the Chinese, and for good reason, and since nervousness about an uncertain future ruled over Lhasa, the caretaker, Khyenrab Tenzin, sent his ten-year-old son, Thorpe, in the convoy of caravans, to be our abbot. He was hoping he'd be safe in exile and that a better life awaited him elsewhere. However, as chance would have it, they encountered the Chinese while on their journey. The Chinese were far better armed but the terrain was to their disadvantage. The Tibetans were much better prepared for the mountainous roads. Therefore, the Tibetans crushed the

Chinese, but at greater costs. Only three people escaped, including our abbot. He is now the only living person, the only eyewitness to an event that happened almost sixty years ago."

"And the point?" Aviel provocatively urged for an explanation.

"The point is obvious! Everyone knows it," Kromen scorned his listeners. But the listeners only raised their eyebrows and thought nothing of it. Eagerly, they awaited a resolution. Both had begun to suspect the truth, but they wanted to hear it from Kromen, who directly and didactically explained: "The point is that three people couldn't tow the caravan. It's a large, non-compact monster, so one important piece of treasure has remained hidden in a certain rock cleft near the road from Zikac to Sikkim. Period."

"So, there's nothing but money behind it..." said Vitas disdainfully.

"Not only money!" Kromen sharply defended. "Invaluable treasure, inheritance from our ancestors..."

"Our?" Vitas interrupted him mockingly.

"Our, like our human race, you disgusting prankster. Given your limitations, can you please try to understand how this could increase Tibet's prestige, not to mention the pressure of public opinion on China."

"How? By filling your pockets with treasure that doesn't belong to you?"

"Alright, alright, enough – I have no problem handing over all treasure to the Tibetan government-in-exile! But it's obvious there would be some basic expenses..."

"Exactly, and those expenses will be pretty high, right?" Vitas broke in incessantly. Aviel watched the whole back-and-forth with great interest.

Kromen ignored Vitas' impertinence without comment and continued: "Most importantly, I want people to talk about the problem in Tibet. People can't forget about the invasion of Tibet as if it were something that happened long ago. We can't come accept it, even for the sake of losing business, though some people would do anything for a dime."

"How generous," Vitas growled in disbelief. "Why didn't you become a politician? You were planning on it at one point."

"And how do you want to get to this fortune?" Aviel interrupted them with a rather pragmatic question. Kromen had to divert himself, so he could avoid the relentless questions from Vitas.

"Our abbot is the only one who knows where it is, but it's not easy to get him to talk. I've been trying for months. No result. Although…" Kromen raised his finger importantly. "One day, after an exceptional session, the Lama called me to tell me that he'd reveal it. I must only complete one task, however. I must bring him one Christian and one Jew. Don't ask me why, I don't know. You realise that my journey in life is such that I only know pragmatic, matter-of-fact, sensible people. Atheists are all strangers to your religious ways. Apart from the two of you, I don't know of any fools who'd meet the given criteria and be willing to come here. And that's why you're here, you lunatics."

12.
Slapy

Vitas felt like he was standing on needles. He and his crew, including the cameraman and sound guy, who was not only the technician but also the driver, were driving up to the dam in an old, rusty Skoda. The crew received instructions on exactly what to do and when. Vitas also saw it as a pivotal moment in his career. He was to speak to one of the most significant gangsters in recent times. It was as if he had received an invitation from Al Capone himself, the murderer, thief, lobbyist and illusionist. It was an exciting situation. He realised the uniqueness of such fleeting moments.

He didn't know what he would or would not be able to shoot or what it would lead to. That's why, apart from the bulky standard camera, he also had a then-state-of-the-art analogue Beta-cam in his briefcase, which had an inconspicuous hole on the side with a small camera lens. He also had a midi-disc recording device with the microphone tucked inside his shirt pocket. He had sufficient experience with this combination of equipment. Since either the source, contact or camera deflection often broke down, he always had a back-up plan for the most exposed situations. After all, even as a journalist, he would walk around with a microphone, without people ever noticing. Not that he'd use everything, most of it being scrapped in post-production.

After the meeting, Vitas went through the recording and jotted down important notes. This was far more authentic and accurate than if he were to take notes on paper at the time. He was never able to take accurate notes on the spot. He wasn't able to take notes while thinking about other related issues or questions...

When he was a TV reporter, he frequently kept a hidden camera, not only to prove to the producer that the villain had refused to confess, but because it also made the report more interesting. And if the respondent actually said, "OK, I'll talk," he later acted as if he had never been shoting.

– – –

The crew turned off the main street towards the Slapy Dam. The nice but narrow road led through a dense forest. Vitas was looking among the trees attentively. He knew that Russian war veterans were supposed to guard the former Communist premises, but he couldn't see anyone.

After three miles, they were driving beyond the dense forest and right up to the former Czechoslovak Communist presidency. There were only a few low-rise, angular homes. Perhaps only thirteen buildings neighboured the Slapy Dam, on about seven hectares of fairly hilly land, covered with pine and larch. A hotel dominated the centre, not especially tall but larger than the others and with a swimming pool, a restaurant and a perfect lawn all around, as if cut with nail clippers.

Vitas turned on the hidden camera in his briefcase and the midi-disc in his shirt pocket. An eighty-yards long and narrow road with a pond and fountain led to the main entrance of the hotel. The Divine Nike, the ancient goddess of victory, identical to the Nike of Samothrace located at the Louvre in Paris, lorded over the fountain. This one, however, had a certain perfection, undamaged, not like the one in Paris, with only its central features remaining. Its long, outstretched wings seemed poised to take off. And instead of a branch, she held a sword aloft in her hand. The tip of the sword pointed downwards and water gushed out of it, shower-like. The lawn around the pond bore a bronze-plated, life-sized horse with elaborately detailed features. The horse's left front leg was slightly raised and thanks to the muscles and mane, it appeared at that moment to be trotting around the pond.

At the moment the rusty Skoda stopped before the main entrance to Kromen's hotel, the lord himself was exiting the building. It was impossible to tell if this was some theatrical display, a boastful gesture, or just sheer coincidence.

Vitas noticed him immediately behind the fogged-up window of the poorly ventilated car. He felt his eyes strain. He remembered the "picture" he took one year ago in Prague, when the window had opened and out popped a head of tangled hair over a miserable face, wearing a dirty, dark t-shirt. Here was a confident, smiling man in a three-piece suit and new boots. Everything he was wearing was brown. He was also wearing a tie with an oriental pattern. His hair was perfect. If there was a strand out of place, it had to be intentional.

"Welcome, editor," Kromen shook Vitas' hand, staring at him attentively, making the moment seem all the more significant.

"Hello – nice to see you again, at last," said Vitas quietly, emphasising the word: again.

Kromen noticed the obvious irony and smiled a little. "I'm sure you've noticed that things have changed since last year..."

"Absolutely," nodded Vitas, scanning the premises. His eyes stumbled on the bronze-plated horse. "That's a beautiful horse, where did you get it...?"

"I had it made to my liking," Kromen explained with a touch of humbleness and continued dreamily. "I hope you won't blame me for my artistic inclinations. I love sports. I love horses. I've already had a few horses here, but they didn't fit in. I had to clean up their – excrements – they smelled, flies were all around, y'know."

"But this one doesn't move much and movement's a pretty characteristic trait for a horse, isn't it?"

Kromen smiled wryly and raised his index finger. "Let it be. A crane moves the horse around the pond several times a day, based on my mood. You should see the beautiful view when you stand here to the left and only see the horse's shadow through Nike, with the glowing edges of the huge sun…"

"Sounds … fancy. I had no idea you were such a romantic…" sighed Vitas. Kromen looked at him inquisitively. It wasn't clear whether Vitas was making fun of him or whether he truly meant it with admiration.

"As an expert, you could actually shoot me a neat presentation. It would be good business for you. Shoot it without the crane in the background, just shoot the horse jumping, with Nike obviously in the forefront and then edit it, so that it's a continual shot, with me sitting here on an armchair or in the saddle, smoking a cigar…"

"I'm sorry," smiled Vitas. "But I can't. As an investigative reporter and especially with you, it'd be a conflict of interest…"

"Oh, you and your conflicts. Everyone nowadays keeps talking about some conflict or other and the country's economy is going down the drain. Let's continue," Kromen quickly changed the subject, as if he were turning a page. He shook the cameraman's and the sound guy's hands very energetically. "After you …" he nodded towards the hotel's glass door.

The receptionist stood up at attention right when they walked in. Kromen leaned over the receptionist's desk and uncompromisingly said: "Call Mila and have him take care of them. Make sure they get whatever they need. If they'd want to fly over the premises in a helicopter to get a shot, arrange it. And you – come with me," he grabbed Vitas by the shoulder and they walked into the hotel's restaurant alone.

A large room, about sixty-five by fifty-square-foot opened up in front of Vitas. There were about thirty-five tables in the room. Vitas stood in astonishment. He felt like he had walked into a chateau. He was surrounded by baroque paintings, mirrors, candle holders, even the cutlery was stylish. Everything was prepared to stun a visitor into amazement. The view out of the window was enhanced by blossoming pines, the surface of the Slapy glistening through. In such an environment, one would expect to see a tourist or two, or perhaps some leisure area, with antlers, canoes, worn-out veteran bicycles, a paddle on the wall rather than those mid-fourteenth century paintings of the Madonna besides an art nouveau candle-fixture. The fact that there wasn't a single person in this room seemed awkward and filled it with a subconscious flow of wrongness.

Kromen was watching Vitas out of the corner of his eye, urging him to sit down.

"Where?"

"I think there's enough room here, your choice. How about here in the middle and please put your briefcase over there."

Vitas knew that the picture from the hidden camera would be useless. The only thing he'd see in the editing room would be shots of Kromen's legs. He couldn't lift the lens without giving the hidden camera away and he could take as many shots of the local environment as he wanted with a professional camera. At least the sound from the midi-disc would work. In fact, he was only realising now that a constant series of sounds had been coming from hidden speakers. The noise of plates and cutlery banging and people chatting went almost unnoticed. There was a quiet, gentle commotion all around the restaurant. But the noise was subliminal. Impossible to notice unless focused on. There was no way this noise could interfere with the recording.

Everything seemed absurd to him. Alone, sitting with a major mobster. He was imagining how great a shot it would be, if the cameraman were here. The camera would show the both of them staring at one another, a cat and a mouse, impossible to tell who was the mouse and who the cat. The mobster has his elbows on the table, his hands clasped just below his chin, both his index fingers thoughtfully stroking his nose, staring at Vitas. The camera is slowly zooming out into the wide lens, so everyone is slowly beginning to see the wide... emptiness.

"What am I to do with the money?" Kromen began without any foreplay. Vitas shivered with surprise. "Am I supposed to eat it? So, I've decided to invest in sports."

A moment of silence.

"I will set up a political party."

A moment of silence.

"What do you think?" asked Kromen impatiently.

"It's very generous. Which party? Right, or Left...?"

"It doesn't matter, I wouldn't even label it as such. I want it to be of benefit to everyone. Of course, I'm lean right-wing, I hate Communists, but I have a rather social feeling, so I wouldn't want it to be exceedingly *right* or *left*. I just think that we're missing a party that wouldn't be burdened by the interests of individual parliament members..."

Vitas was only partly listening. He would play it all

back afterwards. He was concentrating on the questions he had prepared and was running through them in his mind. He knew he couldn't rush anything here. After all, it was nothing unpleasant, the waiter having soon brought in a few appetisers and a choice of drinks. But he opted for sober drinks only, needing to think clearly. When the waiter brought the menu, for a long time he merely flipped through it, as if reading a lengthy novel before hopelessly pointing at something. A fresh and well-prepared meal had been served within fifteen minutes. Vitas understood these first impressions were the key to luring him in. True, he had a hard time remaining cool headed.

"You're not listening to me at all!" Kromen interrupted Vitas' thoughts.

"Sorry, I was just thinking about your explanations," lied Vitas, looking into Kromen's dark eyes with exaggerated attention.

"So, you're a Christian or not?"

"Yes, I am," Vitas blurted, as if wanting to emphasise his calm, while watching closely, although this hardly seemed the case. "True, true, I'm a little unanchored. I don't like personifying God or Christ into some specific form or too precisely defining something indefinable…"

"But you are baptised, right?"

"Yes. Why?"

"How old were you when you were baptised?"

"A bit older than most: fourteen."

"You should've had your head on straight by then," Kromen said grimly and continued with slight contempt. "I feel sorry for you. Not that I'd care that much, but I consider it misleading and more importantly, a dream-hindering. And that's another problem, though I've never been to a christening, children are usually baptised," he interrupted himself with a scornful laugh, "… when they're young and really have no idea what's going on. It's different when they decide to get baptised at twenty. I believe that's your own foolish doing. But a baby a month old?" snorted Kromen.

"Anyway, this has nothing to do with age but rather spiritual belonging. This tradition is common for all religions, including giving someone a name, which is of course to say something about that person..."

"Y'know what? – let's get down to brass tacks. I think we live in a different age now, the world has spun on its axis a few times since the beginning of Christianity and everything has shifted its place. We're now swimming in a different pond!" he shouted daringly. It was as if he had suddenly woken up and realised that he was jumping out of the coat of a wise businessman, always on top of his game, waving his hand amicably and immediately changing the subject.

"I have a sense of charity," he said airily with a grand gesture. "I really do like sports and I really want our small country to have greater success in the world. I would like to help parents raise talented athletes, I would like to help others to victory...To help others to win!" he bellowed unexpectedly. "It's an amazing slogan!" Kromen withdrew his Walkman, pushed the record button and aptly began: "Slogan: Help others win!"

– – –

"You can't judge it like that," explains Kromen angrily in front of the camera. A composition of takes: Kromen's villa on the hill on the right, lush pine trunks, thirty-yard-long beaches and the take ends with a shot of the Slapy to the left, with the perfectly flawless Kromen dominating the foreground.

"What do you mean disappeared? Where did the millions disappear to in your opinion? Are you saying I pocketed them? The transfer was completely legal. Y'know something? I even tried helping the bank above and beyond my responsibility. The Vietnamese market-sellers in Cheb offered me fifty million for the building. Yes, you heard me, fifty million! Only to turn it into a warehouse and a market. But I personally offered these fifty million straight to the bank, so they'd get back the thirty million that they lent out. And y'know what they told me? That they can't change a contract that they'd closed with a previous subject. D'you get this nonsense? This inflexibility? There's no wonder banks are going bankrupt one after the next!"

"But what about the other real estate? And what about the far-fetched estimates?" refutes Vitas. "What about the other millions? The scenario is the same for all of them …?"

"But what scenario?" Kromen threw his hands up pleadingly, looking so naïve that Vitas didn't know whether to laugh or to cry. "What are you accusing me of…?"

Kromen was fidgeting for a good ten minutes, making it clear that Vitas wouldn't get any further. He understood he'd been mistaken thinking that he'd get the infamous Kromen into a chokehold. They were standing on a piece of grass not far from the beach. Vitas noticed a spent cartridge on the ground. It all fit right in, though he acknowledged some talent on his own behalf. He discreetly informed the cameraman of his discovery. The cameraman quickly zoomed in on the cartridge and then directly to Kromen.

"Where did Mr Rypanek go?" Vitas immediately changed the topic.

Kromen looked at Vitas with a blank look on his face. Aware of the camera, he quickly switched to his innocent smile, like the moderator of some popular American TV show: "And what deal do you have going on with Mr Rypanek, Mr Editor?"

"He disappeared. And you closed a pretty profitable

advertising deal for over 150 million. Did anyone collect the VAT on that sale? I assume it'd be around thirty million. And Mr Poke-His-Nose-In, the one doing the advertising business for you, the one who should've paid the thirty million VAT to the state, has disappeared – he's gone..."

"Should I have drowned him or what? I'd like to talk to him myself. He was such a nice person ..."

"Was or is?"

"I believe he still is. I don't understand what you're implying."

"What were his advertising responsibilities?"

"Plenty of them, something for the newspaper, some billboards and so on..."

"Can you show me any of the billboards, or a magazine running the ad? And I don't mean some poster at a bus stop in Rabyne or some other little village."

"Mr Editor, be so kind and don't push me into any one of your fabricated imaginations. That deal is long over. It has fulfilled its purpose. I'm sorry Mr Rypanek disappeared, but I believe that he's sure to resurface and pay his debt to the financial bureau. What are you trying to accuse me of?"

It wasn't the evasive answers that bothered Vitas so much as the fact that Kromen seemed to constantly be playing with him. Despite revealing what Vitas knew (and in Kromen's eyes it was a surprising amount), Kromen smiled, remaining sincere towards Vitas. Vitas was expecting Kromen to "freeze" and kick him out. If this were the case, then Vitas could use the following headline: "Public TV Station Editor Kicked Out of the Mobster's Den" or something like that. But consistent politeness and hospitality prevailed.

Unlike the tired staff, Kromen was still smiling when they said their goodbyes. It was late in the afternoon and the sun was slowly setting. Vitas was watching the Nike of Samothrace from afar, before driving away into the forest.

It was as if it was threatening him, saying: "Come here one more time and I'll chop your head off." Kromen was posing next to the fountain. He was standing between Nike and the bronze-plated horse, smiling and confidently waving his hand, in a kind of slow-motion. A whooping crane approached this red-halo, framing the holy trinity.

13.
The Hunt

"Tsampa might be a hearty meal, but I hope we won't have it every day," complained Aviel, hungrily devouring the brownish matter from the bowl, while munching on a radish. You couldn't say that the monks here starved. They had plenty of vegetables, grains and an abundance of dairy. But the cooking and serving were unusual for new guests.

"I wouldn't fight over this tea, either" a sour-faced Vitas adds, drinking his butter tea.

"True, the meals aren't that great here," confirms Kromen. They are sitting in the dukang again, a prayer room that apparently serves many social purposes. They had prayed several more times before this humble lunch.

"Some things can be grown here, but a lot has to be imported throughout the summer and stored, because there's no way in or out in the winter," explains Kromen. "A lack of meat is another problem here…"

"… but there are so many animals outside, cattle…" interrupts Aviel.

"Yes, but local customs prohibit the killing of any animals."

"So is everyone here vegetarian?" adds Vitas to the discussion.

"Not at all," laughs Kromen heartily. "They're hypocrites!

They eat meat but they can't kill any living creature, so how d'you think they do it? When the Muslims were here, they slaughtered the poor living animals for them. They had someone kill the animal and then they ate it. And then they prayed to their Buddha, saying they wouldn't even kill a fly! Haha! Once the Muslims disappeared, there was no way of getting meat. Of course they sometimes found a way – neither poultry nor cattle die of old age here. But careful, you know me," he raises his eyebrows and points his right finger to his chest. "We always find a way to figure it out ourselves, right? Finish your tea and follow me, I want to show you something."

Kromen was dragging both companions down from the lamasery towards the pond. But they didn't make it that far. They got to the pastures, walked along a narrow path to the left of Mount Jadhang, until the lamasery was completely out of sight. Mount Jadhang rose sharply to their right and there was a steep slope to their left. They walked down the path until they reached a small tributary of the Jadhang Gad. Yaks, goats, sheep and bharalas were grazing on the surrounding pastures. Fences were clearly useless. The terrain was hilly but the green pastures were only in the lowlands around the tributary. Although they had nowhere to run, some animals, especially the more agile goats and sheep, wandered off. The sheds, stables and hayshed glued to the surrounding rocks provided food and shelter for them in the winter.

Kromen dragged his companions beyond the pastures. Along the way, they met a few monks, or rather herdsmen, who tended the animals for their livelihood. There was a small hut on a remote outcrop, hardly a likely place for the small abbot nearby. The inside of the hut continued on into the depths of the rocks adjacent to Mount Jadhang. Various tools, such as a log rooting an axe, some chains and something resembling an anvil were lying around the hut.

The trio were approaching the doors of a house. Kromen began to tip-toe quietly, cautiously looking around, but all the time he contradicted himself with a smile. He was slowly reaching for the door knob, when a sharp, swift arrow suddenly cut through the air and darted right next to Kromen's head.

Kromen cursed. He jerked and shouted: "No! Kushok Cheng, I'll never get used to this!" He turned his back to the house quickly. Only then did Vitas and Aviel notice a short man with a moustache, flowing hair (which was very unusual here) and a large bow and arrow. He was smiling from ear to ear as he came towards Kromen with open arms. "Kushok Kromen, it's so nice to see you after such a long time. And you finally got your friends to come here from the land far away?" he said in shaky English, looking inquisitively at Vitas and Aviel. Vitas' English had improved a little, he knew quite a few words and although he didn't have much opportunity to speak, he caught up quickly. Their Tibetan was far worse, both of the new guests having only learned some of the basic words. But since they were in regular contact with the locals, who spoke little English, there was hope for quick improvement.

"This is Lu Cheng," Kromen mutually introduced everyone. "Cheng, I am afraid I don't have the nerve for this kind of welcome," he scolded, smiling at his friend.

"Come on, let's offer up some sacrifices to the gods," said Cheng wryly, opening the doors to the house, nudging in his guests and clarifying with a shy smile: "The gods are demanding. Maybe they'll condemn the gifts and then there'll be more left for us..."

Vitas and Aviel felt strangely uncomfortable, as if they had walked into a canteen or a kitchen. There were assorted plates and knives lying around everywhere and a large working table... The sweet air also wasn't all that pleasant. But

Cheng pulled them into another, more comfortable space. Candles lit up the room, the guests were seated into a plush corner with blankets and pillows and offered the traditional tea and butter.

"And today we have something…" Kromen passionately smacked his lips.

Cheng smiled without answering and disappeared, then quickly returned with a bowl full of dried yak meat biscuits. The guests went at them unscrupulously.

"I would like to show our new guests our footbridge in action," said Kromen to Cheng, with a sparkle in his eyes. He was like a fish in water and soon they were off. The group split up, Cheng heading closer to the pastures while Kromen and his companion climbed up the rocky path.

In the meantime, Kromen explained to them that Lu Cheng was a butcher. A relatively despicable profession in Tibet, this being the reason he lived in such isolation. Nevertheless, he and Kromen had grown close, supposedly as a result of some minor business deals, he smiled slyly.

They climbed onto the ridge, along which led a long, narrow path above the pastures. They stayed close to the rock, a 168-foot-high cliff to their right. They soon reached a twenty-foot-long unsupported footbridge, and crossed it.

Kromen pulled out the rope hidden between the rocks, which inconspicuously led under the whole length of the bridge to the other side. They waited. They were perfectly hidden. No one from below could see them. There was a small overhang underneath them but that wouldn't have saved anyone if they'd rolled off the path. He would have to fall off helplessly, slide down like on a toboggan and shatter to pieces down by the pastures or be pierced by one of the many rocks sticking out at the bottom like stalagmites.

It didn't take long and there was a bleating goat on the other side behind the footbridge that Cheng was chasing from behind. He was beating her with a stick, yelling "Shoo," the way he yelled at chickens, but quieter, so that no one would hear him from afar.

Once the goat was in the middle of the footbridge, Kromen pulled on the rope and a strut that was holding the bridge shifted all the way from the end, where Cheng was standing, and sharply crashed in a spiral onto the shore, where Kromen and his friends were standing and staring. When the goat fell onto the overhang, its legs dangled helplessly. There was nothing to hang onto. The skills to overcome mountainous terrain were of no use to these animals. It swung over the overhang and the only thing heard was a short, hopeless bleat, then silence, interrupted by a muffled crunch a second later.

"So, what do you think?" Kromen chuckled. "This is what I came up with! What're you gawking at?" he bombarded Vitas and Aviel. They were still speechless. "Everyone's happy and guess what's for lunch tomorrow? Goat goulash of course!"

"I still have to perfect it," says Kromen on the way to the lamasery, as happy as a hero returning from a victorious battle. "I have to come up with something for the yaks. You can't get these giant animals up here and the footbridge is completely out of question. This'll be your task, what d'you think? You could also help make this region a little more lively and civilised."

The excited Kromen was suddenly taken aback. He was carefully watching the monk, who was running from the lamasery towards him. It turned out to be Lao Puwei, who had accompanied Aviel and Vitas from India to the lamasery. "Something's going on," Kromen said grimly, walking towards Puwei.

"Where are you, where are you?" wheezes the out of breath monk.

"I was showing our new friends around. There was a tragedy. A goat fell off the cliff and died."

"Again?" Puwei whined, clenching his mouth. "We all have to pray for her." But his attention was quickly diverted back to the concerns that led him to Kromen and his companions. The Tibetan view of death is far less tragic than that of Western civilisation. "I come to you for another reason. Our enlightened Rinpoche Lama Thorpe Tenzin wants to speak to our guests immediately."

14.
The Information Battle

The phone was ringing off the hook in the newsroom. Vitas felt on top of the world. His colleagues, his friends, the inquisitive police officers, even anonymous callers came through every now and then to congratulate him, supporting him in his efforts to continue. The report caused uproar. It showed a system which had resulted in the banks losing hundreds of millions. The Rudolfinum case one year ago was the only one which had presented some kind of a breakthrough, but it was still only one case. But it had already become an implemented model, which given the current legislation, made it very difficult to legally fight against. Vitas analysed another case in the report, the estate in Neprevazka, which resulted in the Czech Savings Bank losing ninety million. More importantly, he had warned against this system and that other cases were bound to follow. The *Bad Penny* TV show had guaranteed viewership.

"It's Vitas," he said abruptly into the phone. There was silence on the other end. "Who is it?" the feared reporter nervously growled.

"Petrovsky. Inspector Adam Petrovsky," said a cheerful voice on the other end, seeming to imitate James Bond with his introduction. "I would like to meet with you, is that possible?"

It took Vitas a while to figure out who he was. "Oh, you. The one who invited me to a reciprocal interview last year. And then you didn't show up and it all turned into an interrogation. No, I'm not interested."

"Wait, wait," called Petrovsky pleadingly to prevent Vitas from hanging up. "Don't be foolish. We've been working on something for several years now and all your show says is that you'll broadcast it as a 'to-be-continued' fairytale. You're going to wreck everything. You can't…"

"But you had your chance to talk to me and you know damn well how that turned out. Thanks, but I've received so many calls from other officers since then, that one more or less…"

"Exactly! On the one hand, the question is if they were even police officers at all, and on the other hand, I'm truly offering you a solid discussion. It's not that simple but a number of things have changed. It's even bigger than you think. Even bigger than we thought a year ago. But please, understand, it's really not possible to discuss this over the phone. The district attorney, three investigators and five operatives are sitting next to me. We will all be here, so no one will be pulling anyone's leg. See you at the Congress Hall in an hour. Deal?"

After giving it a moment's thought, Vitas agreed. "Fine, deal. I'm curious…"

Vitas touched upon another important aspect in his report. In addition to describing the structure of the whole scam, he also mentioned Kostka. The biggest post-November mobster, later commonly referred to as the Godfather. Together with Kromen, they milked the con to the point of bankrupting several banks for all they were worth. Just like Kromen, Kostka was a bootlegger during Communism and just like Kromen, had even spent some time in prison.

After the revolution, Kostka worked his way up to capo

in the criminal underground. An unscrupulous man, he didn't hesitate to get rid of anyone who stood in his way. He had control over many politicians, no matter if they were right or left-wing. He played with bankers and managers of large construction companies as if they were chess pieces. The name: Kostka. Although this name was often hidden behind other code names, it appeared whenever and wherever it came time to discuss larger privatisation, grants, foreign investment, large state tenders or any business deal worth the name.

– – –

The described Congress Hall is a tall, modern building by the Nuselský Bridge, not far from Vyšehrad Castle. A man who may have been a police officer or a secretary picked Vitas up in the lobby. They took one of six lifts up to the twelfth floor and Vitas was taken into one of the many offices.

The members of the Renovations Team, as they were introduced, were either standing or sitting around the small, smoky room. Vitas even shook Inspector Adam Petrovsky's hand. Petrovsky was a tall thirty-year-old man with very sincere eyes and thick, black hair. When he was holding Vitas' hand, he was staring firmly into his eyes and the left corner of his mouth twitched into a slight, inner smile. Vitas couldn't help but take a few snaps.

"So what are you working on next, editor?" asked Petrovsky. The police officers were suspiciously eyeing Vitas' bag. Although it looked like a regular plastic bag for beer and smokes, it was clear that there were some envelopes with documents in it.

"I am obviously working on a number of other cases…" he paused for a moment as if anticipating his opponent's card in the game. But since they had nothing in mind, he pulled the documents out of the plastic bag with little hesitation. "I have the Jenštejn Glassworks, which is 400 million at Hana Bank. It seems this bank is going down the drain because of it. The Bohemia Bank was also involved. I have all transfer agreements, lien agreements and stamps from the Land Registry..."

"We're working on that right now," he said cheerfully, everyone else nodding along. "Now imagine you'd bring this information to light. Any traces would be disposed of straight away."

"And what do you have?"

"What else do you have?" asked Petrovsky, looking frankly at the plastic bag, as if he hadn't heard Vitas' question.

"I have some two more documents, what about you?"

"That's difficult," the district attorney cut in unexpectedly. Vitas was taken aback having a feeling that everyone but Petrovsky were mute. "You have to understand that the criminal code prohibits us from sharing any details with civilians. However, I can guarantee that you will be the first journalist to find out about our next steps."

"I see. So, I'm supposed to tell you everything, find out nothing and leave. Is that right?"

"But Mr Editor," Inspector Petrovsky comforted Vitas. "It's really not easy for us. The Criminal Code makes this clear. And if someone here says anything, then, ad A: he would violate the Criminal Code by exceeding the authority of a public official, and ad B: he'd be laid off, and ad C: he'd be prosecuted by the Ministry of Internal Affairs and finally, ad D: the lawyers representing Kromen, Kostka and other scoundrels would use this against us and over two years of work would once again be made useless. Would you want that to happen?"

In his mind, Vitas laughed at the way Petrovsky used the

Latin preposition "ad," only to realise this was Petrovsky's usual cliché used to emphasise the dramatic nature of the information he provided.

He was, however, unpleasantly irritated by the whole situation itself. Angrily, he snapped back his words: "No, of course I wouldn't want that, but I'm sure you know what I do want. I have a job to do. If my job helps you, that's great. But I don't understand why I should be doing your work. And if you're not willing to say a word, I of course guarantee complete confidentiality regarding the source, I have nothing more to say to you and it's the same bullshit you put me through last year. I guarantee that no one will find out who you are or where I got the information from. I'm sure you realise that it'd make my life more complicated if I ratted you out. No one would tell me anything at all after that." Following a moment of silence, each looking defiantly at the other, he added: "Well, what d'you say?"

"Well, it's difficult," the district attorney uttered his favourite sentence.

"Okay then, goodbye. There's nothing more for us to say." Vitas decisively got up to leave.

"But the Criminal Code considers you an accomplice if there's proof that you knew of these crimes and didn't report them to the competent authorities," said the district attorney in one breath.

"Well then accuse me," Vitas snapped back calmly, slowly making his way to the exit.

"I'll accompany you," Petrovsky got up, adding in apology: "Here, you can't even leave by yourself."

"… so I don't accidentally peel any information off the building walls or what?" Vitas grinned ironically and left the room without saying goodbye, not caring if he was or was not followed by a police officer.

Petrovsky caught up to him in long strides and they

silently walked up to the six fully occupied lifts. They stood next to each other in silence, grinning slightly. The commotion around stopped for a moment as some people boarded and others went into their offices. Once there was peace and quiet, Petrovsky leaned over to Vitas' ear, both still staring into the dark lift window and mumbled between his teeth, his lips barely moving:

"Six o'clock under the tail."

Vitas was so startled, he jumped. Afterwards, no one moved an inch and no one said anything until downstairs in the lobby and Petrovsky shouted, as if there were several deaf spectators sitting around.

"Goodbye, Mr Editor."

– – –

Based on the President's pardon, Maya was immediately released from custody and following several media spots on the controversy, everything calmed down. However, as she hadn't accepted the pardon, the formal court proceedings continued.

A pivotal event took place two months after her release. While moving house, Maya came across some documents bearing the header of the former financial prosecutor's office behind a wardrobe. What a surprise. Finally, a genuine document that would prove she had been entitled to the property. In her view, the previous documents, which in truth had been skilfully falsified, had been forged by mean Premonstratensians, tenants of the building that was supposed to be hers, or even by vengeful Communist undercover spies. She was holding a pile of about twenty officially stamped documents with headers in her right hand, referencing her grandfather, the millionaire painter.

Maya hired three renowned lawyers, who launched a

campaign proclaiming her innocence and unquestionable entitlement to all the property – this is the role of a lawyer. However, she forgot to tell them to never, under any circumstances, speak with a reporter named Vitas. And that was a mistake.

Vitas shot a simple, almost primitive report. He set out with his crew to the prearranged interview with the incriminated, unsuspecting lawyers. He shot the interview, in which the lawyers questioned the innocence of their client and backed their claims up with documents from the financial prosecutor's office. When innocently asked if they'd be so kind and provide a copy of the documents for the camera, they did it without even thinking. But why not?

However, Vitas took the pile of copied documents and went with his crew to the Land Registry Book located at the Prague Fruit Market, to present these documents to the unsuspecting head of the office, Mrs Braun.

The camera was on. It took a shot of the head of the Land Registry with shelves containing thousands of books and various documents stacked all the way to the ceiling.

"Could you please say something about these documents?" Vitas hands the officer the folder with the documents.

"I don't know. I'll try. I see the first document has no Land Book number, which means this document did not go through our Institution, so I can't say anything about it… But fine, the second document says 5090 from '47, LB – meaning Land Book – yes, this document went through our office. So, let's take a look at the collection of documents under 5090 from 1947." Braun put on her white gloves and began to peruse the immense archaic shelves, which stretched out into the distance. The corridor of books led to a large window, letting in sharp, milky light, a cameraman's nightmare. The cameraman tried turning this distorted effect into something intentionally artistic, and

Braun ended up surrounded by a fog that intertwined with her blond hair, seeping into the contours of her face.

"… following the revolution, we didn't even know how all the documents were intertwined," she tapped her white gloved index finger, focusing on the spines of the books. "We received a collection of documents not long ago from the courthouse on Jagellonska, so all the documents can easily be linked. Here it is, 1947…"

She carefully pulled out a tired, dense book, pulled it towards her, thereby also obscuring the milky light. Braun caressed its cover tenderly, as if it were her young daughter, who came home from school with an A on her test. Then she stopped, apparently realising that she was on camera. Her facial features rigidified, as she coldly flipped through the pages.

"Here you are, number 5090. No, wait–" she twitched and shouted. "The document, which yours references, has to do with receipts in Holešovice Bubny… Look…" she thrust the information right in front of Vitas' nose, pointing at the exact place with her white finger. Vitas pulled back, the cameraman desperately sticking the camera lens between the two of them, so that the camera saw Mrs. Braun and the book, her white finger dancing around the black print. "… Look again. Not Hradčany, as your document stated. Receipts for the Bank of Agriculture for Bohemia and Moravia, dealing with some issue regarding a ladder and the driveway up to the building in Holešovice… and here it says B 1941 sash 86, so let's take a look at this number in the Land Book…" the head of the office turned as if on a dome, the book almost flying out of her hands, skipped two rows, heading straight for the shelf, where she removed the second book. "You see? This document, labelled B 1941/86, references the same collection of documents. Not Hradčany, no ancestor of your Maya, this document has been forged.

Truth told, even digging this up you'd never have it registered in the Land Book. We have an employee code that's been observed here for centuries." she gave Vitas a spiteful look. Vitas nodded, accepting the criticism, as if it were him who had forged the document and as if he were the scoundrel who had made the error.

"What else do you have there?" Braun scornfully removed all the other documents from Vitas' hands. She was letting loose on him, as if she had lost all respect for him and the camera. With every document she looked it over carefully, analysed it, all her reactions the same: "Forged, forged, forged…"

The head of the office, who was rummaging through several shelves, quickly inferred the absurdity in the presented documents.

"Well, Mr Editor," she addressed Vitas the way she would an impolite student, pointing her white index finger at his nose. "Your documents from the financial prosecutor's office may contain some unique and genuine stamps, signatures or dates, although I doubt it, as every piece of paper as a whole is forged, with some truthful features here and there, scattered quite at will throughout. Whoever forged these documents knows nothing of the Land Book. That said, I'm willing to admit that we too, weren't all so clear on a handful of references of late. But I'll have you know that every document that goes through the Land Book, has to have the number of the Land Book, as well as the year. When a document is filed into the Land Book, it's assigned a number and is filed under this number and date into the journal. Then, a decision had to be made as to whether or not to archive the document. If it were to be archived, it is recorded into the books under the same number and is also filed into the Journal of Collected Documents under the same number. It's not possible for a document to be filed into the Land Book Journal without being archived or registered into said Journal. Every property had its own land sheet, which ought to include the name of the owner and the journal number..."

"I'm very sorry, but three renowned lawyers declared these documents real, is it possible that they are mistaken...?" provoked Vitas in his favourite way, playing dumb, which often drives the other party insane.

"If your 'renowned lawyers' consider these documents to be genuine, I expect they would go to the archive of the former financial prosecutor's office, or better still, come and pay us a visit. No one has ever done such a thing but for the district attorney and the former judge! I assure you we would take the pleasure to explain that forged documents cannot be genuine. And perhaps even your 'renowned lawyers' could understand that..."

— — —

The term "tail" is a common expression in Prague, referring to the well-known spot by the statue of Saint Wenceslas on Wenceslas Square. Not knowing the layout of Prague and wanting to meet someone, the easiest thing would be to use this expression. The horse's tail faces the museum, as if ready to gallop through all the events that had occurred on this Square. Every major national event of the past several centuries had taken place here: the welcoming and defamation of Hitler, the revolutions and the counter-revolutions...

Someone suddenly bumped into the pondering Vitas, almost knocking him over, and quickly walked away without saying a word. Petrovsky. Vitas followed him quickly. He understood that he didn't want to start talking right away. They wandered the streets of Prague for about half an hour, heading towards the central station, where Vitas really had to try hard to not lose Petrovsky in the crowd. Discreetly, they window-shopped, watching the passers-by in the shop-glass to see if any were following, before heading back towards Wenceslas Square, coming to Bartholomew St, renowned for its police history. Some of its buildings were formerly used by the Communist State Security Guards, now investigative authorities.

There was a bar with a fitting name, The Al Capone, on this street. The display windows were decorated with various sizes of fired cartridges, old Communist police hats reading "Public Security", batons and clubs… It was shelter for out-of-uniform police officers, who came here to wind down. A bottle of beer washed away the uniform dust and they were transformed into regular people, at least in their own eyes. This is where Inspector Petrovsky and Vitas walked in. He pointed to a small table, hidden in a dark corner.

This was probably the first time since wandering the streets of Prague that he looked into Vitas' eyes. "So, ad A: except for the Congress Hall, we did not see each other today and ad B: I did not say anything to you. Is that clear?"

"Of course," said Vitas casually.

And then a whirlwind followed. There seemed no other way to describe it. Inspector Petrovsky began explaining the entire case, about Kromen and Kostka, uncovering all the connections from every point of view. From the personal perspective – forensic specialists now-bribed, White Horses, usually in the form of disappearing Ukrainian citizens, who had many companies to their name, every company owning various properties, acquired for cheap – dilapidated old cha-teaus, estates, mills… all atypical property. Any "minor" change in data, such as size, resulted in exponential differ-ences in financial estimates. It also involved people disap-pearing or coming to a mysterious end.

Vitas was busy making notes. He already regretted not

recording this, impossible to track all that was said, let alone write everything down. He had even avoided the most discreet voice recorder, not wanting to lose trust at the point of case-disclosure. Petrovsky was producing more and more information. He spoke informally with him after just a few minutes, toasting to general conversation with a sip of beer and a shot of good whisky.

"… imagine that Kromen even got involved in sports!"

"But of course," said Vitas ironically. "He loves horses, he's even got a bronze-plated one! He's no athlete, he's a snob!"

"Y'know, I'm kidding too," said Petrovsky scornfully. "He loves anything that brings him money. And that includes sports. He's taken over the SAZKA betting company. D'you know anything about that?"

"Honestly, I start one case and the others just fly past me. And I hardly intend on chasing after them. I have to leave some bits and pieces for others," smiled Vitas.

"The SAZKA betting company is a gigantic monster, invented to finance gambling in sports," Petrovsky ignored Vitas' irony, as if he'd said nothing at all. "Naïve people bet, hoping they'll win, as long as the ball keeps rolling. But the mathematical probability for first prize is 0.000007 percent."

"But good luck doesn't depend on maths," refuted Vitas.

"It's a passion. The whole world knows that no one can put a stop to gambling. If the state prohibited it, people would operate it illegally, without any audits. So, it's better off being legal, but higher taxes imposed on it. That's logical. That's why all of the SAZKA betting company's profits (all of its billions) are intended for sports.

"The SAZKA betting company is a rich, bloated demon, the target destination of all the financial gains earned through the much-condemned act of gambling, owned by various sports associations, thereby able to redistribute the money to its shareholders. And that's exactly what they do. At the beginning of the nineties, officials from the Ministry of Finance ran it, entirely public and legitimate.

"Kromen's only in the game recently, however. Discreetly, he's taken control of the whole goliath. Kromen's a gambler. No matter who he deals with, he always performs a thorough background check, to know who he has the honour of meeting, how to deal with them, how to blackmail them, when and where to tickle them, how to make them feel utter and complete bliss. But one thing's for sure, he's only interested in the final result, still leaving each interviewer feeling like the winner. Like they're the one with the upper hand, even though they're the one at the bank, asking for a loan. A bank clerk has to feel like the bank will self-destruct if it doesn't immediately pay Kromen the required amount. A gambler. He's a gambler," the police officer continued excitedly and persistently to drill into Vitas' head.

"I even find it a little basic in a way," objects Vitas. "Like a snob, like…"

"Yes, no doubt he's a snob but he's definitely not basic. He's a gambler. His appearance, expressions and gestures are all part of the drama. His gestures are as thorough as a professional mime. Only to serve its purpose."

"But what good is it to you as a cop? You can't put him in prison for imitating Hitler's gestures or ego."

"Definitely not, but there's money on the line here. Ad A: he abolished the Ministry of Finance's supervision over the redistribution of money into sports. It all went down behind the SAZKA betting company's back and no one can see a damn thing."

"Ad B: The money cycle is clearly given. In the past, you could trace the fate of every crown. Kromen usually started financial operations that were generally not profitable for the SAZKA betting company, leading us to a minor crime, allowing him to disrupt the well-established flow of money while he obscured various pockets until he was finally on his own. He managed to get money out and then created a deliberately unlikely network of purchased items, from all kinds of state-of-the-art equipment, down to gold-plated faucets at the company's headquarters. And we'll give the rest to sports, right? We are completely honest and generous. Everything for sports, once we deduct all the expenses. True, it's still a lot, but not as much as it could be."

"Ad C: he created a corrupt network of shareholders' representatives, who took courtesy bribes and money from the SAZKA betting company itself. Overweight officials from various sports associations don't care that boys living in small villages kick rags rather than footballs. They're only interested in making sure they've got their bread and a splash of good wine at home."

"Look," Vitas frowned. "I get it, I even find it interesting, but it's more of a moral issue than a criminal one, don't you think? Thieves are meant to steal, especially when you give them the key to your house and contraband to steal with a message saying: 'Enjoy it...' No, no..."

"I'm telling you, these are clear penalty shots: damaging others property, uneconomical management of others property... Don't even ask. And ad D: cultivating and protecting one's image. Kromen's created the perfect wall of defence, so that he can defend the whole honestly tendered kingdom. The main thing is to have control over the media. Kromen invests a lot of money into media advertising. No one cares if a small part of it doesn't go into sports."

"So, that's probably what he's not successful with here at the Czech TV station," smiled Vitas.

"For now! For now," the Inspector prophetically raised

his finger. "You should watch the case. But let's get back to our properties…"

Petrovsky kept talking and talking. Vitas was most amazed by the lengthy wired recordings of Kromen and Kostka, citing several testimonies, as if he were learning them by heart. They were oftentimes absurd events that even police officers were involved in.

He laughed about the situation, when he was watching Kostka and Kromen meet the Minister of Finance and his business partners at upscale restaurants in Prague. These meetings were monitored by four different police units without even knowing the other was involved. Since everyone from the industry was more or less familiar with each other, a representative of the Group Against Organised Crime and the Service for Uncovering Corruption stood side by side with long remote microphones. After some small talk, when everyone greeted themselves ironically, everyone focused on their equipment.

"Man, there were fifteen of us there. Fifteen!" The Inspector laughed uncontrollably.

"I was standing in a waiter's uniform and the chef was standing next to me. If this chef had ever brewed anything, it was tea for the SIS, the Security Information Service. You get that, man? We were staring at each other like crows for a second, then we blinked at each other like gays and he pulled out a leather diary with an unrecognisable lens, which turned out to be a camera. I took out my glass case, which was also a camera. We both covered each other and snapped one picture after the other. We stood there like two snuggling homos. Under normal circumstances I'd like him but now I'm like a thorn in his ass. Not to mention the other thirteen agents or cops, who were dancing around in masks, acting like inconspicuous shrubs. And so we were snapping pictures and recording and discussing how and where to stash away a billion during the privatisation of two of our biggest banks."

By nightfall, Petrovsky was barely wheezing, but the amount of beer he had drunk kept his vocal cords moist enough to share more information. Inspector Petrovsky felt responsible despite being reckless after drinking alcohol. They knew they were stepping on thin ice, so he soon suggested going elsewhere.

"I don't want to risk a colleague seeing us, even though there is an unwritten rule that says: whatever happens in this pub, stays in this pub... Come on, let's go to Hybernská..."

They bought a bottle of wine along the way and Petrovsky kept on talking and talking. They walked into the well-known police station on Hybernská. Petrovsky took Vitas into a room which didn't resemble a police den at all. It was an ordinary room, only the furniture evoked the feeling that he had stepped back into the 1950s. They sat in an armchair, drank wine and talked about what it would be like if there were no criminals here. Laughing, they agreed that they'd be sad and nothing would be of interest to them in their own profession, if they would have ever entered law enforcement as heralds of great truths. They reclined in their armchairs, falling into a righteous sleep, completely drunk.

Two of the biggest state mobsters met at an elegant restaurant near Wenceslas Square just when the drunken Vitas and his new friend were falling asleep in the police den. Kromen and Kostka looked comically different side by side. Kromen was tall, his hair combed perfectly, dressed in his best, most desirable suit, while Kostka was shorter, wearing a simple suit and ordinary shirt, making him look rather plain standing beside Kromen. He obviously considered his clothes as "overalls" for specific occasions.

"Get rid of him," he was grinding his teeth at his partner.

"No, no, no," Kromen shook his head almost dreamily.

and then bluntly stated: "We should pray for the goat," and peacefully walked away.

Kromen and Vitas simply stared, their mouths wide open. Tungjur was still sitting at his spot, still spinning the prayer wheel, smiling a little. Kromen took one step back behind Aviel, but this was just a helpless attempt. He knew he had to stay put because it was now Vitas' turn to talk to the Lama.

"After you, Kushok Vitas, Lama Rinpoche Tenzin is expecting you," Tungjur interrupted an awkward situation without moving, making it seem almost telepathic.

Vitas slipped inside. The room had no windows yet the air was clean and fresh despite the seven candles that were emitting quite a bit of smoke and odour. Since the abbot's room was next to the main "central heating", there was an artificial stone fire pit in the corner of the room. Now, it only had cold ashes and pieces of charred wood. Vitas thought it had to have been ventilated. The yak butter candles dimly lit a relatively large room with many Buddhist artefacts and hanging thangks – painted canvas with sacred scenes and statues dominated by a three-foot tall Chinese bronze-plated statue of Buddha Vairocana from the late Ming Dynasty. The swaying flames created movement, scattering flying shadows all around. Words of various mantras were peeling off the walls. The words: "ÓHM", "PARASAMGATE",[15] "SVAHA",[16] and "PARADJODAJAT"[17] were visible on the walls of the dark corners. However, the tetreng, a rosary made of human bones, was the most morbid for Vitas. The Lama was wearing this tetreng around his fossilised and wrinkled neck. His luminous torso of human remains

---

15 Tib. – "That which stands behind everything else."

16 Tib. – "So be it."

17 Tib. – "Dear God, enlighten our intellect" – a mantra for intuition, enlightenment, inspiration and cosmic consciousness.

was amplified by the mysterious and glittery surroundings. Despite all of this or maybe because of it, Vitas realised that this was the right environment for a person to dig deep within himself.

Vitas was quietly and carefully observing all the details in the room as the Lama watched him intently, while sitting in his traditional pose on a pillow in the dark. "Kushok Vitas," he said in his school-learned, easy to understand English. "All these words are only empty words until they are pronounced. It's only fog in the open water unless it is sounded out. And even after it's pronounced and then slowly disappears in the silence, even then it may not be more than the sigh of an old tree. You have to be ready for the word, it has to flow through you, and your whole life has to flow through it, a feeling of birth, your sins, love, death and continuation, the infinite samsara."

It was as if Vitas was just now slowly beginning to wake up. He came up to the Lama, knelt down and handed him the khatag, a white ribbon, a ritual object, used to pay tribute to every respectable person since the beginning of time. Kromen imposed it on him and he acknowledged it as a fitting welcoming object despite his contemptuous attitude towards everything non-pragmatic, intangible and all non-atheistic practices. Vitas held the khatag correctly in both hands, palms up. The Lama accepted it with heart-felt gratitude.

"I have a feeling you know I'm Christian," objected Vitas immediately, following the Lama's previous explanation. Not so much in contradiction rather than out of curiosity, in order to better understand the situation.

"Yes, I was also hoping you're Christian. That's what was agreed on in the first instance. This however, doesn't deny the fact that your understanding of enlightenment is just as close… But we're probably getting too ahead of ourselves," he smiled slightly, offering Vitas a pillow to sit on. "I assume you'll have tea," offered the abbot, without even expecting a negative response, gesturing lightly with his left hand. Monk Tungjur soon brought in a tray with a tea kettle and cups.

"How long has this lamasery been here?" Vitas dared to ask after a moment of silence.

"For many, many years. Its origin was lawful. If the body is sick, the disease has to get out somehow. The ulcer represents the healing process. It may seem like an ugly comparison, but eruptions are nothing more than volcanoes looking for a way for the tension, the lava, all the evil emotions as well as the good ones to get out, so that balance and reconciliation can be restored..."

"I don't like comparing Tibetan Buddhist monasteries to ulcers, it sounds a little awkward," objected Vitas.

"The words may sometimes sound unusual," the Lama smiled. "So many monasteries have been destroyed, so many monks have been killed or spiritually beaten and so many of them had to flee to the nearby Small Tibet. The so-called Chinese Cultural Revolution then came after all those flames, as if to sprinkle water over a smouldering fire-pit or bury sprouting seeds in slimy mud. So, let's not say the word, but just like the occupant's land, our land is a place, where everything can go out. That's why these lands are suffocating. They are full of pus, the evil, the good and everything else is rolling around under great pressure, it's bubbling and waiting to erupt. You don't even have to be a Buddhist to understand. You can even be an educated Christian to understand that this is all just temporary. When the time is right, all will be released, and I know this time will come..."

"But will we live to see this day?"

The Lama laughed. "If you keep asking like this, it won't

come. If you keep asking like this, you won't even wake up, you won't be close to enlightenment. I know, I know, you're not a Buddhist, you're Christian. But that doesn't matter. You have to be patient, because if you're not patient, it won't come. It will come when you least expect it."

"I think I'm far more patient here than at home in Europe," Vitas apologised, embarrassed. "I'd just really like to know why I'm here."

"I don't know," said Lama Thorpe Tenzin calmly.

"What?" Vitas' mouth gaped. "You were the one who initiated all of this?"

"No, no, I am only the mouth. Nothing more than the mouth. I only ask that you devote your time here to Christianity, practice Christianity, practice the dharma,[18] albeit in your own way, but most importantly, keep your eyes open and follow the words of the Buddhists, the Hindi and the words of your colleague, Aviel and try to come to an awakening, even if as a non-Buddhist, you may not believe in it. However, let's call it something different. Let's use a word that is more familiar to you – Prajñā – knowledge, wisdom."[19]

"Sorry, what do you mean by devoting my time to Christianity? I don't think there's a Church or dignified father here, no bearer or interpreter of the Christian faith, is there...?"

"Yes, there is."

"Is there?"

"There is."

"Who?"

---

18 Dharma – "a way of being", a path to universal truth. It represents an individual inner law, which has to be followed if one's individual life is to be in accordance with the laws of nature and the universal essence of being.

19 Prajñā – Buddhist term often translated as "wisdom", "intelligence", or "understanding".

"You."

"Wait, wait," objected Vitas. "I'm afraid you're idolising me. I might be a Christian, but I'm no longer practicing and there's no way I can teach anyone. I am not a priest. I don't have enough theological knowledge to teach anyone. I am not even consecrated. What's more, I'm a sinner. I've committed the cruellest sins. There's no way I can teach. I'm afraid I'm not the one you're looking for."

"No, no," smiled the Lama. "I know you're not all that educated in those ways but all you need is the will to learn the Holy Scriptures and to teach it to others."

"Honourable Lama Rinpoche, the last time I stepped foot into a church was around ten years ago. Maybe as a tourist, I'll go to a church some twenty times a year out of curiosity."

"Exactly. And how can you be a tourist at church? You can't deny yourself. Christianity is in your blood. It's your unforgettable genetic makeup over the past centuries. You know all too well, that even if you naively claim to be atheist, you'd still be Christian. Only a fool has no idea where his roots are. No blind man, but a fool claims he has no roots if the roots aren't visible on the surface."

"Ok, but why? Why all of this" Vitas shook his head.

"The only thing that I want to tell you today and the only thing that I can tell you today is that you will definitely be able to answer this question yourself. I am sure you'll have an answer soon, but definitely not today. Therefore, now, I am asking you for the most necessary: Learn, so that you are prepared. You know there's an abundance of wise books here. Teach others, meditate and… please be patient. That's all."

Vitas felt hopeless and outraged. He wanted to defend himself but the Lama only raised his right hand sharply: "I will tell you as much as I told your friend, Aviel – wasn't it Moses, who also refused to accept God's mission before the burning shrub on Mount Sinai? We're through for today." The Lama suddenly cooled down, slowly grasped the dordze, which was lying on the floor hidden behind his body and slowly started spinning it in his hand. He completely detached himself from the present, thus making it clear to Vitas that any further discussion would be useless.

Vitas got the hint, stood up and walked away. He tried to get by Kromen and Aviel in the same way. He didn't feel like talking or explaining anything. "A bit of patience and self-repentance wouldn't hurt," he said mysteriously to Kromen, his index finger raised in an attempt to cut off all his efforts. He was holding him by the shoulder, hissing "So what? Stop your gossiping and tell me everything he said…"

"Like I said, I'm asking for a bit of humbleness." Vitas gently yanked himself loose of the angry Kromen and disappeared behind the door. Kromen's furious eyes moved around the room until they landed on Tungjur, who was still sitting on a pillow by the entrance to the abbot's office. He was spinning the prayer wheel, mumbling his mantras.

"I would like to speak with him," Kromen said in a reserved yet vehement voice, pointing his finger to the wall, where he envisioned Lama Thorpe Tenzin to be.

"I'm sorry, but Lama Rinpoche has no such plans," monk Tungjur said softly, with the utmost effort to not cause conflict.

"He doesn't? He really doesn't?" Kromen articulated almost threateningly, approaching Tungjur, who got to his feet in the situation's pressure. "Be so kind and tell him to include it in his plans. I am asking you, I am begging you, please go tell him that."

Tungjur opened his mouth, wanting to object, but once he saw the relentless, determined stance and Kromen's rigid features, he sighed: "Fine…" and disappeared behind the door.

"Enlightened Lama Rinpoche," said Kromen very coldly

with a fake bow when he was called to the abbot. "Where I come from, if there is an agreement or contract, it is followed. If two parties freely agree on something, they follow through with it. I assume I have fulfilled my duty. Is that so, your honourable Rinpoche?"

"Yes, it seems that you have," said the abbot, half-smiling.

"And now it's your turn. May I ask you to keep your part of the agreement?" said Kromen softly, slowly, but all the more vehemently.

"Yes, yes, you deserve it. However, I'm not sure how satisfied you will be."

"What do you mean?" Kromen raised his eyebrows in disbelief.

"There really is a grand fortune in Tibet, near the Sikkim border. But might not what you consider a fortune and I, the enlightened Dalai, consider a fortune, differ? Certainly not gold or jewels… They're only the feeble means to something greater. Books, ancient manuscripts and most importantly, fulfilling the dharma, the path to freedom – this to me is the authentic fortune…"

"Are you telling me," the red-faced Kromen interrupted the abbot, "that you lured me in on a fortune like a hare on a carrot? And this treasure is nothing more than some Buddhist nonsense? Do you know what that's called where I come from? A scam. It's a scam, your honourable Rinpoche. And every scam deserves punishment!"

"Oh, come now, Kushok Kromen, do not exaggerate. On the one hand, the books are of extreme value, while on the other hand, I cannot say you won't find other things of value to you together with these books… And don't forget that we also have your beloved yellow metal here. However, I didn't make any promises as to when I will pay you for your services. And personally, I think that your greatest payment will be received in the next life…"

"Are you serious? Please don't make fun of me, honourable Rinpoche…"

"I am not…"

"Yes you are. I know you honour rebirth. Yes, I was witness to a monk's loan, who had agreed to pay the other party back in his next life. However, as a witness, I wanted and got my commission straight away, not in the next life. It was truly a lot of fun, a show suitable for Broadway, if you know what that is. But I'm not looking for fun! I want the price paid immediately. Right now!"

"I'm sorry if there was such a misunderstanding, but there's simply no way it will be possible right away."

"In that case, we're through," Kromen pointed his index finger at the abbot, making his decision definitive. He turned around and headed for the door.

"I am deeply sorry, but if you'd be a bit more patient, I am sure you'd also satisfy your interests."

"My interests, you say?" Kromen turned at the door. "You know all too well that I only have a few days left to return. Winter is coming and the whole lamasery will be cut off from the rest of the world, no one will get in or out. And you keep telling me to wait. I have no intentions of waiting any longer! I lack your generous patience, because everything moves a bit faster in Europe, y'know? How much does Europe produce in comparison with underdeveloped regions? We have to work, everything is fast-paced, we don't have time to dream in our enclosed chambers and meditate on something we will never have!"

"That's a pity. I thought you had learned to look deeper into things, to see the blind spot. It doesn't matter how many tons of toothpaste Europe produces in a year, but which wise steps it has taken, what it has discovered and how it has helped people… There are many things that can't be explained right away, though later, you will understand them…"

"No, I'm just on my way out, but I'll be back and rest assured that I am going to want my investments back."

"Fine, I'll gladly be expecting you. And for my word, here is a ring. It will be extremely valuable to you, and I'll be glad to be rid of it when so much blood gushes away from it. It has very bad karma, but perhaps you will know what to do with it..."

Kromen grabbed it into his lustful hands and caressed it with disbelief. He was examining it intently in the dark room, his eyes were sparkling from the reflections of the red stone, which was held by a dragon's open mouth, his scaly, golden body circled an imaginary finger and his tail completed the circle at the top by crossing the neck of the dragon's head. Precision, extremely elaborate detail.

"Well, we'll see," said Kromen, a little more concilia-tory. "We're definitely not through with each other yet. Goodbye."

16.
The Way Up

Vitas lived a very fast-paced, fruitful and satisfying life in the nineties and at the turn of the millennium, shooting one case after the other. He directed the *Bad Penny* Show under the strict supervision of producer, Rokos and met with several police officers and mobsters…

In essence, he had become friends with Inspector Petrovsky. This essence was under the provision that they had to remain discreet. Their meetings took place under the strictest security measures. If they agreed on a meeting over the phone, the call was always recorded one day and one hour earlier. For example, if they were to meet on Thursday at four o'clock, the telephone recording would state Wednesday at three.

In retrospect, the other phone calls at the time were amusing. Cell phones were not yet commonplace. Since he directed the *Bad Penny* Show, he got his first cell phone from the TV station. Back then, reports were shot by driving from telephone booth to telephone booth in order to arrange the time and place of the next meeting. But most importantly, people were a lot more trusting than today. If you agreed on something, everyone stuck to it. Often the dates and time of the meetings couldn't be changed, so there was nothing left to do but trust that the other person

Surprisingly, he laughed. "What would we do without them for god's sake? We have to have some self-reflection..."

"What are you mumbling?" Kostka stared at him with astonishment. "Where'd you come up with such vocabulary? Are you high?"

"We'd be bored without him," Kromen continued as if Kostka didn't say a word. "We'd miss him and Vitas is just doing his job. We can't get rid of everyone who stands in our way..."

"Get rid of him," Kostka exhaled, leaning deep into his chair. "This is the only way. It obviously has to be an 'accident'. But leaving this psychopath loose can put an end to half our activities. You're making yourself look like a man of virtue, but if you think the prison scrubs don't come in your size, think again..."

"That's enough! Maybe I am making a mistake, maybe it's foolish, I could care less about the snoop, but I don't intend on making myself look like a raging murderer."

Kostka laughed. "And what are you trying to say? That you're completely innocent, or what?"

"Certainly not, but I'm no longer involved in this matter. That's definitive. I'm taking this risk upon myself. D'you understand? And if you disagree, we're through!"

And so from whatever angle presented, Kromen saved the life of a sleeping, drunk and snoring Vitas. Somewhat ironically, exactly ten years later to the day, it was Kostka shot dead by an anonymous professional assassin, in 2006.

– – –

"DON'T DRILL HOLES IN OUR HEAD," Vitas, bleary-eyed in the morning, read the letters in the office and helplessly grumbled.

15.
A Meeting with the Lama

Kromen was sitting in the shape of a lotus leaf, hands clasped, nervously fidgeting with his thumbs in an endless circular motion, while watching monk Tungjur, who was sitting in the same position, spinning the prayer wheel in unison with Kromen's thumbs and reciting different mantras in a low voice. Despite his eyes being half shut and the defencelessness of his attitude, he perceived his surroundings well and was able to instantaneously react to anything. Every muscle in his body was as tense as the calm before a storm. Monk Tungjur was sitting by the front door of the abbot room of the local Lama Thorpe Tenzin lamasery. No one could tell if he was guarding the door, or if he was just sitting like that by coincidence. But his position rather confirmed the former. No one would dare to simply walk into the abbot's prayer room. Vitas was sitting next to Kromen, also in the same position, but completely motionless. He was absentmindedly staring at the door behind Tungjur's back. It took about half an hour for Aviel to walk out.

Kromen and Vitas jumped up. "So, what did he tell you?" they were interrogating him the way he would a student, who had just walked out of an exam room.

Aviel looked at one and then the other, as if he were surprised that they didn't know what had happened in there would turn up. Nowadays, since people have cell phones, everything is flexible, everything can be changed at any time, everything either works out or it doesn't, nothing actually matters...

Once cell phones became commonplace, wired tapings became a major concern. The measures were prosaic. When Vitas shook hands with someone from the Security Information Service, the anti-corruption police or anyone authorised, including Inspector Petrovsky, there was a ritual that took place before the meeting. Everyone took their cell phones apart, most importantly taking the battery out. Then, unless the meeting took place in a discreetly parked car somewhere in the dark, both parties laid the parts of the cell phone out next to each other. Vitas later recalled it as a comical situation, a measure which his profession had to take at the time.

Later on, this ritual became cause for laughter.

"Are you kidding me?" giggled Muller from the Security Information Service when Vitas disassembled his cell phone.

"In order to keep everything confidential, not risking anything, right?" Vitas apologised, offended as anyone would be whose old habits were being destroyed.

"But that's foolish. Anyone can eavesdrop on your – or especially my – conversation. But tell me this – someone has to give an order to wire-tap a conversation. Who would do such a thing? Someone has to arrange the tape-wiring. This is probably the easiest thing to do. However, someone has to really listen in, evaluate and propose a solution. Who'd do that? Someone has to propose measures and decide which steps to take next. Who'd do it? Do you know how many people this tape-wiring would employ? And honestly, do you really think you're such an exposed person? Yes, we definitely wire-tap the conversations of Kostka, Kromen, the premiere, and dozens of other people all the time. But do you really think you're on this list…? No," Muller answered his own question.

Vitas gradually began to deal with the SAZKA betting company case, although he began by scoping around it remotely, simply recording facts.

"Yeah, I started with the SAZKA betting company case a couple years ago," nodded Tomas, Vitas' younger colleague from the Nationwide Journal. "Useless. I've been working on it for months, already uncovered the flow of money, a deliberately unprofitable business for the SAZKA betting company. But once Kromen finds out about it, he calls the publisher, the publisher calls the editor-in-chief and the editor-in-chief calls me. So, I don't think you're working on it."

"We'll see," refuted Vitas confidently. "And nothing since then?"

"Like what? Nothing. I'm good. And it damn well paid off. Kromen then sent me to Las Vegas with a bunch of other journalists. He even gave us a few chips for the local casino to get us started. Not bad, right?"

"Hold on, were you really in Vegas? And just because you wanted to write about him before?"

"I don't think that was the reason. I'd probably have gone there either way. Kromen arranges various trips for journalists in nationwide media, anyone who could potentially write and film something about the SAZKA betting company. Who knows?" Tomas started laughing. "Maybe you'll send me a postcard from South America in a year."

"I doubt it," Vitas frowned. "I'm fascinated by his megalomania."

"Do you know that he has a TV studio at his house?"

"Yes," nodded Vitas. "There's nothing strange about that. He shoots the lottery bets from his house because it's a lot cheaper for him that way…"

"Don't get confused. I know guys from the editing room.

Do you know how much money goes into the studio? No editing room at the Czech TV station matches his editing room. If you're speaking in gigabytes in 1999, they're dealing with terabytes. They throw money around everywhere there. I wouldn't be surprised if they start using bank notes as toilet paper one day. And then have a look outside at the demolished playground, or look into how much hockey-parents have to invest in their children in order to turn them into Jagr. So much money and so much time. It's only a huge ordeal because no one is willing to put in long hours playing hockey anymore unless they get something in return..."

"So what? Are we in this together?" snapped Vitas.

"No way," Tomas replied as expected. "But good luck..."

— — —

"Hi, honey," said Vitas to the CTIS, the Czech TV Information Centre. The CTIS was a services centre and a source of information for editors. Five of his employees had an excellent database and several renowned foreign agencies available to them. If an editor was assigned to a task during the morning meeting that was supposed to be ready for the evening news, he often knelt down in front of the CTIS as if he were at a church asking the gods for help.

The CTIS employees could provide him with information even during his trip to the respondents. There was no doubt they needed the service as much as they needed oxygen.

"I'd definitely need to know everything about the SAZKA betting company..."

"No, no, Vitas," Catherine, the head of the CTIS, said, rolled her eyes at him sadly. She was a small, lively creature with huge eyes. Her short, ebony-coloured hair shot out of her head in all directions. She was very intelligent and educated. This is perhaps why she was also inordinately humble, timid and insecure. "We really can't do anything now. We are all working on Inunhost. Do you have any idea what 'Inunhost is?"

"What's that?" Vitas rolled his eyes. "What's Inunhost?"

"That's what we don't know. Zajickova ran in here this morning, saying she was assigned the task of shooting some Inunhost. We've been trying to figure out what this may be for over three hours now. Possibly some feast or something like that…"

"Why don't you ask whoever assigned her the task? I don't mind waiting. I'm not in that much of a hurry, but if you want, I'll find out what he actually wanted you to do," Vitas winked conspiratorially, smiling.

"That'd be very nice of you. You'd really do that for me?"

"I'm on my way," saluted Vitas, striding off to the head of the local column, Hermik. He knew they were on good terms.

"Look, you assigned Zajickova to some case, right?," Vitas got right to the point, without sugar-coating it.

"Yeah, yeah, but how come you, such a snoop, are interested in such an insignificant case like the pumpkin festival in Unhost?" Hermik was shocked. "Yeah, I told her to go shoot something in Unhost, why?"

"Oh, Unhost, it's in Unhost," Vitas gasped and chuckled uncontrollably. "Sorry, my mistake, I confused it with something else," trying to elaborately get the words out, despite his laughter.

Hermik was shook his head in confusion as Vitas disappeared behind the screens in the newsroom.

"Ok ladies, I finally know what the Inunhost is," he exclaimed at the CTIS. Everyone turned to face him, eagerly awaiting what he would say.

"It's very simple, but I hope the SAZKA betting company

will get top priority after this. I'll tell you," Vitas swung his hands like a messenger delivering an important message in a theatrical role, almost bursting with pride.

"Exaggerate, Vitas…" Catherine encouraged him.

"I see it as if I were present at the morning news meeting. Hermik looked lovingly at Zajickova, wanting to give her the easiest case he could, so that she wouldn't screw it up again. So in order to not make everyone think he's favouring her, he said: "and then we have the pumpkin festival. Veronika, could you please shoot something in Unhost."

Vitas interrupted his monologue and looked inquisitively at the surprised CTIS employees. "You get the difference, right? I'm not saying inunhost, but 'in' (pause) 'Unhost."

The CTIS simultaneously burst out in laughter and rage.

— — —

Vitas became very temperamental as a result of his quick stardom, a series of successes and self-confidence which strengthened his belief in the fact that he could match any case he set his mind to. He felt powerful. When at rest, in thought, he let darkness and rhythmic music (preferably blues) engulf him and immerse him in a feeling that he had total control over his body, or rather detached himself from it. He was floating gracefully, entering a new space, another dimension. At this time, he couldn't help but remember his mandatory military service, when his blood pressure went up at the thought of being out-of-uniform. He was so against the military at the beginning of the 80s, during the time of deep socialism. It was a waste of all human values. It was impossible to stay. According to the instructions of his doctor friend, he lost consciousness several times a day. They always took him to the first-aid station, just to throw him out immediately, shouting something like, "Simulative ties."

Vitas was persistent. He 'lost consciousness' at least once every other day. They measured his blood pressure every time. Normal. So, he said, I'll try to change it. But how? He had no blood pressure monitor, no advisor, no literature, nothing. But after some time, long consideration and practice, he figured it out. He had to completely relax, as if he were floating on water. He lost his perception of time and noise… He wasn't paying attention to anything around him, his concentration completely focused in his head, and when his calves and then gradually the rest of his legs started tingling, he knew that was it. Tingling in the legs was a symptom of high blood pressure. From a regular 120/80, he was able to achieve a personal measured record of 170/100.

He collapsed many times, he faked a head concussion. He even underwent a risky lumbar puncture at the hospital, which left him paralysed for fourteen days, without simulating anything. This was when Leonid Ilyich Brezhnev had his funeral and some Communist nurse recorded everything, including the half-dead patients, to watch the funeral. She was standing over Vitas, who was unable to move from his bed, berating someone about reactionaries and good-for-nothing socialists, how they couldn't even bow at the memorial of one of the working people's greatest leaders. Vitas also felt sorry, especially when he found out how Brezhnev's coffin landed in the hole in the ground. He had now spent more time at the hospital and the first-aid station than at the army unit, so the doctors at the psychiatric ward decided to diagnose him with neurocirculatory asthenia. But there were cameras everywhere, including in the bathroom, in the rooms and in the corridors. The only thing Vitas was grateful for was that the psychiatric ward was where he played his best chess. But after three days, he had no choice but to lose consciousness and raise his blood pressure. He was very proud of the fact that he was able to get his blood pressure to 160/110. At least until a young doctor shook her head in astonishment. "That's strange, blood pressure usually goes down when patients are diagnosed with neuro-asthenia…"

'Now, I'm going to have to learn to decrease my blood pressure,' Vitas thought angrily, but his efforts did bear fruit after a few weeks. A Colonel, the head of the psychiatric ward called him in, sarcastically saying, 'Private Vitas!'"

"Here!" Vitas replied with an ordinal step.

"We probably won't win the war on imperialism with you, right?"

"I'm afraid not, Comrade Colonel!"

"Are you sorry, Private Vitas?"

"Very sorry, Comrade Colonel. But I will at least try to fight imperialism in poetry."

"Go home, Private Vitas and stop provoking!"

And so Vitas left the military. Never again did he try to change his blood pressure or control his body. He only knew that under certain circumstances, people could do almost anything with their bodies. But he had no idea where the boundaries of possible and impossible lay. During times of great tension and chaos, he recalled his 'medical' experience and sometimes relied on it to ask for some much-needed rest.

17.
Preparing for a Spiritual Pilgrimage

Vitas and Aviel got to work. Over and over they said they weren't prepared for their mission, but they wouldn't let it get to them. It's a theatrical performance. It's a second life. They have nothing to lose and everything to gain. The environment they were in was so soothing, they almost felt free of any petty feelings of shame and indecency. It was as if someone had cut them free of regular, atavistic feelings, as known to them in their "civilised" environment. The ideas of having to behave in accordance with position had disappeared. They left the world of regular European and American traditions behind. No one was watching them, no one was tracking them and they felt completely free. It was as if the ocean had washed them up onto a beach in a large wavy seashell and they could finally take the right step towards freedom. When Kromen disappeared from the lamasery, they finally felt more relaxed and behaved in a way they never could have in a "civilised culture." They understood that it was a matter of perspective and of tradition.

Both of them were beginning to understand Tibetan. Since they were in regular contact with Tibetans, who didn't speak any English, their Tibetan was constantly improving. They were discovering hidden corners of their new home, which was becoming more and more isolated due to the weather. It began snowing and it was getting colder.

Each of them got their own hole in the rock. The rooms were closed and relatively spacious. They had intended to rebuild them to their own liking rather than to the image of their God.

They got to work. They searched the premises of the incredibly large lamasery. They found many objects that could be used as sacral symbols. Vitas even found a crucifix in one of the sheds. It was perhaps made of tin or some mixture of lead and something. They weighed it and argued about the origin of the material. Aviel cheered Vitas up. He didn't care that he was dirty and surrounded by cobwebs. After cleaning the crucifix, they put it on the table, which turned into an altar. Aviel wasn't that lucky, so he had no problems making David's Star. He put a mezuza[20] on the door frame of the "synagogue." The mezuza had Moses' text on it: "Think about the past, try to understand the years of the past generation, ask your father, he will tell you and ask your elders, they will tell you…"

Most importantly, there were so many books to choose from that it was difficult to navigate through them. They humbly admitted that they were far from being scholars. Both of them borrowed a lot of literature on their topic. Akhum, the librarian, was very helpful in their search. They were not only in awe of the diversity of the sacral and worldly literature but also by its relevance. The latest books included educational textbooks, dictionaries and others, until about the middle of the twentieth century. Then, it was rather sporadic, depending on "who brought what," the librarian clarified with a mysterious smile.

---

20 Mezuza (Hebrew: "door frame", "door case", "door post") – A small box containing a rolled-up parchment with two passages from the Torah. It is placed on the door frames of Jewish households, flats and Jewish businesses in order to fulfil one of the commandments of the Torah.

Curious monks sometimes came to see them. They were incredibly kind-hearted, but terribly, almost annoyingly curious, like small children. They wanted to know what they were doing, why they were doing it, they even asked about details in the biblical text, which neither Aviel nor Vitas were able to properly answer. Vitas didn't dare call his temple the Lord's temple, but the visitors easily solved that problem. They called Aviel's synagogue and Vitas' temple the gonkhang. This is what monks called several smaller chapels in the monastery, where they could mediate without interruptions and isolate themselves from everyone else. They smelled of yak butter and they were covered in thangka. Every free space on the wall was covered with holy images or mantras.

Aviel and Vitas were very busy, they were swamped. They had to improve their Tibetan, partake in several meditations and read sutras. The readings mostly took place at the dukang, the main Buddhist shrine... They even attended Hindi meditations from time to time, all while renovating their own shrines, which also served as their private dwellings.

The weather outside was getting colder and colder. The beginning of September was cold and frosty, with heavy downpours and the occasional snowfall. Ideas of going on trips were soon scrapped.

– – –

Aviel had an idea. He never confided it in anyone, but he continued to search for something. Even in his eyes he seemed absentminded. He later admitted that he disappeared a few times to snoop around the local stables until he found what he was looking for. The shofar is a traditional Jewish musical instrument usually made of ram horn and played like a flute. Rosh Hashanah, the Jewish New Year, was fast approaching. Blowing the shofar is supposed to create the sound of wailing, thereby awakening reason, consciousness, feeling and a desire in people for improvement. But Aviel's craftsmanship with his shofar didn't so much create the sound of wailing, but rather evoked wailing in its listeners.

"This is no ram horn! Where'd you get it?" Vitas yelled at Aviel in an attempt to prevent his concert performances.

"It is a ram horn!" Aviel claimed stubbornly.

"You had to have torn it off some poor goat…" Vitas persisted, trying to disappear into the more remote rooms of the lamasery.

That year, Rosh Hashanah was on September the thirteenth. Many monks came to Aviel, who informed them of what was perhaps the biggest Jewish feast. He told them of Judgment Day, the creation of man, who wronged the Almighty and then received repentance…

Needless to say, the monks enjoyed this feast so much that they added drums and shells to Aviel's shofar to accompany and liven up his band. The 5768th Jewish New Year turned into a Buddhist séance. Aviel was desperate at first, but then waved his hand: "Forget it, at least they accepted it and liked it and as for YHWH? He has to see how desperate I am…"

Vitas laughed mischievously at him, but appreciated his reading from the Torah. Aviel had turned it into a form of play, so that everyone understood Rosh Hashanah. The monks thought he was very creative and even the Lama smiled a little when he met Aviel in the days following the weekly Jewish ritual. Yom Kippur, the Great Day of Atonement, another important Jewish holiday, was just around the corner…

18.
Euro-Hut

Cypros was a political commissioner during Communism. He didn't have any problems. He preached to soldiers about how wonderful life could be in a beautiful socialist country, he sometimes confiscated someone's Bible from his locker, imprisoning him for twenty-four hours in the local military base, and always transferred most of his worries to the agitator squad, who had to teach his comrades-in-arms to sing the Bolshevik anthem, The Internationale.

He was a happy fellow. Although his wife was a bit of a wishy-washy grey mouse, not much fun to be around, but she did cook for him, clean and do his laundry. What more could be asked? She gave him a son, who was almost his double. He was a wrinkly, scrawny little boy, just like he later saw in that stupid movie, in which the boy was born as an elderly man. He moved awkwardly. When they were together, everyone looked at them like they do strawberries in the winter and he smirked like a drunken Santa Claus. But this so-called Velvet Revolution had ruined everything. Suddenly, he was out on the streets, just when he was waiting to receive a higher military ranking on his epaulette, making him a captain. When the commander of the unit fired him, Cypros told him that he wouldn't mind switching lanes. He left the Communist Party and preached about the prosperity and peacefulness of the capitalist way of life.

"Lieutenant Cypros, I don't even know if our unit will survive this period," the Colonel said in a hoarse voice from across the officer's desk. "And if it does, then you," he pointed his index finger at him strictly, "you will definitely not stay here. Or do you believe in God or something?"

"If necessary, I will also believe in God," replied Cypros bluntly and modestly. The Colonel didn't buy it. Apparently, there wouldn't be political commissioners anymore, only chaplains.

And what next? With retirement nowhere in sight, he's trying to figure out simply what path to take in life, everything being different for him now too and always hearing that his father was a bastard... What could he do? He has to provide for himself, but since he lost his job, the way isn't clear. This isn't good. This really isn't good.

For several years, he was a fish on dry land. He closed a deal every now and again, but nothing exceptional. What else could he do? He was only qualified in humanely preaching about socialism to soldiers, who, in their minds, merely told him to go to hell and that manual labour was as good as Greek to them. The extra money he sometimes earned on odd jobs here and there really wasn't much.

Moreover, his mother was no longer independent. His father died years ago. There was no way that Cypros could take care of her anymore. She was sick and in every possible way, she couldn't even go to the bathroom on her own, a situation so many others must come to know. The solution: a long-term care facility. He put her in the Bohnice Psychiatric Ward and then told everyone that the state put her there, while waving his finger from side to side like a windshield wiper during a downpour.

True, a long-term care facility isn't all that mentally

encouraging, especially as a final destination. I could imagine better, pondered Cypros, when he saw about forty groaning women. It was a large room, about 400 feet squared, with dark, ochre latex on all surfaces and various women hollering nonsense. The windows were barred and there was one large, fully tiled bathroom, where the nurses sometimes hosed the screaming women down with water.

It was really not that great at all. But Cypros' monthly visit to his mother paid off each time, it being payday from the welfare office and his mum signing off the whole cheque in his name. This was even worth buying the bouquet and box of chocolates that he always brought her, so that he wouldn't look so standoffish, only there to cheat his own mother. He did always take the box of chocolates back however, because his mom always forgot that he'd brought it in the first place, and that way he could at least return it to her next time, though he never thought to touch the flowers.

Firstly, he was not alone. Dozens, maybe hundreds of people were like him and only went to see their loved ones on payday. Secondly, he was a saint compared to the son of the lady who lay across the aisle from his mother. He sat on a bedside chair, crying and shaking like an aspen. Not because his mother was dying, but because he'd gotten into some trouble and wanted his dear mother to help him. Imagine pleading help from his helpless mother. Cypros thought that a step too far!

He listened attentively. Either way his mother didn't pay much attention. Maybe she didn't even realise who he was. She had already signed the paper and now Cypros was there as a gesture of pure love. He leaned over her bed as if they were talking, but he was eavesdropping in on the vaguely familiar voice of the son across the aisle.

"Ma, if we don't write it in *your* name, they'll take away our house and what'll I tell your grandkids then?"

"But I've already given you the house. I don't own anything else."

"Yes, but you could take on the three-million…"

"But Vince, where would I get it…?"

"Mama, my dearest, you won't take it from anywhere, it'll only be on paper and everything will be fine."

"What do you mean, fine? People will come here asking me for it."

"No they won't. Not even the devil takes where there's nothing. You know that. Believe me, ma, I swear, no one will ever bother you. And I'll pay everything back next month when I close this huge deal…"

"Vince, dear, you have already made so many promises in your life…"

"Don't worry, mama. Look, there's a notary waiting outside. I'll go get him and he'll take care of everything. Don't worry. Don't fall asleep on me. Your granddaughter got an A on her art project, she really takes after you. It's a God-given talent, really, it is. Hold on, I'll be right back."

Cypros also left. He only took the paper and didn't even wait to see how everything turned out with Vince. It was clear that everything would turn out just fine and that he'd end up debt-free.

He paced from wall to wall, like a lion in a cage, thinking hard.

"Damn fool" he cursed himself. "Why didn't I already think of it? I can be persuasive, when I want to be. Epaulette aside, persuasion is just about the one thing that stayed with me once I'd left the unit, the one thing I remember well how to use…" Amid his wandering around, he ended up in the bathroom, staring at himself in the mirror. He was puckering his lips, making grimaces, greeting the person across from him, informing him of a wonderful business proposal!

Before long, Cypros found a debtor owing twenty million on a building and received two million in return. He and his mother managed it all very professionally, without a single mistake.

He exchanged the two million for 100 crown bills and his wife went for a dip in a bath of money. She was also quite surprised. Before long she was feeling frisky, and jabbed poor Charles IV over and over with her nipples. Cypros couldn't help himself and cut old Charles IV from two of the notes, placing the cut outs over her breasts. The beauty! Life instantly adopted an entirely new meaning. He understood that this new system really was a gamechanger, and once in good hands, life really could be good.

Two months later, his mother died and the loan died with her. Not a problem, until the time came to meet with the notary. Apparently, his mother owed twenty million (plus interest) and if Cypros wanted to accept his inheritance, he would also have to pay off the twenty million. Enough. He caused a scene, claiming it impossible, but to no avail. It was all no good. This of course was awful, as he would have to decline the inheritance, meaning he would also lose his mother's four-million-crown flat that, until now, they'd lived in for nothing. Overall, the whole deal cost him two million. Two million washed away. Helpless, Cypros booted around the furniture, screaming: "Such a fine deal, oh – oh, fuck it!"

After exhausting himself in this manner, he reclined in his armchair, took a shot of liquor, and embarked on a long train of thought.

In the morning, his wife found him lying on the coffee table, dead drunk. He snored like a freight carriage, empty measures of plum brandy encircling him on the floor, and he himself covered over with scribbled-on sheets of archive paper.

Cypros took it rather to heart. Yes, he admitted to screwing up this little transaction, but the ones to come would surely be profitable. Through the years, he developed a strategy that he began to perfect. He selected various social institutions, retirement homes, long-term care facilities, oncology departments at hospitals and so on, scouring their lists in the hope of finding those ones to whom he could transfer his debts. He became such a consummate professional that he began to attend social events at retirement homes, posing as the manager of a foundation, bearing gifts and running various charitable events. In the end, they even liked having him around. That was good. Very good. Oh, to picture him arriving at a Christmas celebration, brandishing an artificial Xmas tree (easy to repack and reuse on another occasion) and some stuffed tat... the old folks sometimes fouling themselves, but him smiling no less with those starry chaps, going so far as to do a sort of chicken dance, or a conga line at one party or another. But even then! He always found a soul.

Notwithstanding this usual business, he thoroughly examined business registries, cadastral offices with foreclosed properties, attended court cases, met judges and clerks, always searching for debtors who were looking to dispose of their debts. Cypros was their last and only resort. First they would kiss his hands. Then they would bow down and kiss his boots.

In the aftermath of several successful deals, he was sitting in his (now new) armchair again, considering some new method of restructuring, some quick boost. Everyone must believe they provide salvation in some way, that they somehow resemble Christ. It was a company he needed, a place for the people to shelter as Jesus had found in Bethlehem. "A home, a barn..." No, that was short-sighted. It wouldn't need to be extravagant, his ambitions were neither high nor mundane – "A roof! Yes, that's it: a roof. To tell these poor individuals that I'm giving them a roof over their heads – No, no. That won't do. Even better: a hut. Yes, something a bit more modest. But it's missing that financial element. Europe's in fashion these days, so it should be the European-Hut. Perfect. No! The Euro-Hut! That's everything! That's actually really good."

Still sitting in his armchair, Cypros was laughing like a little boy, already picturing himself at some party in Dubi in North Czechia, where Euro-Hut were organising an unforgettable spectacle for the doddering elderly. "Come unto me, my herd of sheep, come hither and thereupon be sheltered in the warmth of this Euro-Hut…"

Out there he'd be buzzing around with his butterfly, pollinating flowers long thought to be worthy compost. And old age was supposed to be repulsive? On the contrary, it is the most beautiful time of all…

19.
The Death of Hermit Tao

Vitas and Aviel quickly adjusted to the local ways. They studied, took part in sutra readings, read poems by a renowned Tibetan saint, meditated and prayed. Their Tibetan was good enough to understand the basics, but it wasn't good enough to hold an elaborate conversation yet. The questions of the curious monks, who peeped into the Christian and Jewish tabernacles, later became Bible readings, glimpses of the Torah and the various testimonies of the saints.

In truth, both novices could be proud of their relatively privileged positions. The vast majority of monks had assorted practical jobs, such as maintenance work, cooking, grinding barley, making yak butter (whether for food, tea or candles) and so on. Other groups of monks were responsible for a rotating number of services, like cleaning and washing the dishes. It was a deep-rooted and fairly sophisticated regime, dating back many years.

Then there were about forty monks whose status was special relative to the others. These monks held loftier positions in the hierarchy, so they weren't involved in regular work. They were responsible for church service and studies. The librarian and the main representatives of the individual religious groups, including the Hindi Maasai Mangaung and our two novices fell into this category.

A group of eight monks, led by the local abbot, Lama Thorpe Tenzin were at the very top of the hierarchy. A council called the little Kashag made decisions on fundamental issues. However, the Lama was responsible for the ultimate decision, meaning he always had the final say. Truthfully, he never intervened in fleeting things such as the technical operations of the lamasery. This was the responsibility of the maintenance upheld by monk Tungjur, one of the eight chosen ones.

The whole community was preparing for winter. The feast day on the twenty-fifth of October marked the official start of winter and was also the death anniversary of the glorious Buddhist teacher, Tsongkhapa, who had lived at the turn of the fourteenth and fifteenth centuries. He had founded Gelugpa, one of the central schools of Buddhism.

Preparations were in full swing. Yak butter was being stirred and poured into marching lanterns and everyone was busy cleaning… when suddenly came news of the death of one of the walled pilgrims.

The news came from monk Wung Pien, the guardian of both of the Buddhists who had intended to reach a state of total dissociation. Based on what Kromen had told the newcomers, it had been the Chinese pilgrim who had arrived quite recently. The bowl with tsampa and water that Wung Pien brought to the hermitage regularly remained untouched for two days afterwards, and no one would accept any callers.

This was no tragedy for the local monks however, not interfering with preparations for the feast of the upcoming winter, although they did have to figure out how to deal with what remained. Several monks had suggested simply to wall up the opening where the food was served and to leave everything else the way it had always been. Nevertheless, the council unanimously decided to break the last stone abode of Hermit Tao.

Sharp pickaxes were stuck into the stone. For around half-an-hour following, the Lama communed with the spirit of the deceased through the *Tibetan Book of the Dead*, introducing him to the bardo[21] he would pass through on his way to nirvana.

The butcher, Lu Cheng, who seemed also to be a grave-digger, then put the remains on a cart and took them far away to the other hillside behind the lamasery. Most of the monks accompanied him on the half hour trip, piping flutes made of shells, beating drums and dancing in the rhythm of a bear that stomps from side to side. Then, they parted and prayed. There was no way Vitas and Aviel would miss this occasion, even though the ritual that followed took them strongly by surprise.

"O ye Compassionate Ones, defend (so-and-so) who is defenceless. Protect him who is unprotected. Be his forces and his kinsmen. Protect [him] from the great gloom of the bardo. Turn him from the red [or storm] wind of karma," said the Lama in a soft voice, as if immersed in the depths. "Turn him from the great awe and terror of the Lords of Death. Save him from the long narrow passageway of the bardo…"[22]

Using a long, curved knife, Lu Cheng the butcher and now the gravedigger, carved a swastika into the dead hermit's back. He separated the legs and arms from the torso and cut the skull with a single, precise swing of the axe. The vultures were circling one by one, stuffing every inch of their lustful beaks, leaving nothing but a skeleton by the time another thirty minutes had passed. Nearby, Lu Cheng watched attentively how the wild game feasted. When vultures cannot break their nourishment from bones, they are

---

21 The state of existence intermediate between two lives on earth
22 Bardo Thodol – *The Tibetan Book of the Dead*, or *The After-Death Experiences on the Bardo Plane*, English translation by Lāma Kazi Dawa-Samdup, downloaded from http://www.holybooks.com/the-tibetan-book-of-the-dead-2

known to soar to great heights, dropping them onto the rocks below and shattering them, so that their sharp beaks can reach into the marrow.

Unlike Vitas and Aviel, the rest of the monks were completely calm. It seemed that this spectacle was no different from the process each morning at breakfast. In their eyes, the hermit had reached a bardo state, a period of transition between death and rebirth, or onto the path of deliverance. Properly prepared, he would be liberated to reach the state of nirvana, an eternal peace. If not, his soul would only wander in the samsara of continual rebirth. He would be born again, either human or non-human, perhaps as an animal. Reincarnation, a core element of Buddhism, gives believers a clearer view of death. It becomes no more than a part of never-ending life, or of constant death and rebirth – samsara. During the funeral ritual, they prayed, sang psalms and read other excerpts from the *Book of the Dead*.

The situation had left the Jingzhi somewhat speechless, and seeing this Lama Rinpoche had summoned them to his chambers. He clutched his essential dordje. He quietly asked how they had understood the hermit's transition to another dimension and how far they were in preparing their mission.

"You know, we're just not used to that sort of thing," Vitas politely assessed the ritual that had just taken place. "And then…" he added timidly, "I'm not really sure what you're expecting of us. Do you want us to become Buddhists, or to stay true to our own faiths…?"

"Do of your own accord, that to which you feel closest. But also be grateful if you have learned a bit of our literature, which is very intertwined with your faith, although I am not saying there are no contradictions."

"We were obviously shocked by the hermit's funeral," Aviel dared to say.

"Be assured that he did not suffer. He reached the true state of nirvana in the final stage. He freed himself from his physical body."

"And who is the other monk, the one walled up a bit higher?" asked Aviel.

"Monk Sonam. The Chinese murdered his whole family. He was one of a few partisans, remnants of the fight against Chinese invaders. He survived the eradication of his kind in the Mustang region of Nepal. The invasion of Tibet was difficult for him. He fought long and hard and when the final remnants of the partisans were scattered, some went into exile in India, Nepal and Sikkim, but Sonam couldn't. He had no choice but to stay on Tibetan soil. He was very bitter and couldn't find comfort anywhere, even though our faith offered him a path and the belief in a better future. He chose the path of solitude, so that he could concentrate on freeing himself from his body and achieving enlightenment. He has been locked up in his cave, searching for enlightenment for almost a year."

"He's been walled up there for a year now? He must have already gone blind."

"Maybe, but his vision has transformed into a completely different form of perception. And since everything around us is only a spiritual construction, with no existence beyond our consciousness, he has no problem with seeing the way you do. I'm sure you are beginning to understand meditation through learning our practices. Have you in your previous lives never experienced the ability to control a lot more than your physical body alone? This can be achieved by merely concentrating and relaxing for long, uninterrupted periods of time."

"I have plenty of experience at that," Vitas nodded vigorously. Aviel turned to him, alarmed.

"Can you describe it?"

"But it's a bit… odd" Vitas timidly replied.

"You think we have no time for laughing here? It's our passion!"

"It was some time ago, many years really. I learned to control my blood pressure and I think I'd still be able to do it today. I believe that under certain circumstances, people can control their bodies to such an extent that it just can't be explained through common reasoning. Simply by relaxing and concentrating…" Vitas summarised the time when he tried getting out of military service.

"Yes, that's exactly what I mean, you might be a Siddha[23] yourself," the Lama responded cheerfully, closely observing Vitas' every facial movement. "I see that you are very close, on the way to Tantra, in essence. Many Buddhists have been searching for this throughout their entire lives, while you are quite capable of doing it. The goal is not of course to increase one's blood pressure, but one's vision, our way of concentration, an understanding of the imminent emptiness, to lose all reception of sensory stimuli… This is how it begins, on which you must build. I'm thoroughly impressed." Happily, the monk rubbed his hands.

"You have already completed our spiritual exercises without knowing. I refer to our ways of dealing with emptiness, when we focus so much on our inner selves that we no longer perceive our surroundings, we detach ourselves from shapes, noises, smell, taste, touch and all sensory objects, just as it reads in the Diamond Sutra. Your senses are isolated, uninterrupted. If one truly falls into this state of perfection, all temporal space opens up to us, allowing us to master it, as we too, become a part of it… This is not possible however, without many years of practice," the Lama nodded in acknowledgment. "You may be able to master the

---

23 Siddha – one, who has mastered a high degree of physical and spiritual perfection or enlightenment

art of tumo, the ability to survive frost naked by accumulating body temperature, you can learn lunggompa, become a man who runs a mile in under a minute... And what's more," he continued enigmatically. "If you study and practice hard, you will learn to fully overcome the consciousness of your body. This is especially helpful at the moment of death, when you want to free yourself of the tormenting samsara."

"But I'd say for me, it's more a matter of chaos," Vitas humbly admitted, not too enthusiastic regarding his possibilities at the moment of death.

"This may seem true, but you have the possibility to overcome it. And it also seems you have enough humility, an essential condition for continuing on this path. There are of course many paths to take, and our means to achieving deliverance is Mahayana Buddhism. You still have a lot to learn."

"Oh, please," added Aviel, who had been paying close attention, quite viciously amused by Vitas' options at his moment of death. "What's your aim? On one hand we should absorb Mahayana Buddhism, yet be immersed in our own faith at the same time: Vitas into Christianity and me into Judaism."

"It is second nature to you, that is the reason why you must improve in your own faiths but also learn more about ours, especially when your companion is so obviously more inclined to it. However, please approach it with due diligence. If you had brought about the conditions you were describing," the Lama turned to Vitas again, "yourself, without thinking, or had even demonstrated them for the sake of amusement, your health and future would be in great danger. If a person finds a way to open up, he also has to be able to close himself off, otherwise he risks his mind openly wandering, capable of incurring great evil, without the owner of this mind knowing anything at all. A person can do incredible things with the body. One can float, sit outside in the freezing snow, all the while believing an enchanted warmth, but this person must also be aware of the limits of his abilities. Either way, I am very happy that you are here," the Lama concluded simply, ending the conversation.

"And why are we here?" asked Aviel, unrelenting.

"In preparation," the Lama briefly surmised.

"In preparation for what?"

"I think it's time…" the Lama gave Aviel a very generous verbal slap, ending the conversation once and for all.

20.
Untouchable!

Vitas, having composed a heart-breaking piece on the harshness of fate, darted off north to Velké Březno to see a big fish who owed millions. A White Horse. Yes, a White Horse. Just as the famous Czech author, Karel Čapek, had come up with the word "robot" in the first half of the twentieth century, so too, was the term "tunnelling" (also-known-as large-scale financial fraud, or asset-stripping) was first widely used during the Wild West era following the then-Czechoslovak Velvet Revolution, to express a bank robbery without any bloodshed – a bank robbery that entailed no more than white limousines. The term: White Horse, was much the same. In English, it suggests a Guarantor or a Straw Man. In its simplest form, it is a person who takes on someone else's debts knowing there is nothing to lose. Generally, this person will receive some cash in return, or is perhaps simply jettisoned into a lake, a concrete block on his back, to ensure he wouldn't resurface to testify. Or perhaps he would remain ignorant...

This was nothing new. Among other vices, the end of the nineties, the end of the second and turn of the third millennium, was known widely for debts that only a few fools paid off in this recklessly expanding republic. Many of these debts were never recovered. Only the naïve spoke of ethics, considered almost an obscenity at the time.

The Indian summer painted the surrounding landscape in flagrant colours. It seemed that God himself had been dreaming of what he had done on Earth, dropping his palette and leaving every colour splashed in smudges and droplets all around. Vitas and his crew arrived at a gardening colony. He lost all sense of direction in the labyrinth of miniature houses and gardens.

He stopped and asked an older lady, who was helplessly trying to rake the leaves that the wind had cleanly plucked from under the rake teeth and mockingly swept around her in colourful patches. In essence, she was running around like a butterfly hunter with a net on a rod.

"Good afternoon. Where may I find Lavicka? Zdenek Lavicka?" he tentatively interrupted the leaf hunter, who was wearing a scarf over her head. She was completely thrown off guard by Vitas' remark. It seemed the world had at that moment spun around her. Snapping back, she stared at Vitas, then carefully put the rake down, teeth up, and composing herself, leant on the rake. She pointed her free hand behind Vitas. "Over there."

Vitas turned around and saw an elderly man, impossible to tell how old, standing under a large walnut tree. He was tiny, hunched over, leaning forward on his cane like a baseball player waiting for the pitcher to throw the ball. He was wearing something that could be described as a blanket that he must have slept under at night and wrapped around himself in the morning like a long-faded, now only grey-brown, Eastern palette. He had a very wrinkled and attentive expression on his face. His lips were clenched so tightly that they hinted to the absence of at least one row of teeth. His eyes were wide open.

The creature started shaking and moving slowly, then threw his cane up. That's when his body stopped and stared curiously with his head tilted back towards the flying cane.

The cane flew into the tree, taking down some leaves and nuts, which fell on the ground but the creature was so full of the passion to succeed that he had obviously forgotten about his cane altogether. The cane fell on his head, still facing upward. The creature screamed in surprise then, waving his hands around helplessly before falling onto the grass. Then he got up as if nothing had happened. And this process repeated itself, including the cane, the surprise and the hit on the head…

"Mr Lavicka?" called Vitas uncertainly, the camera rumbling in the background.

The creature spun on its axis.

"Yes, Lavicka. I'm Lavicka. Do you want a nut?"

"No, thank you, I don't want a nut," he echoed Lavicka, without ridicule and quite sincere. "May I have a word with you?"

"Yeah, yeah," he said willingly and quickly made his way to the fence that divided both of them, in swinging strides. Vitas could now take a closer look at him. The baggy rags on his legs, a combination of pants and the aforementioned blanket were held up by several suspenders, which had been clipped onto the baggiest parts, so that these garments remained tight on his body. He had tangled, chestnut-colour hair and big and kind-hearted round eyes. His unshaven, wart-infested face was bruised from the cane. His mouth was still slightly open and remnants of salami or bacon flew out of it each time he spoke. Vitas inadvertently stepped away from the fence. He was glad there was some type of barrier separating them, otherwise he had a feeling that this creature would jump up and hug him. This way, he only stuck his fingers through the holes in the fence, looking in like at an animal in a zoo.

"Hello," greeted Vitas politely. "I'm Vitas from the Czech TV station."

"Howdy, I'm Lavicka, from round here."

"Can you confirm that you are the owner of Spedinter, Bonnie and Clyde and some five other companies?"

"Not at all. Someone must've written it in my name."

"What do you mean 'written it in your name'?" snooped Vitas, trying to act less apprehensive than Lavicka, although that was a difficult task.

"Well, I was there with him and they wrote it."

"Where were you and who were you with?"

"He drives a Skoda, I was there with'im and he damn well written it."

"Slow down, slow down, I don't understand. And why did you sign it? And how much did you get for doing this?"

"A bottle of beer and a fifty. And we went to Prague," Lavicka explained, smiling proudly.

"Hold on, right – you went to the Commercial Court in Prague and that's where all the companies were transferred to your name? And you spoke with the judge?"

"I don't know his name from judge, but there was a chap sitting at a desk going on with'imself."

"And what now? There are lots of people who come here asking for money these days, right?"

"I don't know anything and I don't have anything. I'm not giving you anything."

"I don't want anything. And you live here in this house?"

"Yes. I live here. I have a room there. It's mine. I have a towel and bread there."

"Right. And you're happy."

"Yes. I live an'appy life."

"And what do you get up to in your spare time?" Vitas hunted for a personal topic that he could elaborate on, making the film a little more humane.

"Well, there's no lady in the picture, no woman…"

"What do you do all day?"

"I work on everything here, on the garden…"

"Did you graduate from elementary school?"

"I failed out grade five."

"Then can you tell me who took you to Prague? Do you remember the people, the ones who took you to Prague?"

"Yes, they gave me a bottle of beer and a fifty."

"And what did you do with the fifty?"

"Had another beer."

"And one of the guys who wanted you to do this was Koulicky, right?" Vitas dropped the name of a previous owner of one of the companies, prior to its transferral to the hands of this nut hunter.

"Koulicky? Yep, Koulicky, if that wer'im, yes, then that were him."

"Koulicky used to own the company."

"Yep, yeah, yep, yep – that was'im… that was him… a bit stout. And back then, there were two lads, two chaps."

"Hold on, which chaps?"

"Well, lads. Cyprous or something or other, had a hut."

"What hut???" stunned, Vitas was still trying to figure out the loose ends.

"Som'fin' from Euro, from Europe. Seemed though they'ad safe shelter in a European hut. Yeah, yep, it was one of those Euro-Huts…"

Vitas couldn't unearth anything else. An intensive search through the Commercial Register and the Land Registry followed. He also had some of his lawyer friends involved along with anyone else who could help him crack the case. But in the meantime, he continued to shoot his more or less demanding work.

– – –

"Gentlemen, I'm telling you: if you come up with it, I'll pay.

So I don't have money, what's money? Pchaaa… Production isn't an art, but selling is! – Right?" Shama asks defiantly, turning his head, curiously observing his audience like a rooster keeping an eye on his hens to ensure their safety, all while anticipating a round of applause.

A meeting in total secrecy of four individuals and another three hidden cameras is taking place in Zličín, on the outskirts of Prague, at the residence of Vitas' friend, who is on the verge of bankruptcy. He's an unconventional individual, who universally maintains a very optimistic viewpoint, right until the last minute and long afterwards. Even so, he owes money in all directions. He too, entered into business at the fall of Communism. He had become highly involved, like a new settler in the Wild West, under the impression that it's sure to start raining gold at any minute. Innocently, he began his life as a businessman as a physical entity, but this was ill-fated. He paid off millions in debt, fed dozens of people in stores and bakeries, kept ostriches running in his backyard, enough cats that they fell on his head… A less pragmatic person would call him mad.

But Vitas had developed a soft spot for him as a result of this extreme generosity and his enormous heart. He built castles in the sky, attempting to climb imaginary clouds to eternal happiness. In reality, he was rotting away, bound by handcuffs plagued with ill-conceived laws, cancer, debt and the usual consumerism in all directions. His employees, however, had hit the jackpot. His generosity knew no bounds. His grey hair too, made him appear a soulful, Olympic god.

His unpredictable reactions were dangerous though, and Vitas feared them. Common logic and his own fairness suddenly forced him to act completely against what the common person had ingrained in their mind. It later transpired that Vitas' fears were justified.

The other two attendees were none other than one Cypros, of Euro-Hut, and his son. Together, they were almost identical, but for the fact that one of them was more wrinkled. Both were wearing suits with a bowtie, commissioner-style; a total contrast to the scruffy Shama, who wore jeans, an ostrich-feather suit and a hat also made from the feathers of his own ostriches. Three chairs were not enough for him. Shama appeared more like some deranged cowboy, who had confused the saloon with a dairy bar. His fiercely abrupt and chaotic gestures were contradictory to his own divine appearance. He waved his hands around so profusely that it was impossible to get closer to him, no matter the angle. Contrastingly, both of the other attendant businessmen had terse gestures, shy and tense. In this light, the older Cypros came across as very sovereign, even a little conceited. Vitas sensed the difference in these two different worlds. He considered himself neutral. As such an ingenious reporter, he must remain above it all and keep all things under control. The only thing that could make him nervous in such a situation was the question of whether all of the hidden cameras were working, it being impossible to check during the process of this incriminating shoot.

"Do you know why the financial office doesn't bother me? Honestly? Because I pay thirty-five people! If they ruin me, that's it, finito, I'd go belly up – toast! Let the welfare office pay, they're squeezing me dry and blackmailing me like the Italian mafia!"

"That's not good. That's really not good…" says Cypros.

"It sure isn't good, but I'm not giving up, they have no chance, I'm untouchable! They already wanted me to…"

"Get to the point, man," Vitas interrupts him in the middle of another wild gesture. Vitas knows that even theatrical grandeur won't let Shama's soul reach all corners and he needs to keep him in check. "Here, the gentlemen need clear instructions on how to get rid of you as a physical entity, yet stay alive."

"Yes, that's true," Shama grimly descended from the cloudy heavens, keeping his verbal and nonverbal expressions as vainglorious as before. "And you know what, go to hell! I have no problems being homeless, but do it to those people! The poor souls I employ, who see me like a brood hen. What's going to happen to them??? I bought them a bakery for eight million and now it should all go to waste?"

"That's not good..." said Cypros.

"But man, they don't care. Get to the point," Vitas still attempted to guide this alleged brother.

"Yeah, fine. What are you going to do about it? And another thing – did you come up with the company name yourself? It's genius."

"Yep, yep," the businessmen nodded humbly.

"Well, hurry up and shelter me in your Euro-Hut."

"First of all," said Cypros, "don't worry. It'll all work out fine..."

"There's no doubt about it," Shama interrupted Cypros. "Otherwise you wouldn't be here, right?"

"However, we need to know all your receivables and liabilities to the tee."

"Of course," exclaimed Shama confidently. "Consider it done. I'll have my brother do it," pointing to Vitas. He obviously liked his new relative.

"We need to know exactly what obligations you have and who you owe money to. We need to know whether it's a common expenditure, like the electricity bill, money owed on healthcare, or money owed to private subjects, and so on... We also need to know what you own, what's on lease, any loans you may have, what's clear without any liens, and so on..."

"It's definitely necessary to get rid of you," said the younger member of the Euro-Hut.

"Yes, do it!" yelled Shama.

"No, no, he obviously doesn't mean physically," clarified the older Cypros.

"But physically too," Shama waves his arms divinely, reclining comfortably into his chair and stretching his legs out under the table, all the way to the other side of the room. "Do you know how many people, including my wife, would sleep better at night?"

"But that's really not why we're here."

"No, no, I really didn't steal anything. Yes, I borrowed like twelve million from the Bank of Commerce, but I paid everything back, although not right away. The interest piled up on the delay of payment, but they got all their money back! And then they put tape around my TV at home with stickers saying: foreclosed, like some collector. I'm surprised they didn't wrap a piece of tape around my wife."

"Cowards are always the biggest thieves," the younger Cypros wisely philosophised, sadly nodding his head, without anyone in the room understanding his statement.

"So, you're going to give us all the information on receivables and liabilities as well as the status of your property, as a physical entity," the older Cypros tried putting an end to the matter.

"Yeah, it's probably at a 180:110:40 ratio. Liabilities 180, receivables 110, property 40. In millions of crowns of course."

"Alright well, you're going to give me an exact breakdown, including all the clear references to the company in question, its registers, and so on. It must be scrutinised and then it can all work out in the end."

"Yeah, you can count on it. And what are you going to do with it? Can you also get rid of it if it's a physical entity?" Shama hesitantly asked.

"It's harder to do, but why not?" said the younger Cypros.

The older Cypros launched himself in: "But we're not going to get rid of anything! It would take too long and cost too much."

"Then how *are* you going to do it?"

"If we got rid of you as a physical entity, you'd still have to repay most of the debt, and they'd foreclose everything, including the bakery, which'd be the end of your business activities for the indefinite future."

"No way, what would I do at fifty-eight???"

"Right, so we'll have to go about it more sensitively and more discreetly. Find someone we can transfer your debts to. Based on the agreement with the Business Court, we have to wait six months, because they can ask for all of it back and cancel everything within six months. So, we're talking a year from now, thereabouts."

"Hold on, hold on, what agreement with the Business Court are you getting at?"

"I can't go into it right now, but I'm on good terms with the court. On very good terms. I know someone there."

"Alright, so that would work... and who is this guy – the one who's going to take on the debts?"

"I don't know yet," the older Cypros shook his head. "We have a database of White Horses. People suitable for these purposes and we have to choose the right candidate."

"What?" Shama waved his hands, sitting up from his almost horizontal position, showing interest. "You have a database of White Horses? Like guarantors, right? How did you get this database?"

"Well, only potentially discreet White Horses. We collect information nationwide, especially in social institutions, et cetera and so on... everywhere... different places..." Cypros attempted the vaguest answer possible. He had to back down a little. "But be careful, this person has to be legally competent to decide on his own, so he needs an ID card."

"Your ID card," added the younger Cypros.

"And there's not too many of those."

"And, so you keep a record of these poor souls?" asks Shama curiously.

"But we also keep a record of young teenagers, who would do unbelievable things for a new cell phone or car. They don't care what happens tomorrow. But in their case, it has to be quick because once they're old enough they're not going to want anything to do with such business deals, right?" the older Cypros laughed at his own joke and everyone joined automatically. Mistakenly, as Shama's laughter was decidedly false. Cypros had underestimated him. Over the years, he had become so used to dealing with a certain kind of person that he classified them into specific boxes. When it came to Shama, he opened the wrong box.

"Or people," added Cypros, listening to his voice with adoration, proof of his own abilities, "who could care less about everything, there could be a flood tomorrow for all they care. But the most common cases are those of the dying, who still want to have a bit of fun before they go. We cater to everyone…"

"Really?" Shama's eyes were wide open, as he was wiggling around on his chair, his vicious divinity long gone. Meanwhile Vitas perched on pins and needles, completely wordless. "So, if I wanted to throw the towel in, and I'm only saying *if*, we'd shake on it and you'd…" he first pointed his index finger at both Cyproses, then at himself and then at them once more.

"… Yes, if you want, we could write something in your name, we'd give you three percent of it, so that you can make the best of the time you have left here, then you make the best of that time and everyone's happy."

"But I won't be happy for long because I just won't be."

"But you'll make the best of it before then."

"And someone will shed a tear, because he'll never see that money again…"

"That's life," the older Cypros shrugged his shoulders. "We don't have room for everyone in our Euro-Hut…"

"Life is hard," Shama noted tragically, gazing into space, full of gloom. After a moment of virtual silence, he took a deep breath and sighed: "Fucking life!" He pauses, raises his eyes towards Cypros and asks coarsely: "And what about the poor soul who you transfer it to? He's then stuck with the short end of the stick."

"No he isn't, there's no way, because he has nothing. And usually these people are in such a state of mind that they aren't bothered by it. They live a beautiful life…"

Vitas had to nod in agreement, Lavicka being living proof.

"Alright lads, I probably can't do this," sighed Shama.

"Hold on," refuted the older member of the Euro-Hut with a patient smile. "Such a person could really care less, and more importantly, what about your responsibility towards your employees, your family and what about your property? Do you want to lose everything?"

"Don't be a fool," added his son. "This is a game of false ethics. It's not going to help anyone."

"It's going to help me, gentlemen!" exclaimed Shama, poking his index finger into his chest. "Me, me! And THAT'S of the utmost importance to me."

"Don't be foolish, man!" Vitas couldn't take it any longer, turning on Shama. He understood that his friend could instantly ruin his case simply through his senseless, moody, and rather unconventional whims. "We knew what we were getting ourselves into and that's why we called them!"

"Fine, so let me tell you something, my darlings. I've got cancer in my brain and in my thyroid gland. By now it's perhaps spread everywhere – a real coincidence, no? That would make me one of your perfect targets. Well? We could have made any number of other deals but forget it. I'll fight this bastard on my own! I'm not backing down. I'm untouchable so far and they're not going to touch on me so easy! You can count on it. As for you and your retarded, impoverished old men, or your moronic teenagers, I don't need it, so get out!"

"But – pal!" Vitas shouted desperately.

"And you!" Shama brushed him off and added, sneering hugely: "*Pal.*"

"That's not good. That's not good at all," cried the older Cypros. As he stood up with jerky and trembling gestures, he grabbed his briefcase with such anger that it fell open and all the contents spilled out onto the floor. Nothing but papers. He and his son quickly gathered them, thrusting these documents back into the briefcase before quickly taking leave.

Vitas went outside and attempted to bargain with Cypros, hoping to convince him, but they (with their insulted egos) solidified, making it very clear that they would accept nothing. "This is really no good. I've never met such a fool before," the older Cypros yelled from the partially opened car window, and slammed his foot on the accelerator.

That was the end of Vitas' very promising case on the Euro-Hut. No less, he broadcasted it but it was a mere fraction of what he had hoped for during an interview that had got off to such a strong start.

He came across Shama every now and then. He was still cheerful, talkative and boastful over his willingness to fight. "I'm untouchable so far!" he yelled at Vitas, while theatrically waving his fists. His fight came to an end approximately two years after the meeting in Zlicin. He was not untouchable anymore.

Cypros remained untouchable, though he did close the

doors on his business after the idea went out of date and it became difficult for him to acquire new clients, especially once some desperate creditors had taken discreet perpetrators in social facilities by storm. But this didn't bother him so much anymore. He was already in the clear. It was only a side job, like extra pocket money with added rent. He was hired as an advisor for the Minister of Labour and Social Affairs. Apparently, it would be a shame to let all that field-experience go to waste.

– – –

"HOW ABOUT MAKE A LIVING SOME OTHER WAY???" read the anonymous letter. Vitas gloomily put it into the folder that was slowly getting heavier and heavier – the same folder where he placed all these letters from the same anonymous author.

'Who are you?' Vitas asks in his head, caressing the yellowish folder without thinking. 'What do you want? Why are you doing this? How old are you? Are you a fat, stupid misanthrope? Probably… What do your eyes look like? Don't be shy! Lift your head up and show me your eyes! Let me see them!!!' Vitas clenches his lips tightly, slowly takes a pen off his desk and writes: "BRETISLAV" on the folder.

"So, Bretislav," says Vitas loudly and enthusiastically, like some celebrated actor of the early twentieth century. "DON'T PISS ME OFF!"

21.
God's Blood Versus Chhaang

All the preparations for the first day of winter were winding down. Lanterns and candles were eagerly being prepared with great zest. Barley flour was being roasted for the tsampa and everyone was cleaning... Vitas dared to make a humorous remark at Aviel, saying that it reminded him of military service, which he so desperately fled. They were both so busy that their heads didn't hit the pillow each evening until after midnight mass.

It was no surprise that the local climate took the biggest toll on their biological clock. The air was brisk like a blade, the higher altitude caused lower blood pressure, echoes could be heard from further away, and the aromas here were more vivid. Vitas' senses felt more agitated, almost aroused. The awareness of new stimuli, which fade over time but soon return, was vital to this feeling. He also felt a return to earlier experiences, such as when he had quit smoking. He absorbed the fresh air, the various emotional fragments of memories emerging from the dark oblivion to merge into this difficult-to-grasp nebula, sending tremors down the spine.

He had smoked for nearly thirty years and had fought a cruel fight with smoking. The fight had taken fourteen years with numerous breaks in between. At one point, he had smoked some two packs a day. Over and over he had tried to quit, sometimes for a day, sometimes for a month, and once he even stopped for two years, but he always went back to his old ways. These moments of change (especially from smoking to not smoking) or vice versa, always brought back memories of his childhood. The aromas he hadn't smelled for twenty or thirty years, suddenly resurfaced and started pounding at his emotions. If possible, he would quit smoking continually, if only to have the incredible ability to perceive his surroundings more intensely.

One of his failed attempts to stop smoking immediately came to mind. But he didn't consider it a failure at all. He hadn't smoked for more than six months then and it was right after the Revolution, in which the Communists formally stopped playing their role. He had never crossed the western border, which had now finally opened up.

"Y'know how it is, you old fleabag. Pack your bags and get out into the world," said his very understanding Eva generously, noticing how nervous he had been examining the map of Europe.

Vitas packed his rucksack with mountains of canned goods and clothes and set off alone. He soon arrived at Ceske Budejovice, facing Austria. But lo and behold, some eight hitchhikers stood ahead of him, several of them couples. Realising the wait would go on for some time, he pulled out a crumpled paperback of Nietzsche's *Thus Spoke Zarathustra*. Before he even got through the first sentence, there was a German, from then-West Germany, standing beside him. The other hitchhikers started off frantically.

And they followed. He was a thirty-something travelling businessman from head-to-toe. He sold everything from wine to screws. Vitas said he'd like to go to Austria.

"Kein problem," the young man said bluntly.

Vitas, who spoke better English than German, tried to say: "I would like to find some work…"

"Kein problem."

Of course, the borders had opened up and nothing was a problem. Vitas started tearing up at the thought of all that freedom. It was an unbelievable feeling to cross the border without even stopping because the officers considered him to be German as well, so they only nodded and let him through. No person can truly understand this feeling without having lived under Communism. His whole body was burning. 'I am in a bully-free world, everything is truly possible and attainable…' Insane thoughts raced through his head. Even so, he couldn't quite accept the reality of the situation. There had to be some mistake. He was waiting for a betrayal.

"Are you going to Germany?"

"Me."

"But I can only go to Austria. We're on good terms with Austria. I still need a visa to go to West Germany and I don't have one."

"Kein problem," shouted the driver bluntly, revealing his disregard for any restrictions. It was June 1990, six months after the fall of the Berlin Wall, there was one week left until the unification of Western and Eastern Germany, one more week that Czechoslovak citizens needed visas to get to Germany.

They drove near the Alp border between Austria and Germany and Vitas knew that he had to be on his best behaviour. He had just illegally crossed into Germany. He arrived in the spa city of Bad Tölz, not far from Munich, where they visited a restaurant for lunch. Of course, Vitas didn't have any marks, the local currency. His new friend generously waved his hand, as if saluting, enough to say that he'd cover it. But the waitress scowled when it came time to pay and he called out his "Kein problem, kein problem, aber Ich habe keine Gelde," Vitas understood that his new friend had no money. He pictured himself behind German bars, an illegal immigrant, a thief, thinking about how much he'd have to pay. Fortunately, the businessman's passport was sufficient collateral.

Vitas got by as a dishwasher and cleaner. All his jobs were strictly under-the-table. He got a sense of something that was completely new to him. He was in Munich at the time Germany was unified. There was an important evening at the Central Marien Plaza in Munich. The utterly drunk and screaming delegation of the former East Germany arrived in their infamous Trabants among the cheering crowd. They were ecstatic over the new freedom for all of Germany, while Vitas was ecstatic because he'd become a legal visitor as of midnight.

Afterwards, he hitchhiked in mania all across Europe. He went to Stuttgart with a man on his way to Garmisch-Partenkirchen, so he went there next. He was near Innsbruck. Who could resist such a gem of a town, truly a divine teardrop on the edge of the Alps? But the next person that picked him up was on his way to Florence. And who could resist Florence?

By September, he found himself in Merano, Italy. In Tibet, he would immediately recall seeing those Alps. The top of the world seemed like a mass of flesh to him, but the Alps were more like a human worm writhing helplessly on a bed of nails. Back then, he had no money and he was hungry. He pulled out his Czech-Italian dictionary, headed towards the beautiful village of Lana, and picked apples for one season. He greeted everyone with a polite "Buongiorno." Most people stared at him, answering: "Grüss Gott." Hard to say if this was incomprehensible rudeness, the citizens of the South Tyrolean region more Austrian than they are Italian, or if he truly did look untrustworthy. There was no way he'd find a job as an apple picker.

He had been roaming around for two days when he came across a tall man, whose grey hair blended in wonderfully with the slightly whiter mountain tops all around, standing proudly by an apple orchard. His striking blue eyes peeked vividly through his silver glasses. 'This is not what a true orchard owner looks like,' Vitas thought in his head. But he also thought triumphantly that there was no obvious reason to discriminate

"Buongiorno," Vitas greeted politely.

"Grüss Gott," said the man, cheerfully smiling, visibly amused by Vitas.

"Do you need any workers?" asked Vitas in German. The answer was brief: "No."

"Well, have a nice day then."

But the grey-haired man began to laugh and asked Vitas slowly, so that he'd understand: "Do you know what you just asked me? You asked if – *I* – want to work. And *I* don't want to," he burst out laughing.

Definitely amusing. Vitas smiled sourly, not wanting to spoil the fun, all while thinking he'd probably make himself look foolish for a lot longer.

"Where are you from?" Suddenly, the man stood to attention and although Vitas was relatively tall, he reached only his shoulders. The man stood like a teacher at the front of the classroom.

"From Czech," Vitas exhaled briefly.

"Oh, from Czech? Franz Kafka!" he barked briefly, raising his palm to his ear, making a gesture as if waiting for an answer that he'd need to use his ear for.

Vitas had no idea why, but he adapted to the game. He also stood to attention and started listing off the works of Franz Kafka. The man clenched his lips and nodded his head derisively. When Vitas finished, the man yelled out: "Max Brod."

Vitas was horrified and started saying something about being Franz Kafka's friend, but retreated as best he could. He was fast realising that his poor German meant that there was no way he could properly describe him. But the grey-haired intellectual was quite pleased then, and asked Vitas about his educational background. When Vitas told him that he studied at the Academy of Arts in Prague, the man threw out his intellectual demeanour and said: "I accept!"

Later, they would become very close, but only after Vitas showed this Tyrolean his paperback copy of Nietzsche's *Thus Spoke Zarathustra*, and before that they remained on strictly boss-and-worker terms. Nietzsche and Schopenhauer were his employer's gurus. As visionaries, he had desired to emulate them by not completing his studies in Munich and Strasbourg. Gols, as Vitas learned to call him, wandered among the fruit trees, attempting to muse on their philosophy. Vitas worked himself to exhaustion, carefully picking a minimum of three apples at a time, making sure not to break off the stems, putting them into the basket without damaging them. Given his bad German, Vitas had neither the intention or the capability of arguing with his intellectually dissatisfied employer about the buzzing of poisonous flies, which Nietzsche himself had classified as swarms of petty humans.

In his desire to philosophise, Gols came up with an ingenious idea when two Poles came to him asking for work. He hired them immediately, as one could speak German and the other spoke English very well. Once, in a good mood, he called Vitas and both the Poles and asked Vitas a tricky, philosophical question in German. The Pole, who understood German, translated the question to his fellow countryman, who translated it into English for Vitas, then Vitas responded exactly the same. Gols was in fits of laughter.

Gols had inherited his orchards. Far from being his

fulfilment in life, he did earn a bit of money this way. Like any amateur philosopher, he went for a charismatic appearance, but also like any philosopher, he was hard up most of the time. Therefore, he was grateful for the orchard and worked it for all it was worth. Unlike dedicated agriculturalists however, he didn't offer any accommodation, which was rather risky for Vitas. He slept under the apple trees, ridding them of all its fragrant fruit. That typical smell made his nostrils tremble slightly. Vitas saw vertical orange lines shooting alongside the stars, licking into the sky. These were no more than the cars high up in the hills above him circling wildly through the serpentines. It was a clear day in autumn and the nice weather wouldn't last. One of the Italians he worked with took pity on him. He gave him the keys to his house in Lana, about three miles from the orchard, so that he could live in it. The house was under reconstruction, it wasn't furnished, the walls were bare and the only running water was from a garden hose. But this being fairly common in Italy, the cellar had wine enough to fill any heart. There was also a furious dog running around on a steel leash. This dog hated Vitas to death.

He rode his bike to work, and in the evening he sat on the large patio, drinking fine dry wine, propping his feet on a table to stare at the stars above, which pierced the bed of nails. At that moment, he realised a certain absence. It wasn't a woman that was missing from the scene, but a cigar. The next day, Vitas rode by a gas station to buy smokes. In the evening, he inhaled the dense fumes and made the bed of nails dance, piercing the stars that slid down the tips of the rocks, leaving behind a comet-like tail. He never blamed himself for giving in again. There are situations that cannot be regretted, even through bad behaviour. In other words, sometimes one has no choice but to misbehave.

– – –

Vitas and Aviel had become so involved in the local life of the lamasery that they had stopped asking "why," a question that had long been juggling with their thoughts. They understood that if something is to come, it shall come. They started feeling decidedly happier with the numerous local activities. Vitas enjoyed meditating. It was relatively easy for him to learn the secrets of Buddhism to reach towards the human soul.

The Eucharist is one of the central rituals of the Catholic Church. The Holy Communion, the Last Supper, when the priest presents the attendants at mass the Body of Christ, and the Blood of Christ, the wine. Vitas knew that he was committing a sin simply by entertaining such thoughts. Under normal circumstances, there was no way he would administer this to non-Christians, especially without confession. Nobody present was Christian and more importantly, he was in no way sacralised to perform this act. "I have committed the deadliest of sins and received no remittance yet," he called out in desperation, looking to the heavens, as if he were waiting for God to tell him what to do.

"I'll tell you what to do," smiled Aviel. "You have to crucify yourself before and after mass, pray and ask your Saviour for forgiveness. Don't worry, he'll forgive you. He's probably shaking his head anyway with all this earthly havoc…"

But then he added quite seriously: "I also have a feeling that reformist Judaism is not as reformed as it should be, so I was thinking I'd reform it more myself…"

"And where will I get the wafer and wine?" whispered Vitas, without reacting to Aviel's complaint.

He took care of everything in the same way. He went to the bakery, located at the lower productive part of the rock formation, the monument forming the lamasery. The bakery roasted barley flour, the base ingredient in tsampa. Various meals were made by adding different ratios of assorted ingredients to tea and yak butter. The best he could do was make a wafer similar to tsampa. He received a blessing from the abbot himself, so everyone was doing him favours. Vitas used the tsampa base to fry small pancakes. It was also useful that he found cookie cutters that helped keep the shape. Lo and behold, the wafer was made. Then, he blessed it with fresh water from the pond under the hill, near the Jadhang Gad tributary. In truth, he strongly doubted that this act helped bless the Body of Christ, but he performed it nonetheless.

The wine was another problem. There was no wine in the lamasery. The only solution could be… well, Chhaang was the Tibetan beer. It was milky and made of barley. It was far from the world-class quality of Czech beer, but that's beside the point. Beer was only served here on special occasions and feasts. It was impossible to drink this beverage on a regular day. Nevertheless, this holy act was fated to take priority over petty worldly restrictions…

Vitas is standing in front of the crucifix, holding a priceless gold chalice, which he received from the abbot, in his right hand. Apart from the crucifix, this is the only dignified sacral artefact anywhere to be seen and it is filled with beer. He is holding small pieces of tsampa in his left hand and the darkest thoughts are racing around in his head. The only words he can utter: "Forgive me, God."

He didn't believe in God's tolerance, let alone the tolerance of any Church authorities, had he met any. Fortunately, there was no chance of meeting anyone like that here. As he stood in this absurd position, he started seeing things differently. Now it was as if he was seeing himself through his other eye from far above. The whole ritual slowly became a theatrical performance, in which he constantly repeated: 'This is not me, this is only a game, and it's all make-believe. I'm not even responsible for my own actions.'

He stared at the crucifix in front of him for several minutes, holding the beer in his right hand and the tsampa in his left. He felt very light, as if the burden of responsibility had really been lifted from his shoulders. He no longer felt embarrassed, knowing that he could do whatever he wanted. Since he knew he only wanted the best for everyone, he could really do anything at all. He lifted the cup with the beer, smiled, and winked at the Crucified, nodding his head towards him, as if he were toasting to his health, drinking down the whole cup of beer. He wiped his mouth on his sleeve and slowly put the tsampa into his mouth.

Vitas' spiritual focus didn't seem abnormal to him at all. He read the sutras, the Psalms and the Bible. Mahayana Buddhism dominated here and it didn't seem to be in contradiction with his consciousness. As for Christianity, he tried to learn more about it and spread it among anyone who showed an interest. Even so, he was suspicious that for the vast majority, the allure of Christianity was primarily the promise of receiving God's blood. He understood that all religions are intertwined in many ways. The Tibetans use saffron water instead of the Christian Holy water, their Ten Commandments are very similar, and the rosary is almost the same, though it has another name. Even Buddhist reincarnation runs parallel to Gilgal, the Hebrew Promised Land.

He began seeing Buddhism as more tolerant, offering a wide range of possibilities, not only in the diversity of its schools, but above all in its tolerant approach to mankind. Contrary to these notions, Christianity seemed stilted, one-sided. He could hardly comprehend the difference between right and wrong, and therefore how to proceed.

Vitas' thoughts were flying around from side to side following each most recent scent, and though he was still missing something that he found indefinable, he was the happiest he had been in many months – since the time he'd found himself alone... Of course now and then he was still overcome with Chebness, that nostalgic feeling of unforgiving guilt, turning moments of meditation and past reflection into his greatest antidote.

22.
The Seventh Higher-Power

Vitas was at the height of his investigative success, he only came home to sleep. He hardly had time for much else. The chickens were all gone and he didn't take care of the children. Moreover, since they were teenagers now, they couldn't care less.

Eva was used to his stubbornness, obstinacy and most of all his greed, especially when he embarked on a news report. Their many years living together occurred in phases, when he was "working on the Revolution" or was preoccupied with some other work, while she took care of both children on her own, considering him as her third, most demanding child. The time Vitas spent with his family was exceptional and sporadic, usually when he needed to take a breather, which would then allow him to dive that much deeper into his unhinged projects.

He expanded his activities to such an extent that his cases made headline news most of the time. Though his cases dealt with more than just Kromen and his gang, they were the reason he was responsible for new assignments. He was on the merry-go-round of reporting. He felt right at home and enjoyed his time there. But without even realising it, it had become a hectic dream, in which he had no time to stop or look back.

At this time, Kromen completely trusted Vitas, there being no other way to explain the fact that Kromen continued all-too-willingly confessing on camera, even when Vitas completely shut him down. Vitas could only shake his head, as it seemed almost unbelievable. Not even his colleagues could believe it.

"How did you fool him, man? How d'you get him to speak over and over with the cameras rolling?" they'd ask, before agreeing on one possible explanation: "He doesn't care if you shut him down or put the halo of innocence above his head. He just wants to be on TV. He's conceited..."

Let's use the head of the Czech Interpol Section, Travnicky, who had become the subject of a media scandal at the time, as an illustration. He was forced to resign overnight after news services revealed corruption and serious economic fraud, through which he was associated with the criminal underworld. All media stations were trying to decode just what criminal organisation supported him, but no one dared point fingers. The media created speculations on speculations, this being second nature to them. This international scandal was dissected and analysed from all angles, always failing to pin down the culprit.

Unsurprisingly, Vitas pondered and pondered. His colleagues made fun of him: "What do you think, Mr Investigator, seems like we've come up short, eh?"

Vitas finally told them he was willing to try and so he picked up the phone.

"Hello, Mr Kromen, Vitas speaking. Hope I'm not bothering you. Can we have a word...?"

"No problem, what's on your mind, Editor? I'm driving, but no problem, I'm listening."

"Have you seen Mr Travnicky from the Interpol on the news? I would like to know...?"

"Editor, don't even get me started," Kromen interrupted

him. "Such an honest fellow! Sure I know something about it, he comes to Slapy at least once a month and this case is just driving me mad!"

"You really know him? He spends time at Slapy?"

"Sure, he has a cabin up here that I let him use, on-the-house. I do favours for solid, honest people."

"And you'd vouch for how honest he is on camera?"

"It'd be my pleasure, Editor."

"But…" said Vitas, pacing uncertainly from side to side, "you know, it's headline news and I'm shooting it for the station. Do you think we could cut it before the end of the day?"

"You mean the shoot? Of course. You're in luck Mr Editor. In fact, I'm just leaving Slapy now, heading to Prague for a meeting. Well, it's eleven o'clock. I could meet you at the headquarters of the Czech TV station around twelve. That should give us plenty of time. Is that alright with you?"

"That's great. I'll be expecting you."

During the shoot, the only thing Kromen seemed to be worried about was whether his lips were too glossy, taking a glass of tonic beforehand, or whether his tie looked straight.

Vitas couldn't help but wonder whether Kromen was really so foolish and clueless, or if he didn't much care about anything but getting media attention at any price. There was obviously one other possibility: that he actually did trust Vitas too much. He mistakenly thought that Vitas understood his arguments and saw them exactly the same way. Difficult to decide.

Either way, he celebrated success again and his colleagues from the newsroom could only shake their heads in disbelief. They couldn't accept that Vitas had managed to get one of the major mobsters of the day to head straight to the newsroom to confess that the former boss of Czech Interpol was his friend.

The head of the newsroom, Hermik, kept fidgeting during the local news meeting, as if he was tasked with arresting Travnicky, convicting him and shooting the evidential report himself. "Gentlemen, gentlemen..." he tried to silence the noisy reporters, "and ladies, of course, keep in mind that a positive report is not news for me!"

He paused for a moment to emphasise the importance of the spoken words. "Although our colleague Vitas is flying between journalism and news like a frightened swallow, he fits my bill for a well-run local column. Follow his lead, please."

His colleagues shook their heads, partially in acknowledgment and partially from their telling off, puckering lips, squinting eyes, and examining Vitas from head to toe. He was blushing humbly, all while considering how he would react to this praise, though he wasn't sure if he should consider it as praise at all.

"The truth is what's written or presented in the media," Hermik continued mentoring, "not the truth."

Vitas couldn't take it any longer. He raised two fingers like a schoolboy and piped up in a timid, defensive voice: "But I did broadcast the truth."

"No doubt about it!" Hermik growled morosely. "I'm just saying we are the seventh higher-power, so we determine the public's opinion. We decide where society will go."

"It sometimes gets out of hand," shouted a rather ill-mannered voice from the crowd of editors.

"Who said that? Who said that?" Hermik asked angrily. "Whether you like it or not, our top priority is viewership. We want people to watch us more than they watch commercial television. If you don't like it, go somewhere else, perhaps commercial TV would suit you. Keep in mind that my rules apply double there!"

"We know, boss," moderator Bradla took over. Bradla

later befriended Vitas. He had a special ability to always get the last word in even though everything was resolved. Obviously this scored him some extra points. "I'm hereby declaring a battle over viewership."

The silence of the editors indicated a white flag had been raised and Hermik nodded in satisfaction. Putting their weapons down was the only thing they could do in the interest of preserving their existence.

— — —

The extravagance of Kromen became so extreme that, together with Kostka and a few other notable public figures, he established the Inter-Guard Foundation. This foundation was established to take care of the children of police officers who were killed on duty. Vitas and Petrovsky could only laugh.

"So, buddy," tears of laughter streamed down Petrovsky's face. "Once they get rid of me, they'll go to my son and say: 'Your dad was a hero and now we'll take care of you...' and I'll roll over in my grave."

Vitas however, was rather upset that he couldn't open any murder case that involved Kromen or Kostka. No necessary evidence existed and it was hardly worth risking the potential lawsuit that would undoubtedly appear after pursuing accusations lacking in supporting evidence. He was aware of several murders, several dead White Horses that had profited as a result of Kostka's or Kromen's business deals, but what good would that be without any proof?

Even so, Vitas was overjoyed with the incredible pace of his profession. He had picked up a fair number of reporter's tricks. In addition to the hidden or covert shoots already described, where several recording devices were placed to cover all of the shots, he gained plenty of other experience.

In one case, he came up with a rather slick trick for presenting information about Kromen, which he believed was true though he lacked the supporting information.

He made a deal with Inspector Petrovsky that he'd shoot an interview with him if he had the same opinion regarding this "truth." And since there was no way that this could be a simple dialogue carried out with Petrovsky's consent (only the spokesperson could make such statements, not an operator), Petrovsky would be attacked by a "furious reporter named Vitas" along with his camera crew on the steps of the Congress Hall.

"Inspector Petrovsky, is it true that your supervisor banned your Reconstruction Team from investigating the Jenštejn Glassworks case?"

"How… how did you find me, Mr Editor?" Petrovsky went along with the theatrics. "I'm sorry but I'm not at liberty to discuss these matters with the public…"

"Then is it true that Kromen and Kostka have their red hands all over the police headquarters as well? In which case, how would you explain the fact that you can't handle a case that has siphoned funds from the Bohemia Bank and the Hana Bank…?"

"But I can't discuss this, Editor. Please make way and leave me alone. Please, contact the spokesperson. He's competent to discuss these matters."

The interview finished but the information was out. Everything would suddenly be clear to the viewers and there were no complications from the ethical point of view. 'Well, it was a bit out-there, but I'm a fierce investigator, right?' Vitas inwardly laughed, always expecting a pat on the back for such work. The expression: *to take someone down*, became second nature to him, no different from breakfast and sleep for others.

Despite all the conflicts in his profession, Vitas boldly

defended his work and could even get into heated arguments. He was proud of the fact that he was never taken advantage of, but he avoided direct questions relating to whether he remained convinced that no one had ever taken advantage of him, answering: "I don't know, I don't think so."

Vitas also became a relatively popular social celebrity. He could easily attend VIP parties for judges, state prosecutors and lawyers.

He had begun talking to the Prague District Court judge at a birthday party for one renowned lawyer. He was a bit under the influence, when they quite openly started discussing some cases.

"You know, Editor, I do civil cases but I also settle disputes between companies and those are unbelievably frustrating."

"Tell me," Vitas pondered, "how do you know for sure that this party is right and this party is not? I often get a pile of material from an angry person. I study it for hours and hours and often I can't even understand it. And even if I understand the material, I don't even know whose side I'm on. Then I can send that person to hell, but you can't. You have to state your verdict: guilty or innocent."

"No, I don't say that. They say that in the sentence. I only say: you're right, or you're not right. I deny your request or I confirm it." She then suddenly started laughing. "Often I myself don't even know who's right. It's really that complicated... And when I'm desperate, I toss a coin in my office. Why? If the other party doesn't like the verdict – appeal."

A little tipsy, she leaned over to Vitas, hiccuped and whispered in his ear: "But Editor, I wouldn't want to sit in the City's appeal room.[24] I used to think that the Court should be the God's truth. But if it's truly God's truth, then I get why it works the way it does here... ha ha..."

---

24 City Court in Prague

Regarding current cases, Vitas was relatively knowledgeable, so when he saw another judge talking to a state prosecutor, to police officers and lawyers, he knew that they were all working on the same case. They all perceived it differently however, meaning he quickly lost faith in the current justice system. Although he couldn't swear they were all talking about the same case, or how it was going to turn out, he knew that in certain cases, the lawyer simply sinks one client for the victory of another. Vitas was frustrated that he couldn't comprehend this process, no matter the steps he took.

– – –

During these cases, he met a lawyer named Markyr, a specialist in criminal law. In addition to the most significant criminal cases, he also became famous for defending several undercover Communist spies. Following the Revolution, which had completely altered all perspectives on morality, there was sufficient interest in the field to no surprise. Vitas discussed several cases with him and even received some of his interesting feedback.

"Get this," he once told Vitas. "Professor Zabicka, a renowned doctor of philosophy, a much respected, unsuspecting gentleman who teaches at the university, honoured by the intellectual upper-class, the old-school type. What a shock, the *YouCommie Donkey*[25] newspaper unearthed him as an undercover Communist spy. When asked by his colleagues and friends, he always said that he'd never had anything to do with such things, but he saw no reason in suing anyone about it.

---

25 *YouCommie Donkey* – uncensored newspaper by dissident Petr Cibulka, in which he published a detailed list of undercover Communist spies and collaborators.

Unfortunately, everyone, including his family, started looking down on him. He had to give up his professorship soon after, before completely stopping all teaching at the university. Then, he worked as a regular teacher, sitting at the front of a classroom full of no-good teenagers, somewhere way out in the sticks, licking the wounds given to him by the staples that the brats shot his way whenever he wasn't looking, and he finally said enough was enough.

We filed a lawsuit, waited almost two years for the trial and when it came time for the first hearing, where the Ministry of Internal Affairs was the defendant, it was like a theatre performance. Everyone present had to be identified at the beginning of the trial. When it came time to introduce Professor Zabicka, the lawyer for the Ministry of Internal Affairs interrupted the hearing for technical reasons and said: 'Excuse me, are you Professor Zabicka, born on so and so day in village XY?' And he said: 'No. Everything is correct but I wasn't born in XY but in the neighbouring village, AB.'

The lawyer said: 'My deep apologies, we must have the wrong person. The registered discreet Communist file refers to a different person, coincidentally with the same name, but from a different village.'

And that was that. But his life was still in ruins."

"That's an amazing case," Vitas burst out eagerly. "Could you give me the professor's number, please?"

And there he had it. He was so eager that he picked up the phone and dialled the number the following day. "Hello, Vitas speaking from the Czech TV station, the *Bad Penny* Show. Is this Professor Zabicka?"

"Yes, he's speaking – Zabicka. How can I help?" asked the respectful baritone voice.

"Hello, hello. I know your lawyer, Dr Markyr, rather well

and he's told me quite a lot about your case. I have a favour to ask. I would like to shoot an interview with you about what you encountered in relation to your alleged work with undercover Communist spies."

"I'm sorry, but there's just no way. Please understand."

"Why not?" Vitas shouted, almost in disbelief. "This is a great opportunity for you to come clean. It's an absurd case and you have the chance to come out of it victorious! Or is it your relatives? You want to protect them?"

"Not at all. There's no doubt that I'd come out victorious, but it would hurt the other Zabicka, the one from the neighbouring village."

Vitas gasped and sighed in desperation: "But he's the undercover Communist spy, the one who actually hurt you. What does it matter???"

"... but he's only human, too." the Professor concluded the interview and hung up.

Vitas stared vacantly into space for a second, before mentally closing the case for good. Somewhere deep down inside, he had a feeling that if he pushed any harder, he'd end up on thin ice, something he was quite unfamiliar with at the moment and could hardly grasp the thought.

He was on the same page as the vast majority of other reporters, in that everyone was obliged to consent to giving a testimony. It is in the interest of "higher moral principles," in the interest of society, which he (and other investigative reporters like him) must raise to a higher level. And *he* was the chosen saint, who was to proclaim this truth.

But Vitas had a knack for provoking people to confess on camera. His wife often witnessed him successfully persuading a respondent to interview with him. She herself claimed that she'd run for the hills. "You'd convince a dead man. I've been listening to you for half an hour now and I know that I will never speak to any editor. If anyone ever introduces himself as an editor to me, I have to hang up immediately or I'm afraid it's all over."

He saw things quite pragmatically: it's necessary for the culprit he wishes to take down to make the best possible statement on camera. The easiest way to get someone to confess is to directly approach the respondent in question.

Using an indifferent tone, he'd inform his correspondent that he had such and such information on him, meaning he would like to conduct an interview. If the correspondent turned him down, he'd answer in a dull voice that it really didn't matter, he couldn't care who's right, there was no way to force him to defend himself, but that he had ten minutes to make the case and that he must present the defence in the interest of objectivity, and if he doesn't want to, then no problem. His answer would probably take up two or three minutes in any case, so the time could simply be used to let his opponent speak instead…

The person in question immediately becomes offended and begins to defend himself. He explains his total innocence and usually agrees to the interview. If not, then a telephone discussion covering the basic information, followed by the subject's rejection is shot in exactly the same way.

— — —

It seemed Bretislav couldn't sleep either: "THE PITCHER THAT GOES SO OFTEN TO THE WELL, IS ALWAYS BROKEN IN THE END…"

23.
The Feast is Interrupted

The lamasery was glowing with candles and lamps. The whole place smelled of burnt yak butter and there were monks engaging in hectic discussions in every corner. Lama Thorpe Tandzin, dressed in a festive yellow sash draped over a red robe, was telling a large group of monks about the life and teachings of the famous teacher, Tsongkhapa, of the major Gelugpa School that even his Holiness, the Dalai Lama followed. Others were reciting mantras and singing. There was an even bigger party going on outside, despite the frosty weather. The snow conquered the ochre colours without resistance. Not only was there plenty of chhaang to be consumed, but one group also built a stake, wrapping it with cloth to form the shape of a person, at a real stretch of the imagination, and held an archery contest. It's a well-known fact that many Tibetans are talented at shooting. They achieve excellent results even while riding on horse-back. But it was considerably harder in the piercing cold. It was clear that the competition was far from being close. But then again, they also claimed that it was too easy in the summer. In the end, there was one thing that mattered. That their competition brought them great joy.

Diverse music, sounding from drums, whistles and the notes of seashells could be heard all around. But it was a little tempo-less when one group's music blended in with that of another's.

It was October the twenty-fifth, the feast marking the first day of winter. The celebration was planned for the evening, which was fast approaching. Vitas joined one group and then another. It was as if he only partially soaked up the assorted atmospheres, moods and inputs. He suddenly felt a little submerged in his nostalgic Chebness. He was spiritually above this feast. Slightly under the influence of the Tibetan beer and with only a slight overview of the situation, he felt a little homesick. When he was too sad, he clung to a group of drunk-but-happy monks, led by Aviel preaching on Jewish feasts. When he noticed Vitas, he winked at him cheerfully, hugged two monks nearby and called out: "These are the first two monks that've converted. They've decided to be faithful to the Jews. I bet you and your Christianity have nothing on me!" Both monks were merrily, but incomprehensibly, almost foolishly, nodding.

Vitas wandered around outside, dressed up warm. He let himself get carried away by the incredible sound rising from the lamasery and the dark shadows of the mountains. He gazed up at the stars, which gradually popped up on the sky. It was as if someone was fixing them up there. Someone lay up high, with their head resting on their left hand and their elbow leaning up against a cloud, rummaging through an old, rusty tin box with tweezers. They shove the poor, damaged ones to the side, carefully and cheerfully plucking out the right ones and fixing them up there. They squeeze the two parts of the tweezers together too, and place each star exactly where it should be. In doing so, they hardly even notice that one of the boxes falls, crashing to the ground, leaving a long, hot tail behind and burning out before hitting the earth. Before shoving the other star into its correct place, the Electrician raises his head slightly from its resting position, looks down at the ground in curiosity, then raises his eyebrows with defiance and says: "So what, you miserable stain, you like it? You want more?"

Vitas is awakened by the sudden silence, like the sound of a thunderbolt. Something must have happened or the festive parade is already underway. 'I shouldn't miss out on that,' he thinks to himself, reluctantly leaving his place on the cliffs.

But as he approaches the lamasery, he hears noises that have nothing to do with the festivities. Monks are running around, whispering to each other, the gestures of their hands expressing incomprehension, amazement… Vitas searches for someone who can tell him what has happened. Then he notices monk Wung Pien, the guardian of the pilgrims, meditating on some rocks, as a group of huddled monks approach the lamasery. Pien makes vivid hand movements, asserting that he only went to feed his dependent. The sentence is repeated as if by the hero in a movie. "I only went to feed him, when I saw them there. They looked dead, right? But they were moving around a little. The dead don't move, right? Please, if they still have some purpose left in the world, let them live. If not, let them enter their bardo, so they can be reborn and continue from the previous. It's only God's will. And mine too, since I found them…" Nobody paid attention to what was being said, interested instead in two lumps of cloth, one somewhat bigger than the other, that some of the monks were carrying into the lamasery.

The whole feast concluded at once, everyone focused on a happening so critical to the smooth operations of the lamasery, that it engaged every living soul present. A middle-aged, adult female, if it could even be identified given the mutilated features, and a little child. Likely a girl, but no one could tell for sure. Now, they were in the hands of Dr Sithar. But the lady was not doing well at all. Who are they? What path were they on? That took care of the monks' entertainment. Everyone joined in a heated discussion, speculating, flying from logical premises into speculative nonsense, trying to piece together odds and ends of information. It was clear that no more was needed than such an extraordinary event and the lamasery was turned upside down. Regular operations were indefinitely postponed. Vitas and Aviel came to the conclusion that this would all pass in a few days and that everything would be back to the old ways again. When a stereotype of monotony suddenly changes, it can only be thrilling. But there was no way that a well-functioning cog-wheel would stop on the spot after decades of smooth running. It did, however mean the end of these festivities.

The following morning, the mind of every individual in the lamasery was preoccupied with a single problem. Everyone wanted to find out more about the mysterious couple. Morning mass was rushed. The Lama didn't even partake in it. There was silence. No loud instruments, no rag dangas, drums or seashells were heard. Everything had changed. Dr Sithar was surrounded by monks who bombarded him with questions. He only nodded grimly and waved his hands in chaos, suggesting he would hear nothing about it. Everything made more sense before lunchtime. At first, it was rumoured that the woman was already in the bardo, awaiting rebirth. This was all confirmed early in the afternoon, so a ritual open-air funeral ceremony took place early in the evening. Butcher Lu Cheng reigned over the proceedings.

There was another rumour that spread at the same time. That the other one, the young girl, was fine. Dr Sithar strutted proudly around the lamasery. He was clearly pleased by the looks of admiration. "She's completely fine," he explained graciously, repeating the same words all around the monastery catacombs. "She's just a little exhausted, suffering from hypothermia, hungry, but she'll be up and running by tomorrow." Sithar was a master of alchemy and knew well how to use herbs. He stored various roots and studied their influence on the human body. He boasted about being able to put anyone to sleep using no more than tea vapours. He could make a person dance and speak the truth. The truth is that Sithar came from the eastern part of Tibet, and had inherited this knowledge from his ancestors. China was the birthplace of these miraculous ancient medicinal discoveries and since it was a neighbouring country, the manifestation of these practices were clear in Tibet as well.

Vitas and Aviel soon drifted from this happening, which had seemed to shake the walls of the lamasery for a while. But they both remained interested in where these two females had been travelling at the time, mulling over various possibilities in Aviel's learning session. By now, it was hoped that they would have learned compassion, tolerance and sensible foresight, allowing them to await resolutions peacefully, even when there was no means of escape. They were rather taken aback therefore when monk Tungjur, the Lama's assistant, sought them out himself.

"Honourable Lama Rinpoche Thorpe Tenzin is asking you to attend the Grand Council, right after morning mass. Please make no errors in being there."

"Of course," they both nodded. But Aviel wasn't able to hold down his curiosity. "Can you tell us anything more specific?"

"Yes, you will find out more in the morning, after mass," replied Tungjur sharply. Both friends almost burst out laughing, but controlled themselves out of politeness. Moreover, it was clear that Tungjur didn't reply so mysteriously from foolishness. It was merely a game, or his preference for words that remain ambiguous. In essence, he had a perfect formula when it came to reacting to questions that he didn't feel like answering. Each smiled at the other mysteriously, like agents who had recently uncovered the intentions of an unfriendly enemy, each showing the other that they were in the know. All they could do was to wait for tomorrow and hope that a revelation would come. Both Jingzhi had no choice but to arm themselves with patience.

24.

... Even Higher

Vitas reached a point that he humorously referred to as sadomasochism, later proclaiming that he had even wanted to take himself down. His friends and relatives also jokingly called him Egon, just like the manic reporter, Egon Erwin Kisch. He dove into situations, truly earning the reputation of an editor with low survival instincts. He discovered that Kromen would be holding a Christmas party in Slapy, with the vice minister of Internal Affairs and several other interesting people in attendance, most of whom definitely wouldn't want their names associated with Kromen in the media.

What did Vitas do? He rented a van with tinted windows, hid in the nearby woods with his cameraman and spied on the cars passing by. The camera was on a tripod in the car, it was fifteen below zero and Vitas made the cameraman take a shot of every license plate of every car that drove by.

He then crept up to the edge of the property under cover of night, like an Indian in a Western movie, only to soon abandon this effort when he realised that Kromen's premises were well guarded and he was likely to be caught. It'd be rather hard to explain the embarrassing situation that would follow.

After many years, once he was able to talk to him about

almost anything, Kromen would react with great astonishment: "And why didn't you come inside? It would've been fantastic if you'd shot a charity event intended for children, the orphans of police officers who were killed in the line of duty..."

Without question, there were many interesting people in attendance. He was ready to broadcast it but Rokos was already yelling at him: "You have completely lost your judgment. What do you want to do there? See if the Vice Minister of Internal Affairs came to a Christmas party, or if Kromen is a paedophile for organising an event for children? What do you want to say in this report?" The report was never broadcasted...

Vitas' father passed away. It was the blow that everyone expects, but that no one is prepared for, and has to deal with in their own way. His wife, Eva, softened all the personal hardships in his life. When he was down, she always lifted his spirits. Vitas had long walked around like a sleepwalker, mumbling to himself a lot. Eva always explained with an understanding smile: "He's talking to his dad..."

His father's death affected him so much that any of the limits or survival instincts that he may have once had all washed away. This was the age when mafia cab drivers raged through the streets of Prague, and their main concern was finding a lucrative parking spot. These parking spots were the reason fights broke out, resulting in several deaths and many destroyed cars.

Vitas couldn't think of anything wiser to do than transform his car into a "droshky," a colloquial term among cab drivers, by putting a flashing sign on the roof that read: TAXI, sticking magnetic stickers all around it, borrowing a meter, and parking in the most lucrative parking spot of all: Republic Square in Prague, to be precise. Of course, he remained wired from head to toe with cameras and microphones, and had a microphone on the roof rack as well as a cameraman waiting on the tram pier in the distance, equipped with a telescopic lens, to shoot details from afar. The cameraman was dressed up like a foreign reporter, capturing the gems of a Prague evening.

Three cab drivers had their vacant signs turned on, standing next to several civilian cars. All the cab drivers remained sitting in one vehicle, engaging in a friendly conversation, waiting for a nice score.

They immediately fell silent upon Vitas' arrival. There was piercing silence not only coming from the taxis themselves, but also from the cars and trams passing by. It was as if in a silent film, when the protagonist focuses on his world alone, dwelling on his own problems in which nothing else matters.

Vitas got out of his car cold-heartedly, leant up against its side, elbow resting on the roof-rack, tiredly ruffling through his hair. He chewed so loudly that his jaws were pumping. Any passer-by would call him a barbarian. He hardly even saw the other cabs, and seemingly had no idea that they were near him, or likely didn't care.

And lo and behold: a tourist walks by, completely ignorant of the Prague transportation system, staring at a map truly clueless. Clearly this is Vitas' friend, who speaks French perfectly. Her job is to act like a grey heron, accidentally bumping into Vitas.

"Where you off to, madam?" asks Vitas in the indifferent, foolish voice of city folk.

The reaction is immediate. The cab doors open, first letting out white cigarette smoke, then running shoes, two pairs of jeans, one pair of black dress pants and then all three strung out droshkies. One gently grabs the tourist by her shoulders and guides her away from Vitas, who is simultaneously addressed by the two other gentlemen – "We'd like to go to Prosek, Pod Baní."

"Sure gentlemen, have a seat," Vitas says, very helpfully, with a naive look on his face. To put it politely, the reason he enjoyed playing dumb, was that it never failed to disarm the other side. The other then has a tendency to thoroughly explain everything to the fool, so that he can comprehend the problem at hand. This is exactly what he wanted, especially when dealing with fraud and embezzlement, cases far more difficult than this.

The rotund cab driver with bad breath sits next to him in the passenger seat and the other one sits behind, constantly leaning forward so his head is right behind Vitas' headrest. His heavy breathing is accompanied by grunts as if these were his final throes, both hands holding on tightly to the side of Vitas' seat in front of him. In consequence, he'll continue to sway with Vitas helplessly at each bend in the road. Vitas turns on the meter, observes his friend safely getting on the subway alone, and they set off.

"Do you take the line?" asks the passenger.

"Do I what?"

"Take the line," gasps the dumpling, quite rudely from the back seat, bellowing a "Ha!" four inches from Vitas' ears, yanking so much that the safety belt locks. Vitas quickly burrows through his mind, consulting cab driver slang and habits with his friend, another cabbie, to prevent immediately giving himself away. Taking the line refers to using the cab company's radio, and this cab company would assign him jobs depending on his current location, all for a flat rate.

"No, I don't. It's only my job-on-the-side, just earning pocket change."

"And what d'you do?" rasps this cabbie customer, breathing down Vitas' neck.

"Y'know, I'm a teacher... a dead-end job, the brats are demanding, they keep on whining about wanting awesome cell phones, and my wife's constantly on my case about a vacation by the sea because it's good for the spots on her skin that popped up on her belly because she works as a maid in a hotel and probably got it when she had to clean up after a group of filthy Arabs who stayed there six months ago… or maybe they were Jews, now I'm not so sure. Anyway, major problem: the chef accidentally served them pork, very well prepared, I might add. They loved it, devoured it, even had seconds before the boss asked what delicacy they were actually chomping. Once the chef told them, all that delicious fodder suddenly turned right back up on their plates, I mean they were full, of course… all because the chef told them the truth. So much for the placebo effect. All you need is one word. Say it at the right time and the effect is unbelievable. Physical force has nothing on it. I've seen a hulk, a mountain-mover, be defeated by a clever dwarf. Do you know what he said to the goliath that had him hanging onto every word? He said…"

"Enough! Shut up! Turn around!" The dumpling interrupts Vitas' babbling.

"What am I supposed to turn around?"

"This droshky! And hurry up before I change my mind."

"I don't get it."

"Listen pal, there's more than one thing you don't get. Do you know what it means when someone says they're going to Pod Baní? That you're getting an ass-whipping, my friend. We're cab drivers, is that clear? Believe me, if we got to Pod Baní, you'd never get behind the wheel again. But listen pal, you're such a nutcase that even a mamba would take mercy on you if it listened for half-a-second…"

"What mamba?" The other cabbie behind him yells across Vitas' ear.

"Y'know man, the snake."

"What's a snake got to do with it?" resonates from the back seat.

"Nothing, I just used it as an example, you get it? Figurative speech!"

"Did you see it on TV or something?"

"Bullshit. I didn't see anything on TV! You better shut up too! Don't piss me off," The first cabbie glances at Vitas again with a sheepish look on his face. "My friend, you look like an idiot. What subject can you possibly teach?"

"Sewing."

"What???"

"I can sew."

"Like sew what?"

"Clothes, dresses."

"Pal, that's what women do."

"And so do I," said Vitas proudly.

Vitas drove back to Republic Square in the midst of these shenanigans. The cameraman, who could hear everything through the radio, was watching it all unfold from a distance in the dark.

"Pal, I feel real sorry for you. You're unbelievably lucky, though. Last time someone barged into our space, thinking he'd take our money, we got rid of him. They were then putting his limbs back together like a puzzle in the morgue." He nodded his head convincingly, looking at Vitas as if he were an exhibit in a museum.

"But I wouldn't even want to put my hands on you. If you want to make some money, go to a droshky company and take a deal at a flat rate. Screw it, you're putting your health at risk. You could get the flu. And compared to the others, I'm not even a big contender."

"I'm immune to the flu."

"You nutcase, you ain't immune to this," He leaned in towards Vitas, letting him have a whiff of his bad breath, sticking his hairy fist in front of his nose.

Back at the newsroom, he took the precaution of leaving

out the verbal provocations and the mamba messages, keeping just the heavy drama instead, adding in some statistics, some standard interviews with cab drivers, and that was the end of the story. Although the result aroused the manager's enthusiasm, the cameraman, editor and everyone else involved refused to have their names in the closing credits. There was only one name to this report: Vitas. And only because his burned-out survival instincts had led him to it.

– – –

The *Bad Penny* was outsourced. No one, except for the producer, would be employed by the TV station. The TV station paid an external company 55,000 crowns for one report. There were three reports in one show and it was broadcast every week, meaning four times a month. But the costs for one case did not exceed 20,000. Except for the editors and the camera rentals, the TV station paid for everything else, such as the editing suites, the phones and the offices. It was then relatively easy to figure out how much money was unnecessarily taken from the TV station, to line private pockets. The net profit came in at around 400,000 per month. Frank Bozik was the owner of the hard-to-decipher but suitably named firm, NBM, Ltd. Once, during a moment of weakness, he revealed the meaning of these words: "Nothing But Money."

As long as everything ran smoothly, reports were being made and shot, Vitas remained the script editor, and there weren't any problems. They just shrugged their shoulders, worrying about nothing. But Bozik and Rokos' appetites flourished. They sometimes got on Vitas' case, asking him to slip in not three, but four reports into a single show. Moreover, they started motivating the journalists to film their piece in one day, instead of two. This obviously affected the show's overall quality. Over time, the viewership even started to decline.

Vitas began to resist political shoots and royalties. "We should motivate the reporters who do complicated reports, uncover big shot vices and not these shit-bags and boring PHTs: profoundly humane tales."

"But our expenses are high, we have to save money somewhere," the producer and businessman defended their steps.

"Don't be crazy, chaps. You make thirty-grand on one report. Everyone's using free reruns from the archives. No one goes anywhere to save on travel costs. I can hardly bear watching it any longer. What more do you want? What do you want to achieve?"

But this was a very non-diplomatic move. Both his bosses' features hardened. The sturdy bow of Rokos' Napoleon complex flexed, and the conversation was cut short. Vitas felt so bulletproof and innocent that he didn't even realise he was walking a tightrope.

– – –

"YOU'RE TURN WILL COME, EDITOR..." commented Bretislav, persistent.

25.
First Steps

The Great Council, called the "little kashag" are sitting around in a circle on pillows in a dark room next to the Lama's. The candles and lamps make theatrical shadows and it seems like this will be the height of all upcoming activities. The Lama sits immersed in himself, eyes closed, head down. His lips are moving slightly, mumbling or praying aloud. The whole Council consists of less than ten of the most important people in the lamasery.

But they are not here alone. There's a six or seven-year-old girl sitting on a pillow in the corner, her hands around her knees, her chin resting on them and her thick, black, greasy hair sprawling down. From around her knees, her hands clutch a repulsive clown – a thirty-inch-long wooden cylinder at a diameter of about three inches, with dirty cloth balls hanging on either end. One ball seemingly represents a head. There are two elongated balls at the other end, which could be feet at a stretch of the imagination. The whole monster is on a short stick, wrapped in cloth, representing hands, forming something of a cross under the head. Since the girl is clenching the clown, it's clear that she is putting all her energy into it, freeing herself of all her problems and transferring them into its form. She's wearing the red garments of a local monk, clearly a desperate man's hand-me-downs that she dug up somewhere in the lamasery. Baggy as they are, no one can tell whether she is wearing pants, a skirt, a sutana or a modern sari, it being five times her size. She stares around the room with a not-too-startled but tenacious look.

Looking into the huge black wandering eyes, half-turned and Eastern, her hair and her hands wrapped around her knees, clutching the clown, all fades until all that remains are those eyes. Vitas plunges into those eyes like into a duvet, helplessly hanging onto them. He manages to free himself only through the shadow performance, which simply interrupts their eye contact, freeing him of the spell. Immediately, he shivers with the cold that engulfs him.

Silence. Every monk is accustomed to deep meditation, so no one is disturbed. But here, it seems that everyone is awaiting an open door, followed by a scream. Akhum the librarian, head slightly leaning towards a candle as if a bodhisattva were about to jump out of it, is taken by surprise. The Hindu Mhosai Mangcug studies the fingers on both hands, their bellies touching.

The directness of Monk Tungjur's question sounds like a shot: "What do you suggest?" He looks at everyone inquisitively, adding: "What do we do with her?" His expression implying that he and the Lama have known the answer to that question for a long time already. His sole interest is in the opinions of those present.

"Did she at least tell us her name?" Lao PuWei dares to ask.

"She hasn't said a word, let alone her name," says Dr Sithar. "She only nodded when I asked her if she's in pain, so we know she understands."

More silence.

"I would send her out West more," Lao PuWei says unexpectedly in a resolute voice. "She's only a threat to our solidarity, putting our meditation in jeopardy. It wouldn't be a change for the better. She could mean the breakdown of our whole lamasery." He sinks his eyes down to the ground, before adding, as if wanting to convince himself that his opinion is correct: "Away with her. They'll take better care of her there."

Wung Pien, the guardian of the walled-up hermit quickly rises to his feet and steps in front of the girl, who was still staring into vacant space.

"What's your name, young lady?" he asks in Tibetan.

No response.

"What's your name, young lady?" he asks in Chinese.

Nothing.

"What's your name, young lady?" he asks in English.

Still nothing. Wung shrugs his shoulders, raises his hands, then lets them fall freely and walks away.

"Rmi-lam," a whistling noise is heard from the girl's mouth.

Everyone stops. Wung turns around, comes closer to the girl and asks in Chinese: "What now?"

"Rmi-lam," the girl repeats, staring him down. Her glare implying that even the famous Wung is not only an idiot, but a deaf one too.

Everyone spontaneously bursts out laughing, except for the Lama, who remains seated, leaning over and mumbling something to himself. Vitas and Aviel also laugh at the girl's reaction, though they have no idea why they are laughing. Their laughter only eased the tension caused by the single word that the girl had uttered. Like popping a balloon.

"Rmi-lam? So, a dream? So, you're our dream?" chuckles Wung. It isn't until this moment that our Jingzhi understand that Rmi-lam (pronounced: "Milam") means dream in Tibetan. "Well, let's hope you're not our 'bad' dream," he continues with an ironic smile before retaking his seat. "That wouldn't be good for us…"

Akhum the librarian is trying to calm the situation: "Hold on, at least she said something, no? At least we finally know her name..."

"Yes, and now that we know it, we should all wake up from our dream and our dream should go onto its own destiny," Lao PuWei insists.

"If she came here," the Lama's strong, stern voice is heard, "then it's God's will and we cannot and shall not oppose it. MO[26] clearly showed me the way. If she is here," the Lama directs his finger at the girl, pausing "then she will stay here until it is time for her to go and none of us shall push her away. On the contrary, we must take care of her, we must raise her, for I doubt that anyone will come forth to acknowledge themselves as her mother or father, who took her away."

"Honourable Rinpoche, I want what's good for her," Lao PuWei tactfully objects, apologising slightly for his previous objections. "I was only taking into consideration the purity of our monastery, free of women. The continuously spinning wheel of life, the constancy and purity of thought could be interrupted by her movement." Lao turns to everyone, in an attempt to find someone with the same opinion for his defence.

"First of all," the Abbot cuts in sharply, "she's not a woman, she's a child. If you are speaking about the circle of life and its continuity, you must also consider its evanescence, the evanescence of everyone sitting here and the evanescence of the whole monastery. If the destruction of the lamasery in its entirety is important to the gods and if she is to be the cause, thus it must be so."

When Vitas recalled these prophetic words some time

---

26 MO – a type of Tibetan prophecy, which takes place in the case of important decisions related to health, work, travelling or fundamental issues about the future.

later, he couldn't help but wonder if there was something that the Lama wasn't trying to tell the others. Everyone, except for Lao, now respectfully inclined to their superior and it was clear that no one intended on joining in Lao's argument.

"I was only thinking that the Buddha's teachings and our traditions could be threatened by her presence," Lao insisted uncertainly.

"Tradition? Which tradition are you referring to? The wheel has been spinning at a different rate ever since the Chinese trampled our soil in the fifties, digging everything up, stomping across all things and destroying everything in their path. The traditions have long been disrupted. There's no way we can tolerate our lives here in such isolation. Everything has changed and everything must move forward with every new day to pass, from the arrival of our new Jingzhi, to the other happenings. It will not move away from Buddha, we must preserve Him, whether it is here or abroad. Every intruder changes the direction and speed of the eternal wheel. By means of culture, everyone leaves an imprint of his God, whoever that may be. Our world is decimated, hundreds of thousands of people, lamas and monks are murdered, the land is sucked dry and you persist to discuss tradition? Lao!"

The Lama directed his flow of feelings, accumulated over years of time, to the poor PuWei. But it was clear that the tirade as a whole was not intended for him alone. "How many years have you been here? Instead of using those years to understand the futility of labouring for your own personal gain, not allowing yourself to get carried away by harmful greed and deception, you suddenly deny the samsara, the circle of life that you yourself refer to, during a random test. You want to protect the cloak, a mere piece of cloth, instead of protecting what the cloak is covering. Consider how you have spoken."

Jiří Ovečka

The Lama gazed over the audience with a strict, commanding eye, refusing any further discussion. He stopped on everyone, as if talking directly to him.

"If the gods sent us this girl, then it is our holy duty to take care of her. To take care of her education, to ensure that she is happy and healthy here. We must handle everything. We must all grant her what we know. Starting with myself, I will personally teach her the words of Buddha and the history of Tibet, Tengyur Confucianism, and the history of China. Dr Sithar will be responsible for natural sciences, biology, botany, anthropology, and in essence, all things related to the human world. Mhosai Mangcug shall teach her Hindu teachings and Hindi. Aviel shall teach her mathematics, Judaism and English, and Vitas shall teach her Christianity and of European culture. And if Lao will finally comprehend his place in the eternal wheel, he shall be responsible for bringing any necessary items from the outside world to raise her and keep her healthy."

The Lama paused for a long time again, watching each reaction, all quite hard to read. Everyone humbly accepted their role, without further dispute. No one could peer into another's head, however. If brains could speak, the room would be so loud that no one would understand a thing. Vitas' head would moan: 'God, why didn't I study more? I'm completely stupid and I don't remember anything at all...' Gazing into another's eyes, Aviel's especially, he knew he wasn't the only one having this thought.

Abbot Thorpe smiled as if he understood the inner embarrassment of those present. "I think there is a deep well of wisdom in our library. Using it, you can study and prepare for your teachings. Now, for organisation, Akhum the librarian is responsible for Rmi-lam's upbringing and shall receive help in the form of sources of information. Not everyone can teach her at once, of course. No complicated

formulas, Aviel. Start with fairytales, epic tales and biblical stories. You must begin with games. Everything must
include allegories, symbolism and metaphors to broaden her
field of vision." The Lama suddenly let loose, as if a weight
had been lifted off his shoulders and clarified in a very cold,
bureaucratic voice: "We must meet here once-a-week, not
only to assure the smooth running of the lamasery, but to
also evaluate the curriculum of the week prior. We must
meet to advise ourselves on the methods for her instruction.
I understand that this will not be easy for us. But for now,
off to work."

26.
A Court Battle with Kromen

The Czech TV station's Legal Department had sent an internal envelope containing several documents.

Re: Kostka and Kromen's lawsuit against the Czech TV station.

Although Vitas had received several similar notifications throughout his career, it always made him feel a little uneasy. He immediately asked himself if he had done something wrong. Whether or not he really had done anything wrong wasn't at all the deciding factor. The defendant always had to be the one who issued the suit, meaning in this case the TV station, not the editor, who was only a witness. At this point, it was up to the lawyer representing the TV station to decide how much time he would give Vitas, the witness, to speak, and what he would use of the information provided. From experience, Vitas knew that even though advocacy is one of the most lucrative professions, a corporate lawyer is often unable to support himself in the legal field. This at least, had become the rule at the Czech TV station. Heaven forbid that anyone would feel offended by publishing information claiming that day breaks after nightfall. The TV station would in all likelihood lose this lawsuit.

Even so, it must be said that many judges themselves were often desperate, not knowing how to close an absurd case. The one who issued the suit could even be sentenced for truthful information, if it caused harm to anyone. It was frequently no more than a game, a juggling act with words, where the deciding factor could have been the use of the continuous tense, which didn't express the exact facts. So, if the issuer is being sued by a thief, who was caught because his crime was recorded, yet still wins the case, such a blind man's decision leaves the editor frustrated and helpless.

Vitas could never be sure how the trial would turn out. Mentally, it was so demanding on him that he started flirting with the thought of having a cigarette again. He held an unlit cigarette in his hand, considering whether to allow nicotine to clear his thoughts or not. Knowing what he had gone through to free himself of this habit, he crushed the cigarette in his hands, absorbed the smell of raw, unlit tobacco and tried to leave the world of nicotine by fully concentrating on Kromen. Their "good" relationship was clearly over. Why the sudden turnaround? Although the explanation was simple, he was oblivious to it. Kromen and Kostka were getting ready for another bank and just when they were supposed to squeeze out millions, a report came and screwed everything up. It was a major turning point in the relationship between Kostka and Kromen, as Kromen was of course constantly subjected to the remorse of his partner, who had long wanted to deal with this annoying louse his own way.

Vitas came well prepared for the trial. He had plenty of information, especially from Inspector Petrovsky and his colleagues.

Of course, as a witness, he couldn't be present at the process. Over thirty journalists, mostly friends and people dressed in everyday clothes, broke into the courtroom. Some of them were police officers that Vitas was familiar with.

Judge Vasicek thought that thirty minutes would be

enough for the summoned witness, Vitas. When asked if Vitas agreed with everything that he had claimed in his reports, especially regarding the fact that the petitioners, Kostka and Kromen were to rid Czech banks of about three billion crowns by means of their activities, Vitas convincingly replied, "Yes."

At the same time, he used the opportunity to add a word of his own. "Above all, I would like to point out that if Mr. Kromen feels his reputation is being damaged by the proposed lawsuit and the reports in question have had a negative impact on his life, I would like to cite the municipal court here."

"What is this?" growled the judge morosely, having been hoping to go home early.

Vitas took out about twenty stapled pieces of paper. "This is the verdict of the local Municipal Court in Prague from 1996. It deals with the process of a certain Matulik, accused of murder and the stealing of a dead body. He admitted to the crime in the preliminary hearing, stating that Kromen, present here, ordered the murder. He withdrew his claim during the course of the hearing and only confessed to stealing the dead body. And if I may cite just a few short sentences from the Municipal Court's verdict…"

Vitas' voice sounded very modest, all the more so comedic for those present. The quoted passages, formulated desperately using broken and artificial legal language, evoked laughter among the counter-party. Only Kromen's and Kostka's lawyer, one of the most renowned lawyers in the country, spoke on Kromen's behalf. After the hearing, police officers, thoroughly taking note of everything, told Vitas that the lawyer was yelling at Kromen for not telling him anything about this. "How could I have known that the snoop would bring that up here?" Kromen objected, crying out furiously.

"Defendant Matulik denies the death of the victim and points out the connection of the murder with actions of Kromen's witness," cited Vitas, looking apologetically at Kromen. The expression on his face implied that he was deeply sorry for bringing it up here, but that there was really nothing else he could do. Kromen gave a very cold expression in reply.

"The defendant confirmed that he and Kromen had prepared versions of the testimony, depending on whether or not the victim's body was found." Vitas went on to another part of the verdict, "According to the witness, witness Kromen is wealthy and ranked highly in the underworld. He also knows many police officers… And so," Vitas searched enthusiastically for further material like a botanist just stumbling upon a new plant: "…in no way does the court consider the testimony of Kromen's witness credible, given all the facts and circumstances surrounding this person. The court has uncovered that this person is identified as a chief in the criminal underworld and concludes that this person is not credible."

Judge Vasicek looked at Vitas, submerged in papers. The hearing was suddenly over, adjourned for an indefinite period of time, to be exact. He discreetly called upon Vitas in the hallway in front of the courtroom. "If I were you, editor, I'd get a gun. This case is over for me. I don't want to be involved. Do you realise what you're getting yourself into?"

Soon afterwards, another hearing was ordered with a new judge, who took over the case. She gave Vitas four hours to speak. The TV lawyer was crocheting while Vitas broke down the entire network of mobsters, intertwined in complicated webs, comparing all alleged fraud in terms of the personnel, location, and company, also providing supporting evidence in the form of Land Registry statements…

Kromen and Kostka simply stared blankly into the papers on the table before them. Vitas put an end to the whole case unquestionably, with a secret police report that assessed Kostka's and Kromen's activities in the same way and asked the council for "permission to implement measures to put an end to the criminal activities of both named…"

After winning the trial, Vitas had the upper hand. He seemed to be an invincible investigative editor that everyone could admire. He ignored various warnings that drew his attention to the transience of this happiness. No, life was beautiful…

– – –

"Alright, I'll think of something," growled Vitas, who by now hated writing down ideas. Unlike in the past, it now seemed only to be stalling and insulting. He never really knew how the shot would end up, the case frequently turned the wrong way, or went off in a completely different direction, and then the bureaucrats harassed him for drifting from the topic.

Vitas brought up the SAZKA betting company in front of Rokos. But this topic frightened him, the bow of his ego collapsing like the wet sail of a sailboat on a calm day. "Make sure you check everything thoroughly with the Czech Press Office," Rokos repeated, over and over.

"Sorry boss, but there won't be anything there. I can't even get anything from the Press Office because the TV station closed it down."

"What?" shouted Rokos. "What do you mean closed it down…?"

"Simply closed it down. Apparently it was expensive…"

"But that's impossible. That's like taking away a bricklayer's brick trowel, tying his hands together and telling him to build a wall. Where do they get information for the news now?" Vitas stared in astonishment.

"That's what Wikipedia's for…"

"But there's no supporting evidence there, you can't take over responsibility for the information there, anyone writes whatever they want!" Rokos was fuming.

"I don't know, I really don't know," Vitas said in defence. "That's just what I heard from the ladies at the CTIS. They said that editors no longer even need the Czech Press Office because it only proves their illiteracy. It's basically a mirror. The editors can see how stupid they actually are and then they quickly form a complex about it that prevents them from doing their work. There's nothing you can do with a timid editor who knows he's foolish. So they were better off getting rid of the Czech Press Office."

"God, I hope you're kidding. Stop pulling my leg and get to work," sighed Rokos.

Vitas quietly began meeting with former SAZKA betting company officials and shareholder representatives. He only addressed those who were in dispute with Kromen. He knew that otherwise, Kromen would find out and he wasn't prepared for that yet. He needed time. A lot of time.

He got so wrapped up in the SAZKA betting company case that he ignored everything else going on around him. He put all of his energy into it, as if he were waiting for the final blow, leaving nothing but a flood behind. After less than a year of snooping around, it was all just routine work. This time, however, tolerance did not follow like before. This time, it unleashed a harsh and ruthless duel.

Even Vitas set completely different standards for assessing Kromen and Kostka. Kostka was a ruthless murderer. It wasn't words, but projectiles that should be used in a dialogue with him. He would take a revolver with him to the bathroom, even at home, after all "one never knows…." He pictured Kromen as a gangster who knew how to kill (for god's sake only not with his own hands), as well as a charismatic nobleman and philosopher. Having a cup of coffee with him was far from boring. Thanks to the SAZKA BC, he could sit high up in his nest and sometimes throw an extra worm or a chewed up bone to a passer-by, as long as he was easy to see! Politicians, too, would hold their voting ballot over the ballot box, waiting for journalists to take a picture of them voting. In terms of wealth, the SAZKA BC definitely didn't save money on Kromen. His office and the services it incurred cost upwards of 150 million a year. Two personal assistants, two secretaries, a personal treasurer, two drivers, a Bentley, an aircraft… Kromen had boarded a bullet train, got rid of the slow locomotive, and had taken the wheel, taking it to an entirely different station than the one that the satisfied passengers thought they were going. Poor people couldn't notice the difference between a lethal desert and a life-giving forest.

"Vitas is a very dangerous psychopath," Pozounek would characterise Vitas to Kromen using the most frightening colours, suggesting the difficulty of taming his activities. "He adopts the image of a poor man, living in a worn-down house, wearing a smelly sweater, but that's nothing more than an impression! He acts like he's the messiah, but he's a bastard!"

Kromen was keeping up with the times. He acquired a rather expensive but flawless PR team – lobbyists and messengers, who would clean up after him and successfully create an immaculate impression. Pozounek was the head of the SAZKA BC media protection. Whenever necessary, he would be the first one out in the field on the front lines, eliminating any potential threat. He was the knife in Kromen's hand. Of course, he had to defend his means of existence at the SAZKA BC, and he was certainly well paid to do it. The billions that would otherwise all end up in the hands of the athletes had to be filtered a bit first. For this reason, he would sometimes discreetly create risky situations, which he would immediately resolve and then rightfully so, expect a significant restitution from Kromen.

At one time, Pozounek was a journalist, and he was well aware of the operations of the media. "Well, this Pozounek completely screwed the status of journalism in the Czechia," said an older colleague to Vitas. "He was the one who introduced marketability and… not so much corruption, but rather… an intentional swaying of public opinion through lies and white lies, plainly manipulating people for the sake of business, or just for the fun, because he can, and after all, he's Mr Almighty. He devalued the currency of the word to an insignificant sigh that lacks all meaning. He treads the earth, heels crushing anything in his path, simply because the focus of his interest is elsewhere and he'll do anything to reap benefits financially or for his career. He's a completely unscrupulous man."

"How should I deal with Vitas?" asks Kormen directly, piercing Pozounek's eyes like a harpoon into a whale. "I tried being on good terms for years. It's no longer possible."

"You know, it's hard," Pozounek, frowning, sighs distinctly, trying to free himself of this harpoon, though to no avail. His efforts were to make it seem to Kromen that he could sooner stop the world from spinning than stop Vitas.

"Should I deal with it?"

"No boss, I can handle it," Pozounek defends himself with his arms outstretched as if wanting to stop a tank with his hands. "You don't have to worry about it. I only want to emphasise that this is a first-class bastard. He won't let anything get in his way. Watch out! Several celebrities have already tried to stop his slanderous false campaigns, but it's not that easy! He's got an external contract with the TV station, so there's nothing anyone can do. When you pick on someone in their hierarchy, it's immediately an infringement on freedom of speech. And they're very sensitive to that over there. That's why these ruffians get away with so many lies. I only want to point out that you have to go about it in a completely different manner. But I mean," Pozounek exhales very modestly and with all the more emphasis, "I have a way. His past, his psychopathic present… It won't be easy, but… he'll definitely take it," Pozounek offers the solution on a platter.

"Surely not," Kromen ponders the idea of bribing Vitas.

"Absolutely! I've tried it, but he's not cheap!"

"Nonsense. I know him all too well. But sure, try it. How much?"

"Hard to say," Pozounek backs away. "I think his price will range somewhere between five and ten, whether a bride or discrediting, or… something else," he chuckles sarcastically. "Something will work."

"I'll give you eight, not a penny more. And I know nothing about it, but you guarantee that we're out of harm's way. I'm warning you, if anything goes wrong, you have to inform us immediately. Otherwise, I want to have progress reports on my desk every other day. Only words written on a computer, no signature and don't send it by email. Attacking the director of the TV station will be my last resort. He'll have a fit if I tell him that I'm not going to include the lottery draw in the broadcast. One hundred million a year is a good enough reason to have him kiss my feet. But if you fail and leave me no choice but to take these steps, everything is over for you as well. Is that clear?"

"Crystal clear, boss. But you don't have to worry about that. It'll work out one way or another."

– – –

Eight years and four judges later, the final verdict in the Maya case was approaching. Thanks to the pardon, there was no risk of punishment, but Maya clearly didn't want to hear the word "guilty." This too, had to be the real reason she accepted the pardon approximately fourteen days before the final verdict was made. Then it all suddenly came to an end.

Well, not everything. There were several civic court trials involving real estate with incriminated forged documents that took place over the years. Maya singlehandedly lost all these lawsuits, it being relatively easy to prove who the real owners were, so the property was transferred back to its rightful proprietor. Although it was impossible to point the finger at Maya without a non-verdict, saying – girl, you're a criminal – the old-fashioned Latin expression, cui bono,[27] could easily apply in this case, which would give everyone the right to say that someone here, was the ugly duckling.

But it didn't end there!

The ugly duckling filed a complaint at the European Court for Human Rights, asking for compensation from the state for tangible and moral damages totalling ninety-six million crowns. The court acknowledged the fault in the length of the court proceedings (which was almost exclusively caused by the wading of the whimsical duckling) and the right to respect private correspondence.

In the end, Maya was awarded approximately 700,000 crowns. And that was the end of charismatic Maya's whimsical ways.

– – –

Vitas recalled Inspector Petrovsky's account of how Kromen and Kostka met with the Minister in secret. Back then, the

---

27 Lat. – in one's favour

meeting point was surrounded by different secret police agents, internal affairs and the Security Information Service. In essence, they all picked their brains in order to acquire any convincing information. Now Vitas was sitting (equipped of course with all of his recording devices) by a table in the back room of a discreet Prague hangout, talking to "some" Pozounek, who had no idea that Vitas knew who he had the honour of meeting. There were two more occupied tables in the room. A couple of tourists, probably husband and wife, playing with their camera, were sitting at one table. In reality, it was Vitas' lawyer friend and Vitas' colleague. There were another two young guys sitting at the other table, looking at each other with blank stares, as if not knowing what to say to each other. These were employees of the SAZKA betting company, who had accompanied Pozounek be to his witnesses. They too, had a hidden camera.

Right then Vitas had his lawyer and friend in his corner and he was also aware of Pozounek's "agents" at the other table. Neither Pozounek nor his "agents" were aware of Vitas' lawyer and friend. He regretted only putting an insignificant fraction of this manic, absurd world into his reports, but that too, was what fascinated him the most in his job. These were bizarre situations that he would never get the chance to experience under normal circumstances. Yet, they were simultaneously like the abbreviations of myths that he'd only read about, seen in movies, or on stage, but never experienced. And only a fraction of it he would be able to 'get over the ramp' as they say, meaning show the audience. He would be unable to describe his feelings, to include the thousands of things that he is convinced are true but lacks the supporting evidence. There would be neither enough time nor footage to contain any emotions and come to think of it, that would be off topic in any case, meaning it would never be included.

Finding themselves in a smoky room, in an awkward situation with people watching one another, they dealt with Pozounek's mysterious offer. Vitas had no idea how or when he would come, but he knew he would come. The whole meeting was summoned according to a telephone call, during which Pozounek offered him a PR job at some obscure company. Vitas knew what he was getting himself into. Therefore he warned the other editors in advance, especially Rokos, that he would probably receive a financial offer at this meeting that he wouldn't be able to refuse immediately in the interest of discovering more information. Rokos was horrified, jumping around like a ping-pong ball, inciting the whole legal department.

"Well, what do you say to a nice trip, a nice vacation… to some other continent… with your wife of course … Where would you like to go…?"

"We don't fly anywhere, we get dizzy."

"Right, but you don't get dizzy from everything…?"

"Why the special treatment?"

"I admire people like you. You're such an adamant warrior. Such people should be appreciated."

"I get my pay."

"But that's a joke," Pozounek waved his hand scornfully. Then he stared at Vitas, rubbing his hands on the bottle of Coca-Cola, leaning over to Vitas and growling softly. "I have a job for you. I know you're a completely honest man. I need you to shoot a clip about three minutes or so, for 200,000. Not bad, right?"

"Who's it for? You spoke about some PR job over the phone…"

"Doesn't matter. And you've got plenty of time for editing. I don't care if you finish it in one year, or two. It's cash in your pocket."

"For the SAZKA betting company?"

"It doesn't matter," growled Pozounek, still leaning over, almost flat to the table, staring into Vitas' eyes. There were some eight inches between them, as if they were discussing the biggest conspiracy.

"You know what, I'd take it. But I get dizzy," said Vitas slowly, without budging.

"If you close your eyes, the dizziness goes away," whispered Pozounek. "Do you know what'll happen if you don't succumb to the flight? You have to take a deep breath, close your eyes and imagine the unparalleled beauty of the clouds, the luxury…"

Vitas could only laugh mockingly. This surprised and probably also offended Pozounek. His features hardened. His eyes narrowed. At once he jumped away from Vitas like a bad actor at rehearsal, performing a silly gesture with his outstretched hand, as if to say 'step away, Satan!' Then he yelled, for the whole pub to hear: "No! I won't give you the 200,000! Broadcast whatever you want about the SAZKA BC, but we're a solid institution and we're not going to give some easy-to-bribe journalist cash not to broadcast his lies about us!"

Pozounek rose in the middle of his heartrending speech. He continued to make a silly gesture with his hands, preparing to leave, but talking anyway.

"No, no, no. You can't expect us to do that. Fortunately, I have witnesses here," he glanced around to the other tables. Everyone was speechless. "Did you hear that? He wanted me to give him 200,000."

"We heard it," the two young guys nodded, siding with Pozounek.

"We didn't hear it," said Vitas' lawyer friend in a loud, naive voice, clearly finding this all very amusing.

"Well, if you didn't hear anything, don't talk about it," Pozounek brushed him off. "If they heard it, it's true and valid."

"No it's not," articulated the lawyer slowly with a smile on his face. "Because we were listening and recording and that's not what happened…"

Pozounek walked out of the pub angrily and his two allies followed soon after him.

"That would work!" Pozounek was yelling at his poor co-workers from the SAZKA BC, "but now, the bastard has to play fair! He had no other choice but to play fair! He knew that he would then screw everything up! He had so many witnesses there. There was no way he could accept the money that he'd otherwise normally accept without batting an eyelid."

Pozounek thought nervously for a long time before arriving at a clear conclusion: He has to move on to Plan B – to discredit his name.

– – –

"I GUESS YOU DON'T KNOW WHERE TO DRAW THE LINE, DO YOU?"

27.
Introductions

At first glance, no changes took place in the lamasery during the weeks that followed. Rmi-lam sat shyly in a corner, not reacting to anything, until asked several times and once it was clear that the one asking was losing his nerve. She was like an inconspicuous, grey mouse that disappeared somewhere in the catacombs and would probably never even emerge if it wasn't for hunger. She kept on dragging her ugly clown around everywhere and didn't even let Aviel touch it. At one point he almost got into a fight with her over it because he wanted to give it a wash. Rmi-lam's past was taboo. No one could ask her about yesterday, the past month, or the previous years, unless she herself wanted to talk about it. And she really didn't want to talk about yesterday. Given her restless sleep, it was clear that she led a very nervous life up until now. At first, there were guards at her door, who took turns guarding her. The guards slowly disappeared as Rmi-lam grew used to the local environment.

Vitas saw Rmi-lam as a ripple in a calm lake, as a distraction that probably meant nothing for the future. Most importantly, since he didn't speak Chinese, he couldn't fulfil any of the Lama's instructions. There was no way of communicating with Rmi-lam because she could speak Chinese alone. And the same was the case for Aviel. But

Vitas searched for another way. He and Rmi-lam were learning languages together in class, in Vitas' "chapel" as well as when strolling around the lamasery. On occasion, they even learned the meaning of words outside, where it was getting colder and colder, using very non-traditional methods. He ran her hands along a rock that formed the corridor to the lamasery, repeated the words on the wall, corridor and floor in English, Chinese and Tibetan and then only described the features of the wall, saying it's black, rough and hard. It was a search and discovery process for both of them. The truth is, Rmi-lam quickly outperformed her teacher.

When Rmi-lam stared in awe at the bodhisattva-Avalokiteshvara,[28] decorated thangka in the Buddhist chapel, they began analysing the word: beautiful. It turned into a word association game. Its thousands of hands depicted in the symbolism represented the crowds of people he helped. But what feelings are evoked when people look at him? Fear? Mystery? Despite their awkward communication, often just shouting keywords at each other, they suddenly began to understand one another. Beautiful. Although something can be ugly, it can possess inner beauty. She began to see what makes humans different from animals. Together, they started associating words, searching for those with specific meanings, which signified something completely different when put together.

"That's terribly beautiful…"

"How can you say 'terribly beautiful', it's an oxymoron…" she stumbled for words.

It's one thing to describe a word, but it's something completely different to describe what's happening in the soul. In this way they translated the words of Lama Anagarika

---

28 Avalokiteshvara – one of the most important bodhisattvas in Mahayana Buddhism, embodying the compassion of all Buddhas. The current 14th Dalai Lama is considered his reincarnation.

Govinda from the *Basics of Tibetan Mysticism*: "There is no adequate word to describe the essence of the mind, for there is nothing to grasp or define in the pure essence of the mind. We only use words to free ourselves from words once we come to the indefinable essence…"

There was also a similar language barrier between Aviel and Rmi-lam. He had given up on teaching a similar level of Judaism and set his sights on teaching mathematics and English. But Aviel found communicating with Rmi-lam a lot more difficult. "One stone and one stone equals two stones," simultaneously, he pointed at two stones and showed her two fingers. Rmi-lam stared at him without making a sound. When he told her to try counting like that on her own, she was clueless once again. Aviel found this very irritating. He obviously didn't have the skills to teach her this. When she finally improved after several months, it had become like a game of stones to her. She found it very amusing to pick them up without thinking, hide them and throw them into the candlelight. Aviel later complained to Vitas that he didn't have the nerve for it. Vitas could only laugh.

Once Rmi-lam adjusted to the lamasery and its people, she greatly enjoyed going to the library, where Akhum was king. He showed her a few illuminated codices on various sacred themes, where she witnessed horrific snakes, dragons and portly men in the typical seated position… But the library was not only full of picture books with sacred topics. It also had works on world history, art and photography. When Rmi-lam found Aviel, Vitas, or any of her other teachers boring, she simply ran away and hid in one of the dark corners, the gonkhangs, or in another cave corner of the vast lamasery and examined bewitched pictures by candlelight.

She didn't dare misbehave so much when she was with

the Lama. She listened to him with great respect. On top of this, his teachings were far more intense, there being no language barrier between them. The Lama was relatively strict, but more benevolent in the case of little Rmi-lam for her age. He helped her understand the basics of Buddhism, leaving Taoism and Confucianism for later.

All the teachers found it hard to keep Rmi-lam's attention when Wung Pien went to see hermit Sonam into his walled-up hermitage with a bit of food. He brought him tsampa, some fruit and vegetables, and a pitcher of water, always on a daily basis. But only once a day. Rmi-lam could never miss this daily happening, no matter how cold it was outside, and no matter how much wisdom anyone was trying to impart to her. She jumped around Wung, who grumbled constantly at her to leave him alone, or else he'd spill the water, fall down the cliff, and then she'd be taken away by demons, by the naga, but it was all no use.

When they arrived at the stone hermitage, he would forbid Rmi-lam from getting any closer than ten feet from the opening, where he served Sonam his food. First, he had to tap hard on the rock with another stone, so that Sonam would be mentally prepared. The light, though a mere flicker, must not distract him from his meditation, which would cause him harm. Then he would move the stone that covered the opening, remove the empty bowl from the hole, and replace it with the new, full one.

Wung managed to keep Rmi-lam on a short leash for some time, but once she lost her shyness, not only was he not able to keep her within ten feet of the hermitage, she even tried sticking her head into the opening, getting her eyes used to the dark, so she could see inside. She longed to see the hermit. She had pictured him in her head as a huge warrior with a moustache and a sharp sword by his side... Wung had told her about how hermit Sonam fought against the Chinese during the invasion of Tibet many years ago. The only thing Rmi-lam had adhered to, perhaps simply out of respect and fear of the hermit, was secrecy. Even though she violated it constantly, once by the opening, she was bound by the seriousness and temperance of the mysterious unknown, only whispering each of her questions.

Rmi-lam found her happiness and kingdom in the kitchen, however, which she would have no doubt come across sooner or later during her expeditions and escapes from her teachers. She discovered two kings, the chefs in the kitchen. They each had two assistants by their side. They really had their hands full, with around one-hundred-and-forty hungry mouths to feed.

Rmi-lam would escape to this kingdom again and again. Of course, many delicacies awaited her there. Neither the chefs nor their assistants could resist an attempt to get the youngster to warm to them with a few treats. But what does the word treat mean here? Does it include the dairy products of yaks, goats and sheep? Supplies of barley bags were abundant. Legumes, vegetables, fruit and products imported from elsewhere that would only reach the monks' menu sporadically, were stored in the basement. Chocolate was another delicacy to be discovered. The only time there had been a large presence of meat was when Kromen had stayed at the lamasery.

Though Rmi-lam enjoyed being spoiled, no one would let her grow on them too much. Instead, she would take advantage of her influence, devouring every treat she was offered, sometimes even stealing it and then… farewell! Like a wind that would blow through the kitchen, she would devour everything worth devouring, escape through the other window, and leave a mess behind.

Rmi-lam also enjoyed music. She couldn't produce a sound from the huge, thirteen-foot-long rag-dungs, so the monks had to hold it for her and laughed when she tried to sing into it. But the real fun was playing the drums and shells. The sounds she created were so offbeat that sometimes they reached ultrasonic tones. At first, her approach to these instruments was chaotic. But later on, the monks tried teaching her how to play the shells.

After several months, Rmi-lam felt completely confident in the lamasery. Its inhabitants too, had gotten so used to her that they saw her presence as a matter of God's predetermined course. Vitas was quite wrong in thinking that not much would change with her arrival. Straight away, everyone started to develop a much greater sense of their activities, from cleaning and cooking, to conducting mass. They also felt greater responsibility. The isolation of the lamasery didn't bother anyone much, this falling in line with the mission of Buddhism. Moreover, it was better that no one drew attention to their own non-existence to those in the outside world; given the attitudes of the Chinese forces, any interest from the public or official authorities could be tragic for the lamasery.

But after many years in isolation, each activity had become commonplace and typical. Rmi-lam brought something to the lamasery that seemed to awaken everyone from their lethargy, from their dreams, forcing them to examine themselves through newly perceptive eyes. They began dusting places that had never been dusted before. Almost overnight, the cooks began to try preparing well-presented meals instead of slopping the usual blob of tsampa into a bowl. Rooms, although still mysterious with the lack of light, all at once seemed brighter. There was a new whiff of fresh air running through their veins. Since Rmi-lam was a gust herself and no one ever knew where, when, or how intensely she would blow through, they were always prepared for her. If people didn't see her for longer than three days, they asked what had happened to her. Our teachers would say the same thing after a single day, if she didn't try to scare them, or catch them off guard first.

Rmi-lam made her way around to different liturgical ceremonies. Out of curiosity, she closely watched Aviel's Sabbath, which started on Friday at sunset. She'd play the shofar while he was reciting the Sabbath's Kabbalat, or the Torah. Aviel would roll his eyes repeatedly, asking God for forgiveness for dishonouring such a feast day, though where there's no plaintiff, there is no judgment. No one but he knew how the Sabbath should be celebrated. "Hopefully God will see how helpless I am and he'll forgive me," said Aviel offhandedly. It was more difficult at celebrations, which were sometimes attended by the monks. Thanks to Rmi-lam's interruptions and entries (Orthodox proverbs would call this dishonour), these rituals were closer to humorous stories.

As the Christian holiday of Christmas was approaching, Vitas went out into the harsh winter and brought a fir tree into his holy room. He "consecrated" the tree and he and Rmi-lam decorated it using every usual and unusual trinket. From some distance, Aviel observed them in contempt, and commented on the ugliest decorations. "There's no way I'm decorating a tree for Christmas. What if we do it together and Santa Claus comes here?"

"Don't you dare try," said Vitas menacingly, trying to decorate a branch with a fragment from a broken mug. "As a Jew, tough luck. This is solely a Christian thing."

"Hold on, back in the States, I'd celebrate your Christmas all the time, and we had a Santa with reindeer and a sleigh."

"Sure, but you also have a turkey dinner on Christmas Day, so once the turkey is ready, get Santa and call me. Until then, you're out of luck. You and Santa are already trying to take over Europe, ruining our culture, and now you're going to try doing the same thing here?"

"Hold your horses." Aviel got up, making his way to the Christmas tree, which looked like a well-groomed broomstick.

"Enough of that, Rmi-lam." He grabbed a wooden board used for drawing or making inscriptions. Though the lamasery did have paper intended for Rmi-lam, it was only used on occasion, being very rare. If the writings weren't needed for future reference, the board and chalk were used. Aviel tried drawing something that looked like the map of the World. He left out the territories of Africa, South America and Australia... "We're here, right? This is Tibet. Buddhism reigns here. This is Europe and Jesus Christ reigns here. This is America and Christ..."

"And where is your God?" Rmi-lam interrupted him.

"Well, He's here all around us too..." Furiously, Aviel ran his index finger over the vicinity of Europe and America.

"But how can both of them be there and there. Do they understand each other?"

"Wait, wait, that's not the issue here," Aviel tried to free himself from these intrusive questions that caught him off guard. Tapping his finger on Europe, trying to drown out Rmi-lam, he continued, "This is Christmas, the day Jesus was born, baby Jesus is celebrated and baby Jesus brings presents..."

"How can he bring presents when he was just born?" Rmi-lam found another discrepancy.

"He was born 2000 and some years ago and this is how it's celebrated every year. He brings presents here," Aviel banged on the board, pointing at Europe, then America, showing the difference in the bearer of gifts, "and here it's Santa Claus, driving a sleigh pulled by reindeer, that brings the presents."

"Well, I want both of them!" Rmi-lam resolved the whole issue, not leaving room for further discussion. "Baby Jesus and Santa Claus will both come and you will be on your best behaviour because both of them will bring me presents."

Vitas chuckled quietly, preparing the tree, while Aviel shook his head in disbelief, although fighting to suppress his laughter. Rmi-lam glanced at her clown and clarified: "I'm getting both!"

"Of course," Aviel nodded understandingly, with a slightly ironic undertone.

Rmi-lam quickly began to frown, and asked rather aggressively: "Since Europe has baby Jesus and America has Santa Claus, what do we have here?"

"The Chinese," Vitas shouted spontaneously, trying to concentrate on putting up candles on a fir branch, all of them bending until the wicks faced the ground.

"Leave her alone," Aviel snapped and turned to Rmi-lam. "Forget it. These feasts are not celebrated here. They celebrate others here…"

"Which ones?"

"Well, which ones…" Aviel thought.

"Mönlam," Vitas interrupted him. "Mönlam feasts are coming up. They celebrate Buddha's victory in a dispute among several teachers. And then Losar in February. Those are New Year's celebrations. I've already studied it," he boasted proudly.

"Yaaaay," Rmi-lam clapped her hands. "We're going to be celebrating all the time!"

"And Losar will celebrate New Year 2135, also the year of the Earth and the Mouse," added Vitas.

"He alone," Aviel pointed at Vitas, "as a Christian will celebrate the New Year right after his Christmastime, right before Losar. It'll be 2008."

"And what about you?" Rmi-lam asked curiously.

"I celebrated the New Year a couple of months ago, I'm in 5768 now."

"That much? You're old. And how old am I?" Rmi-lam wondered.

"Calm down, little one, you're about seven years old."

Rmi-lam frowned indignantly, closing her eyes, now perceiving Aviel as her nemesis. "That's impossible…"

"No more questions," Aviel tried to be relentless but tender. "Go see the Lama for your next class now. Go, go. No discussions," he defended himself from Rmi-lam's attacks, who would of course have ever more questions.

28.
Something's Going On

Vitas knew that something was going on in the criminal world. He'd had a heads-up from various sources that something was going down, but what? Petrovsky kept grumbling and mumbling something like, "It needs time, don't worry, you will be the first…" They had already agreed to meet the day after tomorrow at 10 pm, as usual. This meant tomorrow at 9 pm at the Al Capone pub.

"Vitas, someone's on the line for you," Balek, the head of the edition called grumpily the following morning in the control room, "and be so kind and tell your sources that I am not your secretary."

Vitas picked up the phone with an apologetic smile. He was immediately floored. "Hey," he heard Petrovsky's voice. Given their security measures, this phone call was hardly expected. "Ad A: we are currently arresting the director of the Investment Bank and his deputy. Ad B: forced corporate governance. Ad C: I can't say more at this time. We're on for tomorrow (equals today). Period," Petrovsky said abruptly, with an ending typical for the greenest of brains, which Vitas recognised during the course of the compulsory, Communist military service.

"I have something sweet," said Vitas simply to Balek, who raised his eyebrows with curiosity. "The Police have just arrested Rolnik, director of the Investment Bank, along with his deputy. Forced corporate governance."

"Seriously?" the head of the edition opened his mouth in awe. Management arranged a meeting within five minutes, assigning Vitas the whole case, providing him with all the necessary facilities. He was also assigned a crew that waited at his command.

Vitas sat by his favourite table in the newsroom and picked up the phone.

"Investment Bank, General Director's Office," said the secretary in her monotone, trying to sound happy and welcoming as she was trained to do, without knowing who is calling.

"Hello, Vitas speaking, editor at the Czech TV station." The whole situation suddenly seemed very embarrassing to him and he didn't even know how to pose the question. "Could I please speak with the director?"

"I'm sorry, he's busy. Can I give him a message? He'll either call you back or send you an email."

"And could you please tell me what he's busy doing?" Vitas stopped for a second, thinking how to sound more formal. "Isn't it because he's busy being arrested by the police?"

"What?" a long, deep emphasis fell on this monosyllable, elongating the high-noted ending of the question.

"Are the police present?" Vitas exhaled in surprise.

"You're out of your mind, Editor," briefly, officially, but with a polite undertone, the secretary concluded the call and hung up.

Could it be – a red herring? Vitas froze. He had to shake it off once he realised how foolish the secretary and general director Rolnik would think he was. The secretary was probably just giving him the "news flash," while laughing.

"So what, back to trees?" Balek, the head of the edition smirked, with his fingers clasped behind his head, leaning so far back in his armchair that he was almost lying flat. "I'll keep an eye on what's going on," Vitas cut him off, nervously making a call, but Petrovsky wasn't picking up.

"If there really is something going on, I want to broadcast it on the news at noon," Balek expressed his not-so-wishful wish.

He missed the noon broadcast, but the wave of information about the bank's forced corporate governance and the arrest of Rolnik and his deputy were already making its way around the newsroom. Everyone bombarded Vitas with questions about what was happening. He had no answer. Nevertheless, he set off with his crew to the bank, which was completely surrounded by police officers clad in black head-gear. Wherever possible, he scanned for information. He didn't get back to the newsroom until thirty minutes before the main news broadcast. It had all been true. The morning mystery wasn't uncovered until after the news, when the spokesperson for the Czech National Bank came into the studio for a special interview.

"Where is the editor, this Vitas?" he called as soon as the production team led him through the tourniquets of the main gate.

"Mr Editor, you have unbelievable information," he grinned at Vitas, his arms spread out, as if they were child-hood friends. "The whole banking world is entertained by your information. You've caused uproar. First of all the managers at the bank laughed at that red herring you called in, but five minutes later, armed officers burst into the bank, and arrested two men. Mr Editor, my hat's off to your deep foresight. I'd like to see your crystal ball," he chortled uncontrollably, going straight through to the studio, to the chair, confessing to the moderator why the Czech National Bank and a team of police officers had put the axe to one of the biggest financial institutions in Czechia.

– – –

Eva left her home to pick a few mushrooms for the soup. There was a small pond not far from her house, where she knew she'd find some good ones. On the outskirts of Prague, the place was so idyllic it was almost unbelievable. She herself had been the one who taught Vitas to pick mushrooms back in Cheb. The untouched landscape by the German border, a restricted area during Communism, was a haven for mushroom pickers. Vitas would watch Eva dash by, her basket filled, while in his own basket he had only one or two cracked mushrooms. But over time he became so involved in mushroom picking that even when working on some hectic investigation, he'd swish through the woods with his phone to his ear, snapping his fingers, showing Eva the white mushrooms that were now popping up everywhere before him.

"How can you be on your phone in the woods and delegate tasks at the same time?" she reacted, angry at his disgraceful finds.

"It's the other way around – I'm picking mushrooms while at work. That sounds better, right?"

In truth, mushrooms were a central theme in their meals, especially when times were harder and Eva was on maternity leave, not earning a penny while Vitas raved on in his manic dreams. That was back in 1986, when Chernobyl, the nuclear power plant in the Ukraine, exploded. Since that time, Vitas liked to say that Chernobyl saved their lives. Although Cheb stands around 800 miles from the source of the fallen radioactivity at its epicentre, Vitas would bring home basketfuls of mushrooms every day, all of them, thanks to the new radioactivity, popping up everywhere like burst springs in a sofa.

Mushroom-picking really meant a lot to Vitas. Above all,

the woods were a form of relaxation for him, where, briefly, time stood still.

– – –

"Are you the editor Vitas' wife?" a sharp, arrogant voice pierced the divine peace by the well, where Eva was just plucking a mushroom.

Jolted with fright, she turned around. She was surrounded by three men, who she recognised at once. One of them was holding a large professional camera on his shoulders and the other, the very young fellow, was holding that long rod that she knew from her husband's slang was called a boom pole. There was a "zeppelin" at the end of it, the cylinder covered in fur, used to protect the microphone from the wind.

The third man was standing right in front of her with a defiant smirk on his face. Although she hadn't met him personally, she knew it was Pozounek. He had both his thumbs thrust in the pockets of his jeans, his fingers sticking out. He stood on the grass, legs slightly apart, swaying gently from side to side, and squished a large mushroom with his left heel. He didn't step on it directly; he only crushed the cap and the thick stem, just scratching it, bending it into a crippled angle.

"What're you doing here, man?" screamed Eva in place of an answer. "You're stepping on my mushrooms!"

Pozounek backed away startled, immediately resuming his sovereign stance. He hadn't expected a reaction like this. "Are you the wife of that oh-so-easy-to-bribe journalist, Vitas?"

"I don't know what you're talking about, but you can get out of here!" Eva said abruptly. Having lived with Vitas for many years, she knew that the best thing to do in a situation like this was not to say a word. Don't say a word. DON'T

SAY A WORD! No matter what. Don't let them get to you. Instead, she simply picked some two or three more mushrooms before calmly heading home. That is, on the outside she appeared calm. Inside she was dreadfully shaken-up, but didn't let it show at all.

"Hold on ma'am, hold on," the entire crew pivoted and followed her. "This awful house belongs to you and your husband, Vitas?"

This of course was said only to provoke her, but she withstood the pressure, not saying a word.

"What was I to say to him?" Eva later complained to Vitas. "That as a family, we were looking for a place to stay in Prague, but we had no money? That no one had ever given us millions because my husband is crazy, always setting his mind to something and going after it like a bird with its prey, and that nothing can stop him? That's the last thing on his mind, no one gets it…" Eva rose above it, and there was no bitterness. She accepted their financial hardship as the toll she had to pay for a life of intrigue and joy with a boisterous chap that needed a good grab by the ankles to keep him grounded.

The truth is the house wasn't all that nice. It was a small abode built back in the thirties. But at least it had electricity and real running water, with two rooms. Nothing special for a family with two children. No one knew that Vitas was preparing to renovate the home. Vitas had saved up some money and generously gave Eva 20,000 crowns to take care of the household. This would barely be enough for a few bricks.

Pozounek followed in Vitas' every footstep. He arranged to wiretap his conversations, had him followed, making himself a constant reminder. Sometimes, there was a "nondescript" car parked across from the semi-solitude of Vitas' front garden. Sometimes, he was delivered a letter with a blank piece of paper in it. Sometimes, they received a prank call from an unknown number. Bretislav also intensified his activities. Not a week went by that Vitas hadn't received a message from him.

"SO WHAT, SNIPER? WHAT YOU GEARING UP FOR NOW? DIDN'T YOU BITE OFF MORE THAN YOU CAN CHEW? IT'S NO LONGER WHAT IT USED TO BE... ARE YOU GETTING OLD? YOUR SNOOPING DAYS ARE OVER..."

What was perhaps more unpleasant for Vitas was that, in all his cases, Pozounek also followed in his footsteps. He was far from prepared to broadcast his report on the SAZKA betting company. He had a lot of information but nothing on camera. As a writer, he could publish it, but definitely not as a TV reporter. He had no illustrations and more importantly, he didn't have any key statements on camera. He still had to meet with numerous people, and in this environment, he somehow had to earn a living. He had no choice but to shoot other cases. But from the wire-taps and his other sources of information, Pozounek could discover exactly who Vitas wanted to "take down," then contact these figures himself and advise them on how to proceed.

It didn't take long before Vitas was instructed by the director of the TV station to work on the SAZKA BC case alone. Vitas' work became significantly more complicated.

Later on, after the SAZKA betting company affair, Vitas would wonder where Eva had put the money he had given her.

"And what were we supposed to eat, dear?" she laughed at him. I didn't want to say anything because I didn't want you to get nervous, but I needed money for basic household supplies..."

Kromen stepped up in a helpful way almost at once, like

a cork burst from a champagne bottle. He invited some of the founders of the *Bad Penny*, such as Rokos and the cameraman and another editor, to the SAZKA BC Gamblers' Palace Dreamland, where everyone hoped to hit the jackpot. He invited everyone except for Vitas, that is. The SAZKA BC was off limits for him.

Kromen loved theatre so long as he was the playwright, the director and the main character in the play. Unconditionally, the audience's applause had to be addressed to him. When the TV camera crew entered the building, they were greeted by the cold and proper prelude.

"Please put all your metal objects on the tray," said a security officer.

It was as if they were walking through the security checkpoint of an airport, but at an airport it's all quite normal, while here, it seemed completely unjustified. With all the cameras and stern eyes surrounding them, each of the guests felt as if this security frame would reveal their genitals as well.

They were chaperoned around the building as in a gallery. They were afraid to touch anything, tiptoeing around in their shoes, in awe of all the luxury. This was the intention. They were made minuscule, until they felt like ants visiting an anthill. No matter where they looked, there were employees standing on guard, motionless, expressionless. There was nothing human about them. There weren't even personal belongings on the tables. There were no pictures of loved ones, no diaries, no food, not even an apple or a yogurt, nothing. It seemed it didn't matter at all what table anyone sat at, after all, the pencils, keyboard and monitors were all the same at every seat.

"One second, gentlemen," Kromen addressed the people arriving from the TV station. He remained seated and didn't even bother getting up. Comfort ran from floor to ceiling, including the carpets, the furniture and the pictures on the wall. It was hard to tell if the cost was in the tens or the hundreds of millions. Rokos' bow drooped and his ego lay crumpled in a dark corner on the floor.

The representatives of shareholders were silently sitting like spectators in the dark behind Kromen. Like young boys three visitors stood by the doors, waiting for Kromen to finish whatever he was writing. Apparently, it was a prologue that was supposed to create tension and clearly show who was to play the main character, who would have the loudest voice, and around whom the world would spin around.

After two minutes of total silence, Kromen slowly closed his gold ballpoint pen, a mark of his old-fashioned tastes. He placed it ever so slowly on the table into a precisely aligned position, as if some kind of marking indicated this, and finally looked up at the people who had arrived. He clasped his hands, leaned way back into his chair and sighed: "Well, what are we going to do with you, you snoops?"

He shook his head in disbelief, seeming to regret the fact that he and his spectators had to waste their time on such nonsense, gesturing them to sit down across from him at the table. These ordinary chairs were in clear contrast to the surrounding luxury. This was all part of the performance.

"Well then, let's get right down to it," Kromen cleared the air and grabbed a large file that showed the name VITAS in capital letters. "Here's all the information on your Vitas. When and how much money he accepted as bribes and in which specific cases, his legal battles, his whims, his fetishes, his psychiatric diagnoses, and so on. "

"But come to think of it, this is really your problem. I will only pull this out if necessary, if you or someone from the Czech TV station doesn't come to their senses. Only then will it become clear who you've entrusted such a VIP position to, and who is this man with such public influence? "

"What remains clear is that you're attempting to harm sports associations and above all the athletes who depend on our activities. We help others win. This is more than some meaningless phrase or a catchy slogan. This is a fact proven by our annual reports. We invest hundreds of millions into sports every year, and you want to jeopardise these efforts because of your desperate colleague. How will you explain yourselves to them? What will you use to make up for the losses they'll feel?"

Kromen's monologue took over half-an-hour. The astonishment they felt at this incomprehensible and ill-intentioned meeting was interspersed with threats, and a realisation that their actions could affect the world of competitive sports, and worse still, harm the TV station, not only in the eyes of the athletes and the officials, but of the general public, along with the court verdicts that would result from lawsuits filed.

"So, the choice is yours," Kromen concluded his theatrical performance. None of the TV reporters, not even Rokos, had a chance to speak. Rokos felt like a balloon punctured by a needle, his life coming to an end with erratic flight and the usual sad deflating sound.

What could he have done? He wasn't as far into this case as Vitas himself. More importantly, Kromen's theatre was so impressive, that there was nothing he could argue against. The cameraman and the other editors were only here to take up space – they were only messengers, witnesses to the whole episode. Moreover, it was clear that Kromen would sweep every argument into a hidden nook. Surprisingly, the satisfied spectators, those semblances of shareholder representatives, did not applaud. Kromen's performance was so convincing and so impressive that he himself was grinning like a pre-schooler, amused to find that the pigs had fallen prey to the wolf.

The three representatives of the Czech TV station left the SAZKA betting company's building feeling that they'd just departed a sauna without a shower to cool them off. They left the wooden benches and that eucalyptus smell only to be driven at once out into the cold.

– – –

Behind his back, Vitas had no idea what was going on at the SAZKA BC. He knew that Kromen was up to something, but he saw no reason to fear him. Once the TV reporters had left Kromen's sauna, Vitas was off to see Petrovsky, who had recently been promoted to Chief Inspector, despite still preparing for his first career attack.

Vitas knew there was more to come; there would be a reason to keep the camera rolling in the coming days. His allies in the police force gave him hints, trying to imply the significance of the truth, without putting an end to the Investment Bank case. Unfortunately, his informers simply couldn't reveal any more at that time. It was early, and there could be no risk of evidence coming to light before its time.

Vitas was always tolerant in these situations. But now the ice was about to break. He knew he'd be the first one to get any insider information. His main concern was that since the footage and the deadlines were longer in journalism than in operations, the news would be brief and less interesting for him. He had no clear opportunity to get involved with the case, to reveal its many characters, its background information and its relationships.

Spring was in the air, all was in bloom, painted anew in colours of joy. It was a warm, balmy evening. Vitas strolled into the infamous Al Capone pub on Bartholomew Street. Petrovsky was already seated in the smoke and the mist of the dim corner, waving mysteriously towards Vitas.

"I have some exciting news for you," said Chief Inspector Petrovsky, with an air of superiority. "Ad A: we'll launch it tomorrow. As of yet, this is unrelated to the SAZKA BC. Now, it's only the real estate, the VAT and the various loans and scams. All over the country a number of figures will be arrested over the next five days. We plan to forcibly enter twenty companies, shut them down completely, seal them off and confiscate their computers for analysis. Ad B: tomorrow, we will also ask the Chairman of the Parliament to extradite three members of parliament for prosecution. That's the stuff!"

"Which ones, which ones?" Vitas asked excitedly.

"Tomorrow! Wait until tomorrow! Let it be for now, we can't spill it all just yet. You'll be the first to know."

"And the most intense spot: where? Kromen and Kostka in handcuffs, I'd like to get that on camera. How and where's it going to go down?"

To their surprise, neither of the conspirators clashed heads, as they bowed low, scribbling one over the other into Vitas' generous notebook. Petrovsky sketched the buildings and the entrances through which the police squad would make a forced entry, and Vitas copied the key points again onto the same sheet, but sideways. Times, places and names. Gradually, he glugged one beer after another. "Ahh, we can't get hammered today," Petrovksy said with a sad but conciliating look. "It's bedtime! Ad A: it's eleven o'clock, and Ad B: we have to be fit and ready in the morning," he concluded abruptly.

Bartholomew Street was all an orange glow outside the pub. The night's stars foretold the pleasant day of tomorrow, the fresh air blowing tight to the walls as both men felt the slowness that precedes all storms, the tension of unspeakable expectations. Raising their fists as if in ritual, they looked at each other, gave the thumbs up and went their separate ways.

This was the last time Vitas saw Chief Inspector Adam Petrovsky alive.

– – –

The next day at eight o'clock in the morning, Vitas steps into a small, but nevertheless luxurious building in Prague, District Four – Kostka's residence, where Kromen is to also arrive in the early morning hours. His cell phone is turned off, leaving him blissfully unaware of the calls that Rokos is assailing him with, trying to call off the camera crew and summon him to the office... By now Vitas knows already that things didn't go as planned for the SAZKA betting company, but he sees no reason not to film Kromen, when, he notes well, so far it has nothing to do with the SAZKA betting company.

The crew is ready in the car, the cameraman is holding the camera in his hands, waiting to hit the record button. The sound guy, too, is ready with his boom. But time is running short and nothing is going on. Kostka's home is silent with not a sign of life. He doesn't want to interrupt the radio silence that he and Petrovsky had agreed upon. They had laughed about such conspiratorial terms, more suitable for an operative of the CIA.

After an hour, he joins the bored crew, who obviously remain unaware of the situation. The sound guy flicks through the radio stations without thinking. "Only gossip, no music on any station," he mumbles, constantly pressing the buttons, looking for something better to listen to. Sometimes he hears buzzing sounds, sometimes squeaks, always returning to the news.

Vitas suddenly freezes. Sharply, he raises his hand palm-first before the sound guy's face, and snaps: "Don't touch!"

The moderator reports in a cold, absent voice: "... Chief

Inspector A. P. of the economic crime department was found dead in his office this morning at five o'clock. Evidence suggests that the wound was self-inflicted by his service-issue weapon. No evidence has been found to suggest suspicious involvement. An elite officer of the police, A. P. dealt with the most serious economic offenses. According to the spokesperson for the police department, there is an embargo on the case, pending ongoing investigations. Now to the weather. Sunny all day with showers coming in from the west in the evening…"

Kostka's home resembles a long-forgotten but heavily-adorned fort. Dead silence looms around it.

– – –

"You took on far more than you could manage," Rokos yelled at Vitas." "If I could, I'd put a stop to it. But, we were planning it and everybody knows that we've already started with the SAZKA betting company case, so where does that leave us?" he paced around the office in despair. The *Bad Penny*'s budget, too, cast a shadow between Rokos and Vitas. Though no one dared to mention it, bitterness and suspicion showed in the producer's eyes.

"What do you mean 'Where does that leave us?'? Shoot it," snapped Vitas, reclining in his chair. In some sense, he had already surrendered, anticipating another sentence, but he remained ready to fight. Petrovsky's death was still fresh in his mind. "But first, I'll shoot the police officer's murder."

"Do you have any proof regarding this 'murder'? Apart from your confession, of course, clarifying that you and he got trashed the night before and went on a pub crawl?" Rokos' grim eyes gazed helplessly at Vitas.

Nothing! The end! Period!

The head of the TV station decided to hold off, declaring that work on the SAZKA BC had been brought to a halt. "We didn't find anything ground-breaking or circum-stantial. There will be no SAZKA betting company case," declared the director of the studio on behalf of Kromen and his accomplice, Pozounek.

All surveillance and pressure immediately subsided. Celebrations were underway at the SAZKA BC and Pozounek's suit was worn out at the shoulders from the con-stant shoulder-patting he received.

"We did a great job," Kromen and Pozounek toasted with a glass of Cuba Siglo, one of the world's most valuable rums. "You deserve your eight million, but you'd be lost without me. So be it, athletes are generous and hereby express their gratitude," Kromen chuckled.

"But it'd still be worth trampling the louse a little more," he said in full modesty, proud of his sway, his abilities, and especially the fine print: "My services are unique and irreplaceable…."

In its entire being, the SAZKA BC building danced drunk with its blameless authority…

"Calm down! Don't upset yourself," Rokos told the impatient Vitas. "Let's go back to the SAZKA betting com-pany, keep working on it, but focus on the public and keep Kromen out. More importantly, no one can know a thing, or we're through."

"We need to give it to him!" Vitas said, hot with anger.

"Fine, soldier, as you like. But we've got to create an utterly inconspicuous and tranquil atmosphere. An illusion of peace and serenity," Rokos expressed poetically, waving his hands as if he were soaring above in the clouds. It wasn't until he had landed from heaven and looked into Vitas' furious eyes that he realised that it was the whip that would tame this fighter, not sugar "Don't be impatient. Tomorrow you'll be at the news meeting, where you'll be assigned a task. It has to be completely separate…"

"I'm not shooting any other case!" Vitas ground his teeth in frustration.

"Yes, you will. Yes you will or else you won't shoot anything anymore. If it were up to me, you'd be through with the SAZKA betting company case once and for all. Damn it, don't worry, you'll get the SAZKA betting company case back but back off for now. Can't you rise above it? I'll see you at the meeting tomorrow morning, nine o'clock!"

29.
Christmas

Christmas – the Christian holiday celebrating the birth of Christ. The Czech carp waiting to be bludgeoned over the head. Vitas could hardly bring that tradition to the monks, who would never harm a living creature. But the memories were as vivid as the light of day. The scales of the carp bring good fortune, and the scent of Christmas cookies… The intricate photographs of every Christmas past unfolded like cards within his hands.

Among the many monks, even the Lama had gathered in Vitas' sanctuary for Christmas Eve. Vitas had made arrangements with the chef to prepare certain sweets, which in truth would never pass the test in Europe.

Rmi-lam's eyes glowed as she stared at a tree that any Czech family would be ashamed of. But here, at the edge of the world, it looked astounding. She ran to open her present, wrapped in yak leather – a toboggan. Rmi-lam got a toboggan. Vitas made it himself.

Aviel got a gau, a necklace that was essential for every Tibetan Buddhist. Often a scroll bearing a prayer, or a symbolic object with personal significance, was contained within it, in the box hung around the neck. In meaning, it resembled a locket containing a loved one's image. This genuine Tibetan gift was in fact somewhat provocative for

Aviel as a Jew. But this provocation offended no one, least of all its recipient. Aviel carefully removed the folded paper from the gau and read the verses:

> Turn your back on the summits, the current will carry you on.
> The wind with its chaos of spirits wishes to weigh you down,
> Loosed free of their shackles, there, the nagas rise;
> Where they draw you by darkness, by lies,
> Peace, too, is long waylaid.
>
> Here is a codex. You look by courage, perhaps,
> Knowing nothing. The air, numb, gasps
> And the light's fires go starless. Darkness, once rare,
> Now the jurisdiction of vultures.

"We managed to decipher it together with Mhosai Mangcug on the rock by the path leading to the lamasery by the chorten," Vitas boasted, adding benevolently, with a hint of indifference: "If you want, you can put anything you want in there."

"Thanks," said Aviel quietly, taken aback. "We better get to the signs way down at the foot of the rock."

Vitas then spoke of the birth of Jesus and sang carols. The other monks tried joining in. At least they put the effort in, but it hardly dampened the mood in the least. But Rmi-lam didn't give them much room to contemplate, or for Christmas rituals. She dismissed everyone so she could try her present.

At first, she had no idea what to do with the toboggan. Outside it was growing dark. It was snowing lightly and freezing cold... Rmi-lam wrapped herself in the chupa, looking like a furry teddy bear. Vitas sat her down in front of him on the toboggan and went down the slope under the lamasery, while the monks loudly shouted on. Since the snow was powder fresh, they couldn't go more than three feet before getting stuck in it.

"You're too heavy, Chubby," Aviel yelled from the top. The other monks were roaring, whistling and clapping with glee.

After several awkward attempts, Vitas surrendered and allowed Rmi-lam to try it herself. "I'll watch you and you can try it on your own. You'll be lighter and it'll be easier." He pushed the toboggan so hard he fell face-first into the snow and everyone around erupted into laughter.

The toboggan went about ten feet, only to get stuck in the snow again. The monks waved their hands in despair. Rmi-lam kicked the snow angrily and began yelling that she wanted it to hold her.

"Just a second!" Aviel too. plunged in and with his fingers spread out in his furry gloves, stuck his hands out as if wanting to stop a freight train with his body. "We have to flatten the whole surface!" he called out in a decisive voice. "How many of us are here?" He counted one monk after the other with his finger, leaving out himself, Vitas, the Lama, and the honourable Tungjur, who stood some distance to the side. The peel of aristocratic seriousness and dignity had long torn away. "Seventeen! Seventeen of us. Go get the other monks, whoever you can find! We'll defeat the snow, we'll conquer it!"

The monks howled and ran into the lamasery. Within several minutes, they had gathered many of their brothers. Some were excited, others angry, distracted from their meditation or from other activities, but one and all accepted their duty to Rmi-lam. Some fifty monks dressed in dark chupas stood on a slope almost fifty-feet wide and a hundred yards long, creating a pointed contrast to the white background. Aviel had his work cut out for him, shouting and ordering them around.

"Quiet, quiet!!! Ok, listen! Form three lines one behind the other about fifteen feet apart, with about fifteen people in each line. Lay down horizontally in the snow, forming a straight line across the whole width of the slope. And everyone, grab the ankles of the monk in front of them. I said form a straight line! Not a wavy one! Ok, straighten out a bit more!" Aviel was furious, forced to shout so loud that his vocal cords began to strain.

"The first line will start. Hold on tightly to the person in front of you and turn!" commanded Aviel. "The whole row will start turning slowly, rolling the snow in front of the next. Then the second row... then the third!"

Within seconds, all three rows of monks were rolling around in the snow, creating a timid but hectic noise. Their chupas were strewn wildly, pieces of dark red cassocks visible in the white and black. They tumbled uncontrollably down the slope, powerless to control a single movement. Rmi-lam bounded on the spot beside Vitas like a spring burst from a mattress, screaming with joy: "Christmas's fantastic...!"

There was a fraction of time, perhaps some three seconds, when all three rows rolled successfully. Soon, the first row, or rather a few individuals from the first row, went a little faster. The consequences were then inevitable. The row twisted and fell apart, some of the monks no longer able to hold on to the person in front of them. Then, the second row crashed into the first and within seconds, the slope was full of desperately gyrating limbs, heads and bodies, the wings of fluttering butterflies trying in vain to fly away, colliding in the hope of forming a milky halo in the widespread snow. Although the snow was quite flat, it was littered with imprints and holes. Then they did it all once more, but carefully this time. The monks were no longer misled by Aviel's enthusiasm. But in any case, Rmi-lam was cheerfully tobogganing down the hill in no time and the monks screaming to try the slope themselves. Then they bartered with Rmi-lam. Anyone who wants to borrow the toboggan has to pull Rmi-lam up the slope. This was a good deal for both sides and everyone was happy. But the darkness was relentless, and gradually consumed the whole slope. Many monks withdrew to the lamasery for candles. Some of them also grabbed the much-needed chhaang. The wasteland, surrounded by demonic mountains, had transformed into a party, an oasis of flickering candles and human life. 'If there is a god,' Vitas blasphemed to himself, 'he must really be gazing down at us with great bliss right now. At something that cannot be explained, justified or analysed by formulas or natural laws…'

A toboggan, chhaang, the snow, the dancing, the carols… everyone revelled in the evening. Champa, a plump but good-hearted monk put a stop to the outdoor festivities. When he went down on the toboggan, everyone knew the end would be tragic. The plump monk lay in pain by the toboggan. Someone acknowledged the situation, saying: "As the greatest Chinese women far and wide, our Rmi-lam has the right to own her own eunuch!"

"Of course, she's our Empress," replied another monk. The idea evoked more joy, but Rmi-lam didn't notice the comment at all. Her attention was drawn to the pieces of broken wood, which had been to that point the cause of great entertainment. She was desperate. The Lama and Tungjur also failed to find this amusing. They stood in silence, hidden under the cloak of darkness, attentively observing the frolicking monks.

Darkness. Only the sharp outlines of the stars could scrutinise the events around the Jadhang. Everyone returned to Vitas' holy sanctuary, where they sang carols and Vitas spoke of the birth of Jesus Christ. Mhosai even came up with a poem, an ode to the new Empress. Rmi-lam and many others were having the times of their lives. Though everyone was drunk, it wasn't so much the chhaang, but the whole spirit of the lamasery, in which everyone created their own pencil-traced images that forever remained ingrained in the souls of the Jadhang.

– – –

The mornings after such euphoric parties are rough. The brisk air engulfed all local traces of the festivities that had happened the day before. Vitas didn't realise it was daytime until he opened the doors to his chamber. All the blinds are shut during the winter and with no clocks to hand it was difficult to tell the time indoors. The cold outside could penetrate the bones. Blackness. White. Vitas was afraid to stand for a long time, letting the environment affect his mood. He feared being engulfed by the silence and couldn't bring himself to surrender to it. He resisted the pull of his emotions, but became enslaved to them, letting himself be tossed around. He must leave. He shook himself off and went to see Rmi-lam. There was an eerie silence all around. It was as if he were in an endless cave, alone. He slowly opened the doors to the chamber, but Rmi-lam was nowhere to be found. The bed was made and even her clown was missing. No wonder – apart from last night's tobogganing, she never left without it. It wasn't unusual for Rmi-lam to hide out somewhere, so Vitas tried not to worry. He first went to see Aviel, who told him to leave him alone, that Rmi-lam was probably with the chef, or out playing in one of the many chapels of the lamasery. He dismissed the thought of Rmi-lam and passed through doors to brace himself with gasps of the crisp air. He wrapped himself up in a chupa and walked out into the silent whiteness, with only the shards of rock seeping through to his vision. He took a seat on one of the rocks, still one floor above the main open space. The hills, the rocks and the majesty of the mountain tops in the distance of the world had their own soul. They spoke and their words became messages written for Vitas in the snow. The messages surrounded him, and all was alive. Even the chorten seemed a living tenement, frozen in an instant of time, at the moment Vitas regarded it. Taking his eyes from the chorten, he wobbled onward. Footprints. Only now did he notice the many footprints in the clump of sparkling words right down by the main entrance to the lamasery.

He stepped down. Judging by the size of the footprints, it was clear that they were Rmi-lam's. Vitas had to laugh at the swarm of footprints, she must have been dancing. "Rmi-lam!" he called aloud in a voice muffled to protect the tranquil environment. Due to the low pressure, his voice travelled far. Nothing. No reaction. He couldn't bring himself to call out anymore, feeling the disturbance in the holy quietude. He examined the footprints and noticed that they ran along the side of the lamasery. He looked at them. They soon vanished somewhere among the rocks, passing the lamasery along the left and then passing on beyond to the top of the Jadhang. Mercilessly he crushed Rmi-lam's footprints with his large ankle-high boots of leather and fur. He felt like a misbehaving boy, stepping on grandma's carefully tended lawn of snowdrops. He tried avoiding them, but he enjoyed watching his and Rmi-lam's footprints together.

But his thoughts brought him back to reality. His nerves tightened, realising that he was tracing the ruins of a hermitage, formerly monk Tchao's abode. Tchao had long become prey for vultures and wild game following his death. He looked around attentively. The sharp rays of the sun, intensified over again by the purity of the snow, burned his eyes until he was forced to cover them with his hands. Rmi-lam.

He saw her. She was about fifty yards above, close to monk Sonama's hermitage. A furry ball, holding her inseparable clown in her hands, close to her body. He walked faster, trying to gain some ground, while keeping his eye on her, silent.

Rmi-lam was wading through, carefully sitting the clown down on the rock ledge, looking up at the opening that was wedged by a stone. The only opening in Sonam's hermitage.

"Hellooo!" she called out in a childish voice, banging her glove-covered fists on the rock.

Of course, there was no answer. She glanced around helplessly. There was no way she could have seen Vitas, he wasn't in her sight. Stepping in her footprints, he crept up on her stealthily, climbing a little higher than the hermitage, observing Rmi-lam's games from about thirty feet away.

Slowly, slowly, on her tiptoes, she reached the stone in the opening. She tried poking it out of the hole. Her fingers kept slipping, the eight pound stone clearly frozen to the rock. Rmi-lam exhaled nervously, poking until it shifted, but the fight was far from over. Although it trembled, it was still stuck in the stone. She tried grabbing it and pulling it out with her fingers, but her fingers kept slipping, only managing to move it less than half an inch in the direction she wanted. This slippery enemy must have been warm by now, as Rmi-lam began rubbing her fingers as if playing the harp, her fists motionless, only her clenched fingers shooting out, caressing the enemy, which contemptuously moved a few inches, fingers flying up from her fists, caresses, quick motions, caresses, quickly, "one," and a long "twooo…" Her persistent efforts were rewarded, the stone turned slightly, the centre of gravity was helpless, contemplating which side to favour, out, down or backwards into its nest. The pull of gravity favoured its nest, but the angry Rmi-lam poked it one more time, determined to get the eight-pound stone out. The stone fell hard onto Rmi-lam's desperate head. She gave a whimper and fell back into the snow. She saw stars and the world, a dark, fuzzy beast. Vitas made to leave his hideout to get to Rmi-lam, crawling towards the hermitage, but stopped on the spot. He realised that whatever happened in front of the hermitage was a private matter for Rmi-lam and shouldn't be disturbed by any adult nonsense. When he did walk a few more feet towards her, he hid himself so that Rmi-lam wouldn't see him.

She came to her senses quickly, got up and in a half-angry voice, called in the direction of the hole: "Hey, are you there?" She repeated her calls several times, while on her tiptoes, even trying to jump up. Still no response or at least nothing to be heard.

It was too high up for her. She looked around, all the angrier. She soon came up with an idea. She started piling up snow under the opening and every time she made a pile, she tried rolling it down with her body, the same way the monks did on the slope the day before. Her hands flew in all directions, but she remained completely silent, locked into her objective from which no one could stop her. Whenever she rolled one pile with her body, she then tried stepping on it. It collapsed beneath her slightly, but that didn't matter. She jumped and stomped all around, piling up more snow. She was as busy as an ant, making the ground beneath her higher. Then, she even started forming stairs. Kicking openings with her shoes and later using them to dig.

It didn't take long before she was squinting into the hole. The black, silent hole.

"Hellooo," she whispered into it in a long tone that matched the mysterious blackness.

"Are you there?"

Nothing.

"Are you dead?"

Nothing.

"Can you talk?"

Nothing.

"How are you? Isn't it cold in there?"

Nothing but long silence. One long silence. Rmi-lam had slowly gotten used to the dark but still couldn't see a thing. Her arms were spread out, elbows bent upwards, palms glued to the rock. Standing motionless, she looked like a shadow. Like the shadow of a person who had disappeared, with only his shadow left behind, which by the light-source, is monstrously distorted, shrunken and deformed in strange directions. Whatever the source was would be lost, only the shadow remains

"I have an apple for you," Rmi-lam suddenly burst out, removing a small pale apple covered in wrinkles from beneath her coat. This fruit was rare in these places, imported in the summer by caravan, along with various other valuables that couldn't be harvested there. She turned it in the light before the hole for a few seconds, as if waiting for the hermit to see it and then approve that this is the real apple he wanted. No reaction. She shrugged her shoulders and threw it inside. But she heard noises coming from within. Inarticulate, human hums. Only briefly. As if someone was trying to say something, but then gave up. Again, nothing but silence. But it was clear that there was really a human inside, nothing imagined or made-up. There was a real, living person within.

"You know," said Rmi-lam into the darkness. "You're here all by yourself, so I thought I'd make you feel better and come and talk to you." She paused for a moment. Then, she continued, but softly, as if only whispering to herself. "I came here not long ago and I am an Empress."

Vitas smiled to himself. He had no idea that yesterday's proclamation about the Empress would leave such an imprint on the youngster.

"You don't believe me? I can prove it to you but you probably won't be able to read anything inside there. I can't really read myself yet, just a little bit. And I can speak a bit of Tibetan and a bit of English. The monks here are also teaching me many other things. Lama Rinpoche is the wisest one here. He's extremely nice and has a special, slightly sad look in his eyes. But the other monks are nice too. The two Jingzhi," Rmi-lam started laughing spontaneously, "they're confused. They're funny, just by their look and their eyes… And sometimes, they know nothing, not even what I know. And sometimes they know a lot. But at least I have a good time with them."

She paused for another moment and then continued with a sad tone to her voice: "You know, I'd like to stay here now. Everyone kept dragging me around everywhere, they kept running away with me and I couldn't say a word anywhere. They tell me it's all a game, pretending to play hide and seek. But I don't want to keep hiding anywhere. I'm really happy here and I want to…"

The air cut through the hoarse sound of the ragdung so hard that Rmi-lam jumped back.

"Look, I'll come and talk to you again, but now I have to go to mass. Okay, and I'll bring you something again next time. Be good here."

Rmi-lam grabbed her torn clown, which was still sitting on the rock, jumped down from the ornately carved ridge and dashed towards the lamasery. Vitas continued to watch the hairy ball run down the slope and then slowly left his hideout, came to the hole, picked the rock up from the ground, looked at it thoughtfully for a moment and then placed it back into the hermitage hole, where it belonged.

30.
A List of the Dying

"So, what are we going to play today?" asks the head of the edition, Balek, responsible for the evening news. He is sitting at the head of the large, oval table together with the representatives of the local, economic and sports departments. The sports guy has apparently dozed off; his broadcast has nothing to do with this discussion. They have their own autonomous time but everyone's attendance is mandatory at the meeting. Sometimes, thanks to the topic, a sports event may make the headline news. Twelve editors, moderator Bradla and the editor-in-chief. There are also a few active editors present, who long to have their own initiatives heard. These initiatives alone are often more important than the result itself. Sometimes, there are even those who want to push through a fundamental case.

Vitas, who stares bitterly through the flickering monitors hanging from the drywall, is sitting slightly to one side. He pays no attention to the content, a collision of global stations such as CNN and BBC... The moderators and the actors pucker their lips for the news, for the sitcoms or for the soap operas, like jesters in an act. There is also a gameshow, a hockey match and even an expedition to the gems of the kingdom of the ocean depths. Several monitors flicker at different intervals, in varying rhythms, alternating with the greenish faces of the warriors of the seventh high-er-power, their grey-blue-white glow, enough to convince a clueless observer he's watching some reality show in an orbital station booth, where participants try to deal with the fact that their oxygen is slowly being depleted. The control room is a large, open space with many editorial booths separated by screens. The elevated pedestal is dominated by a studio intended for moderators and the ring takes up a relatively small area, generally speaking, intended for fights in the form of meetings like this one. It is partially open, so that anyone can join. It has a semi-soundproof wall made of feather plates and ordinary screens.

"Well, first of all," says Hermik, the head of the local column, "our investigator, Matousek has finally completed the report on Chemapol. He sniffed out where all the billions were siphoned off to, and that left Chemapol bankrupt. Even Andrej is involved, who now has control over the stronger, healthy part of Chemapol…"

"What do you mean CONTROL?" yells out Kos, the editor-in-chief. "What do you mean CONTROL? Didn't you hear that such words cannot appear in such a report? Control implies a pejorative connotation, a negation…"

"But the word is not negative," Hermik argues with the editor-in-chief. "Since he owns it, he has control over it, no? We can say owner, proprietor but not control?"

"No, but!" yells the editor-in-chief. "Look, this is not up for discussion. Take the recording with the report and come see me with the sniper after the meeting. We'll take a look at it with clear vision and foresight there. This is not censorship, it cannot be misinterpreted. It's fairness! Fair and responsible!" Kos tapped his index finger on the table like a woodpecker against a tree.

"We also have some nice accidents here," Hermik tries to salvage the situation.

"But we're not going to start with those," the editor-in-chief, Kos re-entered the conversation. "We are a public television station, not interested in viewership."

"Sure, we're not interested in it, but it's good to have," the head of the edition, Balek, is playing a dangerous game. "And then it can easily be interconnected with another phenomenon – we have footage of suspects leaving the crime scene..."

"Fine, that's not bad, but we'll throw that in somewhere at the end. Let's go to politics, this is ballast," the editor-in-chief glances in disgust. "But I just remembered – what's up with the shark loans? Is that ready to be aired today?"

"Yes, finished with that. It's more a phenomenon. How can people be so naïve and sign off on a loan that they'll never be able to pay while the lender remains well aware of this? Then, some legislation officers want to blame the lender because he didn't do a background check..."

"Do you have a specific person in mind?"

"I do."

"Oh, please," the editor-in-chief, Kos, interrupts the discussion again, "who'd go on TV saying he'd take out a shark's loan?"

"He wants to remain anonymous."

"No wonder. Fine, but make sure it's a true PHT."

"What else do we have?" Balek grumpily cuts off the subject. "I'm looking for something dealing with top politics..."

"Parrots," sighs Hermik.

"What parrots?"

"The EU committee has prohibited their import into the EU."

"And who's interested in that?"

"Then should I scrap it?"

"No way," Balek inconspicuously taps the editor-in-chief, in fear of perhaps deciding in his favour. "I didn't say 'no', I only asked who'd be interested in this topic."

"Maybe it's worth a shot, what with the whole H5N1 virus."

"Why didn't you say that in the first place?"

"Yeah, we'll run it," Kos interrupted the discussion again.

"It'd be great to launch that in the studio," adds moderator Bradla, "like for example, 'the H5N1 virus is returning to the Czech lands…'"

"No, that's too much," nods the editor-in-chief. "It's good, but we can't say it. Let's be specific. I don't know who'll do it, but have the editor assign it to someone, yes?" Hermik offers. "And on the contrary, we will dampen it, claim it only relates to a few drugged parrots, which we wisely didn't let across the border."

"Yeah, yeah, that'll be fine," nods Balek. "But really I'm looking for something dealing with higher political issues…"

"Geert Wilders has a meeting and a lecture in Munich today," he shouts out, disregarding everyone. He looks down plainly into his papers, partially sitting, partially lying on the chair, one leg over the other, the large notebook halfway over his legs and halfway on the table.

"Fine, we can run that, even if it's not related to Czech politics," nods Balek, turning to the moderator. "There's going to be something anti-Islam again, too. When moderating, don't forget to always emphasise the word 'populist' before the name."

"I'd have an important court trial," reports one editor, Ashley Mohelna, raising her hand as if in a classroom.

"Why are you discussing it here, Ashley?" Hermik cuts her off. "We made it clear at the local column meeting that it's yours to deal with, so why are you bringing it up here?"

"Wait, wait, what are you talking about?" asks the editor-in-chief with interest.

"I'm just worried you're going to air it somewhere at the end again and then it'll be put off till tomorrow," Ashley defends herself, almost tearful. "It has to be aired today because everyone will have it."

"Are you ever going to tell me which court case you're talking about?" Kos shouts abruptly.

"Today, the Municipal Court for Prague is going to make its verdict on who is the official owner of the Saint Vitus Cathedral and its adjacent properties," Ashley says in a squeaky, aggressive voice. "Whether it belongs to the Castle or to the Catholic Church."

"And so, who does it belong to?" asks Kos.

"That's what the court has to decide," explains Hermik.

"But WE already know the answer to that question, right?" Kos hums profoundly.

"We really don't," says Hermik. "The Castle and the Christian Church have been fighting over this for almost thirteen years now. The courts keep throwing it around like a hot potato."

"The thing is," Ashley whistles actively, "that the government issued a resolution in 1954, saying that the Saint Vitus Cathedral belongs to the people."

"Right, but it's only for tourists, not for the people," contradicts Kos. "And what are the clergymen going to do with it when they get it? Are masses even held there?"

"We should also check that out. Either way, tourism is a pretty good business there. We should find out how much it makes, too," adds Hermik.

"Fine, we'll make it headline news," concludes Balek. "It'll be the opening report. Don't forget to say something about its history. It'd be a good idea to get the president involved. Get ready for both options: that the Catholic Church will receive it and that it won't."

"Be careful," warns Hermik, "President Havel is off to Austria this afternoon. You better get hold of him in the morning."

"But there's no way this is a definitive verdict yet," argues Ashley.

"Figure it out damn it," the editor-in-chief sighs. "Send a decoy there in the morning and have him agree on two possibilities with the President, one for Option A and one for Option B. Make sure it goes over smoothly somehow…"

"And we should get an editor to cover the Metropolitan Chapter," says Hermik, "to get them to tell him what it means to them if they don't get it. And if they get it, what will they do with it? Will people have to pay admission and will they be biting off more than they can chew…?"

All the words became blurry for Vitas. He only had the SAZKA betting company on his mind and how to go about the case. How to find the right key? Kromen, Kromen, Kromen… How monstrous. The property case died down, as if it had never happened. The cops are dead or the team broke up. Everything is gone. And now, it's the SAZKA betting company! Will it all unfold the same way? Kromen, Kromen…

"What's with you, Vitas?" Balek growls. Vitas hadn't come to his senses until after Hermik grabbed him by the shoulders and shook him violently.

"Right, sorry, what's going on?" Vitas wakes up.

"Will you help Valikova with the report on Sovak?"

Without even realising how, why, or for how much, Vitas dashes over to little Valikova of the CTIS, as if he were her assistant. Although she is quite petite, her generous behind is as agile as a tank's. She waves her arms like a soldier during a march and has enough energy to spare. She is also rather conceited and especially now, she really lets Vitas have it because it'd be foolish to pass up an opportunity to lead a case.

"What is it that we're supposed to do?" asks Vitas indifferently.

"We're going to record the ones who will die."

"What? Can you be more specific?"

"You should have paid attention at the meeting."

"Well, don't let it get to you!" Vitas gives her a hard eye. By now, they're already at the doors to the CTIS. Valikova, full of courage, bangs on the door twice and barges right in. The terribly nervous and tiny Vitas slips in right behind her, inconspicuously, as if he wasn't even there.

"Right then, I need you to give me a list of those who're going to die."

Period. A simple sentence and seemingly, also a simple request.

Catherine, the head of the CTIS, comes over quickly, sensing trouble in the air. She gives Vitas a desperate look, but only for a second, only as in some secret code, but Vitas responds with the despondent look of a martyr. "Pardon me, what list?"

"Of those who will die. We talked about it at the meeting. Vitas could vouch for this, right? If he hadn't been sleeping here…" she kicks Vitas intentionally, who only slowly nods his head from side to side, his lips clasped tightly together. "… that Sovak, a famous actor, died, so one editor will do his piece. However, we arrived at the conclusion that it's worth having these cases prepared well in advance. That's why it's good to have a list of celebrities who we could interview on the camera before they die."

"But we don't have a list like that," Catherine defends herself, frightened.

"Right, right!" Valikova puts her hands on her hips, loosening one leg, transferring all her weight onto the other leg, shaking her head in disbelief.

"Really. Nothing like that."

"Well, at least the Czech Press Office has to have it!"

"They closed that down."

"I'm sure you can order it there."

"No, dear, they definitely don't have any such list there."

"Don't call me dear. They have to have it there. They'd be foolish not to have it."

"There's no way that anything like that even exists."

"Goddammit! Why are you hiding it from me?"

"We're not hiding anything," Catherine shrugged her shoulders helplessly. "There's no such list. We may only know of someone who is seriously ill, but it can't be written down on some list. We know that actress, Ruzickova is very ill, but no one…"

"So, Helen Ruzickova-aaa," Valikova emphasises the "a," venting her outrage, as if catching Catherine at the scene of a crime. "See, it's possible! And there's our first one! I'll make you talk!" she cackles with remorse and bitter satisfaction that even people from this department should treat her with such hypocrisy to withhold information from her. "Please, add another ten names to that list by tomorrow, at least!"

And so Vitas spent the day sitting in the TV station car with his crew and Valikova, who was constantly on his case. This made him think of how happy Cypros would be and what questions they'd ask Helena Ruzickova. 'Why do you plan on kicking the bucket? Give me a list of your illnesses. Are you in pain?'

It was a rather generous expedition, usually only undertaken with an editor and three other people, the cameraman, the sound guy and the lighting grip or the technician on occasion. Since this was a documentary piece on a Czech celebrity, they put in extra effort, seven people making the trip, including the producer and the assistant producer. But not everyone could fit into the truck. The camera couldn't be placed in the car, because it wasn't insured there. The camera had to be in another car that was insured but couldn't fit everyone. So, two cars set off. The interview with Ruzickova was arranged for one o'clock in the afternoon. However, the crew set off rather late and the TV driver went unbelievably slowly, pressing his foot gently on the accelerator, so that no one could ever prove that they were pouring fuel from this car into their own private canisters. No one worried about it, no one cared. They always found a reason for driving slow.

So, when they arrived at Helen's house at two o'clock in the afternoon, she was standing, waiting for them in her signature pose, like in the movie *Bad Joke* (which Vitas had never seen), with her legs apart and her hands at her hips. "What the hell's wrong with you guys?! I told you I'm only free until two. It's two o'clock now and there's a bus full of you no-goods like you're turning up at a summer camp for kids and you think I'm in the mood to tell you something? I'm going to therapy, so you can just turn right around and drive home!"

And so both cars just turned around and went back to the newsroom. Vitas didn't mind at all.

— — —

The next day was more pleasant for Vitas. This was because the court proceedings of a case surrounding Viktor Kozeny, an infamous Czech mobster who had siphoned off Harvard Funds, had to be recorded. They laid it on him at the meeting. At least it was his field of expertise. The bankruptcy trustee, the victim, the court with its independent attorney, and the case as a whole, was all filmed. Vitas had planned everything precisely, meaning everything went smoothly, including the expensive lunch that he accommodated for his crew at the cost of his time.

Vitas was going back to work, some ten minutes away

from the news station and almost passing it, when the driver suddenly stopped. He pulled out the newspaper and started reading. Undisturbed, the cameraman continued with his crossword and the technician stared through the window, utterly carefree.

"Fellas, what's going on, why aren't we moving?" Vitas whistled timidly.

"It's two thirty."

Vitas didn't understand what this had to do with anything. "That's a nice time, right? But I need to work on it…"

"We can't get back before three."

"And why's that? Guys, it went well, but I still have to prepare and edit it…" Vitas was deeply worried about meeting the deadline; apart from the other news reporters, he was somewhat "spoiled" by journalism, and the essentially unlimited time to prepare and put through further edits. The newsroom was very hectic and really tested his limits. He had to admit that editing a case down to a minute and a half was frequently more complicated than making a ten-minute journalistic report, where he could elaborate a little more.

"If we got back before three, production would send us out to another case," said the driver bluntly.

"So, just take me there and then hideout somewhere, I need to work on it…"

"No!" the driver whispered abruptly. "The production manager would see you and we'd be stuck. Don't even think about it."

Then Vitas waited in the car, absently perusing Bretislav's most recent brief envoi: "ALWAYS AN EYE FOR AN EYE…"

31.
"Once Upon a Time, There Was an Emperor..."

"Once upon a time, over 2000 years ago, lived a famous man with great merit. His name was Jing Cheng. In those days, China was plagued with constant battle and warfare. It wasn't even China at the time, but many small states and kingdoms that were continuously in combat. When one attacked the other, the third attacked the first, thinking that the battle had left the other exhausted. The fourth then attacked the third and so, the fifth blackmailed the fourth and once again launched an attack. War upon war alone..."

"It must have been one big mess," Rmi-lam grimly told the Lama, who was sitting at her bedside.

"Precisely. Cheng ruled over the peripheral state of Qin, the battlegrounds of tigers and wolves. The other states in central China despised and underestimated him. However, the people of Qin patiently conquered one mountain after another, one valley after another and one river after another, until they had conquered all of the war-torn states. This is how the Central Kingdom of China came to be. Jing Cheng took over the mandate of the Heavens and declared himself the title Shi Huangdi – the sovereign, the first Chinese Emperor. He was also given the name Qin Shi Huang. He established many beneficial laws and reforms. Once China was unified, he also unified its currency, its units of measurement, its wheel bases…"

"What's that?"

"The distance between wheels. This was of the utmost importance as it allowed the military, the messengers and the tradesmen to get from point A to point B more rapidly. The roads in different places were adapted to various carriages. They had their fixed tracks, which disabled the universal transport of one carriage throughout the whole territory. As a result, the previous means of transportation were very limited and complicated."

The Lama and Rmi-lam had a very special relationship. On the one hand, it seemed he respected her as a deity, concealing this from external watchers, while at the same time, he tried to raise her as a child. When they are alone together, he made efforts to treat her openly and with kindness, like a father. One of the reasons for this was his own lack of children. He had devoted his entire life to Buddha, isolating himself and hiding from the Chinese aggressors. Rmi-lam was having an effect on him, but once she was nearby, he was actually clueless on how to act. The result was a kind of uncertainty and embarrassment.

The relationship from Rmi-lam's side was similar. She had great respect for the Lama, but this respect was diluted by her girlish exuberance, the urge to disregard certain authority figures in order to disarm these venerable teachers in her longing for new information. Either way, the Lama was the only one to whom Rmi-lam paid respects, having seemingly little to no respect for the other teachers, such as Vitas or Aviel. In the end, they both treated each other like vigilant competitors, constantly spying on one another. Every action has its equal and opposite reaction, but in reality, neither The Lama nor Rmi-lam wants to be a competitor, being too on top of things, respecting one another too much and even liking each other.

Constantly gesturing, the Lama continued to tell his stories to Rmi-lam. Rmi-lam perched on the bed, leaning up against a pillow under the blankets, with her eyes seeming to be luring in one sentence after another.

"The first Emperor, Qin Shi Huang, ordered the construction of the famous Great Wall of China, one of the Eight Wonders of the World, and tore down the walls in the individual provinces, making it easy to get to potential rebels, as he wanted to prevent all his provinces from a possible revolt, which would divide China once again.

But the people still revolted, gossiped and complained, making the Emperor feel very sorry. He only wanted the best for everyone. At least that's what he thought. He didn't realise that in reality, he only wanted what was best for him alone, and simply needed the others to behave. He didn't like the fact that all the people criticised the current situation in comparison with the past. He didn't like the gentlemen, the noblemen, who constantly referenced their origins and demanded their privileges and honour. He was also bothered by the common folk, who danced and celebrated any and all divine and mythic personality but him. Most importantly, he feared that anyone could revolt, causing riots based on their former rights. Therefore, he decided to put an end to everything. He had all the archives and written documents burned, he had wall inscriptions covered up and renamed, but that still wasn't enough. The people still continued to think of the good old days, as it's normal to think of the greatness of the past. Then, the Emperor went to see a famous magician and asked him for help.

'I will help you, Emperor, but the only help I can give you is to rid the whole Chinese population of their Past. Is this what you want?' asked the magician.

'That's it!' yelled the Emperor. 'It's all the fault of the Past! If you get rid of everyone's Past, they won't be able to refer to it. The Past will no longer help them. It will not give them the strength. Therefore, everyone will be pleased with the Future that I am offering them, the Future they keep looking down upon. Yes, rid people of the Past!'"

'So be it. But I am warning you, Emperor, if you eradicate the Past completely, you too, will lose it. You only have to tame it, keep it by your side, pamper it and keep it hidden in your chamber,' replied the magician, winking at the Emperor slyly, fulfilling his wish.

The Emperor returned to his palace and rested contently, flirting with his Future, devoting everything his heart desired to it. Jewels, the rarest clothes, opulent delicacies… He drove all the concubines out of the palace so that the Future would not be jealous, saying that they belonged only to the Past, which no longer existed. The Present sat next to the noble, rich and jewel-decorated Future. The Present was dressed in simple clothes, thin and poor, almost invisible and untouchable. It was a mere breath, a semblance. The Present is only a fraction of time, which rolls over into the Past. If you don't say the 'Present', then it's no longer the Present. Most people look down upon it, and few can enjoy it. They frown, they fail to treat others with kindness and fail to enjoy the sunshine and long only for the Future. Therefore, no one notices the Present, all take it for granted and only treat it with ridicule. The only people who appreciate it are the sick ones, the hungry ones, and those who take joy in the intricacies of life.

But what happened when the Past disappeared? Lovers forgot they loved each other. In fact, they didn't even know one another. Children didn't recognise their parents. People went to work, but forgot where they worked. They didn't even know where to return to…"

"They forgot to say good night," Rmi-lam added to the story, "because they forgot what is good and what is evil."

"And so while the whole Empire was falling apart, people wandered like madmen, with no idea where they were, where they wanted to go, and what they wanted to do. Worse still, stupidity reigned, because they had forgotten everything they had learned at school and that's when the poorest one, the ragged and hungry Past visited the Empire to say: 'Please have mercy, noble Emperor. I am not wanted anywhere, I am invisible, no one hears me and no one knows about me, I am dying. If everyone forgets about me, I will pass away,' it begged desperately.

'Shoo, go away, sister,' called the Future. 'This is no place for you. Don't you see that the Emperor only has eyes for me?'

'Sister, dear, what will you do without me once I die? Nothing. You will have only a roof with no home to cover. A well without water, a fire without wood…'"

"Eyes without light," added Rmi-lam and the Lama continued in agreement: "Lungs without air."

"The lamasery without Buddha," Rmi-lam escalated.

"Yes. The famous Emperor interrupted the conversation, completely happy with his Future, wanting nothing to do with the Past anymore.

'Go away! This is no place for you,' he calls out to the Past, driving it out of the palace. He had completely forgotten about the magician's warning.

Then, a hunger fell on him and he called to the kitchen to prepare a meal fit for an Emperor. But the chef had forgotten how to cook, he had even forgotten that he was a chef and no longer had any idea what it meant to be a chef. And what's more, even the servants had forgotten the fame and glory of the first sovereign Emperor, the Lord of the Central Kingdom. And to no surprise, the Emperor didn't mind at all. Why?"

"Because he had also forgotten that he was the Emperor."

"Yes. Although he was completely satisfied with the beautiful Future that lay ahead, he had no Past, even forgetting that he was the Emperor. Even so, the Emperor did nothing but enjoy his Future and so the Future began to wither away, to fade, to disappear. The Emperor didn't realise that the Future was disappearing and dying right before his eyes. Since he had no Past, there was nothing to compare with the Future. Day by day, the misery increased, but the Emperor saw nothing. He began to wander the streets just like all the other people without a Past, not knowing why or where he wanted to go. Everyone met one another but no one recognised anyone else.

In the end, the Emperor lost his Future, too. It became the Past. And since there was no Past, it completely escaped his thoughts. And so the Emperor lost his future as a result of his rejection of the past. There, now say a prayer and off to sleep with you!"

– – –

Rmi-lam needed her daily dose of the world of fantasy in the form of stories, fairytales and liturgical parables, intermixed with different cultures. The Lama, Vitas, Aviel, and many other monks who were carefully selected by Tungjur, were responsible for this. In the evening, they would whisk Rmi-lam away to the world of elves, princesses and nagas, according to the story being told. Rmi-lam slowly acquired an overview of the most absurd fairytales in the world as told in numerous global traditions.

Vitas tried to recall such fairytales as the Golden-Haired Princess, Three Gold Strands of the Wise Old Man, Sleeping Beauty, and various others. Rmi-lam listened to the fairytale of the Emperor's New Clothes enraptured with fascination. She was ecstatic that everyone could be hypocritically amazed by the Emperor's beautiful gown, despite his being completely naked. The people who couldn't see it were idiots and no one wants to admit to that, not even to themselves. Of course, Vitas adapted all the fairytales to Rmi-lam. It was Rmi-lam who shouted out: "But he is naked!" This little girl's cry revealed the only, holy truth to everyone, breaking all the hypocrisy and falseness all around.

The language barriers were long gone. Rmi-lam learned English and Tibetan the same way that Vitas learned Tibetan, and even dug up a few Chinese expressions. If necessary, there was even an international mishmash in the "higher ranks," who spent more time with Rmi-lam. No one minded. On the contrary, Vitas found it very amusing when he began to speak the language he desired, using the expression that seemed most fitting.

Vitas' stay on the Jadhang was intensified by his sense of inner freedom. A strange freedom that surrendered the past, with the constant feeling of fear and the sense of responsibility for everything he must do. He abandoned worries over paying bills, over what his boss wanted him to do, over whether he would make it here or there on time. He abandoned the feeling of being imprisoned in Central Europe, where he was assigned an ID number at birth, branding him and imprisoning him for life. And the prison bars had expanded. He had had no choice but to go to school, to achieve good grades and maintain discipline. He would fear a police officer on sight, making him wonder what he had done wrong, when he was responsible for his career, his responsibility... the bars continued expanding and expanding, until they became a dense wall, for good and bad alike. And then in a single motion it all collapsed and he found himself on the open field, with almost all his sins forgotten and he felt as if he would soar. He could breathe freely, all of the barriers, saving only those that he had built himself, were gone. Despite his broken and unclear relationship with God, Rmi-lam made him aware of a certain understanding. He felt that there, he, Vitas, had a place in the world.

Only the tentacles of Chebness could sometimes draw him into the depths.

32.
D-Day for the SAZKA betting company

Several calm weeks let Vitas work steadily and help out more intensively at the newsroom. He got a few co-workers to assist him, so that all the work wasn't resting solely on his shoulders. Rokos, in the form of a bow-at-the-moment-of-firing, was dashing in all directions, coordinating the entire event. But after Kromen's purge, he was worried, weighing it all in the balance – on the one hand, he wanted to stand for success, but he was paving his way in the case of failure, throwing the responsibility onto someone else. In order to divide forces, the SAZKA betting company was not only prepared for by the *Bad Penny*, but at the newsroom as well. Rokos preferred steering clear of this. A series of shows were being prepared that were supposed to analyse this case from all angles, and in great detail.

"The plan is as follows," Hermik, the head of the local column said confidently, expecting no contrary opinion. "We will run all three episodes in one day. We have to do what the *Bad Penny* does, which broadcasts once a week, dissecting the SAZKA BC from A to Z. D-Day is exactly fourteen days from today and the *Bad Penny* will precede our show, making reference to it. Vitas will provide his information regarding the illegal business on the financial and capital market of the SAZKA BC to Bradla, who will then run it as headline news under Vitas' supervision."

"Is something unclear?" Hermik asked Bradla, who humbly shook his head. Although the central part of his role was moderation, he sometimes lent a hand as an editor, not wanting to lose credit or forget the basics of routine work. He nodded pleasantly to Vitas, as if to say it was no problem for him to help his friend and colleague.

"Vitas will have your back," Hermik reacted to one of the nonverbal expressions sent his way. "It can't all be up to him. The newsroom must introduce the whole SAZKA BC topic. It must hint at Kromen's illegal business deals, which allowed him to siphon off money from the SAZKA BC, leading to non-transparent management of funds and above all, to wresting control from the Ministry of Education."

"I'll take over the *Here and Now* show that follows the News," added Vitas. "I'll have time to do it because the *Bad Penny* will be finished by then and ready for the broadcast."

"Fine," nodded Hermik. "And what are you going to broadcast in *Here and Now*?"

"I'm going to analyse the severity of the sporting situation in precise detail within the context of the frantic and lavish spending of the SAZKA BC."

"Yes. Fine. Be careful, gentlemen, we have fourteen days," Hermik thrust out his index finger as a warning.

The tasks were assigned and everything was made clear. But Kromen drew attention to himself on the same day. There was no question that he, too, had people in the newsroom. After all, Kromen's information was only a few hours ahead of the official request from the TV station for an interview regarding the financial flow at the SAZKA BC. Information about a show being prepared, depriving the famous SAZKA BC, angered him.

"Where are your estimates???" he yelled at Pozounek, who was sweating, eyes gazing at the ground. "Where is your talent? Good thing the accounting department hasn't paid out the eight million yet. And you can forget about ever seeing a penny of it. If you ever want to work in this town again, get rid of the snoop, and use any means possible. Get a shot of him screwing some other woman, or pissing in public, or strolling drunk down the avenue holding hands with a child, I don't care what, but do something!"

Kromen stood glaring down on Pozounek, piercing him with his eyes. He leaned forwards, hands on the table. "Dammit, is that all you can do? Is that all you've got?"

"No, of course," Pozounek finally woke up, trying to put all possible authority into his words. "It's no easy job. I'll shoot a movie on him. In fact, it's already partially finished. We'll launch an ad campaign in the media and completely discredit him."

"And what do you want to do with the movie? Where are you going to play it?"

"We'll demand fair answers to any questions regarding the movie. We'll pay to have it broadcast on our competitor's stations…"

"You have my attention," frowned Kromen. "Now clear off. I'll be waiting to see the results."

A media battle commenced. There were full-page ads in all the major newspapers, in which the SAZKA BC warned the public against a disgraceful media attack launched by a psychopathic, incapable, potentially all-powerful TV station. Vitas was used to such accusations against his popularity, that even children would rank him lower than a poor starving wolf fighting a hare for a bite. Allegedly, Vitas was preparing to do something so immoral, worthy only of the meanest of the mean.

"Get set, athletes! This is the end of sports in the Czech lands! We lifted you to victory but the media and their madmen will defeat you…!"

It was D-Day. Vitas walked by his friend, the bricklayer, who was just putting up walls over the entrances to the new production manager's office. Each time he had torn down the partitions torn down so many times before, it became easier to fix the doors in place again numerous times. Vitas sprinted around the editing room like a fuse spinning over a pressure cooker, waiting to explode. He was assisting Bradla, while also completing his report for *Here and Now*, which was to air after the headline news. Sometimes, he ran into the CTIS to verify some information. Only formal information, as he was clear on all the details. But now was no time for errors, knowing as he did that every second would be subject to legal scrutiny.

"… so explain to me, how does he get it in there???" editor Becvarova said, standing like a conductor in front of all the girls at the CTIS.

Vitas was so preoccupied by his work that he didn't even think twice about the question he heard coming from the CTIS. "I need you to do something for me again," he asked his friends. But he stopped immediately, seeing Becvarova standing red-faced with her arms firmly poised, as if preparing to launch into a light three-four tempo. The girls from the CTIS, and though girls they were all women from twenty-five to fifty years old, were staring at the conductor, mouths wide open like children in a nursery class.

Eventually the conductor lowered her arms, her eyes lowered like some biblical virgin who had recently been asked for a wreath but had walked away in short steps without saying a word.

"Thank god you saved us, Vitas," Catherine clasped her hands.

"What's going on here?" uncomprehending, Vitas glanced around at all the girls of the CTIS.

"She came here half an hour ago and she hasn't stopped asking us horrible questions. I'm too embarrassed to repeat them."

"Well tell me then, or else I'm not leaving."

"I guess she's shooting something with a zoologist and she asked if a whale is really a mammal or a fish. And if it's a mammal then how do they do it? She's been bothering us with this for half-an-hour now. In detail! And what about the baby, does it have an umbilical cord and does the mother have breasts…"

"Girls, I'm really no expert in this field. There are some things in this world that are even too much for me," Vitas summarised ironically. Intoxicated by his "sports" cases, he switched the topic to verifying the exact names of the Czech TV executive committee, the majority stakeholder of the SAZKA BC.

– – –

A lively meeting was taking place in the office of the SAZKA BC director at the same time. The executive director of the Czech TV station was called into Kromen's office. Kromen, apart from "helping athletes win" annually donated hundreds of millions to the TV station for advertising and regular lottery broadcasts.

"You have a choice, Sir," Kromen raged in his pompous office. Kromen's articulation was so precise, that any lip-reader would be almost overjoyed by the ease in reading his lips. The hand gestures were theatrically direct, his fingers too, a part of the act, receiving a thorough manicure treatment by the day. "It's very simple. I will either broadcast ads and the lottery at your TV station, donating hundreds of millions to your corporation, or I will not. You can answer the question yourself."

The executive of the TV station, elected by the Czech TV Committee, which was elected by the parliament, which was elected by the people, could only writhe in agony, unable to give an answer.

"What is your response?" provoked Kromen. "You see, I understand. It isn't easy. But it isn't easy for anyone and sometimes, a decision must be made. And no decision is the right one, but one decision is always more right than the other. A simple question – how many people around you would you like to see disappear? The athletes? Yourself? Let me assure you that a series of lawsuits will follow. Or would you rather it be one deranged reporter, frankly fit for the psychiatric ward. Decide for yourself. Freely. On your own. But please, make your decision with sincerity. Make a difficult choice, but a choice that though not perfect, is without a doubt the one that is right."

During his monologue, Kromen's voice lowered to the voice of a father, teaching his son a lesson. He finally got up and approached the seated executive, seizing him by the shoulders like a pastor compelling his flock to divert to the rightful path.

He gazed directly into his eyes for a moment, then his vision focused, and he quickly removed his hands from the executive's shoulders, addressing him sternly: "And now, please see yourself out," he arrogantly dismissed the executive of a public institution from the office. "Some decisions must be undertaken alone, without external assistance. But should you make the right choice, you can count on my helping hand."

– – –

"...and you're going to summarise it with the police officer's testimony, saying he's handing it over to the state prosecutor to press charges," Vitas explained to Bradla.

"Absolutely, but we'd better summarise it again at the very end, so that it's clear to the viewer..."

"Alright guys, we're done," interrupted the production manager.

"What do you mean we're done? We have like fifteen more minutes," objected Bradla.

"No way, we're finished completely. We're not going to broadcast this," the production manager said flatly, emotionless, as he turned on his heels towards the door.

"What do you mean 'finished completely?'" both editors burst out.

"Orders from the editor-in-chief."

"And what are these orders based on?" Vitas snapped.

"How should I know...? Just clear out. I'm sending in Kreplik with an accident on the freeway involving an oil spill. This has to make today's news."

Vitas could only shrug his shoulders in surrender, half in reaction to the news and half to say goodbye to Bradla, who considered something for a moment, then stood up and said: "I have to get ready to moderate. There's nothing more I can do with this..." Vitas darted off to the editing room, where he had to finish a report on the SAZKA BC for the *Here and Now* show, which aired after the headline news, with a far more generous deadline and no need to rush.

Not fifteen minutes went by before the production manager returned. A single hand gesture was enough, like the felling of a tree. Sharp, vigorous, short. Snap.

'This is it,' thought Vitas, but refused the production manager's order. "We'll finish it either way, there's only a bit more left to do. We have to finish it so that we have some argument in hand, making it clear that the report was finished. And what's more, what if something else changes…?" he skipped past the production manager as if he hadn't even seen him, giving further instructions to the editors, his voice absent of its former confidence.

The square floorplan of the newsroom allowed Vitas to circle it like a lion in a cage. There was nothing more Vitas could do. He could only wait for the *Bad Penny* to air. The news was current. There was no way anyone would notice that something hadn't made it to the broadcast if no one had known about it before. The situation was different when it came to a major editorial such as the *Bad Penny*, something long scheduled in advance, pre-announced, with news reporters, athletes and the general public all eagerly awaiting the investigative report.

One hour before the planned broadcast of the *Bad Penny*, the executive director of the TV station pressed the red button for the third time. Of course, something had to be broadcast. But there was surely a dark sense of humour and a twisted irony in broadcasting the Intolerance Show, instead of the *Bad Penny*.

'That's the end of it,' Vitas said to himself. He headed home, utterly submerged in the rising tide of Chebness.

33.
Sonam's Laughter

The bright sun rays began to dictate nature with its merciless conditions. The snow respectfully left its territory to the rocks and started to reveal their forms, shyly at first, but then quicker than ever. Pink rhododendrons blossomed, as if in a fit of madness a drunken fairy had danced and tossed her flowers in all directions, though they had once been saved for her nesting place. A flock of butterflies, accustomed to the high altitude, flew around carelessly. Long-tailed marmots whistled to their rhythms, perfecting the whole performance, curiously peeking out of their sandy dens, accompanied by the sheep and goats that roamed around. Air filtered through the lungs, stirred up the mind and its piercing scent aroused the desire to move, to eat and to live. At the bottom of the Jadhang, near the stream of the Jadhang Gad, the animals seemed grateful for the abundance of food. The first monks set out to the stream to pan for gold, which they later bartered for food and goods that couldn't be made or harvested at the lamasery.

Many celebrations had already taken place in the lamasery, including Losar, the celebrations of the Tibetan New Year, which, according to the Gregorian calendar, fell on February eight through to the tenth. It was the year of Earth and the Mouse. Aviel also took care of the Jewish feasts, which were, just like Vitas' Christian feasts, only a peek into their respective exotic worlds. Everyone respected the spirit of the Buddha, which dominated in the lamasery. Buddhism guaranteed a special tolerance towards all other religions. But Vitas realised that attempting to open up the world in its entirety to Rmi-lam played a more important role than tolerance.

The caravan was preparing to set off on its expedition into "civilisation" for its first shopping trip. Lao PuWei, the monk who had brought Aviel and Vitas to Jadhang six months ago, was giving loud commands to his entourage. There was a lot of confusion and chaos, but everything was resolved with a smile, as spring brought everyone to life. It was expected that the caravan would return in fourteen days.

Several activities were moving from the inside of the lamasery into the wide-open space. Everything from the large wheel of life on both sides of the lamasery to the prayer wheel was spinning with far more fervour.

"Kushok Vitas and Aviel," Wung Pien addressed both friends just when the outdoor activities were reaching their peak. "You have a strong influence on Rmi-lam. Could you please tell her to leave Sonam alone?"

"What do you mean leave him alone? What is she doing to him?" Aviel asked, not understanding. Vitas was silent but had a pretty good idea what had happened.

"It's extremely strange. I noticed that someone has been going up to Sonam's hermitage, probably to give him food or I don't know what. So, I hid out there for a while and then discovered Rmi-lam. She brought some fruit or vegetables and then continued to shout into the hole. Monk Sonam has passed on to the highest form of meditation, therefore it is impossible for him to be disturbed. His experiences are beyond his body, his soul is highly sensitive and then this girl starts shouting at him. That cannot be permitted!"

"Does Sonam respond in any way?" Aviel asked curiously.

"It seems he does not, but the truth is that sometimes he doesn't even notice the bowl, while at other times, he smashes the bowl against the rocks, as if for the first time he was asking for a second course! This cannot be permitted!" Wung implored unhappily.

"I wouldn't even worry about it," Vitas tried to put the situation to rest. "How do you know what's best? How do you know that Rmi-lam isn't supposed to be a kind of awakening or who-knows-what for him? Try telling her to stop doing it. We'll see how she reacts, but I strongly doubt she'll agree to it."

"I'm not going to tell her to stop it! She'd pose her most inquisitive questions: why, how, for what... and who-knows-what-else. I'd end up losing my nerves and slapping her."

"Don't even think about it! You know that the Lama forbade any physical punishment of Rmi-lam."

"I know, I know but try it yourself..."

"And what about going to see the Lama?" Vitas interrupted Wung with a saving expression. "We'll see what his take is on the situation."

"That's such a good idea, it's almost as if it was mine," Aviel acknowledged Vitas "We'll try it at the next kashag meeting, what d'you think?"

"Alright, that's in a few days. But if something happens to Sonam before then, the girl better watch out!" Wung Pien waved his hand furiously in farewell.

Four days went by in what seemed no time at all, but Rmi-lam's visits to Sonam certainly did not stop. Although she didn't go see him as often as before, only once a day instead, the truth is, as Vitas sometimes observed her from afar, he did see that Sonam had begun to communicate with her in some way. It was undoubtedly very brief, because Rmi-lam spent most of her time by the hermitage talking and talking alone. However, it was clear (impossible to hear from the distance) that Rmi-lam was reacting to something. Once, he even saw her dancing in front of the hermitage. Happy, glowing. The glaring mountainous background lay behind her, dark blue with its sharp sun-rays. It was as if the sun itself was bestowing onto her its divine spiritual energy.

On the day of the kashag, Wung approached his Jingzhi in a hurry. "Kushok Vitas, Sonam sang today! Imagine that! He was really singing! It was more of a scream, but he was definitely trying to sing. That's it! Something has to happen right away, someone has to tell her to stop doing this. The question is whether this can be stopped or whether it's already too late."

"So he was singing, so what?" Vitas shrugged his shoulders amicably, making Aviel laugh with his irony. "What's wrong with a person singing? We sing and laugh here all the time, so why can't he?"

"But that's against all the rules! What of his promise to lead himself onwards to the state of the bodhisattvas? Where will his attempt to redeem all living creatures end??? What would the all-knowing Buddha Amithaba think?"

"No God can object to laughter and song. This is no tragedy. Kashag is today, so let's ask the honourable Lama Rinpoche."

And that's what happened. But the kashag was surprisingly brief. Po Wung emotionally described the situation with Lama Rinpoche, who looked around at the others and briefly asked everyone: "DOES ANYONE mind?" The question came across as something of a threat and no one in the kashag dared say anything against Rmi-lam's activities. "Our task is to broaden her horizons. Present her with the most knowledge and wisdom possible. Show her all the points of the human moral code and teach her to understand it. But what she does is up to her. You are here to guide

311

her, not to intervene with how she uses this knowledge and wisdom. Is that clear?" he concluded strictly in the tone of a professor. "I don't want to discuss this any further."

And so Wung was left to deal with this problem on his own, like a pole in a fence. In any case, he decided to not worry about it. He would take the bowl with the meal, come to the hole, bang the bowl against the rock, and let the monk know that his meal had arrived, before leaving just as quickly. Sometimes, at something, to someone, Sonam howled within the depths of the hole, as if trying to communicate, but unable to form a single word.

"Kushok Vitas, he wants something but I don't understand him," Wung said nervously upon returning from the hermitage.

"Go get Rmi-lam and she'll translate it for us. She will definitely understand him." He picked Rmi-lam up from Aviel's lecture, who of course accompanied Rmi-lam to the hermitage.

"Hey," Wung shouted grumpily into the hole. "What did you want?"

Vitas and Aviel rolled a larger rock under the hole and lifted Rmi-lam onto it, so that she could poke her head through into the space.

There really were some sounds coming from within. A humming, a grunting, a mumbling, a sound like a drunken man asking the way home.

Rmi-lam turned to the three men and said: "He wants to know what year it is."

"Tell him it's the year of Earth and the Mouse," growled Wung.

Rmi-lam said it and Sonam reacted with a roar.

"He has been very close to God on several occasions and he says that I was the one, who screwed it up," Rmi-lam said proudly and cheerfully, "and that now he thinks he deserves something better than this pigswill. So, he wants a hearty meal."

Wung raised his hands in desperation, as if he wanted to catch a ball from the divine clouds, rolling his eyes to the heavens. "This is truly the end for all the gods. Sonam is distancing himself from the most divine Buddha and he was already so close to nirvana, so close to fulfilling his promise," shaking his head sadly, he made his way back to the lamasery.

Vitas, Aviel and particularly Rmi-lam, who had special rights in the kitchen, took care of an exceptional change in the monk's menu. The mumbling and loud chewing that they heard emerging from the blackness of the hole were the only signs of gratitude.

34.

A Victory Lost

There was a media whirlwind the second day following the broadcasted report. Not only did eager viewers react, who had expected an earthquake at the SAZKA betting company, but journalists also had their say, having been prepared for all possibilities. Kromen and the director of the TV station had touched upon the holiest of rights regarding the freedom of information. The word "censorship" was used in all its forms. Vitas was answered everyone. The affair was subject to media coverage for several days.

Kromen fired Pozounek, who could only helplessly wave his arms. He had one argument left up his sleeve: "He's either a psychopath or a bribed news reporter. If you look at his lifestyle, you'll get under his skin, the first option has preference…"

— — —

In the morning, on his way to the newsroom, Vitas caught a glimpse of the news headlines on the bus and subway. The SAZKA BC made headline news everywhere. He however, had no idea what would happen. He stood behind his work but wasn't sure if the TV station would back him up. Rokos, standing firmly upright, facing Vitas and ready for combat, and Bozik from the NBM, were both waiting for him in Rokos' office. The NBM was a means of money laundering for the Czech TV station.

"I have no idea how this will all turn out," Rokos forecasted gloomily. "We're meeting in an hour, but I don't like it. I don't like your aim. You're a sniper with no idea if he's loading the weapon with real bullets or fake ones."

"You know all too well I'm right," Vitas said quietly through his teeth.

Rokos laughed. "Of course I know you're right. Now I don't know what exactly you have in mind because we're working on more cases. Real estate, the SAZKA BC, and then us, right?" he said, ironically emphasising the last syllable of the sentence. "You know, there are so many truths in this world. The truth is that I feel like an honest person and you see me like a fraudulent person, preventing the truth from being revealed. And maybe we're both right. Have you ever considered that?"

"I don't understand you. What truths?"

"Are you after us?!" Bozik interrupted the dialogue.

"What do you mean, after you?"

"You're stalking us and you're out to get us," claimed Bozik.

"Bullshit… All I want is high quality reporting. We can't save money on that…"

"You're out to get us and we're going to keep an eye on you," Bozik snarled. Rokos swiftly moved to a different tactic.

"By the way, while you're working on some fabricated phantasmagoria or other, we have to broadcast something, Mr Playwright, Sir. Well, your colleague, Budil started working on one beautiful case that we approved for him. It's already in the editing room."

"I see, so this is how you bypass me? The SAZKA BC has

precedence now, right? What's in store for it next?" Vitas refuted uncertainly.

"We're not bypassing you at all, but the Ministry only deals with large, breakthrough cases. He won't be interested in some small trifles. The SAZKA BC? The management will be discussing it soon." Rokos suddenly raised his head like an actor at the moment of proclamation, arching his eyebrows, continuing in a sarcastic voice. "Aren't you even going to ask what the case is about?"

"Or rather, who it's about?" added Bozik with a pompous, conceited smile.

"Alright, who or what is it about?" asked Vitas, who could feel the very ground quake beneath his feet.

"About Blikotka. A successful, exemplary businessman, who saved a lot of real estate from redevelopment," nodded Rokos reproachfully, implying that Vitas should have done this a long time ago instead of broadcasting about him in reference to re-financed real estate, banks gone bankrupt and dead chickens.

"Apparently, he breeds the chickens in a very humane way. Experts from abroad come to study his breed. Allegedly, he lets them watch television and their meat develops excellently," Bozik laughed, clapping his hands on the back of the chair.

"And apparently, they prefer country music and hate drum'n'bass," added Rokos with the same laughter.

Vitas left the room without saying a word. The next day, his identity card for entering the Czech TV station stopped working.

– – –

The original was broadcasted one week later. It was about the siphoning off of money from the SAZKA BC, about its golden faucets, athletes who lacked the funds they needed to survive, about the helplessness of the Minister of Education, who could only wave his hands in desperation, saying that he no longer had the energy to change the legislation with regard to the SAZKA BC, about the outrage of the Minister of Culture, who saw the SAZKA BC as a milked cow, in which only a few individuals were getting the milk and those who should get the milk in a glass, were only swallowing water from a puddle. It was also about paid shareholder representatives, some being generously paid by Kromen, while holding important political posts, about lobbying in the Parliament, for which the SAZKA BC secured the finest lottery laws... About the arbitrary rampage of one man, who held enormous power and money in his greedy hands...

Kromen was furious, raging, rebuking all traces of Vitas, the Czech TV station and the *Bad Penny*. "I will destroy the *Bad Penny*, I will destroy Vitas!" he yelled out to everyone. But to begin with he filed two lawsuits against the Czech TV station because they had broadcasted the report. He entrusted the lawsuits to the hands of several renowned legal offices.

The TV lawyer, Berger, took the stage. He was in a completely different class to the regular lawyers in the legal department, who were renowned for their losses. Berger and Vitas spent several days in interrogation and analysis. Vitas continued to talk and introduce him to his secret and known sources. Berger only asked abrupt questions and took brief notes.

"You've really done your homework," Vitas patted him on the back at the end. "I'll be happy to go into this dispute. It'll be interesting."

It wasn't really all that interesting at all. Berger did what any lawyer would do. He challenged a wrongfully filed lawsuit, wrongful formulation, incorrectly used Sections of the law, and incorrectly closed doors to the courtroom… He completely ripped apart the opposition's lawsuit on grounds of fundamental mistakes. So elementary were the mistakes that Vitas had to ask himself whether the renowned legal firm had been ordered to make them, to lose the case on formal grounds, rather than lose on the grounds of merit. Berger simply smiled and shrugged his shoulders ambiguously. Kromen withdrew the other lawsuits.

It seemed like victory was at hand and Vitas could cross another success from his list. He could definitely cross it off, but a victory wasn't certain. He stopped working for the *Bad Penny*, which had been his base and headquarters for many years. What would he satisfy his energy with now? He needed to release his emotions somehow, in order to achieve mental balance… Although the newsroom granted temporary refuge, it was never fully satisfying, being dry and brief.

But it was far from over. The director's chair was unstable and he fell flat on his behind on the cold, hard ground soon afterwards. That was the end of him.

One would expect a revolt at the SAZKA BC, but that wasn't the case. The representatives of the SAZKA betting company's shareholders were paid well and remained silent, the wind blew in the same direction and pears still fell to the ground.

Kromen played possum for some time following the scandal. He could only wait for another affair to headline the news, so the viewers' attention was drawn to something new.

"What were you thinking, you naive fool?" Bradla laughed at Vitas in the newsroom office. "Did you think you'd take the SAZKA BC down, or what?"

"What do you mean, 'take it down'? The athletes

should have demanded justice and taken Kromen down themselves."

"You know what?" Bradla raised his index finger vigorously. "Let it be. I will introduce you to a very interesting person. I think he'll impress you, and open doors to a completely new world. What are you doing exactly one week from now? Let's get together at three o'clock at the Meet-You-Halfway Café, it's not far from here, near the park."

"… I know where it is. What's it all about?"

"It can't be described so easily. You have to get to know him personally. Well then, deal?"

"Fine."

35.
Movie Night

"Ahhh, dignified father, this is an honourable temple of God..." a very familiar and ironic voice resounds, with a certain degree of arrogance, pride and conceitedness. Vitas turns to see a dark figure standing up against the light in the dark room. There's no mistake. Kromen.

"What brings you here?" he greets Kromen with amazement. Earlier, Vitas had thought he did the right thing in running away from himself into a place, where he would find Kromen. After his departure from the lamasery, he knew that this was probably the best choice. He saw no other option, even if Kromen were to be here permanently, which he hoped wouldn't be the case. Either way, Vitas had to reap his own rewards, cut off from Kromen. He had wanted to isolate himself and more importantly, not to allow Kromen to push him into any spiritual or mental states.

"Can't say I hear joy in your voice," frowns Kromen, kindly patting Vitas on the shoulders. He steps inside, looking around at the decorations in the room. "I see that you made a few changes here. I had no idea. You're too masculine for this spiritual world. I'd never have thought of you in this light."

"Thanks, I'll take that as a compliment, while you seem

to be a constant that won't change relative to any variable," Vitas returns the irony on Kromen's behalf.

He looks at him inquisitively. "And that probably was no compliment on your part, but I'll take it. How does it work here? I've even heard of big changes," Kromen quickly changes the subject. "You've even thrown out your marbles and become nannies despite your age."

"You could probably put it that way. But I think it's changed the development of the lamasery for the better."

"What does 'for the better' mean? I've heard a lot about it and you must all have really gone mad." After a brief look around the room, Kromen takes a seat comfortably by the table, also used as an altar, and gazes at the golden cup in awe. "I got in touch with the caravan and came with it. I bought so many things I needed three yaks just to carry my load, including things for your Empress, as you refer to her: ha ha."

Kromen's laughter has no effect on Vitas. "I even brought a computer," adds Kromen a bit less seriously now. "A laptop." Am I good or what?" He didn't wait for an answer. "And a projector. I'd like to run a short presentation here for you."

"I'm not sure it's a good idea to introduce something like that here, and where are you going to get the electricity?"

"Don't worry, I've thought of everything."

"And what about you? Where have you been? At home? How's life in Czechia?"

"I'd say a lot more normal. It's no longer what it used to be in the nineties. It's boring. They exaggerate every case, the laws don't work in the people's favour, there's hatred all around, everyone wants to punish everyone else… Ha, well, I think you get what I'm trying to say," he points his index finger at Vitas wickedly. "They upset me so much in six months that I was truly looking forward to seeing you."

"And what about the treasure? Have you had any luck?"

"Yes, that's what brings me here. The answers to all my questions lie here."

"And you think you're going to get all your answers here?"

"Firstly, yes, I think so. And secondly, despite the apparent poverty here, this is a land of wealth. You've seen how much gold there is here," he toys with the valuable cup, weighing its importance. "And that ring the abbot handed me could feed you and your whole family in Czechia indefinitely. Here, it's only for you," Kromen begins to laugh, placing the cup back on the table, getting up and heading out the door. "I'd need something more... Forget it, I'm going to go look around, I'll go see Aviel. I assume he's gone mad, just like you. Then, I will get ready for the abbot. I have to find the best opportunity in the upcoming days and take advantage of it. So, have a great day..." Kromen raises his fingertips to the side of his head like a soldier then sires them upwards. On his way out, his back facing Vitas, he adds: "Don't forget about the party this evening..."

Kromen spent the whole afternoon hooking up the electrical device. His friend, Lu Cheng, the butcher from the pastures of lower Jadhang, lent him a hand. Over and over he muttered that he would help to improve the local culture and civilisation. There was a swarm of curious monks all around him, who were so captivated by Kromen's gadget that they forgot to spin the prayer wheel.

Kromen had to use two yaks to transport all the things necessary to develop the monk spirit. He installed five "semi-bikes," more like the parts of a bicycle or stationary bike which ran on electricity, in the basement of the lamasery.

"I wanted to bring solar panels, but I had a feeling that the illiterates would break them here, then peddle them off. We have to get twenty-four volts into this projector," he shouted. "If one dynamo can make around six volts, then five monks should have no problem creating twenty-four volts, even if one monk slacks off."

He summoned Aviel, the former IT expert, to be his professional consultant. But Aviel was very sceptical about the entire concept of the projector. "While I'm sure you've calculated the number of volts precisely, you need more power, more watts. I doubt you'll get more than a-hundred-and-twenty out of the bikes…"

"Stop complaining all the time," Kromen interrupted Aviel, "and stop explaining why something isn't working. Try doing everything possible to make it work! I even took a charger with twenty-four volts, which should suffice on its own."

Aviel only shrugged his shoulders and mumbled something to the semblance of where there's a will there's a way.

The whole lamasery came to life for Kromen's installation. Rmi-lam, too, became extremely restless, but the Lama continued to instruct her on the history of Bon and Bonism. There wasn't much room to concentrate with Tungjur interrupting the Lama every twenty minutes to update him on the current situation. Despite the respect Rmi-lam had for the Lama, she was no longer interested in the dö thread of diamonds intended to catch evil demons. She would've much rather been in the room where so many new and completely revolutionary things were happening. The Lama soon understood that Rmi-lam was only looking through him dreamily, so he changed the subject and told her the legend of Dangnan Deru, a Tibetan king, who married the beautiful Lugjal from a land far far away. But the new queen withered away until the maid brought her favourite dish from home, butter-fried frog legs, which she then secretly snuck into the pantry to find again.

"Don't worry," shouted Kromen. "You don't have to pedal

tonight. I took a battery and the laptop is fully charged, so tonight, we're all good. But it will be necessary to pedal later on. Oh, and gentlemen," Kromen raised his index finger as a sign of importance. "As part of your resurrection, I also brought light, the most modern of LED diodes, at your disposal," he boasted proudly. "I'm not here to sniff the odour of yak butter and ruin my eyes for good while I'm at it."

He shouldn't have said this. The agile Tungjur, the provider of regular reports, whispered this latest outburst to the Lama, who was busy laughing with Rmi-lam once more, as he described how the king found bags of butter-fried frog legs in the pantry. The grim-faced Lama then shook his head dismissively and clarified something for Tungjur.

"Kushok Kromen," Tungjur then reported most politely, as if pleading. He continued on in the same tone, but with a full-stop at the end, leaving no room for controversy. "Those lights won't be anywhere. The only thing that the honourable Lama Rinpoche agrees with is to have one small light installed in Rmi-lam's chamber, so that she can see well during her studies."

"Fine, of course, Kushok Tungjur, as you wish. I'll do whatever you say," Kromen bowed, exaggerating his willingness. "In the whole history of humankind, it's common that the one who wants to revive and bring progress to a civilisation, has to beg and still look like an idiot nonetheless. Better yet, they make such a person feel embarrassed. On the one hand, I can be grateful that you have accepted me here and that I have a roof over my head. I doff my hat to your conciliatory Buddhism and that's the truth."

Tungjur listened to his speech and then turned and left without a word.

The Lama had already been struggling with Rmi-lam for a good three hours and it was clear that it had been too much on her, so they took an hour's break. Rmi-lam took advantage of this and ran to fetch her clown, which was hidden in her chamber. She didn't want to be without it.

What a surprise it must have been for her to see an unknown Jingzhi standing with his one leg on her desk (how rude) and the other one at a right angle, leaning up against the wall to help him keep his balance, feeling his way around on the ceiling, trying to figure out where to install a light bulb in this girl's kingdom, covered in colouring books, thangka and colourful canvases adorned with mythical drawings of the Buddha. She could not allow an intruder to barge in without her permission and without her presence, let alone some complete stranger, a man she had never seen in her life.

She crept up to him with mouse-like quietness, standing very close and watching him sourly. When she looked down at his leg, she was horrified to see that he was standing on a piece of her beloved clown. She took matters into her own hands. She first grabbed the clown and when it wasn't possible to yank the clothes from under his foot, which Kromen hardly noticed, being absorbed in his work, she bit him in the calf. There came a cry of terror as if from a python bite, whose venom immediately shot up into the back of the neck. The shock served its purpose. The clown was free, but Kromen lay spread out across the floor. His fall was fortunately cushioned by Rmi-lam's bed, but it hadn't prevented him from hitting his head on the wall.

"So, you're the girl who's been living here, right?" Kromen rubbed the side of his head, trying to not look grumpy or angry. Despite everything, he decided it'd be a lot easier to get on her good side. "I've heard many nice things about you, Rmi-lam."

"I've heard many ugly things about you," Rmi-lam reacted abruptly.

"You can't believe everything Uncle Vitas and Uncle Aviel tell you. They like to exaggerate."

"I haven't seen or heard anything nice about you yet either."

"Seriously?" Kromen proudly got to his feet. "Look at the switch. Press it and you'll see."

Rmi-lam grabbed the hanging switch from the ceiling, as carefully as if she'd wanted to pull a ring from among poisonous cobras, and pressed it. Nothing. She frowned, frowning even more at Kromen.

"See?" Kromen exclaimed triumphantly.

"But it's not doing anything," Rmi-lam scolded him.

"Not now because it's not hooked up at the bottom yet, but this lamp will switch on once Aviel plugs it in."

"So, Aviel is going to do it, not you!"

"But Rmi-lam, I was the one who came up with this idea, I bought it and I brought it here."

"All you ever say is: I, I, I… You like to brag a lot. Go away from here."

Kromen sighed and gave up. He looked at the lamp hopelessly and shrugged his shoulders: "I wanted to tighten it more, but that should be ok. You can't swing from it," he grabbed the wire with the switch.

"And why would I do that?" answered Rmi-lam sternly, her expression enough to imply that she had no intentions of speaking to him any further.

– – –

Kromen's surprise took place in the gloomy storage areas in the lower part of the lamasery. The Lama didn't want to risk having the dukang desecrate the dubious achievements of civilisation, which obviously offended Kromen a little, but he thought nothing of it, especially as he wanted to avoid any conflicts. Everyone looked forward to it. Fifty local monks made their way into a relatively large room that was clearly not large enough for the purposes at hand. Rmi-lam,

Vitas and Aviel were very close to the front. As the main IT technician, Aviel was responsible for running all the equipment. There was a white, silk canvas hanging on the wall.

Kromen clapped to get everyone's attention. The moment they had all been waiting for had arrived.

"It's going to be embarrassing," Vitas blurted into the silence. Kromen glared at him with hatred.

"Blow out the candle," he instructed. Only a faint light came from the laptop monitor, but he pointed to Aviel like a venerable conductor. Aviel already had a laptop running in front of him. This laptop was connected to the projector by a VGA cable. He pushed a button on the projector and: let there be light. The projector really switched on and after a while, the monitor from the laptop showed up on the screen, seven-by-ten feet large. Aviel then clicked on the mouse to change the background. Vitas' eyes widened to burst, as he viewed the familiar scenery of the lake with its Nike of Samothrace, the ancient goddess of victory, illuminated on one side by a luminous sunset. It was as if Vitas had returned to Slapy. He looked at Kromen in disbelief, as Kromen stood proudly with his hands folded drumming his fingers confidently on the muscles of his own shoulders. The entire audience gazed mouth-open at the gadget, as Vitas had once called it. It was a fact that no one in the entire area had ever been presented with such scenery before. Even the spray of water from the fountain was visible evidence that it was a "moving picture," one that no one had ever seen. But the picture was completely static.

Kromen, sitting on the back of a bronze-plated horse then suddenly popped up on the screen after several long seconds that gave the viewers enough time to take in the dense picture. He was sitting proudly and majestically, like Wenceslas on the horse in the middle of Prague's Wenceslas Square, holding a smoking cigar in his hand.

At once, he brought the horse to heel and with the help of a primitive fading effect, he advanced. At first, he began melting from the original position, then simultaneously popping up in another, repeating this again and again, until he came close to the Nike, seeming equal to her in size, though Nike was slightly off to the left and he was off to the right. He carelessly tossed the unfinished cigar into the lake and drew his sword, which the viewer hadn't noticed until now. He raised the sword very, very slowly, building suspense, until it was exactly parallel to the Nike, but in a mirrored position on the screen... then the whole picture abruptly blinked yellow and turned to black.

"Well, I told you there weren't enough watts," Aviel shouted, but the audience erupted in thunderous laughter before he could finish his words. It wasn't the laughter of ridicule, but rather laughter of admiration, admiration at seeing something new. A window from their prison had suddenly opened up to the outside, whichever outside in the world.

The candles glared. The seething Kromen groaned: "The essential, the best, the most unique part was yet to come." Scowling, he selected five monks and quickly shoved them into the room with the stationary bikes.

"Pedal! Pedal! And quickly! Faster!" he spurred on the monks, before sprinting back to the cinema room. "Is it working? Is it working?" he eagerly attacked Aviel.

"You should have had them pedalling there from the very beginning, now it's too late. I told you there weren't enough watts. The projector needs at least eight hundred. And what about your peddlers? A single one can barely produce about a-hundred-and-twenty. They'd have to peddle for a really long time to fully charge your battery. Then, you could maybe enjoy about a five-minute snapshot."

No one really knew what Aviel was talking about, but

they all agreed that Kromen wanted the impossible. He even proposed that he play it again and have everyone look at the laptop, but the viewers saw it as a done deal, worthy of joy, no longer interested in Kromen's proposals.

Rmi-lam observed the chaos surrounding her grimly and then coldly evaluated Kromen's activities: "He probably loves himself so much because nobody loves him."

But then in an unexpected moment of realisation she smiled and added: "This is how we're going to do it – from now on we're all going to show Kushok Kromen a lot of love, so that he won't have to love himself so much. And then that means he'll put more time to do something more useful and not so annoying…"

No one knows whether or not this happened. The monks didn't openly show more love for Kromen and it certainly had no impact on the evening. Kromen didn't say a word to anyone until the next day. At the same time, it was true that the projector had never again been used in the lamasery. The same cannot be said for the light and the laptop, which, given Aviel's assistance, helped Rmi-lam with her education, although in Kromen's honour.

36.
Alex

"Hi. I'm Alexei – well – Alex of you" is what the man with the kind-hearted smile said to Vitas. Bradla also introduced him as his good friend, Alex. He shook his hand with his plump, outstretched fingers, which looked more like spools of thread. Repeating "Alexei, Alex," he vigorously shook Vitas' right hand and gave him a piercing look.

He also grabbed Vitas' right wrist with his left hand, which meant he was shaking both his hands like some kind of a jack-handle trying to lift a tractor with a flat tire. This is what politicians do so that everyone can see their sincerity and equanimity towards the opposing party. However, from another perspective, by grabbing the guest's right wrist with their left hand, they are also implying that they have a proposal to make. This is done to show that they are in control, even if the other person were the Pope or the Secretary General of the UN. This shows that the only good the other person has ever done was done exclusively by his own initiative, with his consent and under his command. There is nothing that the other man can do: it is an expression of benign sincerity, there is no room for objections here. He has to accept it with generosity and a smile. His only form of defence is to do the same – to also grab the other person's right wrist with his left hand. However, a handshake like this then looks more like a makeshift stretcher for the injured, which Vitas had learned to do when he was a Pioneer of Socialist Youth, back in grade school. Above all, it would be this stretcher-like handshake that would undoubtedly catch the attention of cameras regardless of the grandiosity of the essential moment.

"So, take a seat, gentlemen," said Bradla, signalling the waiter that he was ready to order.

Both of them sat down. Vitas felt that he was reminded of someone but couldn't figure out who. He noticed that Alex was constantly glaring at him. With a huge grin on his face, as if it were to cut his mouth open. Alex was of typical Slavic descent, with wide cheekbones and very puffy lips. He could pass for either a blue-collar worker on the railroad, or the head manager of a company. His clothes, his appearance, his behaviour, gave nothing away. It seemed he could switch from profession to profession at any given moment, depending on what the situation called for. He had dull, chestnut coloured hair, and was a good five inches shorter than Vitas, but based on his level of confidence, it was clear that he had never suffered from any kind of Napoleon complex.

"We have watch you many years. Hat's off to good work you did us." Alex smiled sincerely, even though he was clearly rummaging around in his brain for the right Czech words.

"What do you mean... work for US?" sputtered Vitas, glancing in shock from Alex to the smiling Bradla and back. Back and forth. "I'm sorry, this must be a misunderstanding. It's nonsense, I don't work for you!" inside, Vitas began to boil over. It was slow and quiet at first. But once he realised that he was being associated with something completely unacceptable, when he fully realised the true meaning of the spoken words, he blushed deeply, his eyes widened and he gasped for air. Alex could only laugh uncontrollably until his eyes began to tear up. He grabbed Vitas by his shoulders with his left hand and shook him vigorously.

A mental picture of Ivan, a Russian he once met near Moscow while working on a case, suddenly swam before his eyes. Their introduction had meant many sleepless nights, even though, at first glance, nothing harmful had taken place.

That year, 1994, Vitas was still a paper-journalist and had gone to Moscow as a driver, the co-navigator of a truck, via Poland and Belarus.

Not far from the border, in Belarus, three Czech trucks had formed a team. "Necessity," proclaimed one of the drivers. "We have to do this to survive."

Thanks to this new group of people, Vitas could take in all the tales of burned-out trucks, bribery, theft, while on his breaks… "I was headin' up the Ural Mountains with a full, heavy load. Liza[29] ploughed on up the serpentines at a good twenty-five miles an hour, near-out-of-breath, when a littler truck with a platform in front came up behind. Some men on the platform started unloading goods from my Liza, and I could only watch what they were doin', helpless…"

"I met a desperate man who stopped his truck in the middle-of-nowhere, just to piss. Told me there was no one in sight. But when he got out of the truck, God knows where they came from, about thirty people come on out and literally strip his truck bare in a matter of minutes. They didn't jus'steal the goods, they took the side-view mirrors, the door handles, the doors, the seats, pretty much anything what they could get their hands on…"

"I was unloading goods in some town, 'bout sixty-five miles out of Moscow. Suddenly, a shoot-out breaks out. Submachine-guns, assault rifles, handguns… So we all

---

29 A truck manufactured by the Czech brand LIAZ

drop flat, cover our heads. In 'bout fifteen minutes it all just passed like a storm and everything went quiet. So, we got up and carried on unloading. No one was shocked..."

"I was near St. Petersburg once, when the mafia pulled me over, asking me to make a deal to drive for 'em and let 'em rob me now-and-then. Every five times they'd let me go past and then rob me just once, depending on the goods. In return, they'd watch over my travels. Basically, it was a ransom. When I told 'em to go to hell, they told me exactly what me and my colleagues were transporting, so I better count on the worst. They had exact information from the customs officers. Listen man, you got no idea how many people drive for 'em because they just haven't got any other choice..."

The journey through Belarus was long. They slept wherever and however possible, but never in a secure car-park. The dull, wide countryside was sometimes interrupted by GAIs[30]. Elevated police stations, with police officers waiting for any kind of bribe, sometimes shutting off a closed road, carefully inspecting every vehicle.

"On your way to Pskov, lads? For god's sake, don't go anywhere near Pskov," a fellow Czech called out to them from one of the GAIs, who was heading back to Czechia, without a truck.

"No, headed Moscow-way, Pskov is too far up north..." clarified Vitas' driver.

"They stripped my Liza. Two Lizas and one Scania already missin' up there. They robbed me, held a gun to my head, forced me to drive into the woods. When we got stuck in the mud, they told me get running and stole everything. Luckily, I had some vodka and money I took from my stash, but my passport was gone. To get to Belarus from Russia, I had to get all the customs officers drunk 'til they stopped letting cars pass the border..." his eyes abruptly froze on the

---

30 GAI = State Automobile Inspectorate

oncoming Czech truck, making its way towards Czechia. "Lads, I have to catch 'im if I want to get home this year. Whatever you do, don't stop near Pskov…!"

The journey to Moscow was even longer. Sun-fatigue, dust, thirst, greasy strands of hair, thoughtless, dull, empty minds, eyes burning slightly from the sweat. The truck passed a man with a small backpack. The nearest village or any sign of civilisation was two hundred miles behind them. Where did he come from? Why? What was he after…?

In Moscow, they arrived at a large construction site, surrounded by a barbed-wire fence. It seemed to be a prison of the highest-security. Half of the truck was filled with construction equipment, with machinery and material for constructing a brewery that was being built for Czech-Spanish co-production.

"Can we kip on your premises? In the truck?" Dan asked the Russian construction foreman.

"Yes, you can. But you'll be on the premises by six o'clock. That's when we close up and lock up here."

"Thank you," the driver nodded politely, a heavy weight lifted from his shoulders through solving the potential problem of thieves.

"By seven o'clock you can go no more than thirty feet towards your truck, otherwise security'll shoot," added the head of construction.

"Ah, great, thirty feet," Dan agreed.

"At every person moving around here. Is that clear?"

"Yep…"

"You'll be inside your truck by nine o'clock because that's when we set the dogs loose."

"Great… dogs…?" Dan released what could've been a sob or a question.

Then they both drove into Moscow with only the tractors to do some sightseeing. There wasn't much time left before it turned six o'clock, so they only got to see a single, rugged and muddy market, which reminded them of an Ethiopian refugee camp. Here, they bought some beer and vodka, hoping it wouldn't leave them blind. Later that night, they both drunk-danced inside the truck. To relieve their bladders, they urinated from both windows, shooting as high as possible, for fear of the restless Alsatians prowling the site, hungry for a quick bite.

The next day, they drove the rest of the load into a small town, or rather a village, some forty miles away from Moscow, where they reached a newly-built meat processing plant, to deliver more components. They arrived in the afternoon, as unloading wasn't until the next day. They were greeted by three security officers with submachine-guns and Kolya, the gatekeeper.

Vitas was used to seeing retired people as gatekeepers in Czechia who wanted to earn some extra money. Here, the gatekeeper was a young man named Kolya. His eyes were red, perhaps from drinking too much vodka, or perhaps from lack of sleep, or perhaps both. He invited them both inside for a traditional Russian drink. Vitas pointed to himself, meaning to say he was in charge, and set off for the village. The centre was governed by a saldat, a soldier with a machine-gun positioned higher than the surrounding twelve-storey blocks of flats. These high-rises stood out like the tree stumps following an apocalypse. There were also huts, like the ones in war movies, all around.

"Buddies!" yelled the driver, hands outstretched happily, clutching a bottle of vodka and entering the gatehouse with Vitas.

Kolya also greeted them with a smile, confidently pointing to a very well-equipped if somewhat repetitive bar-shelf hidden in the first-aid cabinet. Vodka. Only vodka. An abundance of vodka.

They chatted to each other for about fifteen minutes. Vitas didn't even have time to ask about his family, his pastimes or his hobbies, why he went into this field of work, or his views on the world, on Europe, on life and on his future…

Ivan stepped into the gatehouse. Momentously, drastically, dynamically. With his arm outstretched, generous to hug the whole world. But four pallid men stood around him like winter icicles. Their leather jackets bulged at the armpits. Gorillas. A happy boss and his cold-hearted security guards. The contrast was as clear as a slap in the face.

"Well, give me the cards!" yelled the jolly Ivan.

The whole scene left Vitas feeling stunned. There was a lot of tension in the air, as if they were all waiting for a command, a trigger, to let all hell break loose. The tension was emphasised by Kolya's knocking. He greeted Ivan with a convulsive smile and then pulled out the cards. He dealt the cards with his shaky, sweaty hands. Vitas didn't even know what they were playing, but Kolya lost in a very short time. Then again and again.

The four silent men stood together, the stunned duo from Czechia, the shaken up Kolya and the constantly glowing Ivan with his grandiose gestures.

Kolya lost three thousand Russian Rubbles. A fortune. Ivan and his gorillas disappeared as quickly as they had appeared.

Despite numerous attempts, Vitas couldn't get Kolya to tell him what all this was about. Ransom? A toll to pay? He had no idea. He was only convinced that if he had done something out of the ordinary, he'd have returned home in a coffin, even in the best-case-scenario.

He obviously made a whole mental photo-album of pictures from Ivan's visit to the gatehouse, which he could now compare well with Alex. It seemed that Ivan's carbon-copy was now sitting beside Bradla and himself, a twin. They both had the same terrifying charisma. He wiped his dry palm over his wet forehead to get rid of the chills. It didn't work. He couldn't get rid of them. And somewhere else: a metronome. There was a metronome beating somewhere behind him at regular intervals. At least, at that moment, that's what he believed. Or what else could it be? A clock? His final heart beats? Or something a lot stronger? There were over thirty people at the coffee shop, all enjoying themselves, ignorant of the fact that a bomb was about to detonate, leaving no survivors. This innocence, this gullibility, this ignorance of the impending apocalypse that only Vitas was aware would happen, left him speechless, unable to warn anyone. And even if he were able to say anything, the reaction would only be the godless laughter of disbelieving everymen, before the pressure wave blew them away.

Once he awakened from his thoughts and fantasies, which only lasted a moment, he returned to his senses and tried to say: "I'm afraid there's been a misunderstanding. The only one I work for is the Czech TV editorial, Ivan," added Vitas, sounding as civilised as possible, yet with a hint of provocation, like a test or question...

"Alex, Alex," Alex corrected him with a smile, "I know your job, your work," Alex translated for himself.

"So, what are you talking about here...?"

"Because you not to know..."

"What...?"

"Relatively, you have to worked for us for long time now, the very beginning."

"What do you mean for us? Who are you? Where are you from? Are you Ivan?"

"Ivan? Noooo, Alexei, Alex... Many question. I am East man..."

"What East? The Ukraine? Russia? Belarus?"

"No, no," Alex got to his feet, a little annoyed but still smiling. "It's of course you not yet ready. Next time…"

"Wait, gentlemen," Bradla quickly stood up, trying to calm down the situation, only worsening Vitas' nerves.

Alex continued to smile. With honesty. With modesty. "Our friend needing additional times," he explained.

"But I think he'll understand…"

Alex examined Vitas and after a moment's hesitation, he took his seat again.

There was a moment of awkward silence. Vitas felt anxious. He shuffled in his seat, not knowing where to look. Was Ivan a mobster or not? Vitas could not be sure. He felt he was in some Asian land, unable to find a familiar face.

Ivan Alex, his palms clasped, holding his head up, amusingly gazed at one and then the other, and laughed sincerely. Vitas glared at him in horror, as if everything Alex had done, be it with the utmost authenticity and innocence, was the vile act of Dumas' Cardinal Richelieu, lacking all moral restraint.

Vitas' eyes met with Alex's. Vitas' eyes burst with heat and resentment, but Alex's eyes were full of support and curiosity. Alex promptly grew solemn, banged his hand on the table, got up sternly and left for the other room.

The two others looked at each other with blank expressions and Bradla reprimanded Vitas a little sourly: "Don't be foolish, he's really an interesting person. Wait until you get to know him better."

"I don't want to get to know him better!" Vitas snapped.

"Then, you're a shitty journalist in my eyes…"

"Blah, blah!" Vitas insisted angrily.

"C'mon man, you meet some of the biggest gangsters and you're bothered by one kind-hearted Russian…"

"So he is a Russian."

"Not Russian, but more like a…"

He didn't finish his sentence because Alex returned to the table at a very brisk pace. He was holding a newspaper in his hands. "Look…" He sat comfortably down in his chair, laying the newspaper across the whole table, making the glasses and tea spoons cover parts of the newspaper, creating a plastic map.

"I grabbed any newspaper at the bar and Mr Vitas, be so kind and find any article with good news in it."

"What do you mean?" asked Vitas, frowning, without even glancing at the newspaper.

"Okay, fine, I tell you. Look at this, other from pink pigeon will be survive in year 2000 and Slavia soccer team to run over Croatia five-one in UEFA Cup re-match, no more good news."

"So what?" Vitas shook his head, uncomprehending.

"You drive and everyone only think about how to take down you, trick you, make stop you, cause accident and make your fault…" Alex paused. "The expression, the neighbour's goat must die, no matter what…"

"So what?" Vitas pressed in the same tone.

"You drive down the street and people are angry, frowning…"

"So what?"

"Do you have the idea how good are you in your country here? In history of time you never be more prosperous. Your generation doesn't even know war. But is not enough. Go to East or to South and to see what badly conditions people be to live there. These people eat insects, have no place to sleep, they have to fight for survival every day, just like primate in jungles, they have informal terms with death. According to many agency, you live in the top twenty countries in whole world and now look here," he slapped the back of the newspaper.

"According to another reportages, Czechs are with the

most angriest and most unsatisfied people in the world, with the end of ladder. People only wanting be to see evil, who see mugged or killed someone and where, they want to reading many things of it, they want to seeing it on TV and they reading about it, they become furious to politics and to everything. They wanting to see punish, see how people are punish. Isn't that punish too benevolent? He must to get more! Even if he hit someone accident, he have been probably drunk and incapable police not even found out. We will kick the dead corpse and dance on it. You already with preconceived feelings that enemies being around you, like some alien from one sci-fi film and you are having to fight him for survival day-to-day. That's also why you act like some foxes driven into corner. You are petrificated, suspected, hating, jealousy… Maybe you only positive character is absent cynical and indifferent. And what interest you? Here you are," Alex slapped the back of the newspaper again. "How dare Czech National Soccer team screw news-journalist in Vienna hotel-room after loss of game! She say she to provoking them for to do it and proving any lack of morale that have soccer players? How obscene, this treason! Have they won, they could to fucking whole Opera Houses, including cleaning lady, and Czechs will to applaud these behaviours."

Alex paused for a second, mocking Vitas with his piercing Slavic eyes and then slowly, quietly and with a smile said: "And so our job is this, is what we do."

"Your job?" Vitas stuttered.

"Well, that's true," Alex chuckled, "it wasn't had very much work. It just had ways being fixed itself out in Czechia. And notice," his face turned serious, he raised his hands in a horizontal position, as if he were indicating the water level, "the tension keep to building-up. And even the worst, this be to making people happy. Not to satisfying them, it irritate, provocative and walk them in, like you wanting be to screw a pretty girl here on the table of café. You know it forbidden, but you will want to do it because it will be exciting and beautiful. Forbidden fruit, yes?"

"But I wasn't considering having sex with anyone on the table of this café…"

"So, you either impotent or you joke. But I think you joke. But since everyone is to be doing this…"

"Doing what? Fucking girls on a table?"

"No," Alex explained patiently, ignoring the apparent impertinence in Vitas' voice. "They swear, provocative themselves even more irritable and hating and everyone only release negative energy, so…" Alex pondered for a moment and then hesitantly said: "This is normal. Do you understand what I say? It is become normal, anything common and normal. It's anything like homosexuality is now completely normal. You make reality show actors into real celebrity and real celebrities into nothing and no hope. You must to breaking any names, concept, values and all you totally distort. You are not being happy when you have to or must to be happy and when something going wrong, or anybody something wrong, you are celebrate to say: 'Look, I said it will!' You not to even know how to laugh anymore. Ever since revolution went little bit out of hand, you can only scraping off the foam, like chef twisting egg to sugar. Now you drown, you cannot breath to it."

"Perhaps you may be partially correct," Vitas added quickly, not making his withdrawal so noticeable. "But what can I do about it? Why're you telling me this?"

"Well, because you are the feeder for them. This is what you offer. You are egg twister, our weapon. You do more work than tanks on front lines, even when all nuclear warheads are on west border for Russia. You are more effectively than any deadly virus. You are to be dealing the cards in this country just to then laugh against people who have the bad hand. You to throwing any jokers and high cards under the table. All you must to do is come here, pull out right ace, poke the needle to your bubble and everything will to fall away, decomposition for prime factors. Then, you will just be staring like astronauts from Planet of the Apes, when they learned the sand they were walking used to be Manhattan."

"Dammit, what do you want me to do about it?" shouted Vitas, as people regarded him with disgust from the surrounding tables. Soon realising this, he immediately lowered his voice to almost a whisper. "I've been trying to do my job honestly for years…"

"There is no doubt for that!" Alex agreed convincingly. "However, do not to confuse honesty to greed, determining to blind ambitious."

"I took care of having many things fixed…"

Bradla and Alex's laughter interrupted Vitas.

"You sure did!" he stubbornly insisted. "I can give you the names of people who couldn't receive bank loans after my report aired, I can give you names…"

"Louse! You are a louse!" Alex said with an honest smile. "But very useful with us. And calm down, we need you and we will to please you."

"Who do you work for?" Vitas abruptly asked, sharp and cold.

"It is hard to say this…" Alex shrugged his shoulders evasively.

"And why? You're the one who raised the topic, so answer me clearly. Are you some kind of an agent? Or an armchair philosopher?"

Alex and Bradla laughed again. This boiled Vitas' blood. The feeling came over him that he was clueless and they were laughing, making themselves appear intelligent, as if they were better than him. He had always hated it. They could at least say what's going on.

"Fine, so it's a secret…" Vitas remarked sarcastically.

"Not very much secret, but I don't think time is yet come."

"By time, d'you mean the time as in historical time, or as in my time, meaning I'm foolish for not yet understanding…?"

"You're very clever," Alex reassured Vitas, though he only saw it as an attempt for reconciliation. "But some streets to your mind are stopped about your emotion. Blind mind. You have too many emotion, so it's not open yet. But I think it will come soon…" Alex glanced briefly around the room, then pulled out his business card. "Look, sorry me for offend you in some way. Here's my business card. When you need anything, and that is anything at all, contact me. Any times. I know times will come. I will to expect you. And calm down, I won't to disappearing for any changes. I am eternal," he burst out laughing at his own use of words and Bradla joined in giggling.

"I really don't know why I would contact you," Vitas slowly rose, forcing the business card into his pocket even more slowly, without even looking. "By tomorrow morning, I'll have forgotten all about this insane meeting anyway."

Alex winked at him with a smile, as if to say he knew this wouldn't be the case. He was well aware that the thought had been planted in Vitas' mind and that this thought would quickly grow with all the nourishment it had. Vitas saw this in Alex's eyes and refused to shake his hand good-bye. He only raised his hand a little, as if he had wanted to fix his non-existent glasses, before changing his mind, only waving his hand vaguely, then rapidly to leave the café.

What had happened? Vitas had no answer, though he felt he had just woken from a relatively nice dream into harsh reality, into a completely different atmosphere. As if someone had removed the distorted lenses he hadn't known he was wearing, and now he saw everything in an entirely different light. Alex really had planted the thought deep in his mind, although Vitas refused to admit it.

He even felt a certain self-pity and helplessness, the same feeling he had had for his parents' generation following the revolution. As children, they had experienced the World War with its hunger and poverty, followed by the building of socialism and Communism. And after all this he had told them that their whole lives had been worthless because they had lived in an absolute delusion. Even if they under-stood once they were sixty or older, there was no way they could have admitted it – they would perhaps have had no choice but to commit suicide.

Either way, Vitas still felt like someone had forced his eyes open to show him that everything he had done up to that point was worthless. Had he been fighting against his demons, against nonsense, or had he been serving the devil for all those years? Although he couldn't admit it, an entirely new feeling crept into his sense for life. It was as if he had lost his arm and he was being forced to live without it from that point on.

– – –

Bretislav, too, could get no sleep: "SEEMS LIKE A LOT OF WORK TO KICK AGAINST THE PRICKS, EH?"

37.
Sonam's Awakening

Kromen had to admit that the lamasery was completely different, everything looked brighter. Rmi-lam's arrival poured life into the sleeping castles, like after a rainstorm, when everything is renewed with life, with fresh scents, and a desire to move awakens... The prince has kissed Sleeping Beauty, rousing her from her slumber. Water consumption gradually increased, everyone suddenly becoming more aware of cleanliness, not only of personal hygiene but also of keeping the lamasery clean. They even introduced a stricter maintenance regime. Vitas and Aviel even convinced Rmi-lam to brush her teeth twice a day, despite her initial resistance and fury. The other monks then adopted this habit as well. Over time, toothbrushes and toothpastes became common goods, brought via caravan from the civilised country.

Kromen met with the Lama. Although he was deep in thought and gloomy after the meeting, he didn't say a word to Vitas or Aviel, despite their relentless questioning. He only shrugged his shoulders and said: "Good, good, hopefully we'll come to an agreement. It needs time, but dammit, I don't want to wait! All I do is wait. But apparently it'll be soon..."

He was clearly somewhat satisfied, at least in part, as

he even agreed to stay slightly longer. After two days, he willingly set off with the caravan into the civilised world to buy various things for the lamasery. However, this time, the goods brought back were rather unusual. They were all for Rmi-lam, including books, pencils and pencil crayons… Aviel and Vitas circled Kromen, giving him orders for all the things they needed. A DVD player with movies, opera music and modern music. Kromen simply wrote it all down, proudly adding: "Elvis Presley, no problem. And what about Hansel and Gretel…?"

Two monks accompanied Kromen to help him, and they set off with nine yaks to transport the goods.

– – –

"Help!" yells Wung Pien. He is running from Sonam's hermitage towards Vitas and Aviel, immediately requesting a kashag meeting. "These novelties will kill us all," he bellows angrily, detailing the new events. "Sonam is banging the bowl up against the wall and he wants to leave! According to what he says, he already left his body and entered nirvana, but now he's returning to fulfil his mission. Apparently, it was the light that pulled him out of Buddha's womb and now he wants to leave. Immediately! This is all Rmi-lam's fault, she was the one who kept on feeding him her nonsense!"

The monks frantically started discussing what to do. Tungjur came shortly afterwards, informing them that the honourable Rinpoche had engaged in meditation and didn't want to be disturbed. "But whatever will be, will be. All things will pass. Life's wheel will continue to spin, no one will stop it. Let us therefore do what is necessary."

All the decisions remained in the hands of the monks, so they headed up to the hermitage. Sonam's hermitage was surrounded by a swarm of buzzing flies and the sound of a metal bowl pounding against the rock echoed to a steady rhythm like the blaring of a horn, each strike symbolising suffering, while the monk howled faintly.

Of course, Rmi-lam, Aviel and Vitas were there too. The monks gazed noiselessly at the crescent-moon of the opening. They clearly had no idea what to do. Rather than outrage, they all seemed in awe. Some misunderstanding passed between them about where the world is spinning to. Only Wung Pien stood unfazed, hands on his hips, looking towards the opening like a vulgar, offensive image. Lao PuWei also deviated from the crowd, having originally been against Rmi-lam's staying at the lamasery. He stood arrogantly, eyes partially closed and lower lip curled, as if to say he told them so, and that this wouldn't have a happy ending.

"Well," Wung shouted at Rmi-lam, gesturing for her to go to the hole and solve the problem. "Well, go and talk to him, smart-aleck, and tell him to calm down."

Rmi-lam walked a little theatrically, she felt the dozens of eyes staring at her, but she remained confidently stubborn. 'There's no way you can understand,' her body implied, pushing a large piece of stone towards the opening so that she could use it as a pedestal in a completely habitual manner, making a loud hissing noise. They all watched her tremble, as if saying: "Labour is now your punishment." Helping her didn't even occur to them, but Rmi-lam wasn't exactly expecting their assistance. She pushed the stone under the hole, from which the monotonous sounds of grunts and a metal bowl pounding against the rock still emanated. She stood up on the stone, so even though the hermitage was higher still, she stood a bit loftier than the other monks. She looked over them haughtily, her back to the hole, slowly raising her index finger with an expression, meaning 'Watch out, now, I'm about to show you something'. There was complete silence, broken only by the noise coming from the hermitage, and no one moved an inch.

Aviel and Vitas had to look at each other with a restrained laugh. "This girl has a knack for controlling people."

"Yes," confirmed Vitas. "She knows how to handle her silence and gestures. Beautiful theatre."

She slowly turned to the hole, retrieved the stone and tossed it to the ground behind her. The noises coming from within immediately fell quiet.

"It's me, Rmi-lam," she yelled inside.

"The candle flame," was heard from the inside. Slowly, with bad articulation, as if someone was mumbling with his mouth almost closed. It was clear that his cheek muscles and tongue weren't working properly.

"Almost everyone has come," Rmi-lam whispered loudly for everyone to hear, with her hands covering her mouth. "Do you want anything now?" she asked in a whisper.

"Leave. I want to leave. Help me."

"Is that what you really want?"

"Yes. I have to see you. You woke me up from another sphere. I am old and in any case there's precious little time for me. I don't know where, when or who I'll be when I wake, but I have to see you before I leave into the world of the bardo. That's all."

Rmi-lam slowly turned to the other monks, who remained utterly silent.

"Tear it down," she told them. It didn't sound like an order, there was no threat, no undertone, her voice wasn't raised, it was emotionless, blank. Only a short sentence spoken with a full-stop at its end. There are thousands of ways to say this, but in this unique instance, no one doubted that they had to do exactly what they were being asked. Three clear words, one verb. The end.

The pickaxes bit into the growth of stone. Since it was artificially cemented, there wasn't much resistance. Large chunks fell off and small pieces shattered in all directions. Apart from the noise caused by the demolition, everything around was as sombre as if the friends were digging their companion a grave. But the opposite was the case: their companion was being raised from the dead.

There was a black hole in the stone lump, about five-feet high. It was now relatively easy for a hunched man or for Rmi-lam to get inside. An unwritten rule seemed to state that Rmi-lam was the person in charge of all the matters at hand. All she had to do was raise a finger, and one of the diggers would step to the side, allowing Rmi-lam to enter the black abyss.

But all at once she shot out of the hole, holding her nose with one hand and waving her other like a fan, emphasising the horrible stench, exaggerating the whole super-sensual atmosphere beyond proportion. Everyone laughed. Finally. She motioned one monk to go inside.

Everyone gazed on in suspense. It took a while for the bone-white, shrivelled hands to appear, trying to grab hold of the rock gnawed by the pickaxes. It was then that something that should have long crossed over to another world, crawled out. He had a long beard, was hairy, hunched over, and with black holes in place of eyes. Hermit Sonam immediately slapped his hands over them, the outside light a source of excruciating pain. When he let go, he staggered and he would have fallen if not for the monk who held him up from behind. Another monk stepped forward and put a scarf over his eyes. His cassock was red and black, greasy and seemingly eaten away by mould in places.

Once Sonam finally gained his stability and with the scarf over his eyes and two monks supporting him, he started 'searching with his ears' like a blind man. "Rmi-lam," he called.

She pinched her nose with her left hand, grabbing him with her other from the short distance, and the four of them followed the monks dressed in dark red, slowly descending towards the lamasery. Sonam seemed not to walk, but to float, with both monks supporting him. There was no way he could have walked on his own. His arms and legs were like toothpicks, ready to snap. From a distance, they appeared to be some sort of procession, leading a crucified old man down his final path. Sonam and Rmi-lam were like a staggering couple dancing their last dance of their lives on the dance floor. And this is how they made their way down to the lamasery in complete and utter silence.

38.
Media Death

Bradla became the new CEO of the public TV station! Shocking news! There was no doubt that it was his clever tactics that had won him the promotion. A moderator. In the eyes of a professional, he could barely read the teleprompter, but in the eyes of the general public, he was the ultimate bore, the one who created and perhaps even invented the news. He obviously had to know how to mingle among politicians. His politics were left-leaning and the right-wing politicians always rooted for the party he had recently interviewed. There was no reason for anyone to be dissatisfied with him.

Having such a CEO could be good news for Vitas, or at least this is how he saw it. But it was all resolved too quickly. Kromen met with Bradla and clearly outlined his requests. If Bradla wanted to continue receiving hundreds of millions from the SAZKA betting company, he had to get rid of Vitas and cancel the *Bad Penny*. And this is exactly what happened. Bradla threw Vitas overboard. Berger, an eminent, greying man, became his legal advisor, who proclaimed that everything reported was false. There were numerous mistakes and despite a certain level of positivity, albeit a reporter's naive effort to inform the general public about taboo topics, the result was a failure. This caused uproar in the media, which in the end meant an indefinite, blurred and incomprehensible end to an affair. The *Bad Penny* was cancelled and Vitas' ID card still didn't work. End.

But it was a flagship case nonetheless: Rokos received the Ferdinand Peroutka Award, the highest Czech award for journalism, from the SAZKA BC, for his approach to journalism, for uncovering lies and evil, for revealing essential journalistic information bolstered the nation's high moral integrity... Surprisingly, Rokos walked around modestly, leaving his bow at home. Exactly according to the rule that a "great man doesn't have to act like one," his high heels and award could speak for themselves.

– – –

Darkness. They located Vitas on the street. He didn't know who, or when, there was no warning, no indications. He was strolling down the road and then suddenly there was a bag over his head and what felt like a thousand hands around him. Within a matter of seconds, he was thrown into a car like a bag of potatoes. Granted, he wasn't cautious. He had been wandering deep in thought for several days, considering his destiny, trying to come up with a next step. He was caught off guard for a split second. But these were professionals, and whether or not he had been cautious, would have made little difference.

He had no idea where they were going or how long he'd be in the car. He'd given up. He was simply waiting.

"I'd like to pay you a tribute," Kromen said slowly, once Vitas was able to identify his voice, and once Vitas' eyes got used to daylight, after having the bag removed from his head. His hands were free. He could defend himself or punch him in the nose, even though it was certain that security guards would be nearby. He could do anything, but did nothing. Kromen was looking, slightly smiling, with no trace of resentment or bitterness. As always, he was wearing a suit, a vest and he seemed to have just returned from a beauty salon.

"I know, you could care less for my tributes," Kromen answered for Vitas. "But I have to tell you. I am truly sorry for hurting you. True, I did find it somewhat amusing, but only as a game, nothing personal. And I have to say that sometimes, I was at my wit's end," Kromen emphasised with his index finger pointed and his eyebrows raised, "and I could have started despising you. You certainly didn't spare me either."

He was sitting outside on the patio by the Slapy Dam, the divine Nike giving her blessing, or rather seeming to dictate Vitas' fate like a conductor equipped with a sword instead of a baton.

"What do you want?" asked Vitas with a motionless, grim expression that remained unchanged throughout the whole ensuing non-dialogue.

"I want to express the feelings I have for you. I have no resentment towards you. I don't want to be your enemy. I respect you because you were doing your job and you were doing it well. You can get in touch with me if and whenever you need anything. Anything." A certain Alex came to Vitas' mind, a man who had offered him the same thing not long ago.

"You say you need to improve your karma. You want to make up for your sins with this crap," burst Kromen, who was now conversing with himself on behalf of Vitas.

"I don't want to make up for anything," replied Kromen, again to himself. "I have no illusions about myself, but believe it or not, I really am only trying to do the right thing, though sometimes, there're rocky roads to traverse."

"And as for the police officer? Was it necessary for me

to have him killed?" Kromen asked in Vitas' place. "I didn't kill anyone, but nothing is simple black-or-white. You didn't know him. You didn't know him," he repeated. "Some things are not as they seem."

There came a moment of silence, both rivals staring into each other's eyes. Vitas was downtrodden, but motionless still, while Kromen was accommodating with no signs of hatred.

"I am not going to shake your hand," said Kromen, "because I know you wouldn't take it. Good luck. I mean that honestly." Kromen stood up and made to leave, stopping for a moment to look at the conductor, the Nike, before stepping into his home.

One of Kromen's bodyguards, clad in a bulletproof suit like the entourage to the president, got to his feet in front of Vitas and gestured for him to get into the parked car, seemingly the most expensive of the BMW X Series, which Vitas hadn't even known existed.

Blankly, he stared out at the landscape passing by, weighing his next move.

He was dropped off on a dead-end street, with no one around to be seen, near a metro station. A man in a suit opened the door for him. When Vitas got out, the man closed the door and uncompromisingly shoved a briefcase into Vitas' hands.

"You'll find one million Czech crowns inside. Mr. Kromen says you don't have to burn it, throw it out, or donate it to charity. Mr. Kromen will never find out, so it'd be a useless gesture, with no effect. Just keep it and enjoy it."

– – –

In order for Kromen to show that everything in the sports world was truly functional and that he was the only supreme leader in the field, he embarked on a grandiose enterprise, the building of a sports hall worth billions of Czech crowns. He felt this was a mental necessity that would silence anyone who doubted him, and excite the frenzy of all sports fans. But he bit off such a large bite that he choked on it. He wasn't able to repay the exorbitant loans that he had blindly taken. He himself killed the immortal cow that had fed everyone full. The whole bubble burst not long afterwards and everything came to light. All the beetles, insects and skeletons came out of the closet and suddenly all the sports officials were throwing their hands up in despair, shocked at what had been going on for all those years, the billions that had disappeared and how the poor athletes had been robbed. Instead of looking at themselves in the mirror, slapping themselves and turning themselves in at the nearest police station, they were the ones who let loose the reins on one of the wildest and most Napoleonic scoundrels, who was no longer interested in business in the Czech Republic. Now he would roam the world, in search of various methods of fulfilling his enjoyment.

– – –

Media death is immediate. It comes several days after the person disappears from the screen. After no more than a few weeks, Vitas could walk down the road without even being recognised. Submerged in his Chebness, he asked himself what life had in store for him next. And what should he do with the million? He kept it. Kromen was right. Why should he do anything if no one would notice? But he felt that the TV station and its crooks had physically assaulted him and that Kromen had even taken his soul with this million, although he no longer felt that he even had a soul.

What next? He exclusively filed his acquaintances into

categories: this is a source, take this one down, use that one to confirm various facts, film this, edit this out...

At the same time, he discovered that he had suddenly lost almost all his friends. Once he was no longer a popular reporter, his phone stopped ringing. It was as if Vitas had woken up again, but that everything around him was still in his dream, a feeling of anticipation, a feeling that the dawn of a new day would bring something life-changing and bright, something that would make the dark haze disappear. But nothing happened. Absolutely nothing. He felt anxiety.

"Snap out of it. These investigations are not the only thing you live for," Eva kept telling him. "Wake up and start implementing other ideas. You can make films, so make them..."

He used his exceptional knowledge of the media world in public relations. He taught media training and thanks to his experience, his students devoured every word he said. Vitas uncovered the secret world of investigative journalism. On the one hand, he loved his work, it was something unknown, but on the other hand, his stomach was constantly clenched. In this way, he knew he was quickly making his way back to the other side of the riverbank and that there would be no turning back.

He seemingly presented everything he had ever learned about the secrets of investigative reporting at a media training session for one of the most renowned oil companies, with the highest turnover in the Czech Republic. He ran this training session in front of the board of directors and its top managers in such a way that even the mouth of the oil company's highly confident gaped.

"If your phone rings and a journalist from one of the popular investigative shows like the *Bad Penny*, *Under the Magnifying Glass*, or *Strike Out*, introduces themselves on the other line, immediately apologise politely, saying you're just in the middle of a meeting and you'll be available in an hour. Then hang up the phone. You have to realise that the conversation is being recorded from the beginning." Vitas paused and carefully surveyed all seventeen managers.

"Your task is to immediately find out everything about the show and especially about the reporter who contacted you. This will clarify what kind of a report is going to be filmed... I'm sure you understand that there is a difference in filming for a Christian magazine, or for the *Bad Penny*, or for *Strike Out*. You have to realise one fundamental thing: you just received a phone call from a news reporter who probably isn't employed by the given TV station, but is an external reporter. In order for this reporter to make his living, he has to take someone – anyone – down twice a month. And even if you explain to him that the person who turned you in, maybe your competitor, the one who wanted to destroy you in the media, is wrong and you are right, you will probably not overturn the case. The reporter has to finish his case, meaning he has to finish with YOU. The reporter already has several testimonies on camera, he's employed two film crews for your case, which means money, so you have no idea that the report is in its final stages, it's almost complete, so there's no way he can go back into the newsroom after your testimony and say: 'Sorry, it didn't work out. It's all changed, I want nothing to do with it.' That would be the end of that reporter. I know this is not your problem, you have your own business to worry about, but you also have to think for him. You have to offer him an alternative way out, or else you're putting yourself at risk in your own business..."

Vitas paused, observing the impact of his words, emphasising too, the weight of the words he had spoken. Of course, he had all of them eating out of the palm of his hand.

"But what alternative way?" the Chairman of the Board of Directors interrupted his speech. "Do you mean a bribe or something like that?" Suppressed laughter was heard all around. "Well, we can't do that. We don't have the funds for that."

"I didn't say anything about a bribe, but it's interesting that would be the first thing that comes to people's minds. Obviously, there are news reporters who do accept bribes, and you can always find the funds if you really need them, but there are also reporters who don't accept bribes. It's pretty risky offering a reporter a bribe because you don't know if he's getting it all on camera or not. Then, you might as well just buy a strong rope and find a thick enough branch. Theoretically, it is possible, but then I would definitely leave this up to someone else. By this I mean the agreement and the handing over of the money. However, I mean something else by 'alternative way'. If you really screwed something up, then sprinkle excessive ashes on your head. You have to immediately take any corrective measures necessary. But watch out, like I said, the reporter has to air it, so turn it into your own ad campaign. Be overconfident and say something like this on camera: "Yes, there has been a marginal error – as a result of incorrect information, external influences… blah, blah, blah… you know, 'You can't avoid human error, though corrective measures have been taken, everyone has received compensation for damages and this will clearly never happen again. We are actually quite glad this happened because we know now how to prevent it from happening again… blah, blah, blah.' We will discuss this in more detail and use specific examples.

"Well, if it's really not the way they say it is, and the person was really taken advantage of or abused, you have to calmly explain the facts. However, don't count on it working. Try to turn the case around and to carefully imply that the reporter in question was taken advantage of. You cannot say this flat out because this would offend him and he would definitely take you down. Reporters are very vain and proud of their power. You have to make it look like it was his idea.

"But most importantly, if you feel confident in your own shoes, you have to write a letter to the CEO of the TV station and the manager of the show. Without emotion, clearly and briefly present your arguments and politely imply that there is a possibility that someone had been taken advantage of. This should work ninety-nine percent of the time. The days of the CEO and the director standing behind their people are long gone. In the early nineties, I recall sending an email to my director, answering questions regarding a complaint about a report, only to never hear about the case again. Not today! Today, the one who files the complaint has top priority. So, there's a huge opportunity if you write the email or letter wisely. At first glance, they act like they have excellent reporters and that they stand behind their work, but if there are any problems, they step back and leave the reporter to deal with the mess himself."

"Does this also apply to commercial television?" the Chairman of the Board of Directors dared to ask.

"It's especially applicable there, especially when you imply that you were just getting ready to launch your ad campaign on their TV station, and now you unfortunately have to deal with something else..."

Vitas made a presentation on how to speak in front of the camera so that it wouldn't be turned against the correspondent. He spoke on how to present a testimony without saying a word. He ran training sessions on how to communicate a testimony that couldn't be edited or that would be difficult to edit at the expense of revealing the secrets of manipulation at play. He gave a presentation on how to predict what is being prepared against the correspondent's testimony and how to throw the aces up your sleeve out onto the table, or at least to minimise media damage.

Vitas stepped onto the other riverbank. But he still had to look back across the water. There was a worm working somewhere in the back of his head. He felt there was something unspoken, a sense that this had something to do with the name "Alex" but also with his departure from the media world. This was not the end, it could not be the end. On the other hand, he didn't want to surrender and realised that in any case, he didn't want to die in the media institute. But he was also afraid that this was only an unspoken cliché, and he did want to die for it. He actually didn't even know what he wanted then or had ever wanted anymore… The edges of the riverbank that he crossed over from were blurry and merging with the water in the distance. What next?

So one day, he pulled out a crumpled up, much hated, twice washed business card with the name Alex on it.

– – –

"THE POT HAS BOILED OVER."

39.
The Black Liquid

Over a month went by before Sonam adjusted to the light. He stepped out of the chamber that was assigned to him every two hours for at least a little while. "I need to get moving and start to exercise," he kept saying, firstly, with only a thin scarf wrapped around his eyes. It seemed he could see the contours of some objects through the scarf, so he didn't mind. He looked a lot better after a good wash and haircut. Unlike the other monks, he kept his hair and beard, as a way of adjusting to the sunlight. If he could have been identified as an eighty-year-old man when he crawled out of the hermitage, then following these changes, his apparent age fell to perhaps seventy. His hair and beard were grey, his body hunched over and very scrawny, and his limbs could snap like matchsticks. But it was clear that he was tall. Had he stood up straight, he would have been over six feet. He intended on reaching his original appearance, as he had a big appetite. Rmi-lam brought him all kinds of treats. She either stole them from the kitchen or passed on ones of her own.

Sonam liked to sit on the rocks and bask in the sun. Heat penetrated the scarf, warming him all the way down to his fingertips. The heat rolled back and forth throughout his body and he could feel a burst of energy within. He sat motionless for a long time. Rmi-lam danced and chirped around him whenever she skipped a lesson or had a break in between classes. The happiness this brought to him was visible. He claimed that this brought him much closer to God than when he was in the cold, empty darkness. Then he condemned those words as "happy blasphemy."

He sometimes told Rmi-lam of his harsh past and this was when a crowd of monks would gather around, each listening without a word as they reflected on their destinies.

He recalled how, as a young boy not even twelve years old, the Chinese had invaded Tibet. He was born in Khama. The people of Khama considered themselves an independent nation, venerable, proud warriors with immense, innocent hearts and a strong sense of humour. Even the CIA agents, who later helped the partisans of the Khama people (and others) in the form of supplying weapons, medicine and training sessions, liked them very much. They called them "The cowboys of the Far East." Today? Today nothing but emptiness, the dwellings burnt down and the monasteries destroyed... nothing but the memories of the eyewitnesses that remained.

He recalled the bombing of the besieged Lithang Monastery. Thousands of Tibetans and their families hoped the monastery would bring them safe refuge, but the Buddhist tabernacle with its long-lasting traditions was razed to the ground. The Chinese called forth bomber-craft that no one Tibetan had ever seen. In order to survive, as a little boy, he had played dead among the corpses, including those of his mother and his sister, who was as old as Rmi-lam. That sickly smell, that crackling and whistling in his head, reminded him of a motionless bomb still in the air. The image froze but the whistling remained, indelible. He was one of the few who had escaped; bleeding, he fled to the partisans, who took him in. Not only did they teach him to shoot a bow and arrow, already familiar with the practice of archery, but they trained him in the use of firearms. No one could catch him on horseback. Childhood? Had it ever even started, it was long gone by then.

In the Tibetans' imagination, the word *thamzing* had the most hellish connotations, comparable in sum with the word *holocaust*, and that which took place in the concentration camps of the Second World War. The Nazis for the Jews were comparable to the Communists for the Tibetans. All the villagers were slaughtered, the women raped, and the monks shot or crucified. The monasteries were destroyed, priceless Buddhist monuments were irreparably damaged, or if they were truly of market value, meaning that they were made of gold or some other valuable element, they were subsequently transported to Beijing.

The partisans were often triumphant and killed many of the Chinese invaders. More than once they defeated superior numbers and firepower, but there were ten Chinese soldiers prepared to take the place of any one of their number lost. Chairman Mao couldn't care less for casualties. So, the armed revolt concluded in the true form of a war in the 1970s. The CIA had cut off the supply of weapons and medicine that they had dropped from aircrafts in parachutes long before that point, during the 1960s. Tibetan training at US army bases had also long come to a stop. The partisans scattered in all directions, some fleeing to India, while only a few remained behind.

He too, wandered the breadth of the land. Not wanting to go to the Indian city of Dharamshala, still he knew that this was the residence of His Holiness the Fourteenth Dalai Lama and the Tibetan government in exile. Neither did he want to go into the Indian Army, where Tibetans made up the Special Frontier Forces, or the Ladakh Scouts who had significant military success. He didn't want to go into

Ladakh, also known as Little Tibet, a place crowded with vacant Buddhist monasteries. He wanted to stay, yet not to stay... Until he collided with the famous Lama Thorpe Tenzin and set off on the path of the monk. An escape to Buddha. For him, this was the only possible future he could see, and he had soon settled in Jadhang.

– – –

After a few weeks, Sonam was able to move completely on his own. Although he had to be careful, not going too far, he was quickly getting back into shape. Lama Rinpoche also went to see him quite frequently and after only a few days, he irreverently said that he was glad to see him finally "alive."

This was just when Kromen was returning with his caravan. Upon his arrival, the monks curiously examined the goods that he had brought. His strength was proved by the many books he carried. He brought back many children's stories, such as *Alice in Wonderland*, *Grimm's Fairytales* and ancient Chinese parables, fables and legends, books on the fine arts... Moreover, he also brought back many DVDs, containing movies and music, revealing Kromen's slight cultural illiteracy. There was neither rhythm nor rhyme, with genres from historical American movies, to mindless shooters that Vitas and Aviel destroyed, despite the considerable protests of both Rmi-lam and Kromen, and the monks' grunts of agreement. In anger, Kromen sourly yelled something about censorship, saying that no one could appreciate the money and hard work of others and that if they thought they were so smart, they should've gone out to buy the goods themselves.

"I'd like to see what you'd end up buying in those Indian slums without my bargaining skills, you clever bastards."

"Yeah, yeah," Vitas said. "I have no doubt that, with

your past, you're very experienced in bargaining, but there's absolutely no theme to these choices."

Kromen narrowed his eyes, but deep down he ignored the insult. Very pompously, boasting self-importantly in front of the others, he told Rmi-lam that he had three more personal gifts for her. He waited for everyone to be quiet, both the tension and his own sense of self-importance mounting.

He first withdrew a bottle of Coca-Cola. Rmi-lam grabbed it and examined the black liquid in disbelief.

"No way," shouted Vitas in unison with Aviel. "Throw it out, right now!"

The other monks, too, were staring at this invention of the Western world in disbelief.

"Forget it," Kromen shouted distastefully and reclaimed the bottle just to be sure. Then he withdrew a knife from his pocket, opening the cola and raising it proudly like a flag so that everyone could see it, drinking it defiantly. He then opened his mouth and gave a long exhalation: "Aaaaah" before burping loudly and handing the bottle over to Rmi-lam, adding: "See, I am alive." She quickly grabbed the bottle so that no one could take it away from her and took a long sip. She still had the bottle in her mouth, when she suddenly stopped, the bottle lowered from her lips, her eyes bulging, her face turning red as she spat it out and started violently coughing, twisting her body as if dancing swing. Everyone erupted into laughter.

"See, you can't swallow it like that," Kromen laughed, glad that his gift was a success.

"But it's good," Rmi-lam continued to twist and frown as she gasped for air, having finished coughing.

Kromen pulled out two more well-wrapped gifts. He did this quickly, while he still had everyone's attention, riding the current of their excitement. Rmi-lam glared at them eagerly, wanting to seize them and open them in private, but Kromen wouldn't let her. Slowly, he opened them in front of everyone.

A pink electronic piano for children, made of plastic. Rmi-lam tapped her index finger on the individual keys in disbelief while everyone listened to the penetrating artificial tones that unpleasantly elbowed into their eardrums to such an extent that they all began to squirm.

"You first have to learn a chord and then you can start playing something," Kromen instructed wisely, smiling from ear to ear while everyone else suspiciously examined the fiendish instrument with its repulsive colours.

Rmi-lam soon put the keyboard down and began to unwrap the other present. But Kromen first demanded silence, even forcing her to close her eyes before unwrapping the present himself. Inside was an MP3 player with its headphones plugged in. He shoved in the batteries, set everything up correctly and then put the headphones to Rmi-lam's ears. She grabbed them with both hands, no less apprehensive. Kromen pressed play and clipped the player onto her shirt, just below her neck. Though the headphones fit her perfectly, everyone else could hear a high-pitched howling noise, followed by a regular crackling and tapping. Rmi-lam's eyes widened, standing still with her knees slightly bent, before running towards the lamasery as if she had wanted to run away from the noise.

Fear spread through the crowd and some of the monks even began to mumble that these gadgets could only be harmful to her.

Rmi-lam ran to the top corridor of the lamasery and stood just before a cliff, high above the courtyard where the crowd was gathered beneath. Trancelike as she was, everyone feared that she would fall. But then she started to calm down a little, closed her eyes, her whole body relaxing as it became clear that she was beginning to feel the rhythm.

Not even twenty seconds passed before Rmi-lam began to sway back and forth, waving and swinging her hands and her head, and slowly beginning to open her mouth. Rmi-lam danced like someone who had never in their life danced before, but this was her first experience hearing such music. Her head, hands and legs (independently of course), darted back and forth chaotically, as if the beat was forced on her by the deafening sounds of hard rock.

It soon became a significant affair to remove Rmi-lam's headphones. Her teachers found it deeply frustrating when she began to sway to the beat of the *Epic of King Gesar*. Fortunately enough, the swaying wasn't so spontaneous or animal-like anymore. But in a short time, she was banned from bringing the MP3 player to her lessons, which obviously caused many tears and much shouting.

40.
On the Other Side

"I to wait for you, Mr. Vitas, I to wait. We're needing people like you," Alex welcomed Vitas with his typical warm-hearted smile and slightly distorted Czech.

Vitas had an urge to ask who Alex meant by 'WE', but he didn't feel ready enough for a verbal shootout, so he only smiled and nodded his head comprehendingly. He knew that he wasn't the one on the high horse here today.

Coincidentally, they met at the same café and sat at the same table as he had previously with Bradla on their last meeting.

"I thought you would never want to talk to me again since Bradla got promoted and today…"

"Sorry me, it's sorry," Alex interrupted him, his left hand outstretched towards Vitas like the bumper of a car, clutching his mobile-phone to his ear with his right. "Boss," he smiled slyly. "Yes? Possibly…"

He slowly lowered his left hand and the bumper became a small, thick tentacle that grabbed a glass full of water, slowly stroking it up and down mindlessly, as if applying a condom. Alex went on to articulate something in Russian, continuing to pierce Vitas with his eyes. Vitas understood perhaps every fifth word, but remained very shy. There could be no doubt that Alex belonged to the group of people who are compelled to shout into the phone, assuming perhaps that because the other person is very far away, they cannot hear them very well. The patrons of the café eyed them in disgust and Vitas felt embarrassed by this screaming Russian. He even vaguely heard something about a tank and something about Ivan, something about getting back together with Natasha, a common expression used by the Czechs to address the Russian soldiers during the 1968 invasion of Czechoslovakia… Vitas began to have a perverse feeling that the whole phone call was a ploy (although he did actually hear some noises coming from the other end) in order to make him feel humiliated, disgraced, and therefore easy to manipulate. Or perhaps Alex knew how to take advantage of any situation…

"Boss," he smiled when he finished his phone call, pointing to the silent receiver as if apologising, as if this small, elongated box was to blame for everything. "But all of us report to some boss, right? And then we all have Almighty…" he pointed to the ceiling. "What were we talking about?" he added inquisitively, but from the sparkle in his eyes, it was clear that he knew all too well where they had left off.

"Well, that Bradla got promoted and that we're not the best of friends now, so I thought you weren't going to want to talk to me." Vitas tried adding a certain insightfulness and indifference to his voice, but a more perceptive person like Alex had to see it differently.

"Tsss," Alex waved his hand generously and wiped his mouth, foam of saliva seeping through his puffy lips. "Petty detail… We thought it will to be wise having Bradla in such a position, but is definitely not forever. Otherwise," he laughed amusingly, "no one is forever, right?"

Vitas also smiled tactfully. "I'd like to follow up on the conversation we conducted previously. What did you have in mind when you said I could get in touch with you if I had any problems? I assume you're neither Santa nor the Tooth Fairy, here to grant me any wishes… so…" Vitas was stuck, he didn't know how to go on. He raised his eyebrows to imply a question, so that he could maintain some sort of a position.

But Alex quickly came to his aid. "Of course we think because you are extremely clever and your services would be very useful with us. It's true that since you no longer do your investigations this days, you no longer have such an influences over public but you have many experience, which is important for us…" Alex became slightly apprehensive all of a sudden. Something seemed to surprise him. But it was a moment of tremor that was very difficult to see. As an experienced observer of people and their expression of emotions, Vitas noticed it, but couldn't draw any conclusions. "I will to admit it, you make me a little bit scared."

"Scared?" Vitas asked in awe. "You – scared of me?"

Alex laughed, probably only to ease the tension. "Do you know what people say about you? That you are 'loose cannon'," he answered immediately. "It's relatively easy to fire but not anyone knows where you will to land, possibly even on the head of person who fire you."

They both laughed, as if this was complete nonsense, that neither of them believed it, before Vitas added at once: "Perhaps that was true. In the past. Now, I'm somewhere completely different," he said lightly, as if he happy, trying to blot all remnants of emotion from his words with an eraser or white ink.

"We will to have a lot of work for you," Alex's face turned solemn. "However, you must to decide on right optional. We have any sectors here, but I will not to offer you the financial sector…"

"Financial?" Vitas interrupted him. "What does that mean?"

"We obviously have any activities here and finance is one of them. But relatively, the sectors are all very connected. Why are you surprise? You know we have the bank here, we involve to any advisory services…"

"I probably wouldn't be interested in that then."

"You will to be surprised," Alex broke out so furiously into laughter that Vitas jumped. "Amazing thing. Imagine Facebook. Zuckerberg and Saverin invent for us. Do you know any things people post there? Their hobbies, adventures, a kitten of broken leg, a food they like… ha-ha," Alex laughed insanely again, tapping his outstretched index finger on the top of the glass of water. "Do you know how much easy to know such a people? We know exactly what to talk about, where we will to meet them – Oh, what a coincidence you also have the kitten, too? It's incredible thing. I don't have a time for it and is not my job, but sometimes I go through the Facebook about any individuals just for fun and then tell my people how to go about them. It's very entertaining, unlocking human mind, to be knowing what persons will do, what he will to say and what are his dreams…" Like an enraptured poet engulfed by his Muse, Alex burst with energy. "There obviously are any other influential thing hidden under financial advice…"

"No, no," Vitas shook his head in disgust. "This isn't what I had in mind at all…"

"I know, I know," Alex interrupted him, seeming to understand. "You value anything else. I know almost all for your cases. Me and you boss were give you much praise…"

"What? With which boss?" Vitas hissed.

"Well, with Rokos, of course," full of fake naivety, Alex sighed.

"What were you doing together?

"Don't you know? I involved his media training session along with any others. How to deal with media. I probably saw all reports of yours. They were my learning tools. And Kromen? You almost got him, but there was no chance for you. I know Kromen since long times... A job well done. But honestly, we must to choose our people wisdom and decide to entrusting certain information. Please don't see the sign of distrust, totally not. But like last time I said, anything take time to go ripe. Unripe fruit cannot be picked, yes?"

"And once it's rotten, then it's useless, too?" Vitas returned the irony, but his words seemed to be emanating from a tombstone. It was as if he were losing the ground under his feet, floating but unable to avoid a few teardrops rising to his red eyes. He tried removing them by blinking. He didn't want to seem too defeated in front of his demon.

"Sure," Alex laughed, still jolly and powerful, not seeming to notice what he was exacting on Vitas. Or perhaps he did realise, though didn't let on out of generosity. "What about *Russia Today*? We can to arrange and you will stay in your line of work," he abruptly said.

"No, no," Vitas shook his head bitterly at this offer of a job for the Russian TV station that would continue to primarily excel in demagogy and misinformation broadcast across the globe. At this point, Vitas couldn't even realise the scope of the offer. "I simply don't want to tread the same waters anymore. I no longer want to be a reporter," he snapped sharply.

"I remember, I understand," Alex smiled condescendingly. "Okay, look, this is what we will to do. We will to start with test. Apologise, but it's really necessary," he added quickly, with a remorseful expression, as if to suggest that he may have committed some social faux pas. It was clear that this was all an elaborate performance. A ritual dance around a slaughtered pig that must senselessly and unnecessarily linger on with all its actions, screams, dances and its noises, until it's completely devoured by the local crowd.

"Let's first show to our goal. Until now, you must to stand in front of camera. I am not saying it was easy. And more, you made anything up. But it's like the tinsel, the…" rubbing his fingers together, Alex couldn't find the right word, "… there is perfect word for in English: LIMELIGHT. In our language, the ramp world…"

"You mean the lights on a ramp, the centre of attention, the popularity and so on…?"

"Yes, that. Limelight… Lime… light – perfect sound – lime… light. It sound like the perfect smack of lips. A double smack. Like screwing a girl and she happily smack her lips twice after orgasm. Limelight…" Alex raved poetically, his hands slightly raised, his eyes gazing up like Jesus in El Greco's portrait of the Praying Christ. "Say yourself – lime light."

Vitas stared at Alex, not understanding him at all.

"Try it," Alex insisted again.

"Lime light," Vitas growled coldly and stiffly, as if trying to squeeze drops of nectar from a fruit that has already been pressed three times over.

"That's not it. You must to really feel and say slow – LIME…" he paused for a long time, "LIGHT… However, we prefer to the background," he unexpectedly snapped, quickly and sternly slipping back to hard reality. "Help from behind scenes. Influence things normal people have no mind to and make them to see what we want them be seeing, things they must to see, things related to limelight. Let them enjoy. We pull the strings…" Alex started laughing again.

'You're a real burst of joy,' Vitas thought, a little frightened. He felt his stomach cramp with the feeling of terror.

"Do you like puppets?' continued Alex.

"I don't know, I can't say I like them. I don't know what

there is to like about them, but I don't mind them, if that's what you want to hear."

"I mean to controlling puppets, pulling on strings. We are just to get a group people here together in Czech, who will to involve internet discussion. Discussion for anything," Alex purred like a contented cat whose owner scratched him behind the ears. "Some topic must to be elaborated, whenever we can involve in discussion, divert discussion in right direction, provide desirable motive and question others. Create controversial review for innocent, romancive theatre performance for explain completely different issue, difficult to know. We obviously know everything is related to everything…"

"You mean to troll?"[31] Vitas frowned.

"Oooh," Alex waved his hands unhappily, without losing his ever-understanding smile. "You all have negative expression to everything right away. We must to help people understand how to perceive a world. You know one thing? First, we will to try anything else and then we will to see, okay?" Alex suddenly stopped smiling, stopped using his secret phrases and started speaking completely pragmatically. It was unclear whether he left the subject of trolls only temporarily, due to Vitas' lack of interest, or for some other reason. He took a pencil out of his pocket and wrote down an address in the centre of Prague on a flyer for the café's honey cake. The address was in the centre of Prague's Old Town. "You will to go here. The next days to tomorrow at nine. No public eye to see you and you will not to be

---

31 A troll is Internet slang, usually referring to an anonymous member of an online discussion, chat or blog, who intentionally writes provocative posts on sensitive issues. Its main purpose being to provoke others to respond emotionally or to disrupt a normal, matter-of-fact discussion. Trolls tend to create the illusion of discussion with the intention to influence someone or even change the reader's opinion on economic or political issues.

working for another. There is enough money for you. You are ours from now on."

"Wait, wait, what do you mean OURS??? I have to know what I am getting into. During the Bolshevik era... sorry, I mean during socialism, I refused any cooperation with the undercover Communist spies and I don't intend on signing onto anything related to any secret service now!"

"We are not wanting you sign anything. Today, we don't sign anything anymore," he waved his hands and his eyes regained their sparkle of joy. "You do not know anything. Nothing. You will to only do your work or – if you smell any fish, you won't do it. Easy. You are and will to be pure like the lily." His serious voice rapidly refilled with happiness and he leaned over the table, closer to Vitas and with great trickery, amusement and mystery, whispered: "And calm down, in following morning, you can look in the mirror."

– – –

Vitas was nervous. He had no idea what to expect. He was convinced that if he were to be offered involvement with the Eastern Secret Services, or even the KGB – now the FSB – he'd proudly step away immediately. He had hated Russia from the time they had invaded Czechoslovakia in 1968, even though he had only been a little boy and hadn't understood the situation. His relationship to Russia was clearly defined and he didn't intend to change anything. It was as if he were screaming these beliefs into his mind, defending his plan to go into a completely uncertain company, with completely uncertain people. But he didn't know what to imagine.

To relieve the burden, or at least take one load off his chest, he confided his feelings to Eva. Her reaction was brief: "Don't you dare get involved in any mess! There's no need! We're not dying of hunger, we'll manage. I'm warning you! Don't get involved with the Russians!"

"But I don't know if they are Russians. I don't even know what I'm getting myself into."

"It doesn't look good and you shouldn't have agreed to anything like this anyway. You shouldn't have even met someone like that!"

"I didn't even know who'd be at the meeting..." Vitas lied angrily and slammed the door behind him.

"So, now you know," he heard softly from behind the door.

"Well," said Vitas. "Like every woman, everything is black or white. I shouldn't have told her. It was stupid to tell her. If I'm getting so involved, I'll really have to keep some things to myself. Of course we're not going to die of hunger, but I have to do something. Even Alex said that I can back away from it at any point. So what? And this is only a test, so it will be a test both ways. If something seems off, I'll back down..."

All sorts of existential considerations swayed through him before the given day and hour. But he knew that he couldn't know what he was getting himself into and that he wouldn't be able to deal with anything until the moment he arrived "at the place." He had no choice but to remain patient.

41.
Summertime

Within a few weeks, Sonam became stronger and overall more physically fit, for a man of his age. This was partly thanks to the quality of his meals. His menu suddenly consisted of meat, not only because of the sheep and goats that wandered too close to the rock and killed themselves, but also thanks to the tragic death of a yak. It had drowned in the wild stream of the Jadhang Gad. This left many monks puzzled, as although the current in the stream is strong in certain places, it's rather shallow, making it difficult for a human to drown, let alone a huge yak. But so be it. Sonam, Rmi-lam and our Jingzhi enjoyed the yak steak and Vitas dared to make a conciliatory gesture towards Kromen in the form of a clenched fist and a thumbs up, which Kromen graciously and modestly acknowledged with a mild sigh.

When it came to the Lama, Kromen beat around the bush for a long time, but with the day of deliverance truly soon enough approaching. He came to see him in his chamber, to babble about remorse, to appeal to honesty, to morality and to ethics – the subtext being that all contracts must be fulfilled. Although there had been no contract, not even a verbal one, Kromen already had an image in his mind that could not be changed. This time, the Lama offered no opposition, but he did allude that Kromen wouldn't acquire any treasure without openness, and there was talk of some compensation.

In the end, Kromen received so much of the gold panned from the Jadhang, that he was more or less satisfied. And also something very valuable he wouldn't reveal, perhaps the real treasure of the Dalai Lama, from who-knows-where, it mattered not. He was surrounded by a halo of secrets and mysterious conspiracies with the Lama, making him seem very important, only for him to mysteriously say that he "had some business with the Lama." He never indicated what wealth would truly make him happy, however, and no matter what he received, it would never be enough. Bluffing was obviously a part of the deal, so when closing his agreements, he kept a mean poker face, only letting on how much he had to lose. Either way, he soon decided to leave the Jadhang in the days that followed. There was no reason for him to stay there any longer.

– – –

Sonam could finally walk around with his blindfold off, only using it to protect his eyes from direct sunlight. Soon afterwards, he too, took part in teaching Rmi-lam, though from a completely different perspective. He began to exercise with her. That's when he transformed into a strict soldier, who uncompromisingly demanded the tasks be completed. "The human spirit is free only when the body is free!" he yelled at Rmi-lam.

"He treats her like a boy," Aviel confided to Vitas, when he watched them exercise.

"Maybe so, but it hardly matters. It definitely won't hurt her and she'll be more prepared for life."

Sonam even placed her on horseback and without warning left her to master the horse on her own. Rmi-lam desperately held onto the mane and screamed like a siren. But she held on. Then, he taught her how to ride properly and even do things like hide behind the horse while it gallops and to stand in a single stirrup, or to jump from horse to horse... Other exercises involved a long dagger, a common weapon for Tibetans, who can work wonders with it. She learned self-defence and methods of attack. Her exercises also involved regular archery classes. It was finally agreed with the Lama that Rmi-lam must partake in at least two physical exercises daily, interspersed with lessons from her teachers.

It didn't take long before the other monks, including Aviel and Vitas, gradually joined in the exercises, especially those with weapons, such as knives and bows. It was strangely amusing to see the monks step outside the lamasery, approach the chorten, remove their prayer wheels and begin to fight. When they finished, everyone searched for their own prayer wheel. They were also interested in exercising the body, such as through running and push-ups. The entire lamasery was at once alive in renewed unison and full of vigour. This was reflected in the religious masses, too, which were filled with zeal and fervent. The samsara, the divine wheel of life that Rmi-lam so often ran towards to spin enthusiastically, began to turn at an ever-faster pace.

Rmi-lam was enjoying herself. She had classes in the morning, followed by exercises and if she happened to escape for a while, she listened to music, watched movies or read... And if more than one of these things, both the spare battery that Kromen had brought and the battery in the laptop died, five monks having to peddle at all hours of the night, either until Rmi-lam fell asleep, or at least until the laptop battery was finally charged.

From time to time, Rmi-lam liked to hide away with her clown among the rocks above the lamasery, near the place where Sonam's hermitage used to be. She would sit there and listen to music from the MP3 player, or from the laptop, and gaze up at the stars that broke through the darkness. The stars spoke to her, saying something beautiful or sad in an unknown language. She knew they were speaking to her, persuading her of something...

Once, she put a DVD into the laptop without even thinking about it. The fact that there was a picture similar to the contraption that Kromen had brought – a piano – on the cover, grabbed her attention. But this piano was a real one, a big one. She had her headphones on. She heard strings, flowing slowly and endlessly from one side and then like a returning tide to the other. Then she heard the sharp, hoarse sound of a trumpet, also in waves from side to side, but in a completely different sense. Rmi-lam was sitting in a boat navigated by somebody else, and she swayed continuously in the waves to the original rhythm. And that was where the stars descended from, caught by a stunning, silver voice. The bright moon hitched the Big Dipper in front of the boat and aligned the others in an honorary accompaniment, patiently setting off on a swaying journey onward. The gruff voice of the old, bearded captain, who had sailed the world over, was proof of the tenderness and fragility of the whole expedition. Tears ran down her face. Sitting on the rocks at the top of the world, surrounded by pure darkness and mountains, stones and stars, in the world of Gershwin's 'Summertime', sung by Ella Fitzgerald and Louis Armstrong. She didn't notice the monitor that was only intertwining static images.

More 'Summertime' verses followed, sung by famous and less famous people, but always singers with a special expression, singers that had something to say to the world. And then a bald, ugly Jingzhi appeared wearing a scarf, and began wriggling his hands across the piano like a worm, all across the concert grand piano. It was as if every sound, every tone would first run through his body, then seep through the monitor and hit Rmi-lam first in the temples and then on the top of her head. The tones began to cover and soothe her entire form. Rmi-lam slowly raised her index finger to the monitor and pointed her finger to the detailed shot of the piano with the dancing Jingzhi. She also pointed her middle finger to it and began lightly drumming the keys on the monitor, which seemed to curl up like a muscle where she touched them.

Vitas knew where Rmi-lam usually wandered off to. She liked this place a lot. He usually didn't want to disturb her. However, it was Aviel's turn to tell a story, so he went to fetch a colleague and they set off to see Rmi-lam together.

She was hidden behind a large piece of rock, gently tapping the monitor with each of her fingers, her face lit up grey-blue. She was wearing headphones and tears streamed down her face. The two intruders wanted to take a closer look, to discover the reason for her sadness. Aviel carefully approached the side of the rock, close to Rmi-lam's back, but as he watched his feet, he failed to look ahead and tripped over a loose rock that was waiting for an opportunity to emphasise its presence. It crashed down beside Rmi-lam. She only withdrew, quickly wiped away her tears, removed headphones and turned around.

"Sorry Rmi-lam, I didn't want to disturb you, we were only worried about you," Aviel said, wanting to hide in shame under the incriminating rock, the same source that had revealed his presence. In an attempt to quickly divert attention from his embarrassment, he looked at the computer and said: "What d'you have there?"

She didn't say a word and only looked back at the monitor. She didn't have to say anything, the DVD cover on the floor spoke for itself. There was the black and white keyboard of a large concert grand piano detailed in the image, with fingers spread out across it, with the title, George Gershwin – 'Summertime', on the picture.

Both men realised the depth of Rmi-lam's feelings, knowing that words like: "C'mon little girl, it's time for bed!" would be impossible. They were wordless. They felt embarrassed and spare.

"Is this a piano?" she pointed her finger to the keyboard in the picture.

"Yes, this is a piano," said Aviel wisely.

"And the thing I got from Sir Kromen is also a piano?"

"Well, I'd say it's almost like a piano… for children," Aviel confirmed hesitantly.

"What does that mean?"

"… a little worse," he uttered the words a little unhappily.

"What makes it worse?"

"I'd say the sound isn't that great," he added, feeling almost ashamed. He didn't know what to tell her. He glanced at Vitas, who had settled off to one side, into the darkness. A gesture of his hand implied that they'd be better off leaving her alone. But before they could do a thing, Rmi-lam abruptly closed the laptop, seized her clown, sprang to her feet and sprinted home to the lamasery. Both Jingzhi pursued her. After a moment's hesitation, they mustered up the courage to check in on her before they each went to bed. They could hear the horrible, piercing sounds of a plastic piano from far down the hallway. With great fury, Rmi-lam was attempting to make it sound like 'Summertime'. As the heads of both of the desperate men emerged in the doorway, she launched a pillow at them.

"I want a piano," she screamed assertively.

"Rmi-lam, how do you want to get a piano in here? It's not possible," Aviel negotiated with her. He felt happy and somewhat superior for Rmi-lam's want of something truly impossible, truly impossible to fulfil and he measured several logical arguments against it.

"I want a piano, I want a piano!" Rmi-lam insisted stubbornly. Her squeals attracted many other monks, including Kromen. As soon as he understood the source of her anger, he was touched with pride. His presents (personal gifts!) were Rmi-lam's favourites.

"Sir Kromen! I want a piano! The biggest one in the world."

"And why, little girl? Is this one not enough?" Kormen asked plaintively.

"No, this one is really not enough. I want to play 'Summertime' and I want to play on the biggest piano…"

"… she means a concert grand," Aviel interrupted smugly, in order to properly explain it to Kromen.

"Yeah, I know," Kromen scolded him, changing his tone deftly, elongating his face into a playful smile, while caressing Rmi-lam. "But that's not possible, dear. There's no way of getting it here. There's no way anyone will ever get it in here."

"I don't care," Rmi-lam waved her hand to rid herself of that unpleasant, fake, and forced caress. "It's your job. I want a concert grand piano and that's it."

"Fine," Kromen exclaimed unexpectedly. "I'll be leaving in a couple of days. I'll be gone a long time, but I'll return and you can practise on this one in the meantime," he pointed to the plastic keyboard. "The uncles here will help you. Learn the G-Major scale and so on… And once you learn 'Summertime' perfectly on this one, I'll bring you a piano from the Heavens. Deal?"

"A concert grand!"

"Yeah, fine, a concert grand."

"Deal!"

They shook on it, but neither one believed the other.

Rather Rmi-lam didn't believe Kromen and Kromen was ever-indifferent to any promise made five minutes prior, especially if it weren't of any major significance to him. After all, he was leaving in two days, and could apply a simple adage to anything promised or said: "If I don't remember it, it never happened."

42.
The Making of a Politician

The bell began to ring in its usual way. The paint peeling off the walls in the hallway, the old wooden doors with nothing but a sign that read Vx Studio, which meant nothing to him, except perhaps the name of a nerve gas, but that was probably out of the question. Spacious rooms, typical of Prague's Old Town, sprawled all around. But a breath of the past could be felt everywhere.

The doors swiftly swung wide and a laughing woman stood in the doorway. A man's laughter and other male voices came from the same direction and she seemed the very foam burst from the wild, raging atmosphere of some morning party, of its first wave that would go on to engulf everyone in sight – meaning Vitas in this case. "Hi, you're Vitas, right? I'm Svata." She stuck her hand out to greet him.

His mouth gaped. He hadn't expected anything like this. Before him stood an elegant lady, somewhere in her thirties, and given the feeling she emanated, he could immediately place her in a category of women with outstanding charisma. Her outfit was enticing, though not at all provocative. On the contrary, it was almost puritanical, concealing everything, but only as if to burst open at any minute and invite him into her paradise. A little short of breath, he could only snap a virtual picture and continue to stare.

"So, what are you looking at? Come on in," she blinked. She even turned a little red, Vitas being rather too legible in his shameless thoughts.

She led him down the large corridors of what could have once been an apartment. A maze of five or six large rooms with high ceilings. All the walls were painted white, slightly yellowish with age, with numberless cracks in the joints and edges of the walls, these translucent splits indicating the years of the whole building. The furnishings were modest, practical, with no ornament but for a single wardrobe in one of the rooms, a spacious armchair, a few stools and coffee tables, as if everyone were to sit around and have a confidential conversation. Nothing outrageous. Nothing captivating or worldly for an individual.

Svata, who quickly welcomed Vitas into a first-name-basis relationship, took him into one of the rooms that all the chitter-chatter was coming from. When she opened the doors, a hard to describe image popped up before his eyes. There were only a few glass cupboards, one desk with a computer in the corner and a large round table that dominated the room. There was a young, twenty-five-year-old man, wearing jeans, a white shirt, and giving the impression of a slick, successful manager. But most importantly, Vitas could see another person who, even after rubbing his eyes, was still standing on the round table, with a bottle of champagne in one hand, almost dancing and frozen still at the opening of the door. The right hand holding the bottle was raised and the other hand was outstretched with the fingers apart, standing with his feet separate and with the look of a mime on his face. The man was relatively tall and thin, around fifty years old. Vitas felt only a couple of weeks younger. His face was rather repulsive. He had thin, indistinct, grey hair and a narrow face – which made Vitas immediately think of Zapotocky, the sadly infamous president of the 1950s, during the cruellest beginnings of Communism in Czechoslovakia. A wrinkled nothing with legs, lacking the necessary tail to meet the criteria of a rat.

In his dead stance, motionless, he exclaimed: "The acclaimed, celebrated, esteemed Mr Vitas?"

"Only the last word is accurate," growled Vitas.

"But why the modesty, my friend?" the man sharply adjusted himself, adopting a more civilised pose, still on the table.

"Well, there's no need for me to introduce Mr Vitas any further," Svata interrupted the conversation and pointed to the man on the table. "This is Mr Bedynka. A politician and Mayor of Lhota, running for regional representative, but his ambitions go far beyond that. And this is your job, to turn him into the most successful politician of the loftiest order." Bedynka grinned at Vitas from above, seeming a hopeless primitive in his straightforward joy. "And this is Mira, our co-worker." She introduced the man by the table.

The young man shook Vitas' hand, which was an impulse for Bedynka, who also wanted to shake Vitas' hand. He bent down and stretched out his own bony fingers. Although hesitant, Vitas shook it lightly. "And what are you doing on the table, Mr Bedynka?"

"Self-confidence!" Mira spoke, not giving Bedynka a chance to respond. "We have arrived at the conclusion that the most important thing for a potential higher-echelon politician to have is self-confidence, so we're trying to bestow him with this in other ways, too."

"I'd say that self-confidence is by far not the only thing, and shouldn't a politician know how to talk, Mr Bedynka?"

"Of course I know how to talk," said Bedynka, offended.

"If I'm to make something of you, try not to let others speak for you, if possible. I'm sorry, but if my job is to truly make something of you," Vitas looked inquisitively at everyone present. "And on the contrary, in certain situations, it is ESSENTIAL that you let others speak on your behalf, but we have to discuss this in more detail."

"It's fast-paced!" exclaimed Bedynka, "and I damn well love it!"

"So can you tell me what's going on here?" asked Vitas.

"As I have already mentioned," Mira stepped into the conversation. "Mr. Bedynka is an individual who is required to become a politician of the loftier order. You have unlimited resources at your disposal. You can equip these premises in whatever way you find pleasing. Our resources are global and you're welcome to them. Whatever you need, you must only provide the justification."

Vitas looked back at Bedynka, who only nodded dumbly. "But I need to know that Mr. Bedynka has some sort of a talent for this."

"He does," said Mira, but then paused immediately. "Well, you are in charge here now, but I'd say he's got the basic skills."

"I see," Vitas said doubtfully, slowly walking around the table, still looking at Bedynka. His body remained motionless, only his head turning towards him. When he couldn't turn it any further, he turned his head the other way, to keep a constant eye on him from the other side, once he came into sight again. During this silence, one could hear a piano playing somewhere in the background. Someone was continually practicing the C-Major scale, over and over again.

"Get off the table, please," said Vitas, emotionless. It wasn't an order, it wasn't a plea, it was merely an imperative.

"So, first of all," Vitas began calmly, once Bedynka got down. Without even realising it, he was in the role of the manager, which certainly hadn't just fallen into his lap out of nowhere. But this didn't seem to bother him, and after a few minutes, he felt comfortable in his new position. "There won't be any more drinking going on here. Maybe as an exception in the evening but never throughout the day. As a politician, you are not permitted to drink. Self-confidence is important but you have to gain it another way. You can, of course, help yourself physically, by raising your chest, your diaphragm, practicing speech technique and mentally crowning yourself the king, whatever… But not by drinking or jumping on a table. So, let's sit down and talk. I need to know everything about you. Absolutely everything, your work life and your personal life."

Vitas too, was surprised by how quickly and comfortably he adapted to his situation. He immediately assessed all three men. Mira was young and immature, who wouldn't stand in Vitas' way; Svata was marvellous and his feelings were stronger, a lot stronger, towards her… 'The terrible chemistry!' he screamed in his mind. And Bedynka was a dummy. All in all, his work was well cut out.

"Y'know," said Mira, "they have informed us…"

"Who're they? Who told you?" Vitas interrupted her.

"Alex."

"How do you know Alex?"

"From the café. He invited me there on one occasion and we agreed to…"

"How did he get to you?"

"I'm not sure. I attended business school before this and then I worked as a business representative, in public relations and so on…" She paused for a moment to measure what else Vitas might ask. The piano practice accelerated to a G-Major scale in staccato. When Mira noticed Vitas was remaining silent, she continued. "And so he informed us that it would certainly be a lot of work with Mr Bedynka, perhaps choosing him for his weaknesses. An unattractive name and not all that attractive to look at…"

All three of them were staring at Bedynka, who answered them silently with his utterly indifferent, and even slightly affirmative look. Vitas was amazed at how someone could listen to others discuss him with such calmness. He decided to add fuel to the fire. "There's not much here to work with."

Bedynka agreed with a smile. This was too much for Vitas to handle. He decided that from then on, he had to be sure to avoid any kind of trouble.

"But we're going to fight with it. We'll create a clear strategy. How often can you come here, or in other words, how much time can you devote to your future every week?" he asked Bedynka.

"A day a week."

"But we need to know," Svata continued, "how long you intend on doing this, so that we can make some sort of a schedule and generally ensure your involvement in the elections and so on…"

"Hmm. I can't say off the top of my head. But right now we have to agree on an intense regime of cooperation, once a week for at least six months, seeing as it isn't possible to prolong it. But you have to make time at least one whole week, once every three months. We'd spend it outdoors somewhere in some cabin or B&B. And after about six months, he could get politically involved somewhere, but still under our supervision."

"And what's your strategy?" Svata asked curiously.

"I already have an idea," Vitas smiled at her, "but it's only bits and pieces for now. I need one week to sum it all up. Not only in my head, but also on paper. I'll get everything ready and we'll meet here in a week. Okay?"

"Okay," said the others in unison.

43.

I Am in Your Hands

"No, I'm not going there!" Rmi-lam snaps stubbornly, stamping her feet. Lama Thorpe Tenzin stands some ten feet away from her, luring her with his vibrating fingers, to come and stand by his side, on the edge of the steep cliff. A 1300-foot drop lies ahead of her. It looms high, around 700 feet from the peak of Mount Jadhang, on the other side of the lamasery. Dressed in his red, flowing cassock, standing at the peak with only emptiness before him, interrupted by a few mountain peaks in the farthest distance, the Lama appears like some deity, beckoning humanity to follow in his steps. Rmi-lam stands still, wearing her red chupa, a backpack slung over her shoulders, with her never-to-be-forgotten clown sticking out of it. Her eyes pierce a single point on the ground, her lips pursed stubbornly. It's clear that a major battle is taking place within her, between respect and fear, and the eager desire to discover something new.

"No!" Rmi-lam insists.

The Lama takes a few steps in her direction, stands behind her and grabs her firmly by the shoulders. "Close your eyes," he whispers gently into her ear.

Rmi-lam closes her eyes but her whole body is shaking.

"Now don't worry, I've got you." The Lama talks slowly, with long pauses in between sentences. "You know you're still safely standing on firm ground. Now, I will let you go but I am still standing behind you. You feel my breath, so you feel safe. Take deep breaths. Feel every bit of the air that you are inhaling and exhaling."

Rmi-lam takes deep breaths and slowly begins to relax.

"Keep breathing just like that. Now start to feel your body. You have your own vertical and horizontal axis. You feel your height and follow it from the top of your head down to your heels. As if it was a narrow corridor that you can stretch, expand and lengthen using your body. From the bottom up and back down again. And then from the left shoulder to the right. Now you can feel the axes and lines stretching. Your diaphragm is expanding…" Rmi-lam was expanding in her own feelings. All the muscles in her body were stretching. Both of her hands went up on both sides. Relaxed, flowing, as if they were helpless and someone else were lifting them.

"And now slowly take three steps forward." The Lama put his palms lightly over her shoulders. He didn't move, so when Rmi-lam stepped forward, she moved away from his palms and was standing on her own, with no security, with her arms outstretched on both sides. Her steps were entirely different. Careful but confident. Given her sense of immeasurable height and width, she had no problem stand-ing close to the cliff. The first step, the second, the third…

The Lama approached her quietly and slowly, but no longer holding onto her. "You are standing on the edge of a steep cliff, with vast space in front of you. The sun… You can take two more baby steps to the cliff. Take deep breaths in and feel your axis, your size. To the left, to the right, up…"

Then he paused and only watched her closely. She, breathing calmly and slowly, took a very hesitant baby-step forward, only putting her right foot in front of her left, so that her heel touched her left toe. This made her lose her balance, so she immediately tried again, this time putting her left foot in front of her right and spreading her legs slightly to regain her balance. She could now feel the emptiness beneath her feet.

From her point of view, she had been standing this way for a very long time. Time had stopped for her.

She took deep breaths with her eyes closed. She could feel the large space all around her and herself within this space. She was firmly anchored, but stretched up high and wide out to the sides, as if strictly defining the contours of the space over which she has mastery. But this space extended further, expanding in all directions, high and wide, into infinity, and cannot be stopped. Eventually she felt a soothing warmth. It may have been the rays of the sun, its beams caressing her with awe and respect. Or it may have come from within.

"I am in your hands!" she yelled aloud in a firm voice. It was a completely different voice. More confident, deeper, every syllable expressing a full experience of life. The sentence was long and echoed slightly among the rocks and into the valley. Then, her hands slowly dropped and she opened her eyes. She looked all around her. Completely calm, without fear. On the edge of a sheer cliff.

Then she steps back and looks contentedly at the smiling Lama. She pulls a white, triangular prayer flag hanging on a string from her backpack dominated by the clown. Together with the Lama, they firmly grab the strings on both sides, anchor them to the jutting rocks and take in the flying flag for a bit longer, spreading its emotions, embodied in specific words, far into the distance.

From that moment on, unless the weather was inclement, she'd come here every morning to shout her "I am in your hands," and to send her message far and wide using the prayer flag.

There was a surprise waiting for Rmi-lam when she returned to the lamasery. She came to the door of her room innocently, grabbed the doorknob but then stopped immediately. There was a beautiful filigree silver box hanging on a hook at her eye level. A mezuzah. There were artful but amateurish starfish, leaves and various decorations on its more-or-less eight-inch-long cylinder. A paper scroll shone through the many openings among the individual figures.

It was easy to open the box. Rmi-lam unfurled the scroll and began to read: "You shall love the Lord your God with your whole heart and your whole soul."

Aviel explained the old Jewish tradition of attaching a small box with two scrolls of Torah text on the door frame of every Jewish home, to protect it. Several monks, including Vitas showed up accidentally-on-purpose when Aviel began to tell the story, and they asked detailed questions about the event. Thus Aviel also ended up elucidating the text, which was reminiscent of a biblical event, such as the escape of the Jews from Egypt, where they had suffered under Pharaoh's cruel reign, and how, under Moses' guidance, they stood before the Red Sea that the Lord parted, allowing them to pass. When the Pharaoh's army tried to pursue them, they were destroyed by the waves of the sea, which had returned to its original place.

"I'll leave out the fact," Aviel then told Vitas discreetly, "that this isn't a canonical text to be placed in the mezuzah, and that it's not written in the Hebrew. I'm not even designated to write it, but so what?" Aviel raised his hands helplessly. "It can serve its purpose, right?"

The truth is that the mezuzah was so successful that the scroll was different every day. Not only did Aviel write a new one, but so did Vitas, Mhosai Mangcug and the others. Thus, Christian liturgy and secular, Hindi and Buddhist texts soon began appearing in this authentically Jewish box.

And as Aviel continued to complain about how everyone was demeaning his beliefs, another box appeared on the door frame, in which Mhosai wrote a short scroll about the famous epic, the *Ramayana*. An excerpt from Ramayana's speech, who relinquished control over the Kosala Kingdom: "No living creature is endowed with the power to control the course of things; man is not independent. The destroyer sways him back and forth. Those who experience ascension are doomed to fail; those striving upward must fall; those who reunite must part from one another again and the life of all must end in death."

But this caused an influx of diverse boxes being created and before long, Rmi-lam's door frame was covered with mezuzahs, clearly none of which had anything to do with Judaism any more, but for Aviel's. And as some overly eager monks wrote and switched the texts every night, the morning ritual for Rmi-lam became something of a challenge, beginning with reading, just to then wash it all down from high up on the cliff and start living a new life on a new day by calling out: "I am in your hands."

44.
Just One Step

Vitas had jumped feet first into a new, unknown element. This job, completely different from what had fulfilled him for many years, left him ecstatic. He didn't understand that it was a leap of despair. The leap he needed to wash out the wounds inflicted on him by the outside world. He clung to this new target so forcefully that he couldn't hear the cries of warning all around him. Somebody would point a forefinger full of warning, but he wouldn't see it. He no longer told Eva of the details of his work, knowing that in any case, she wouldn't understand. It was as if he had sharply inhaled the crisp air, while seeking a change in his life. He was also approaching a milestone birthday, with the understanding that he wouldn't be getting any younger, so he had no choice but to seize life for everything it had. A handful of friends had told him to beware of this second flush of life… And this feeling too, was suppressed in a vacuum, giving him a sudden peace of mind. He was no longer living the fast-paced life he was used to, he had more time to think, but this thinking was a feverish spasm. He fumbled around without realising.

He worked hard all week, not consulting or confiding in anyone, not even his closest friends or relatives. Twice a week he "accidentally" passed by the house with the studio, unable to bear it any longer. Once, he ran upstairs and was struck with anxiety – the Vx Studio sign had disappeared. He had no idea what to think, and tried to put it from his mind. There could be no way it was a trick, the charisma that Alex surrounded himself with was too serious. And he hadn't done anything dishonest, not yet. The media training? Everyone does those… He was standing by the door and could vaguely smell Svata's scent. He knew little of women's lifestyle, let alone tell the difference between Chanel No. 5 and Bvlgari. He wasn't much of a ladies' man. He was an eternal workaholic, considered flirting a waste of time, and loved Eva. It was hardly his area of expertise. Despite this or maybe because of it, the thought of Svata excited him. Her faithful likeliness appeared, he began to talk to her, flirt with her… It was something new and unknown to him. He could hardly miss out on a little adventure, older as he was getting!

– – –

The Vx Studio sign had returned to the door, as if no one had touched it for years…

"So, we have all of Thursday to do it," Vitas instructed his team. "Mr. Bedynka, you have a speech technique class with the teacher from eight o'clock in the morning for two hours. Then, two hours of media training, lunch, two hours of rhetoric with a lecturer from the university and then more media training. We will then practise rhetoric on specific topics until the evening. We'll talk about life, then prepare for different situations," preached Vitas with a secretive smile.

"And what's your idea for the campaign?" asked Bedynka impertinently.

"I'm still working on it, it's not that easy. It's years-worth of work. I mean, if you're really going to work on yourself, you'll reap the benefits in three years at the earliest."

"Of course, but you must have some idea about how to proceed, no?"

"Right, but it's still a work in progress. We have to focus on the issues that interest common people, your potential audience. And there're already universal problems that apply to the whole of the Czech Republic, such as Gypsies and retired people that we also have to accentuate..."

"I'd prefer not to speak about Gypsies..."

"Stop there! They're no Gypsies. To you, they are the Romani community, or you can say *our Romani citizens*. I'm sorry, I might've said it before, but I can – you cannot."

"Oh, but that's discrimination," smiled Bedynka, no less clearly agreeing with this approach.

"As soon as you have the chance, move any Romani citizens who are trouble-causers to the ghettos on the outskirts of the city. But it has to be legal. Then we'll tell the media ourselves that you're a dunce. We'll provide them with the most incomplete information – you have to remain clean and, in their case, it has to be about notorious tax-dodgers, thieves, peace-disturbers and I-don't-know-what-else. So then, we're going to file a lawsuit against the media. You simply have to make yourself visible and the general public will warm to you."

"I think I can do this," he nodded enthusiastically. Mira and Svata took notes and listened eagerly.

"It's not going to be as easy as it sounds. You have to be prepared for everything. I'll take care of it in the form of proper training. The next step in terms of Gypsies is to find one smart one among them – and by smart, I really mean smart..."

"Is that even possible?" Bedynka interrupted with a sarcastic laugh.

"Quiet, please," Vitas waved his hand impatiently. "It must be an intelligent and capable Romani. We'll make a deal with him. He'll set up a building company and he'll purchase homes from you, from the city, for himself and the other problematic Romani who you weren't able to move out for legal purposes during the previous incident. And once again they're moved out to some ghetto that you prepare and as for the original dwellings that they were to live in, they renovate them and sell the homes back to you, to the city, it doesn't matter. Then, the media will uncover your dealings again, so you'll be the worst fascist under the sun, but at the same time, adored by the majority of the public. And you'll even let on that you like the Romani community, that you have a weakness for them because you're doing business with the Romani owner of the building company. This also implies that you're in fact not a racist. Get it? They'll be on your case for doing business with your friend and he is a member of the Romani community. But it has to be legal and proper trade, then the media'll be all over it. The people will either hate you or love you, but no one will remain indifferent to you, and that's the most important thing! Of course, there are many other issues involved in this. We'll even come up with a motivational program for Romani that the government should have implemented twenty years ago, such as linking welfare cheques to school attendance and a long list of other things."

"I see you've been busy," said Mira, happily echoing the others.

"I'm just throwing that out there. I still have to work on it. You have to prepare for attacks from all sides. That's why we'll pre-prepare your reactions, the clear answers, the slogans, like: 'I only do what doctors do – cleanse the body of ulcers…'

"Retirees are another topic. You have to, or actually WE

have to, come up with a program. You must visit them at retirement homes and their own homes and win them over. You have to let them know that the whole country will fall apart without them. They're usually frustrated by their own uselessness, so it's our task to redirect their thinking, even if we'll never get rid of the cause.

"Then, we have social media to deal with. So far, political usage has missed the mark, but this is the wave of the future. We'll hire an expert for this. A referendum. A nation-wide referendum – an incredible topic."

"What's so incredible about it?" Bedynka asked confusedly. "You're letting anyone talk about anything. What's so great about that?"

"A great opportunity to manipulate with people and boost your popularity. Every other chap sipping beer with his pals is convinced that he alone has the global solution and that he should be the one in a position of power. And now you allow him to voice his opinion on any subject, and he'll be impressed. What do we need a representative democracy for," added Vitas ironically, "or even direct democracy, when even the biggest fool, the most clueless fellow or doddering elder, without any conception of the matter, can make decisions about the country's future? It doesn't matter that the subject of the referendum is beyond his intelligence and intellectual abilities."

Vitas paused. His eyes darted from one listener to the other, as if he were waiting for the information to be digested. "Do you know how easy it is to manipulate people?" he emphasised every word.

"Next, we'll come up with a whole campaign of varied events, including artificial issues that you will miraculously resolve. We'll push fictional cases and fake news to reporters… And again – this may result in court trials won, manipulation with the media or simply taming some journalists or publishers. It will be a complex structure of steps, gradually intensifying according to the possibilities, which will continue to expand as your political career grows. The more reputable your political station, the stronger the weapons you have at your disposal, and the greater the possibility that you'll be forced to influence the public's opinion. It's not that complicated. The media is by far not what it pretends to be, so controlling it isn't a problem. They fit the ethical and moral authority category without being entitled to it and without it even being true. The people in the media come from the same senility as the environment around them and they want to elevate it to heavenly heights. If they throw dirt at someone else, they throw dirt at themselves, because they are part of the same environment. So if you react to any criticism or insult in this way, the insult or criticism is intended for you. This media is not an island in the swamp. And you have to claim that you're also impacted by the swamp, but that you are trying to get out of it, pulling the others along, saying you have a mandate to do so.

"Thieves are here in order to steal and murderers in order to kill. No one can really blame them for it, because it's their job. But it's up to the government to prevent these people from doing what they do. And you are the one whose name will have to suffice. Understand? Let them throw dirt at you. Whether you like it or not, no matter how dirty you'll be, you're the one doing the good deeds in the end – at least in the eyes of the people."

"Hey, look, I actually turn out to be a good guy in the end," Bedynka exclaimed, laughing.

"But you're going to have to learn to express yourself with perfect clarity, to be convincing to others, and that's a lot of work," Vitas nodded doubtfully.

"He can do it," Svata put in.

"And do you think that people will buy it?" Mira asked a little innocently.

"If you have the media in the palm of your hands, then there's no doubt. We'll use subliminal information, inconspicuous, yet effective passwords that people don't normally come up with. It'll be more work if we don't have the media on our side, but we'll still manage it. Look at the elections, for example…" Vitas pondered, a gleam in his eye, and quickly turned to Svata. "Svata, can you do an analysis of the last parliament elections? You'll discover what the newspapers have to say about it. I want you to focus on something that no other journalist would focus on – the IQ ratio of the elected member in relation to the program and the promised nonsense. And the same thing for his running mate, who lost against him."

"I don't understand," Svata stammered.

"We have to uncover the real reason that whatever politician was elected. This being something the media would never admit to in their exaggerated attempt to maintain objective and impartial. In other words, I want you to come up with some sort of a formula, an equation that should either confirm or refute the theory that the more foolish or the more slick the politician, the more people vote for him as opposed to the one who takes the matter seriously and really cares for the people and for the given region's future. And thanks to that – we will also find the cause."

"You mean like the government we have is the government we deserve?" Mira asked.

"Yes," nodded Vitas. "But I want an analytical breakdown and not just some witticism. An example: take a specific politician and his mindless slogans during the election campaign, something like: 'We'll give more money to retirees, we'll lower the crime rate,' some vague or simply brainless nonsense and do a side-by-side comparison with a reasonable politician, who lost on the grounds of a more intelligent speech, such as 'I can't promise to give retirees more money, but I will reduce the state deficit'. Or, 'since we're better off now, does not mean we'll spend it all on food…' It's not easy to communicate the point. I want… you know what I want, we'll discuss it later so we don't keep the others waiting. Let's meet here, say tomorrow. Agreed?"

Svata nodded without saying a word and although hard to notice and ever-so-slightly, her pupils began to deepen and tremble.

– – –

"The key to learning the piano is to relax. It's a circular motion of the wrists, stemming from the shoulders. Now, I'm going to show you what the C2 to G2 tones sound like when you're relaxed." A relatively clear voice with distinct consonants, seeped through the walls and into the studio (with the sign on the door again), replaced by the even clearer strokes of the keys. "One! Two! Three!" The source definitely wasn't live. It sounded as if it was coming from a computer, the noise stopping occasionally and going back a little to the same stressed notes and rhythms… Someone was clearly fast-forwarding it to the same spot over and over again in order to understand everything. This was then followed by a lovely sounding "Ding! Ding!" Someone was trying to imitate the recording by pounding the keys. Vitas didn't even realise whether or not he had heard the piano playing the day before. Or one week ago? Yes, a vague chord.

"What does the Vx Studio sign mean?" asks Vitas, sitting quite comfortably in the dark, on a plastic chair by the glass table with two cups of coffee on it. Svata is sitting opposite him, sunken in a huge armchair, her legs crouched beneath her. She's practically sitting on her own heels. Even so, she's still sitting about twelve inches lower, in a deliberately submissive position. Comfortable, disarmed, unaware, or perhaps aware no less? Her body implies a prey-like vulnerability.

"The right stroke is achieved by relaxing and bending the fingers at the same time. There are two basic types of strokes; the legato – quite flowing… One! Two! Three! One! Two! Three!

"Nothing. It doesn't mean anything," Svata shrugs her shoulders. "It's only a sign. Just like it's a bad idea to name someone 'Person' on his birth certificate, so they named this Studio Vx. Maybe the 'V' and 'x' mean something, but I don't know what. Maybe there're more of these for various purposes and this is how they differentiate them," she thinks.

"…Now for the staccato – nice and short – One! Two!…"

"How impersonal," adds Svata. "It's like in America, where people say 'Turn from Twenty-Fifth Avenue to Thirty-Second Street' and so on… I really don't know. It's like the Russians and the Americans have the same 'everything-is-bigger' complex. It's always my job to put up the sign when people are working there." Svata takes a sip of her coffee.

"Starlight sparkled out behind a rock…" a melodic rumble resounds within the building.

"Right, just like the flag is raised at the president's office when the president is in his office."

Svata spits out the hot coffee at the moment she drinks it. She even has to wipe the coffee with her hand, leaving a coffee stain on her left cheek. Vitas feels the need to tell her, his hand pointed out, but he likes the stain so much that he let his hand swing back down without saying a word. She looked very childish.

"You can't even play 'Twinkle, Twinkle Little Star',

without knowing how to play the C scale. Scales are a plague for all pianists, but one must practise them!"

"Have you ever thought about who this 'they', the Vx people, might be?"

"Of course I have. It all seems odd to me, but I haven't uncovered anything. And then I had to admit that maybe I'm better off not knowing too much. If no one wants us to assassinate anyone, so what?"

"The average piano player has five fingers on each hand. Every scale has eight tones, played in several octaves in a row."

"Yes, but I'm still racking my brain about it."

"I'm sure you are because you're a famous investigative reporter," she giggles provocatively.

"That hasn't been true for a long time," Vitas waves his hand with an air of nostalgia, but he can't help but admit that it was very nice to hear, especially coming from such pretty lips.

"How should we deal with this problem? Let's take a look at it. The right hand uses a so-called base. This means that the thumb is placed under the other fingers... One! Two! Three!... Ding, ding, ding..."

He wanted to know more about Svata, but found no place to be so frank, realising they hardly knew one another yet, and were far from pushing each other's boundaries. For this reason, he directed his questions elsewhere. "Have you known Mira a long time?"

"Almost as long as I've known you. I knew he was fairly light-hearted. He jumped into whatever came along and at the same time missed most of everything else. For example: he got involved with Herba-Life Nutrition and went bankrupt. All the products were going rotten in his garage."

"Bellissima, now pause and put your thumb under the middle finger..."

Vitas started to laugh. "I reported on Herba-Life Nutrition, on multilevel marketing, that craze that swept the Czech Republic. The key is for the seller to acquire other naïve sellers to sell the product for them, and then have them look for other people to sell the product to others and so on. It's a tree structure, where the business is only profitable for those at the top and the ones at the bottom will lose the shirts off their backs, while everyone in the world drowns in Herba-Life Nutrition products."

"For the left hand, we use a so-called fold, where the fingers fold over the thumb…"

"Herba-Life Nutrition is like a good knedlík, a dumpling," Vitas added as Svata laughed. "Fibre that only congests the stomach. If the person can't eat, they must lose weight. At their sessions, I saw allegedly handicapped people toss aside their crutches after using Herba-Life products!"

"They had to have liked you," Svata smirked.

"I guarantee you, they did!"

"Now stop and fold the third finger over… One. Two. Three."

"I needed a few more takes of them pouring champagne to fool the crowd, and I was so notorious there that I had to use my wife and the TV cameraman at one of their meetings. They'd've strung me up if I'd shown up. My wife was howling, telling me she'd never do anything so horrible ever again…" As Vitas mentioned Eva, he seemed to become slightly uncertain. Shadows came over his eyes.

"Now, let's pause and add the fourth finger… One! Two! Three!…"

"How did you end up in this line of work?"

"Now the third finger again…"

"I'd rather talk about the analysis?" Svata tried to change the subject with a smile.

"And back the same way…"

"That's why we're here, right?" she said ironically, with her head bowed slightly, glaring straight into his eyes. Her thick but light eyelashes fluttered in her high-raised eyelids. Looking up, the glow of her eye's whites intentionally or maybe unintentionally revealed a great provocation, a certain irritating modesty that movie stars embodied onscreen, back in the 1920s and 1930s.

"Yes, of course…" Vitas responded absent-mindedly, trying to calm himself. "If you free yourself from the humane gossip and established rules, the question of what's right and what's wrong, what's formulated based on generally accepted categories and what's not, and look at politics from this point of view…" Vitas had to stop, gulping hard, her pupils like two vacuums drawing him into a vortex he had no choice but to defend himself from being irreversibly sucked into. "If you can fairly analyse why one politician was elected and why another wasn't, you'll arrive at a clear-cut conclusion of which neither common sense nor morality nor free-will are the deciding factors. On the contrary, these are usually the obstacles and the deciding factors are… the deciding factor is… your coffee stain…" said Vitas, without knowing what he was saying or doing, slowly raising his hand as if shifting a stick in an elaborate game, in which even the slightest move of a stick matters, and humiliating her with a coffee stain. But she hardly moved, gazing fixedly into his eyes. When he touched her, a sharp shiver shot up his spine, dissipating by his shoulder blades, until the dizziness came and then…

"… and for your homework, practice the C-Major scale. Both hands separately, legato and staccato. Please, play it only at the tempo that you can handle. And most importantly: DON'T GIVE UP! YOU ARE MAKING PROGRESS!"

45.
The Emperor's Edict

"And do you know when man had to make his first decision? His first free decision?" Vitas clarified didactically, snuggling comfortably into the pillows next to Rmi-lam's bed. Although it was late and Rmi-lam was tired, just like every night, she didn't want to miss out on a single bedtime story. And tonight, it was Vitas' turn to tell it.

She held her never-to-be-forgotten clown in both hands, slowly turning it over and playing with it as if the clown were walking on his own. She didn't seem to be paying too much attention to Vitas. Not only out of tiredness, but also because she was fully preoccupied with the puppet, as if some life-changing event was unfolding. The only lamp in the lamasery that was installed in Rmi-lam's room didn't work. Because of its reliance on batteries, it was only used when something was being read or written. No bright light was needed for storytelling. Candles sufficed, as was also the case now. These candles created a far more pleasant and cosy atmosphere.

Vitas didn't hear an answer for a very long time, so he started telling her. "Well, it was a really long time ago, when the serpent offered Eve an apple in the Garden of Eden. Forbidden fruit from a forbidden tree. And then after that, when Eve offered the apple to Adam. God had instructed them that they could take anything from the fruits of paradise, but for the fruit of the Tree of Knowledge of Good and Evil. They both knew it was forbidden. This was the first time that man was faced with the freedom to decide."

"That's not true!" Rmi-lam interrupted, while still playing with her clown.

"What do you mean it's not true? Why do you say so? Please explain."

"If God said it was forbidden, then it wasn't a FREE decision. Yes, it was a decision but not a free decision. If God hadn't forbidden it, maybe they wouldn't've even thought about taking it and no serpent would have offered the apple to Eve. It was like that time you forbade me to drink the black beverage. That's the only reason I felt like drinking it. If you forbid me to play my small piano, I'll want to play it even more."

"Fine, fine, you're probably right…" amicably, Vitas tried to calm these unexpectedly turbulent waters.

Unrelenting, Rmi-lam interrupted him by saying: "And why would God forbid anything anyway? If he only created him as a stupid toy, who shouldn't know anything, then he shouldn't have even created him in the first place, right?" she looked pointedly at the clown that froze in her hands and turned towards her, as if indigently reacting to the insulting words: stupid toy. "And if he truly wanted to create him in his image, he had to have already known that Adam and Eve would eat the apple. That makes sense. Otherwise, he'd be quite stupid."

Vitas sat anxiously nestled in the pillows thinking how to get out of this mess. He wanted to wrap up this never-ending, yet interesting topic. "But we're now talking about the decision…"

"Every decision is either good or bad," Rmi-lam interrupted him again. "You have to have the possibility to make a good or bad decision. If you didn't have this possibility, it wouldn't be a decision and no one could blame you for anything. Even a bad person has to have the possibility to decide whether to be good or bad." Rmi-lam, although tired, persistent like a tank, insisted on her own way. "Wasn't it then God's bad decision to create man? Why did he create him then? Was he bored, or what?"

"There are many theories about that. The main argument is: out of love."

"But since he created man, he had to have loved him, right?"

"Of course he loved him. He still loves him to this day. After all, he created him in his image and to his liking. So, he has to love him because if he didn't love him, he wouldn't even love himself."

"So, he has to love me no matter what I do! No matter what decision I make. And he has to love everyone like that! Because if he goes against me, he's actually going against himself." As she spoke these words, Rmi-lam manipulated the clown in a way that suggested he was asking himself and then parodying Vitas' answers. As if it were a dialogue between two identical, schizophrenic clowns with split personalities. Vitas watched the clown imitate him and poke fun at him with growing resentment and nervousness.

"You could say it like that. But it can't be abused. You cannot tempt him. Christ didn't make a big deal out of walking on water."

"But Lama Rinpoche said that firstly, there were five eggs, creating wind, fire, water…"

"But here we're talking about Christianity, Rmi-lam. About the Bible, about how the world was created according to the Christian world, where there's only one God, who created the Earth…"

"Fine, but if he created the world, the Earth and the

water, the day and the night and then man... what did he do before that?"

"Oh dear, had I known that, I probably wouldn't be sitting here..." Vitas said ironically, a little annoyed with himself for actually never having seen the world from this perspective, as deeply as Rmi-lam seemed to see. She was unstoppable in her inquisitive questions.

"And what about the soul and reason?"

"What do you mean?" Vitas growled suspiciously, worried that they'd tread on another inexplicable and mainly fantastical topic again. He was right.

"Man and all of humanity must have received some dose of reason and soul. But what depth and value does an individual's reason and soul have when there are so many people in the world? I think the more people there are, the more reason and soul has to be broken down into many little pieces."

"You mean, the more people there are in the world, the stupider they are because they have to share one dose?" the astonished Vitas made a huge circular motion with his hands, indicating a large dose.

"Something like that."

"I hope not..." moaned Vitas.

"Yes, yeah. There's no way for people to just multiply and soul and reason to be created out of nothing. Soul and reason cannot be here for eternity."

"But that's not how it is! Everything is in motion. Everything is pulsating; you cannot precisely stop things or define them exactly."

"There were a lot less people in the world 1000 years ago, is that right?"

"Yes, but you could trace this back to just two people, Adam and Eve. If this were the unit of measurement for soul and reason, which is then shared by all of humanity, then there would only be a herd of stupid worms roaming the earth today."

"Don't be stupid. It's not just about intelligence and stupidity. It's also about size and quality. It's also about the crowd. How do you know? Maybe a crowd can share a small dose of soul because individuals in the crowd have a lot in common. They have similar characteristics, similar corners of the soul, so it doesn't add up, but there's less of it…"

"Are you counting it up like some mathematical equation?" Vitas provoked wryly. "Is that something Aviel taught you? He would compare math to faith and philosophy…"

"Nonsense," Rmi-lam and the clown gave him the cold shoulder. "When Bodhisattva Mañjuśrī created the huge turtle, which then flipped on its back and the whole world, including Adam and Eve were created on its abdomen shell, he must have also created some dose of soul and reason…"

"Rmi-lam," Vitas interrupted her impatiently. "You're mixing three myths together! The Christian with the Jewish and the Tibetan, mixed in with math and I don't know what else. That's not how it works!"

Something in Vitas suddenly snapped, causing a collision of joy at Rmi-lam, anger towards himself in his "adult impatience" and a feeling of extreme maturity. At the thought of the clown in Rmi-lam's hand mocking him and disrespectfully making fun of his teaching abilities, his right hand spontaneously, rather than consciously, grabbed the clown by the head. He tried turning the clown's head towards Rmi-lam, as he was clearly laughing at him. Rmi-lam, surprised to see someone else touch her beloved friend, reflexively clenched him even tighter and yanked it away. But Vitas clutched a piece of the fabric on his head – the top – which detached from his body when Rmi-lam yanked it – the cylinder – making a loud noise, like a lid removed from a vacuum-sealed container. Rmi-lam immediately grabbed the remaining torso that Vitas clutched and screwed the lid with the fabric head back onto the cylinder. Vitas was more than slightly shocked, and didn't move an inch. The only thing he noticed was that the cylinder was hollow. Everything happened so quickly and quietly that, but for Rmi-lam's grunt, it was as if nothing had ever happened at all.

"Sorry," exhaled Vitas, but Rmi-lam quickly eased the tension with a question. "What d'you mean that's not how it works? The honourable Rinpoche said it. The Tibetans were born from a monkey and a female gremlin. You mean it was Adam and the female gremlin, Eve?"

"Definitely not. Both stories, all those myths and legends originated a long, long time ago in different places. However, it's true that sometimes there are multiple similarities. Take for example, the story I told you last time about the Golden-Haired Princess. The King ordered George to recognise the princess among twelve young women in a veil and if he found the princess, she would become his wife. A fly helped him. Songcan Gampo, the famous king of Zangzung, a legendary empire, which later became Tibet, ordered his envoy to bring him the Chinese Emperor's daughter, whom he would later marry. But the Emperor didn't want to lose his daughter, so he gave him three tasks, just like in the story of the Golden-Haired Princess. A butterfly helped him choose the right princess among the 300 young ladies…"

Had she fallen asleep now? Vitas couldn't be sure, so he just kept on talking. Slowly, quietly. "You will find a number of similarities. Just like Padmasambhava, born of the lotus leaf, brought Buddhism from India back in the eighth century, so Saints Cyril and Methodius brought Christianity to Central Europe a century later…"

He only spoke so that the sudden silence wouldn't wake Rmi-lam, slowly lowering his voice at the end, until he stopped completely.

He sat on a pillow at arm's length of Rmi-lam, who was falling asleep with her clown. Several candles drilled his imagination from each corner of the room. Despite his disunity and ambiguity with God, he felt that everyone on the planet had a mission to fulfil. And since he found himself on the other side of the world, this too, had its meaning. 'It's pretty blasphemous,' he thought, looking at the sleeping Rmi-lam. Ebony-black locks of hair stuck out from under the blanket, her face shrouded in darkness, turned to the opposite wall. The clown stared at Vitas confrontationally. Rmi-lam's fingers were loose, she wasn't holding onto it as tightly as before. Vitas slowly leaned towards her and carefully grabbed the clown in his left hand. Lightly, taking his time, pulling him out from under her arm. The thirty seconds it took felt like an eternity, but he succeeded. Rmi-lam was wandering somewhere in a wild dream of elves. Vitas sat the clown on his lap and stared at it for a long time. Each stared into the other's eyes.

Then quickly, as if something inside him had snapped, he grabbed the clown's head with his right hand and unscrewed it from the rest of his body. He placed the head down beside him and looked inside the cylinder. There was a large, circular opening and something rolled up inside it. He pulled it out slowly and carefully. He unfurled the rolled up, yellowish wax paper. It took him some time to realise that he was holding an almost ancient and seemingly highly important document in his hands. The seals were broken, probably so that it would fit into the cylinder, but they were clearly authentic. Vitas hadn't learned enough Chinese, but it was relatively easy for him to figure out the ideograms signifying, "dynasty" and "government"… It was simple to understand the context – the Lama's allusions and "coincidences," which, far from coincidental, all led to one thing and one thing only: to ensure that the little girl, who was sleeping close by, had everything she could possibly need. Because not only did Vitas have a mission to accomplish, but everyone else in the lamasery, including Rmi-lam herself, also had missions of their own to take care of. He still wasn't sure what these missions entailed, and there seemed a possibility that he would never find out, but that hardly mattered. He was convinced that he would not resist the demands of his mission. This was the first time he found himself alone, feeling a certain pride. He finally understood that it was worth continuing in this strange pilgrimage.

He put the scroll back into the cylinder, rolling it up and replacing the head, and carefully put the clown under the blanket beside Rmi-lam.

"Good night," he said quietly, rather more to himself. He blew out the candles and left the room.

46.
In the Devil's Hands

Vitas lived a completely different life than before. He had to absorb new perceptions, meet new people; his former friends hardly recognised him. He loved his new job and didn't want to deal with the past. He met with Alex only occasionally. His new employer was happy with him. It should have been easy to pass the test and then it would be on for good. Though he couldn't explain what 'on for good' meant. Once – and by now they had met in places of complete solitude (in parks generally) or in places with lots of commotion (train stations, and so on) – he had nervously patted Vitas on the shoulders, eyeing the surroundings as if he were searching for every stone that an enemy could hide under, muttering: "Hay una problema, una problema…" And then suddenly, as if by the wave of a magic wand, he calmed himself, as if his previous nervousness was only an act, winked at Vitas with his laser-beam eye, unbottling all his irony, slyness and confidence. "You like forests? What about Brdy, the hill range south of Prague?"

"And what about it" reacted Vitas, failing to understand. Something seized within him, this being where he and Eva would once go mushroom picking.

"Nothing, nothing!" shouted Alex, unexpectedly slipping back into his act of uncertainty, waving his hand like a hopeless hitchhiker approaching the last car before nightfall.

Vitas let it go, and tried not to worry about it. But Alex called him back a few days later. They went for a walk in the park in Prague.

"I have other job for you. Not specific, only theory…" This time, Alex spoke in a deep and confident voice. Very sparingly, as if saving every word and when he did say something, it was clearly thought out and verified. "We have information. American radar in Brdy. No one know about it but they will to talk about at your station, very soon. In the government. We need foundation…" Every word that Alex articulated was as clear as when a child is learning to read. "Czechs must to understanding this is not good step." Alex kept glancing at the ground, accompanying his words with big, precise and triumphant gestures, using his whole body, as if he were sending and receiving mysterious signals, able to perceive Vitas's reaction with his sixth or seventh sense.

Vitas frowned a little and asked briefly: "Can you give me any details?"

"Yes, yes, but is still secret. No one know any details now, but when media involve, we want to be prepared." He cleared his throat a little and then continued, remaining brief, curt, without any emotions, as if already coming to terms with the fact that everything had to be revealed. "It will to be very powerful radar, catch any missile over Europe. And apparent, there will to be anti-missile base in Poland. Missile is set off anywhere in Europe, radar in Brdy catches and anti-missile shot launches from Poland to take it down. However, this it's against every agreement, against our common interest, against us. How will you to fight with this?" Alex no longer looked at Vitas anymore, but he was as tense as an antenna, devouring everything he was emitting, his feelings and opinions, as if he were the radar.

While walking, Vitas stared intently at the ground, thinking hard. "I think there's a lot that can be done, but we need to be thoroughly prepared. I mean the whole project. It's one thing to breach all agreements, I know nothing about that, you should know that. Journalists are another thing – we want to crush and destroy some of them…"

"Yes, yes, we have any options, leave that for me," Alex waved his hand impatiently. "What next?"

"It's important to know what to make them think. One thing is whether this radar will even help the Czechs. If journalists say this act will immediately lead to Russians and other potential enemies targeting nuclear warheads at us, then people will be horrified and oppose it. A referendum should be called and the result will be clear. The worried Czechs will win. It's always the crowd, never common sense that wins in a referendum. And then, what about the waste? Dirty Brdy. Another important thing is whether you infiltrate the places where the radar will be constructed with your people before word gets out. But it has to be Czech people! Genuine Czech people, who work only for you. We have to be able to inconspicuously work the locals, do interviews with reporters…" Vitas waved his hand cheerfully. "There's so much that can be done. If you put some effort into it, I guarantee success."

Alex nodded his head with a slightly ironic smile and narrowed his eyes. "Yes, yes, it look good, very good. We will to that soon. For now, continue work with Bedynka, we take any measures, send our people and then to agree what steps next."

They met a couple more times to discuss the radar. Vitas had prepared a more detailed strategy for dealing with it. But the main event was yet to come. This didn't happen, however, once Vitas quickly disappeared from the Czech Republic. Alex didn't begin working on the prepared

American radar as part of the European anti-missile umbrella until later, once the radar had become officially known and was already being discussed at a high level. It's true that Alex managed to elicit such hysteria (perhaps even thanks to Vitas) that the Americans alone decided to withdraw their intentions.

– – –

Vitas only lived in the present. He disposed of the past like a piece of clothing that no longer matched a new suit and was left in a filthy corner, trampled on by waves of ruthless heels. It was as if he had released a valve and was now attempting to firmly clasp it shut, preventing any of his imaginations and his former principles from seeping into his brain. And without a doubt, it was no less frothing against the valve! In his mind, he concluded everything with Eva, closing one chapter of his life. The end. No looking back. Nothing to deal with any further. He knew what worked with Eva. During all the revolutions, the waving of keys on Wenceslas Square, "determining the fate of the universe," Eva took care of everyone and everything around her, especially him. He was the king, who had no idea how to do laundry or boil potatoes. He lived for today. Tomorrow was another person's day and the past was long forgotten.

Financially, he was very well off. Vitas, Bedynka, and the whole team went to Switzerland almost every month, where Vitas could fully unleash his imagination. He spent days running training programs and improving Bedynka's abilities, while sporadically dealing with the radar in Brdy. He spewed out one idea after another, reaping looks of admiration, pockets of money, and the warm feeling of a professional who is doing a good job, whether that be teaching, gravedigging, or supervising a concentration camp. Any frustrating thought buzzing close to him was brushed away without hesitation. And Svata was the biggest thought-brusher of all. She knew exactly when and how to use her strengths and abilities so that he wouldn't have the slightest desire to look back. She set fire to his male ego to such an extent that he could no longer imagine living differently. As a clever woman, she knew how to encourage him professionally as well. She knew when to flatter, when to tease or criticise him a little, and then let his ego soar, and when to shed a tear and when to laugh… She knew how to spin the ball of yarn and pull on the thread so that it wouldn't rip, keeping it spinning eternally. He was proud of his lover and didn't understand why his long-time friends kept looking down at him with such disrespect.

"You don't understand," he would yell aloud, not always only in his mind. "You don't understand that I've only just begun living. It wouldn't've taken much for me to just rot away here like an absolute zero…"

Vitas felt an entirely new sphere had opened up before him. Everything stood ahead. Even his breathing had to quicken and become more intense. It didn't stop at Svata – all the girls in the world were his. He couldn't waste another second before trying every one of them.

Then there was another sign. The bullet of a professional sniper ended the life of Kromen's friend, Kostka, one of the most significant mobsters who had ever lived in Central Europe. Neither the murderer nor the one who had hired the hitman were ever identified. Since Kostka was involved in a wide range of activities, it was difficult to pin down the author of the whole undertaking. Even so, there was a joke that circulated among the reporters and the politicians: the shocked and trembling Cabinet Secretary runs to the Prime Minister, interrupts the meeting and exclaims in horror: "Prime Minister, sir, Kostka is dead – he was just murdered. Shot," he clarifies. While everyone freezes, the

Prime Minister only frowns slightly, looks at his watch and says nervously: "Is it seven already?"

But no one could truly clarify the source, where the command to fire had come from. Kostka's death didn't really affect Vitas all that much. Of course he took note of it, but it was hardly possible to say that he expressed much sorrow. Given his new-found thrills, there was neither the room, the time, nor the desire to process this information in any more detail.

But all excitement must subside sooner or later, whether by death or simple healing. No, no, no, there was another cause for his awakening – the worst-case scenario that he had never even imagined in his worst nightmare. The news was terribly brief. It was a medical report from the oncology department, where Eva was diagnosed.

It was a rude awakening. All spinning was interrupted and the thread ripped. He immediately stopped everything, he stopped his new life in full swing, but it was too late. He was torn with self-destructive guilt. He was no longer interested in Svata, or the American radar, or Bedynka, who had worked his way up to Vice Chairmen of the Parliament in a few years. But Vitas neither knew nor cared about this information. The yellowed leaves of the photo album were turning in his head, displaying their countless photos, showing Eva in endless situations; he could no longer picture anything else. Chebness.

Something had ended and Vitas wasn't able to come to terms with it. He wasn't able to just turn the pages and jump from chapter to chapter like in a book. He called this experience the "Nusle Jump," referring to the highway-bridge in Prague notorious for suicides. Today, a tall reinforced fence surrounds it. No, no, he didn't want to jump. He only understood that Eva's passing led him to an irreversible plunge as if from the Nusle Bridge. It was somehow similar to a driver who had caused a fatal accident tearing his hair, asking himself why he hadn't left one second earlier or later. It was only a matter of a second!!! But he made this step quite consciously! No fever was to blame! The step from the Nusle Bridge does not hurt. On the contrary, one feels superior, mindful, in a state of matchless ecstasy, a flight of happiness, mingled with endless experiences, personal and professional successes... But Vitas had already fallen. He had nothing. No work. No Eva. Nothing. Emptiness.

– – –

"Look, Vitas," came the voice of Elza, Vitas' friend and screen-editor, on the other line. "So get this, we've spent months working on a project about the IT faculty and I just found out that it's registered in your name."

After leaving the TV station, Vitas embarked on numerous projects that came his way. One of them was a major project with a documentary filmmaker, to which the EU had allocated thirty million, twenty-seven million of which was to go towards research at the faculty and the rest towards the media – so hurrah, let's get to work! He prepared a presentation to defend the television. Everything was thought out and prepared.

But despite everything, the project promptly disappeared from the surface of the Earth. Abruptly, all interest was lost. But he had no idea who to point a finger at or to blame for stealing his project. And now a co-worker from the TV station called him.

"This is awful, what're you going to do about it?"

"Well, look, it's simple, we're either going to flush it down the drain – and you have to admit that would be a pity with all the money already allocated to it – or, you're in this with us, but only as a director."

And so Vitas signed on to the project he had originally devised, but that had been lying in his drawer, rejected, unless someone was to grab it or simply steal it. He knew he couldn't pick and choose. He had to do something. He had to move, to allow a new day to succeed the old one… How should he avoid the devilish mirror in the bathroom? Alex – or actually Ivan – was a huge liar. He'd lied when he told Vitas that he'd be able to look at himself in the mirror. How to avoid an evening that starts off with a brisk trip down memory lane? How to avoid the breath that feeds the album with pictures from his head? The images of endless situations that had taken such deep roots, gushing towards the surface like an inflatable rising from the depths of the sea to the surface. All the bizarre, ridiculous, tragic moments. Tangled, sleeping, enthusiastic, angry, hungry… Alex had lied.

Without preparation, he would set off on a hike to anywhere. He would simply walk and walk until exhaustion set in, or until he found himself alone somewhere in the woods.

His whole existence seemed paralysed. Self-doubt had eroded him, even from the direction he had felt self-control. He had troubles expressing himself normally, he felt overwhelmed by certain feelings, suffocated by extreme pressure, the edge of every object that he observed seemed to emit strong rays, pulsing on his cranium, constantly repeating: "Foolish Vitas! Foolish Vitas!" in a quiet and deep, but profoundly intrusive voice.

"Should I admit that everything I've achieved was through the random and Machiavellian ability to connect words into some semblance of meaning, or that it came through some sleight-of-hand, made possible by the revolutionary period of the nineties? Did I just swing through some situations that were already played in time, moreover, pushed from somewhere out East…? In reality, I'm nothing more than a chicken shit…"

In this mental state, Vitas set off to see Elza, indifferently turning the greyish sheets of the calendar day by day. He consulted on the first edited parts of the new documentary. He emptily stared through the window of the metro-car, into the dark, watching the ominous streaks pass him by, occasionally glimpsing his own reflection. It was deformed, with holes in place of eyes, his hair flowing backwards into the darkness of the tunnel, a numb and crumbling nothing.

BOOK II.

1.

Six Years

"I am in your hands!" sounded over the cliffs and echoed far and wide, flooding everything living and non-living like a ray of sunshine. It cut the edges of the rocks and stones, seeping through the turbulent surface of the sleeping Jadhang Gad, conveying its message in the form of a thousand bubbles, rising wildly and bursting on the surface. But it was no longer the voice of a little girl standing high on the edge of Mount Jadhang. It was the voice of a maturing young lady.

Sleeping Rmi-lam, reading Rmi-lam, Rmi-lam dancing with headphones in her ears, sulking Rmi-lam, Rmi-lam arguing angrily, pleading Rmi-lam, Rmi-lam. No one could take their eyes off her when she was riding her horse, hitting a bull's eye sixty-five feet away, all while carefully keeping her innermost thoughts. She even snatched some fashion magazines from Kromen and tried to sew her own dress. She kept a diary that no one could ever read. Just like every girl, she had her own secrets.

This was the sixth year that the Jadhang had been contributed to by her essence. Without it, the monks would be dull, lifeless, ossified, the lamasery would only be a rock. It had been like a sponge, eagerly awaiting water. In everyone's eyes, this non-living matter underwent a living charge. When Rmi-lam was present, everyone could take in the absolute Presence. They could appreciate the present and absorb it like never before. No one could say they were unhappy with the breath-taking scenery of the seductive mountains, with the sun and the bright stars at arm's length, and moreover, in having a place to feed their starving eyes, so eager to absorb everything new. Sometimes, they suspiciously doubted and sometimes resolutely refuted, furiously protesting, giggling at jokes and crying over tragic stories... But they were never indifferent. They expanded, shrank, burst with emotion and were in constant movement until they helplessly shut-down with fatigue at night, falling into the glassy and dull, milky mass of sleep.

Kromen has been visiting the Jadhang Gad at least once or twice a year for the past six years. He always brought Rmi-lam something of what he arrogantly liked to call achievements of Western civilisation. But in truth, Rmi-lam's demands were escalating. And what's more, his gifts no longer had anything to do with knowledge or culture. Thanks to various books, Rmi-lam sought a glimpse into girls' secrets, to which everyone at the lamasery, including Aviel and Vitas, remained clueless.

It's worth mentioning that sometimes, Kromen even brought something meaningful in order to keep the kashag, the lamasery council, happy. But it was impossible to determine whether the cause of this altruism wasn't pure selfishness, it being clear that everything at the Jadhang lamasery revolved around Rmi-lam. His departures were filled with feelings of hurt and insult. It seemed to have become a ritual. He was always fussy about the gifts he received from the Lama, enough to make any uninitiated outsider wonder why the Lama would bestow such gifts to someone who was so ungrateful. But there was no outsider here. Gold or any other treasure was of no value to anyone of the locals. It was merely a means of exchange, something that could serve the monastery, and thus Rmi-lam. And obviously, in addition to the sacred objects, it had its own spiritual value.

Six years had already gone by and the Chinese year of the Serpent had arrived again. According to the Gregorian calendar, it was 2013, and according to the Tibetan calendar, the year of Water and the Serpent. Rmi-lam was maturing into a young lady of thirteen years old, and the world was beginning to open up to her. But what world? What could the world expect of Rmi-lam and what could she expect of the world? Vitas had kept silent of her secret year after year. Well, after several months, he had confided in one person, whom he trusted unconditionally – Aviel. Both of them assessed the situation and came to the conclusion that this required complete discretion and had sworn to secrecy. But first, they obtained the exact transcript of the Emperor's Edict. This, of course, posed a problem, with Rmi-lam guarding her clown like an eye in her head. It took them a good month to find the right moment. Otherwise, it was clear that no one had any idea about Rmi-lam's origin. Almost no one. Lama Rinpoche Thorpe Tenzin was one other exception, along with his closest monk, Tungjur. Following his discovery, Vitas had tried to find the answers to his fundamental questions in the Lama's eyes at the kashag. His expression was more than articulate. They didn't have to say a word and Vitas knew that the Lama was aware, just as the Lama knew that Vitas was aware in turn.

Kromen's promise to Rmi-lam for the piano aroused great amusement in the lamasery. Rmi-lam expressed incredible stubbornness by pounding her fingers on the electronic piano. Terrible sounds gave away her every step, grinding the wrinkled rocks of the lamasery, crawling down the corridors, sticking themselves in the teeth… During lessons, the teachers had to exert a lot of effort to silence the piano, often resulting in simply taking the musical instrument away by force. But on the other hand, her stubbornness slowly bore fruit in the form of a relatively accuracy in playing the pieces. Vitas also contributed to this, continuing to impel Rmi-lam to learn the technique, the chords and to practice... He tried to direct her endless thirst and chaotic pursuit for results down a sensible path. The result was a version of 'Summertime' that maybe even Gershwin could have listened to, if he had closed his eyes and ignored the pink piece of plastic that was making the obnoxious noise.

"A piano? Of course. A grand piano? Fine, the biggest one. So, the next time I come... It didn't work out this time, but next time, next time," Kromen fended the impatient Rmi-lam away.

"I'm sorry," Aviel shrugged his shoulders with an ironic smile. "You promised a piano, so you're going to have to bring a piano."

"But not just any piano, a grand piano," Vitas added fuel to the fire. The other monks simply nodded, seeming to imply that he would have to do something, a promise being a promise.

"Honestly, we'd really appreciate it, it would get rid of the horrible noise," added Sonam. "I'll probably have poor vision for the rest of my life, but as for my hearing... well, unfortunately, my hearing is far too good. And a big piano will give us the right to trample over this pink monstrosity with our boots."

"You won't be able to bring the piano to lessons anymore because it won't fit into your pocket, young lady," laughed Aviel with a sly smile.

"You've all gone mad," yelled Kromen. "How am I supposed to bring a grand piano here, brainbox?" The answer was always just a shrug of the shoulders, with no more meaning than that he was the one with the suit in his hands.

Almost all of the monks loved all sorts of surprises. This meant all kinds of cultural and religious ritual occasions, put together by no more than a few people, either with Rmi-lam or without her. And if they put it together without her, then it was mainly for her benefit, and with the whole lamasery present. A single performance with no encore was held following covert and demanding rehearsals, and everyone was impressed. Once was enough. Just as the monks had decided to spend the whole day making a mandala with their circular and square-shaped symbols. They created extremely intricate artwork out of different coloured sand, gold and limestone dust. It was a ritual generally intended for some sort of feast. The circular shapes of the images signified more than the samsara, the eternal rebirth, the infinite, but also the heavens and the almighty powers that affect living beings. In contrast, the square binds us to the ground, identifying man and his powers, strengths and weaknesses. All these incidents force one to meditate, breaking everyone who perceives them down into an atom, until he becomes aware of transience. After a hard day's work, everyone enjoyed looking at the incredibly detailed masterpieces, prayed and blew everything away like dust in a matter of seconds. Everything, including life, shall pass. Everything will come to an end. Even if only to begin again. All is vain and all earthly goods useless, a burden.

Rmi-lam had tremendous influence over the whole monastery, on its cleanliness and all its happenings. She even had influence over the Jingzhi, who were teaching her their religions, thereby also learning more about their own with her. If they wanted to add anything, they had to have it in them and it kept piling up. Aviel and Vitas were convinced that applying their faith was far from the proper rituals. They even thought they'd be removed from the Church if anyone of the church dignitaries saw them in action.

However, they gradually became more and more devoted to their faiths, so it was no wonder that Aviel grew a decent beard over time, and wore certain hats more often. He even made his own tefillin, prayer bracelets, which he used sparingly. No one said a word about it. It was a matter of fact. A natural development.

One day, Vitas, too, began to prepare his own contribution to the local, ritual, Gregorian chorales. He went from one monk to another and rehearsed their singing. Aviel made fun of him and secretly hung a large piece of cloth with the words: "Jadhang's Got Talent" over the sacred booth, with the following words in fine print underneath: "Auditions here. Clean shoes, a clear mind and a vocal range of at least five octaves required. Parents not allowed. They must wait outside until the results are announced!"

Vitas was red with anger and promised he'd avenge himself against Aviel and then some. He stubbornly rallied up the monks until he had fifteen. In the meantime, he studied the history of the Gregorian chorales all the way up to Pope Gregory the Great. Following the example of the time, when there was no notation of this type, he started rehearsing old Latin texts with the monks by singing them himself. He tried raising false tones up or down, stretching them to the correct tone and putting the correct emphasis on them using a stick. And since Vitas didn't want to be the constant source of humour, rehearsals meant trips out far beyond the lamasery, under strict supervision, all the while ensuring that no one, especially Rmi-lam or Aviel followed him.

The truth is, while the monks initially took this rehearsal as a simple source of amusement, the first results soon materialised, and many more were enraptured by the singing. They were overcome by the strong melodiousness of the song, its purity and clarity. Once they had technically mastered the chorales, they let themselves get carried away into landscapes they had imagined only in dreams. Chorales are a matter of harmony. But here on the Jadhang, there were but fifteen people, confessing their inner lives through the means of song. Vitas was in no hurry to put on a concert. There was no rush there. But he deployed a few of the easier liturgical chorales at mass now and then, and left everyone present quite clearly impressed.

2.
The Agreement

"A grand piano? Since when is day night? Since when does black glow in the dark? Since when does a doe tear up and devour tiger meat? You're crazy!" a quiet echo resonated, emphasising every word as if every syllable were to explode. Every word implied resentment, misunderstanding, remorse, superior contempt. Major Li C'cheng was leaning his arms on the armrests so much that it seemed he was sitting in mid-air, merely holding himself up by his forearms like a gymnast in a parallel bar routine. "Why not a recorder? Or a guitar? Why not…"

"Because it has to be a piano. A grand piano," specified Kromen. "There's nothing we can do about it. That's just the way it has to be. If our interest is… our COMMON interest is… to please your Empress, to reassure Lama Tenzin, then bring me a piano. I need the absolute respect of everyone in the lamasery. I need to settle this with the Lama and then you can do whatever you want. That's your problem. But first do what is necessary."

They stared at each other intently. Major Li C'cheng relaxed a little, as if someone had put a missing cushion underneath him. He took his arms from the armrests and put them under his chin. "Fine, I'll locate a piano…"

"A grand piano," clarified Kromen, a little provocatively.

"Yes, of course, a grand piano," Li said, grinding his teeth. "But this will cost you your life if things don't happen the way we agreed upon."

"There's nothing that can ruin this. There's no reason to doubt anything. Everything will be served on a golden platter. The rest is up to you, your abilities and the abilities of your people," mentored Kromen.

"Have no doubt! Now that China's dream of a magnificent rebirth is coming true, nothing can ruin it. No hindrance. Not even you or some insignificant girl." Li's voice was harsh and low. It fired shivers down the spine, and whoever his words were intended would understand that the speaker was willing to lay down his life for every syllable.

"You know," Kromen's face suddenly went solemn, "now, I'm going to say something that I probably shouldn't, but I can't help myself. You've got a bit of a problem. And it's that YOU are creating it. YOU are creating a problem that isn't there and you so desperately want resolved. It's not the insignificant girl. You're adding fuel to the flame. She's really insignificant. She's nothing. A bundle of emotions that perhaps has some special abilities. But definitely not supernatural. You're turning her into something she is not, a monster. You're the ones attributing something to her, which she eventually gains, but only because you attributed it to her. You know, an emperor doesn't become an emperor on his own. He could scratch his behind and not look like an emperor at all. The people around him, his servants, his generals and the environment are what make him an emperor. They are the ones who kneel before him and not because they put some gold scrap on his head. He can be wearing ragged clothes, but respect is what makes him Someone. But if someone walks by him without raising a brow, the emperor is an absolute zero. Nothing. You are the ones turning her into an empress. But why am I trying to talk you all out of it?" he laughed suddenly. "This suits me perfectly. Barge in there, deal with your complexes, but above all, give me what I want. No," Kromen corrected himself radically. "What's *mine*! Because if it weren't for me, you'd still be wandering the streets of Beijing, dreaming of China's magnificent rebirth. But it would still only be a dream that only your superiors would wake you up from. And since you already gave the girl this much power, be careful that all of China doesn't wake up from this magnificent dream. Or," Kromen suddenly thought, "what if she truly is your magnificent dream, ha? In that case, you should quickly wake up from this dream!"

Kromen paused, as if suddenly not knowing what to say. He had fired every round. Li glared at him thoughtfully without saying a word, one hand under his chin, waiting for whatever else Kromen had to say. He couldn't see into his soul or mind. His thin, narrow head was tensely focused, unmoving. Not one muscle moved, but perhaps for his nostrils alone, which twitched unnoticeably, as if ticking away the time left until the world would end.

"Fine," said Kromen uncertainly after an awkward pause. "I think we've agreed on everything. I'll be expecting you in exactly three weeks, approximately half-a-mile from the Jadhang."

"Good bye," Li nodded his head rather coldly. "Deal."

"Wait," Li stopped Kormen, who was already holding the doorknob in his hands. "Take this walkie-talkie," as he pulled out a small, black device with an antenna from the drawer. "It only has a three-mile radius, but that's enough. Don't change the frequency. We'll get in touch as we get closer with your piano. Is it possible to charge the battery on the Jadhang?"

"Yes," nodded Kromen, raising two fingers, signalling a military salute and taking leave of Li.

Li C'cheng smiled mischievously. He was rather impressed, though he didn't let on. Everything was going according to plan. Wu Kuang of the Central Military Committee could report highly satisfactory news. His mission and his well-thought-out theatrical performance before Kromen had paid off. Well, it actually hadn't been a performance, but an adaptation to the situation. He had promised what was necessary. He had done what he had had to in order to achieve the desired result. Kromen's requests wouldn't be dealt with until the basic requirements were met. This meant that no one had to deal with anything. He had no illusions about Kromen's future, or the future of everyone at the Jadhang lamasery.

It had taken five years for him to track down an actual clue. A stupid, insignificant ad. "A businessman with information." After reading this, he immediately knew he was standing on a goldmine. How else would Kromen draw attention to himself? Had he come to the Central Military Committee or the Political Bureau with such great information, everyone would be hitting themselves on their foreheads (best-case scenario), saying that this European fellow had gone quite mad and, in a worst-case scenario, they'd simply put him in prison. And in the worst of worst-case scenarios, though less likely, some fool would actually believe him. Li had only made one, but no less very significant mistake. He had revealed to Kromen the identity of the girl at the lamasery. He'd rather have pulled the rest of his hair out, but he was convinced that Kromen had already known it! There was no way he could have known that Kromen had known nothing and that material gain was his only concern. His undermining the lamasery, a training ground for an anti-human movement of deceived believers, manic for their Buddha, was only for money. "Everyone's gone mad over their Empress," Kromen said clearly. Yes, that was it.

Li had no idea that there was an absurd joke going around the lamasery, which was more than true. This too, is why Li had jumped at the news. "Where is this Edict?" he reacted all too impatiently at the time.

"What Edict?" Kromen wondered, picking his brain.

"Guangxu appointing her emperor..." He hadn't understood until now. He was taken aback, but it was all already too late. Rapid fire. Kromen won the bitter eye battle.

"So, that's how it is..." sighed Kromen. Dollar signs sprung into his eyes, just like some relative to Scrooge, when he began to count his potential profits. Blackmailing the Chinese, doing business with the European tabloids, blackmailing the Lama or perhaps just moral prestige... Or could he have the best of all worlds? It was worth thinking this through thoroughly. Most importantly, this could hardly be rushed.

Li C'cheng had read every one of his thoughts like a book. Only the decision he had already made remained unclear to him. However, after Kromen's didactic outpour, he had hoped that everything would go according to plan.

Li informed the other Supremes that he had established a contact in the centre of this major problem for China. A European, however, and not to be trusted, his only motivation being money. He had no God, which would hardly matter at all, but for his lack of any values. He would only respect himself and the money. On the other hand, this did make it a lot easier to read his thoughts and to predict his behaviour – a clear, transparent relationship. In any case, he must be overpaid, or at least promised an overpayment.

Back in 2012, he had quickly relocated the centre of the ancient Guge Kingdom, with its patterned history and archaeological finds. The torso of the forts alone could truly summon the feeling of bloodshed, the sense that God, too, had walked on this earth. Located in the western part of

Tibet, it wasn't far from Ladakh, in the Zanda district on the outskirts of Ngari, and most importantly, near to the Jadhang. By a straight path it would take perhaps fifty miles, but over difficult and inhospitable terrain, the distance would be tripled for every hiker. This is where the five Supremes met, in the heart of an unpredictable and divine landscape. The fifth Supreme would be the future president, Xi Jinping. He and the others disappeared from worldly existence, leaving only an intense argument over what had happened to him. The media speculated over his temporary disappearance, which had such a simple explanation. At this point, it was agreed that Li C'cheng was to do whatever it took to disappear anything that could ruin China's dream of a magnificent rebirth from the surface of the earth.

The winter of 2012 rolled over to the spring of 2013. It became necessary to quickly put this matter to rest. A motorised military unit and a team of tanks were deployed by the People's Liberation Army. No one was surprised. The army was everywhere. And the western borders with India were yet to be resolved. The fact that the Chinese army withdrew from the short battle with India in the 1960s left no certainty of consent regarding the existing borders.

The five Supremes had hoped that the whole issue would be resolved within a few weeks. And Li C'cheng would be the one to deal with it. Once and for all.

3.
The Letter

Two alpha male blue sheep – one an older leader, the other significantly younger and smaller – are grazing side by side in the lower pastures of the Jadhang. They keep to themselves. And yet Rmi-lam can feel the drama lurking in this situation and, hiding behind the rocks, observes what will unfold. She rests on her stomach with her hands under her chin, her eyes hypnotised by the mounting tension between the two animals.

Though the blue sheep didn't stare at each other, the prelude of a great event could be felt. Their strong horns, sweeping first to the side before curling, flickered against each other. The leader seemed to be the stronger one. Two other blue sheep had already fought for leadership and left the vast space with respect, all that had been necessary was to show their bristled fur. But the younger male relentlessly insisted on fulfilling his animal ambitions, still grazing next to the leader, acting as if nothing unusual was happening. The fifteen females surrounding them hadn't noticed what's going on, or simply pretended that was the case. Rmi-lam knows something has to happen. The younger rival is grazing in front of the leader, who hunches back, stretches his head forward and gently kicks his rival. Although the challenger withdraws, he does so only to the level of the leader, and continues grazing close by. Such audacity. The leader can only momentarily bear it. He stands on his hind legs and leans his front legs against the rival's back. But the rival yanks, pulls away and also rears up like a flame. The battle is on. The leader stands on his hind legs too, both blue sheep bouncing somewhat comically around until coming so close to one another that their hollow horns bang together…

"So, here's our Rmi-lam," Vitas interrupted the performance.

"Psssst," shushed the girl. "It's the most exciting part," she protested, the blue sheep quickly giving up and moving elsewhere, acting as if they had always been the best of friends.

"Well, I have to admit that's nice and all, but wouldn't you rather know about Antigone? We'll be talking about her today."

"No, no, I don't want to," Rmi-lam declared sharply.

"What do you have against Antigone? She's an interesting…" he trailed off.

"Do you not like animals?"

"I like them, why wouldn't I?"

"Did you ever have any?"

"Look, don't go changing the subject."

"I'd really like to know. Have you ever bred any?"

"Look, young lady, aren't you a bit too curious? Why was Antigone so determined to bury her brother? What divine laws have clashed here?"

"What animal?"

"Well, we had hens."

"Hens?" Rmi-lam exclaimed in amazement, staring at Vitas with her mouth open. "Really?"

"Yes, really."

"Tell me about it," Rmi-lam demanded severely.

"Are you really not interested in Antigone?"

"I am interested, but right now I want to know more about how you bred hens."

"No, no, let's please get back to Antigone. It's an interesting tale…" Vitas said stubbornly.

"Yeah, it is," Rmi-lam interrupted his recollections and once she saw she had no other choice, changed the subject. "But I'm interested in something else as well – Joan of Arc. We didn't discuss her in enough detail."

"What more would you like to know about her?" Vitas relinquished, happy to at least stay on one topic for the lesson, without bringing up memories.

"She conquered Orleans and saved the French from the British but I don't get why the French then sent her to the stake and burned her instead of thanking her."

"That's higher politics. The reason can be hidden under the term 'higher interest'. It was really in the best interest of the top ranked heads of the Church and the King, to prevent Joan from becoming too much to handle. It's simple, they were afraid of her."

"But why didn't anyone help her?"

"And who could help her? Everyone had their own problems to deal with and no one had the energy or reason to help some young girl, who'd become a military leader. It was a flame that lit up the whole world and then burned out. Disappeared."

"Does everyone always have to have a reason to help someone?"

"Certainly not, but he doesn't have to, or might not be able to help out of fear for himself, or out of fear for his loved ones. There are many reasons."

"And what if someone would like to help someone but doesn't know if he's got the strength?"

"Aha," Vitas nodded, staring directly into Rmi-lam's eyes, continuing: "And who would you like to help?"

Rmi-lam pursed her lips and remained stubbornly silent, looking back at the imaginary blue sheep that were no longer on their battlefield. They had long been replaced by peaceful sheep.

"And how do you want to help this someone?" Vitas gently continued to ask, in order not to scare Rmi-lam, realising how mature and educated she had become over her years spent in the lamasery. Compared to other girls in Europe, or in other parts of the world, she behaved very differently, had a completely different state of mind, and different social habits. She was definitely missing a friend, somebody the same age. But who could decide what would be good or bad for her, what would benefit her, when she remained dependent only on local possibilities?

"I want to call someone for help."

"Who? I'm afraid that nowadays, it's very difficult to find a person who'd be willing to help someone else."

Rmi-lam stared into Vitas' eyes for a long time. Then, she gestured for him to come closer and briefly whispered something into his ear.

Vitas remained stiff, leaned back and quietly said: "You have to realise that by doing so, you could do something that you could later regret. Do you insist on it? Have you really thought it through?"

Rmi-lam only gulped and nodded her head.

Soon afterwards, they were both sitting in Vitas' shrine with a sheet of the best and whitest paper they could find in front of them. Rmi-lam chewed the pencil nervously.

"How should I address her? Dear colleague…" Rmi-lam looked cloyingly at Vitas, who burst out laughing.

"Probably not. You probably wouldn't offend her, but I'm afraid she wouldn't even read such a letter."

"Is she so stuck up?"

"Definitely not, but do you know how many dozens of letters she must get from such fools every day? Such letters never even reach her."

"Fine, so not 'colleague' but then how? Majesty?"

"Yes. Her majesty."

"Fine, fine," Rmi-lam nodded, absolutely determined to begin writing.

"Wait," Vitas stopped her. "You first have to write something like a header: Care of Her Majesty..."

Once Rmi-lam wrote the header and wanted to continue writing, Vitas interrupted her again. "You have to clarify all points that you want to write about. So, in bullet form, what do you want to mention?"

"First and foremost, that Great Britain was silent in pushing the Tibetan issues at the UN, essentially holding back on the matter and then..." Rmi-lam thought for a moment and then blurted out: "... and then they didn't help at all, even though they were aware of all the injustice that was going on here!"

"Okay, and what are you going to ask her to do? I'm afraid that requesting military intervention would be useless," Vitas explained a little ironically.

"Fine, but she could deny the current situation. Further help would be based on her own discretion..." she exclaimed at the end.

"Well, we could give it a try. And you realise that you have to describe your own situation and present some proof, so that she believes you..." Vitas looked into her eyes inquisitively.

"But I have proof," Rmi-lam looks briefly at her clown.

"Great, so let's get to work..."

4.

The Counter-Revolutionary Grand Piano

When Antonin Petrof, a piano-maker from the Austrian-Hungarian Monarchy, built his first concert grand piano in present eastern Czechia, namely in Hradec Kralove in 1864, he felt like the whole world, the whole human race and mother nature herself, had all turned on him. It was a fight in which his life was at stake. This can only be understood by someone who has devoted their whole heart and soul to an illusion. Who knows that God will protect them from all of life's tribulations because they have been assigned a clear mission – and that is to complete their masterpiece. Until then, God will defend them. They will not be overcome by any illness or encounter any tragedy. Whether or not this is truly the case, is hardly the point. Once the true belief in a Creator, in a Mission of a Higher Order, takes hold, then that becomes the deciding factor.

In his struggle towards eternity, towards immortality, towards the fulfilment of his dream, Antonin Petrof hadn't suspected that he would be appointed a court director of the Austro-Hungarian Imperial piano factory one year before the end of the nineteenth century. He had not suspected how famous a tradition he was establishing in the manufacturing of pianos at that time. Accordingly, he also had not suspected that one of the last "imperialist," intricately-made concert grand pianos confiscated by the Communists would end up at the concert hall in Nanking, in honour of a performance of Dvorak's *New World Symphony*. This was all made possible by the warm cooperative relationship between the cultural monarchs of the Czechoslovak Socialistic Republic and the People's Republic of China, in 1949, during those heady monsoon days of June.[32] And thus they united many cultures into a single heart, which was later exemplified in the movie *People of One Heart*, produced in conjunction with the Czech Cultural events in China. The kind-hearted comrade, Zdenek Nejedly, then Minister of Labour and Social Enlightenment, danced around these cultural orgies on behalf of Czechoslovakia. Meanwhile, comrade San Jang, a fresh-eyed and hopeful twenty-five-year-old orchestrated the entire expression of cultural glory the same year. Thus, the year the Communists reigned victorious in mainland China, the year the People's Republic was declared, amid a breakthrough and revolutionary era and the fulfilment of the grand ideals of the East. San felt he had become the universal emperor. He was overcome with feelings of happiness as cultural messiahs broke down into droplets of sweat. The success was so grandiose that Chinese artists included the *New World* motif in the famous 'Song of the Great Wall'. During the concert itself, comrades almost fainted, while San rode the current of glory, as if he were not only the one who had composed this famous symphony, but also the one who had sung it himself.

He was riding the glorious current until, that is, the Great Mao Zedong asked him what that grand piano was doing right there in the middle of the stage, dominating the foreground like an altar of wellbeing, when no one had played it the entire time. Why had they even ordered

---

32 The People's Republic of China was officially established several months after the event.

it from somewhere out in the boonies of central Europe, and why did a special military plane have to be sent for it? San's delightful drops of sweat suddenly turned into frozen poison. Although there had never been a request from the Czech side for a concert grand piano for the given cultural event, San had mistakenly assumed that it was not only part of the famous symphony, but also a part of the other attractions of cultural artists from the mythical West. During the following thamzing, with his head down and hands clasped behind his back, he quickly defected from his counter-revolutionary activity by intentionally spending the financial means of the Chinese people. During the following relatively brief and dull executions, a few miles away, in a huge cultural centre, Mao could play the Petrof grand. In the meantime, in an effort to repair the embarrassing situation, Minister Zdenek Nejedly had it personally dedicated to Chairman Mao himself. Mao was no longer able to stop the executions, impressed as he was by the powerful sound of this sublime musical instrument. He was an artist too, and with his poems contributed to the Sounds of Ancient China, proving that even he could emulate the greatest poets, such as Wang Wei, Li Bai, or TuFu. However, he had never suspected that he also possessed such a talent as a pianist. Sadly, no one witnessed this virtuosity, Mao barring anyone from attending his purely personal outbursts of artistic emotion. After about half-an-hour, he abandoned his career as a concert pianist and returned to politics, claiming "although the sounds of the instrument are deep, it speaks of aristocratic pride, making it evident that this wasn't raised by the hands of the free working people."

That's how the famous Petrof concert grand piano ended up in a warehouse stocked with antique paintings, amid the busts of Chinese emperors and aristocratic leaders from a time when the People hadn't held the reins firmly in their hands yet. It was a large hall with a huge scrimmage of regressive artefacts, stuffed chaotically one on top of the other. The vast majority were destroyed during the Cultural Revolution some fifteen years later. Only because the keys had been touched by the Great Chairman Mao, did the concert grand survive. Fortunately, the sign with this description remained visibly intact near the piano. The janitor of the building painted a large gold star in a red circle on the huge hinged lid to emphasise the son's inspiration with the ideas of Marxism-Leninism and Maoism. The piano remained in the detritus and oblivion of the hall, ravaged by the Cultural Revolution, forgotten for decades.

Therefore, when in 2013 – the year of the Serpent – there was a request from the Central Military Committee to find a concert grand piano for military purposes, labelled "strictly confidential," it took a long time before any historian realised that this weapon of the Chinese Liberation Army lay hidden under layers of dust, in a forbidden warehouse.

After many setbacks, the large Petrof grand, covered with a camouflage canopy, made its way to Zanda, in the Ngari district, on the back of a large military flatbed truck. Once they removed the canvas, they revealed the exciting shapes of the divine musical instrument in all its beauty, its star obscured by the brightness of the many competitors hanging in the sky.

5.
Growth Rings and the Immortal Emperor

"Look, do you see the grooves? The lines? They're called growth rings." Vitas ran his index finger along the concentration of rings on the stump of an old, recently felled fir tree.

It was an extremely old, crooked fir tree, which had decided to die instead of vigorously climbing its way into another year. It had dried up, and although it had grown in the shade of Mount Jadhang for most of its existence, this had made no difference. It was the only one of this size in the lower part of the Jadhang. Birches and junipers were the only other wood plants that appeared here, forming the base for the local fuel, together with yak droppings.

The felling of this lofty and venerable fir tree – over 160 feet tall – was a symbol of great glory. Although a tree common to Tibet, the uniqueness of its fall here gave the locals a sense of rarity. It hadn't even been a week since it trembled and headed towards the earth, away from those heights it had been trying to reach for the entirety of its life. Vitas truly had to convince the monks not to chop the tree to pieces as it lay on the ground. Wood here was very valuable, but Vitas wanted to preserve some three feet of it above the ground. He was able to defend his decision and also preserve the rough, grey bark. The monks had wanted to peel it away and use it for heating. The cut through the tree was about forty-seven inches. Vitas had smoothed it out thoroughly, so the growth rings could show.

"One hundred or one hundred and twenty-five?" Vitas argued with Rmi-lam, as he counted the growth rings. Some of them were hard to read.

"It certainly remembers the beginning of the last century," Vitas claimed. "Look, here you can see how the tree progressed each year. What the weather was like. Here, you can see the lighter and softer part behind the ring of the previous year – that was spring. That's the spring when you were born and look, it looks like there was plenty of moisture that year, it had a good year and even the dark part – summertime – is thicker compared to the other years – a lot of growth…"

"And what about this twist?" Rmi-lam pointed closer to the centre, where the regular elliptical ring was slightly disrupted by some kind of wave.

"According to the number of growth years, this had to be sometime in the fifties, I think. Something must have happened, a natural disaster, I don't know. The tree suffered some unpleasant shock. See? And something happened here too," Vitas indicated some dirty sediment in the growth ring. "You can read these growth rings. It's as if the tree has written its own resume. Moreover, you still remember it from the time it was alive, a majestic, fierce tree. You can then figure out the long history of this place and everything that went on here. You can learn to read people the same way. The way a person speaks, his gestures, his behaviour… and in time, you'll be able to tell if the person is a liar or a good person… You can learn to read the person the same way you read these growth rings. People who're gifted with this talent are able to read your past in a very short time."

"And if you can read the person's past, can you also read his future?" Rmi-lam asked.

"I can't. That's only possible when more growth rings are added. Now, we know that the tree dried up for unknown reasons…"

"But if we got rid of the growth rings, would this fir tree lose its past?"

"No," Vitas laughed. "It's an expression of its past. An effect. If you get rid of or change the effect, you don't get rid of or change its cause."

"In that case, if you listen to me I'll tell you a story where it's possible to change the past and the future like this. Imagine you have some divine chisel, which could change these growth rings and thereby change the past. For example, use the divine chisel here on this wave, which must have been a terrible blow, straighten it out and that would also straighten out the event that happened years ago. Or, on the contrary, make a wave on this straight line, causing this rock to fall and disappear…"

"Wild imagination, but what story is this?"

"The story of the famous first Emperor of China. This Emperor destroyed the past, thereby also losing his future," Rmi-lam said eagerly, running her fingers along the growth rings of the formerly impressive fir tree.

Vitas settled down comfortably by the stump and clasped his hands together. He had given up. "Well, I'm curious," he sighed anxiously. He was a little worried, not knowing what to expect. After years of story-telling by self-proclaimed teachers, the maturing Rmi-lam had begun to interrupt and complicate these narratives with her own diverse stories. It was a game, a fantasy, perhaps the result of a lack of communication with her peers and no less possibly the imploring search for worlds that she could only read of and hear about, though which, as in a prison, she could never see, never touch and towards which all her senses could only hopelessly desire. Lessons and bedtime stories rapidly developed into discussions and debates concerning what is and isn't right, or Rmi-lam herself extracted some information and retold the now notoriously known tale from a completely different perspective, with everything ending in total chaos, often leading the mentally unstable Mhosai Mangcug to desperately make his way around the lamasery, screaming that this girl would completely destroy him.

"And since he had no past and no future, he could only aimlessly wander around his China, the China he had once united but had forgotten all about. Everything he had once built was of no use now. The Heavens couldn't take it anymore, so they threw him a rope, he had no choice but to climb up and be knocked down a peg or two.

'Well, didn't we give you a mandate to represent us on Earth, to govern everything living and non-living down there, to ensure growth and prosperity, to please both us and the people, and of course also to honour us? And the first foolish thing you do is to rid yourself of the past, so that not only do the people forget all things, but they also forget us, the Heavens. Not only that, but you also close off the road to the future, so no one, ourselves included, can now know what is going to happen!'

'I'm deeply sorry', the Emperor apologised. 'Now that you shed light on the past and into the future, I see how severely I have erred.'

'This must show that you too, are not completely infallible, though almost almighty. You have far too much power in your hands, for such a fool. You must consider your choices more profoundly. Well, you have heard. So, go back down there and rule over the land for ten thousand years for the prosperity of all people in our name. But make no more mistakes! We neither have the nerve nor the time to deal with your matters on Earth, while we rest and take leisure here in the clouds, since the weight of the world lies on our shoulders. Now go! Go!'

And so the Emperor returned to the Middle Kingdom and began to rule responsibly. He knew that thanks to Heaven's mandate, he was responsible for everything living and non-living. He rewarded hardworking and honest servants and punished thieves and dishonest subordinates. He built the famous Great Wall of China and implemented many laws. But beware," Rmi-lam raised her index finger, "they say *trust but verify*. He didn't stay long in the Palace because he was always out on inspection trips, checking everything, praising and rewarding hardworking people and beheading the dishonest."

"Please, how do you know all this?" Vitas couldn't wait any longer and interrupted her. Truly, he did enjoy the fantasy and appreciated how Rmi-lam was able to interconnect historical data with fictional, sometimes absurd stories, giving human reasons.

"The honourable Rinpoche told me a lot of stories about ancient China and I learnt some facts, data and events and then we had to compare everything. And we also discussed what is interesting about these events, what's right and wrong and whether they can even be perceived as morally right."

"That's amazing. Keep going," Vitas urged.

"One day, the Emperor was driving through the deserted land and a terrible, dark storm was brewing. There was no shelter or cave far and wide that he could hide in. It had already started raining when he suddenly saw a large, dense tree that he hid beneath." Rmi-lam placed her hands on both sides of the fir trunk, as if she were speaking about this tree that the emperor had once hidden beneath. "Downpour all around and he was dry and happy. It stopped raining and after some time, the day even brightened. The Emperor bowed to the tree, thanking it for the services it had rendered to him and appointed it an honour of the fifth degree. He clipped a medal to its bark and had a plague built by it, describing its heroic act. And do you know why? Because the Emperor knew that he was responsible for all things – not only the living, but also the non-living. The master of fate for everything under the Heavens," Rmi-lam passionately recounted, still holding the trunk, seeming to draw from it all the ideas of the story in itself.

"On another occasion, the Emperor and his servants were paddling a boat across the wild river. He was on an inspection trip. The land was flat all around, but there was a mountain on the side they needed to get to. And incredibly, even though a mountain lay before them, they continued to row against the strong wind. The wind probably blew around both sides of the mountain, coming together ever-stronger, striking the Emperor's group even harder. The famous Emperor felt offended that the mountain hurt him instead of helping him. Even the mountain was trying to humiliate him. Its duty was to protect him. He felt deeply hurt, so once they got over to the other side after their treacherous journey, he stood at the foot of the mountain, strongly criticising it.

'Why are you standing here if you can't protect me? Such an easy thing for you to do – subside the wind to protect the son of the Heavens, and yet you do nothing. I am utterly disappointed in you.'

Aware of the fact that he could hardly let something like this go unpunished, he called his chief minister and ordered him to immediately have all the trees on the mountain chopped down, leaving it completely bare, and to have it painted an ochre colour, the colour which represented convicts. Yes, that's what happened.

The older the Emperor grew, the more convinced he

became of his mission to rule over everything living and non-living under the Heavens for ten thousand years. But the older the Emperor grew, the older his body became, blighted by ailments and diseases. His knees, his wrists and his back ached, and he suffered from many other ageing illnesses. So, he decided to do something about it.

He invested enormous resources into the discovery of the elixir of life, putting all the chemists under the Heavens at task to try and create it. Vanity. He sent a fleet of ships to the Island of the Immortals, the alleged source of this miraculous potion. There were trees with jade fruit on this island, too. If one of these fruits was consumed, one could live another ten thousand years. But it was all in vain. The whole expedition ended in disaster and only the poor ruins of the fleet returned. The surviving witnesses claimed that many of the ships had sunk and that the wind had blown the rest of the ships far out into sea, never to return again, with only a few ships managing to reach the island. But once the ships got within an arrow's reach of the island, the whole landscape sunk below the surface, leaving them with no other choice but to sail back home.

And so the Emperor began thinking that the Heavens were taking a jab at him, convinced they were only using him for their amusement. And so he set off to see them."

"You mean he tried to return to see them in the Heavens?" Vitas interrupted the story-telling.

"Yes, back into the Heavens. Climbing up the rope. Since he was no longer a youngster, it was quite hard for him to get up there. Once there, a huge quarrel broke out. He could barely catch his breath before the Heavens began attacking him: 'How dare you keep us from our rest. Do you think our time always belongs to you? We must rest and take our leisure in the clouds!'

'And how am I supposed to fulfil my duties and your

duties, when I feel that I'm not immortal? You gave me the power to rule over all things living and non-living, and most of the time, everybody obeyed. And whoever didn't, was punished severely. But I have a feeling that death is inevitable. I feel old and helpless, everything hurts... You betrayed me. You merely fly around in the sky, doing nothing, leaving me to do all the work on Earth. But I am in poor health! So, what am I supposed to do?'

'Look, old man,' the Heavens pronounced. 'We may advise you, but I pray you shall cease your complaints. The advice is simple. Purchase two trucks of fish and journey to the Sandy Hills. That is where you shall attain immortality.'

'As you wish,' bellowed the Emperor, pleased at the coincidence of an already-planned inspection of Sandy Hill. Thus he bought two trucks of fish and headed out there. And that was the place where he died."

"What nonsense is that? How can someone die and be immortal at the same time?" Vitas asked, amused.

"Nothing is impossible," disputed Rmi-lam. "You're only dead when everyone forgets you ever lived. As long as you remain in one person's memory, as long as someone remembers you, you're still alive.

The Emperor's chief minister and his leading eunuch left him in the truck and ruled the Middle Kingdom on his behalf," Rmi-lam continued relentlessly in her story, rubbing the end of the cut on the fir tree with her thumb, apparently aiming to add another growth ring.

No one knew that he had died. The fish that were in the truck in front and behind him reeked, so no one could smell the terrible stench coming from the Emperor's corpse, which had already begun to decompose. Everyone thought the Emperor was alive. He issued commands, orders, edicts – no one was surprised by anything. And no one is surprised to this day. And, so the Emperor became immortal and from that time forth, he has been driving from one side of China to the other, constantly issuing orders. Thanks to the horrible stench that follows him everywhere, everyone recognises him wherever he goes. But in reality, someone else, who has no right to do so, actually rules on his behalf."

"Ugh, so the Emperor is everywhere that smells foul?" Vitas jabbed provocatively.

"No no no, on the contrary. It usually stinks wherever a ruler reigns on Earth. This is your own reading of cause and effect. Sometimes, you can change the growth rings, thereby changing the past and the future." Rmi-lam turned to Vitas and motioned for him to come closer, as if wanting to whisper something. Vitas put his ear almost right in front of Rmi-lam's lips and red-faced, she quietly revealed her secret: "Sometimes, I think everybody stinks."

"Yes, but not everyone who stinks is an emperor. And in any case, your story was beautifully awkward."

6.
Ares and the Muse

The smell of iron, the scent of stained, greasy, iron surfaces, wheels, belts squeaking against each other, causing the teeth to grind jarringly. In defence, one inadvertently grinds his upper teeth against his lower teeth in a circular motion. A deafening, monotonous rumble of dancing iron.

A Model 98 tank, a so-called third generation MBT[33] Chinese tank, launched in October 1999 for the fiftieth anniversary of the declaration of the People's Republic of China. Despite a few limitations, it was one of the most modern tanks ever built. Though for one thing, it did need a four-member crew, as opposed to the typical three-member crew, to operate the non-automatic loading system developed by the Russians. This was all thanks to a special ammunition made in China based on the western model. This tank later underwent several changes, which however, no longer concerned our six tanks, preparing for a challenging journey and a daring operation on Mount Jadhang.

The 125 mm cannon, weighing fifty tons, can annihilate a target with significant force and thanks to its laser viewfinder, with great accuracy, too. Its khaki camouflage is ideal for the desert environment, characterising local Western Tibet.

---

33 Main Battle Tank.

In the eyes of Private Wanjung, this tank has only one key advantage, though a very fundamental and insurmountable one. Wanjung, serving a two-year mandatory military term as a machine-gunner, is a twenty-five-year-old graduate of the famous Shanghai conservatory. His main field of study is the violin, but the piano is the second instrument he loves to play. Although he's had little success in playing the piano as compared to the violin, when he begins performing Ježek's *Bugatti Step*, a masterpiece by a famous Czechoslovak composer, which he so passionately adores, he could bring a dead man to life. The insurmountable advantage of the Model 98 tank that leaves him so impressed is the fact that when two tank-drivers stand regularly in the tower opening, there's enough room for a sizeable grand piano in the ideal position in front of them, on which they could thereby play any masterpiece they wanted – Schubert's *Fantasy in F-Minor* for four hands. No surprise that the almost-ten-foot long Petrof piano with a large gold star in a red circle could only be delivered to the Jadhang by means of a tank. There was a thick layer of rubber insulation, where the piano touched the armour, not scratching it. The cast iron, fully armoured piano frame also guaranteed the piano's continued safety. After removing the front legs and pedal structure, nine soldiers were able to place it perfectly so that the rounded section of the rear wing leaned comfortably against a third of the massive cannon. The rear legs of the piano formed a forty-degree angle with the cannon. For extra safety, firm straps connected the part where the foot of the piano lovingly rubbed against the dark green armour of the 125 mm cannon.

Knowing that perhaps some perverted joining of Ares and the Muse had created such an artistic artefact, Wanjung signed up for the mission voluntarily, aware only of the fact that it had something to do with liberating one insignificant region from the hands of troublesome revan-chists. The only thing that worried him was the prospect of finding a good partner with the same understanding of *Fantasy in F-Minor*. In his worries, he had no suspicion that his decision to partake in the attack would put a damper on his promising artistic career, or rather that this would mark the high point of his ultimate and hardly-appreciated efforts, and his journey in life in general.

A convoy of six tanks, two convoy-trucks bearing forty soldiers, three convoys of supplies and ammunition, includ-ing four mortars, set off upstream along the Langqên Zangbo river. Three water-tank convoys followed them up too, full of fuel. Because of the terrain, the convoy couldn't take a direct route. Going along the Langqên Zangbo river was the most suitable solution and then to follow the steep slopes in the north, up the winding passages between rock walls and mountains, directly to the Jadhang.

Dust clouds rose around the convoy and Wanjung stood proudly by the piano, trying to match the sputtering rhythm of the engine with the pounding of his own delusions.

— — —

Encircled by peak on peak of life's dust,
Man is a bug trapped in a bowl.
All day skittering up its sides,
Ever falling back, never bounding out,
His imagined joys always beyond his reach,
His present miseries ever close by,
Till eventually his little river of years dries up,
And old age takes teeth, takes hair, takes all.[34]

---

34 *Huangshan Poems from the T'ang Dynasty:* A Bug Trapped in a Bowl by Han Shan – Translated by Stanton Hager, Cape Cod: 21st Editions, 2009.

Lama Thorpe Tenzin is discussing the meaning of the verses of the legendary hermit, the Buddhist monk, Hanshan, who lived around 800, with Rmi-lam. Just as the Lama describes the transience and vanity of human life, as expressed in the verses of a poet raised with Buddhism, Kromen stands some three miles north of the lamasery on a jutting ridge, enjoying the feeling of greatness that the surrounding mountains evoke in him. He stands upright, his legs outstretched and his arms crossed. His chest and arms pump to a regular beat as he inhales. He is an antenna, with thousands of oxygen particles rushing towards him as he absorbs each one. These oxygen particles give him the strength to stand domineering over his imperious post.

He can see far and wide, miles into the distance, but a road turns and descends just ahead of him, disappearing right before his eyes after several feet. The word "road" however, might be a far-fetched description for this sandy and rocky terrain riddled with potholes, pitfalls and unpredictable rock projections, protrusions, bumps and protuberances… He stands far from the top of the hill. A rock on his left rises sharply up, its back towards the lamasery, facing north. Waiting.

– – –

"Don't worry, I won't bother you with such sad and difficult verses any further," the Lama soothes Rmi-lam, whose lips are pursed tightly, the stubborn expression on her face indicating just how much she had enjoyed the poem.

"I also have something light-hearted here for you. The poet Li Bai, immortal bard, whose poetic verses flow like the wind that blows across the mountains. He was even expelled from court life in a conspiracy of envy. He wrote this poem at his friend's house in the Songshan Mountains – probably at a celebration and perhaps quite drunk."

Among the blossoms waits a jug of wine,
I pour myself a drink, no loved one near.
Raising my cup, I invite the bright moon
And turn to my shadow. We are now three.
But the moon doesn't understand drinking,
And my shadow follows my body like a slave.
For a time moon and shadow will be my companions,
A passing joy that should last through the spring.
I sing and the moon just wavers in the sky;
I dance and my shadow whips around like mad.
While lucid still, we have such fun together!
But stumbling drunk, each staggers off alone.
Bound forever, relentless we roam:
Reunited at last on the distant river of stars.[35]

— — —

While the Lama analyses to Rmi-lam the unconventional song form and interesting rhyme scheme that alternates through six different forms in the original text, the ground under Kromen's feet begins to tremble slightly. The vibrations are accompanied by increasing thunder. Kromen has lost his confident, on-top-of-the-world expression. His body is now beginning to vibrate. The cells in his limbs and his whole torso are sending emergency warnings to the nervous system. It is at this point exactly, that a colossal tank comes over the hill, the dark orifice of its cannon pointing forth. It's moving slowly but steadily onwards. Kromen can no longer stand in one place. First, his hands fall to his sides, but he immediately raises them again, placing them firmly on his hips. Perhaps he feels like they can't be left like that. His face turns from solemnity to profound amazement,

---

35 Chinese poetry – "Drinking Alone under the Moon" by Li Bai, translated by David Bowles.

attempting tameness, as if able to control it himself, though the opposite is true.

The cannon advances, when a plaque with the sovereign Chinese symbol emerges – a gold star in a red circle. This is followed by the whole ensemble – a piano with a huge cannon. Kromen raises his eyebrows. He can no longer control himself. It doesn't take long before the entire and tangible monstrosity appears before him – a tank with a piano hanging from it like a suction cup, like a huge mosquito, a predator, draining all the power from his body.

At first glance, the final crunching of the tank that stops before Kromen's face shows the musical instrument's clear victory over the military vehicle.

From below, Kromen can't see the top of the tower over the piano, but he can hear the opening of the hatch. Briskly, Major Li C'cheng clambers out of the tank. They look into each other's eyes for a moment, broken only by the noiseless wave of Kromen's hand towards the tank, as if to ask how this abomination had come to Earth.

Li smirks and says contemptuously: "Well, would you prefer your piano brought here on a motorbike?"

7.

A Promise Kept

"Well then, young lady?" says Mhosai Mangcug, "how do you think things will turn out here, well?"

Rmi-lam sits across from Mhosai on the Jadhang rocks in a vigilant position, like a fox prepared for either flight or fight. She has a very contradictory relationship with Mhosai, but no one really knows exactly where they stand with him. Yes, he is amusing, but rather sarcastic. And very loud. Everyone knows where to find him throughout the lamasery. All that's necessary is to be quiet and listen carefully... His double-entendres and ambiguities are often hard to decipher. On the other hand, he's utterly harmless. In his eyes, any fate is difficult to determine. If it is possible to see behind the mask of Vitas, unveiling the mask of Aviel would be a greater challenge, but what of the destinies of all the other monks at the lamasery? So many dreams. The pain, the happiness, the lost illusions... Everyone found themselves with a new, clean and unstained slate. The past had been forgiven. And if it had not been, then everyone, including Mhosai, continues to bear the flame of sin within them. No one has hurt anyone here. But this didn't exclude the fact that he could still be provocative with his teasing humour.

"You mean, here?" Rmi-lam asks carefully. "How it'll turn out here?"

"Look, don't act like you don't know what I'm talking about. Which avatar[36] do you like the most?"

"I don't have any favourites. I like everyone I meet. I can't say who I prefer…"

"The God Vishnu has descended nine times in various forms, once even in the form of a Buddha. I'm sure Vitas has told you about Jesus, so there's another one. You have to choose your favourite…"

"No I don't."

"Yes, you do because only your true avatar can save you once he descends. Just this one avatar can save us all from disaster and extinction. Otherwise, the end will come."

"There will be no end!" Rmi-lam says sternly, but remaining impartial. In no way does she still seem a child. She can no longer be fooled by anyone. As such, she first accepts such situations with a smile on her face, as if they were a game. This obviously irritated some stubborn teachers even further.

"You're mistaken, young lady. We've already said that the worst chaos cannot be prevented. Kalki, the tenth and final avatar will come when there is utter destruction, once man disrupts the balance of the universe by his sinful deeds. And that will be the end of our time. The honourable Rinpoche had to teach you the same thing, except he was talking about the coming of Buddha Maitreya and Vitas had to teach you the same thing, when he was talking about the Last Judgment…"

"No, we haven't talked about anything like that yet. And we're not even going to talk about it."

"You have to talk about it. If we're talking about the beginning, young lady, we also have to talk about the end," Mhosai says, his wide eyes instructive, while Rmi-lam

---

36 Avatar – ava = down, tr = step. Avatar = the one, who descends down (meant like a saviour).

seems to fight a mental protest – her eyes narrow and her lips clench so tightly that several long wrinkles begin to appear on her face.

Aviel, excitedly running up from the lamasery, fortunately resolved the conflicting situation.

"A piano! Kromen has kept his promise!"

He didn't have to say anymore. Rmi-lam shot out enthusiastically, without even asking Mhosai anything, without even saying goodbye. Of course, it wasn't only the piano that had impressed her, but also the chance to skip her Hindi lessons. In the distance, she could hear Mhosai saying something about her responsibility to study, of not interrupting the teaching of others, and that he'd ask the same of himself.

– – –

"Dear friends," announces Kromen with his distinct, over-fabricated smile. "I'm glad to see here, that the fruits of my labour," nodding towards Aviel and Vitas, "are prosperous in this society, bringing their spirit and influencing you in a positive way, just as you have influenced them… and actually even me. But let's get down to it. As you know, I made a promise some time ago and as we all know, promises must be kept… no?" His eyes dart over the audience and stop on Rmi-lam, only briefly registering her glowing face. He hungrily seeks out the Lama's inquisitive eyes and then eventually sticks to them.

"Yeeees, promises are great," Rmi-lam exhales happily. The others fidget in disbelief. "After all, we do all truly love you, Sir Kromen."

Kromen silently ignored this remark and started organising everything necessary for the piano to enter. Yaks are quite lively and unpredictable animals, yet very tough and determined. After a brief consultation, he selected two slightly older but calm, furry yaks with harnesses. They attached to them one thirteen-foot beam and the ten-member group, including Rmi-lam of course, with both Vitas and Aviel, set off.

Along the way, everyone continued to pester Kromen, asking him where he'd found the piano and more importantly, how he'd managed to get it all the way here. Kromen strutted ahead, sometimes saying tersely: "Unless I'm mistaken, no one here, apart from you, had mentioned anything about a piano," he avoided answering any specific questions. "Let yourselves be surprised."

But for the sandy, ochre soil with the occasional juniper bush and patch of grass, the space was lined with mountains all around. They were making their way up the hill to reach their destination. It took them an hour and a half, but they did it. The black mass, embellished with the red star on its lid, gradually revealed itself in all its beauty, modesty and scale, its wood, its keys, its hammers, and its pedals, in the middle of the barren land. Everyone felt a surging potential of energy, but no one had any idea where it came from, or that it seemed to mirror a huge revolution in human thinking, something that cannot be bound by equations, or by the laws of conservation of energy and matter, by instructional manuals or by scientific hypotheses. One of the many things superior to reason. Something which only God has the answers to, yet He remains silent.

No one uttered a word. Rmi-lam sat on a rock that four very willing monks rolled over to her and she began to speak to God. At first, she stroked the keys timorously. She wasn't used to the proper spacing between them. Her fingers hit the incorrect keys, rapidly searching for the right ones. Following its cowboy journey, the piano was out of tune, so many of the notes were completely off key. But none of this was important now. God spoke and the fingers spoke also. They proclaimed something that required neither accuracy nor harmony. The tones curled in the landscape of desolate hills and the scenery of placid peaks and rocks peering around towards them. They crawled into the holes of weathered stone, interweaving with juniper needles and firmly anchoring themselves to the small place where Rmi-lam stood with the piano. Everyone present formed a circle around them, which then collapsed into the shape of a ramp. Thanks to her, everyone slowly set off together and let themselves be dragged between the high hills, the slopes, the rocks and the winding roads at the top of the world. They saw the trembling wind, felt every animal, every plant… The rock mass was speaking.

After their flight, everyone landed back to the earth – softly, gently, slightly intoxicated, and then there was silence.

No one asked any questions, no one wanted to speak. There was nonverbal communication – two monks grabbed the yaks, attached logs perpendicular to their bodies, which then formed somewhat of a track. The others grabbed the piano and after weary effort, placed the piano on the tracks. While Aviel bent over to hold the piano with his back, he noticed inconspicuous oil stains on the ground. Dark, dark blue, like the eye of the devil.

Once the instrument was loaded, the whole group headed off home. Everyone supported the piano, however and wherever possible. The most important thing was to keep the yaks in a straight line. If either of them were to budge or to change speed relative to the others, the piano would, in all probability, fall flying to the ground. Aviel was the only one missing in the crowd. He stayed behind where the piano had stood, having descended like a sudden resolution from God. He watched thoughtfully as the caravan disappeared under the hill and behind the rock, around the bend.

Once they were all gone, he turned impatiently and went straight to the oil stain. He touched it with his index finger and thumb. A bit of slimy liquid clung to his fingers. He raised his fingers to his nose and sniffed it in disbelief. Rotten oil, grease and iron filings. He stood up and looked around carefully, also looking at the ground. He pushed away the dust and stones with his shoes, as if he were looking for something. Then, he circled the area in ever-larger circuits. But there were only two routes of arrival – one, the way from which they'd arrived from the lamasery, and the other leading farther on. There was no other possible access. He set off ahead, still carefully inspecting the surface of the road.

It had instantly occurred to Aviel that someone must have swept the surface. Someone had been sweeping away the tracks. He continued onwards, until he saw the prints of two belts. Clear ornaments of regular lines that cut into the ground. One over the other. Easy to explain – one way there, the other one back. Aviel followed the tracks persistently.

– – –

No one could force Rmi-lam to study that day. The lamasery echoed, interrupted and silenced here and there by insurmountable ragdungs that headed out into the world with their long pipes, spreading the message of Buddha.

8.

Funeral Flowers under Fire

"Where's Kromen?" yelled Aviel, sprinting around the lamasery, his face knocked into a fury like a tenacious horseshoe. He answered the inquisitive responses with a stiff question: "Where is he?!"

Some of the monks then told him that Kromen had spent a long time with the honourable Lama and had then been seen to have speedily disappeared somewhere down by the pastures.

Then, one of the monks saw him running down the rocks.

— — —

Vitas tried to tune the piano. He had everything he needed for it – a handle and a tuning fork. Both of these were amateur creations, and the result of the tuning questionable. It didn't produce jolts as before, but they were far from pure tones. Then, he continued with Rmi-lam's practise. "Knowing the chords is key. Once you can play the Major and Minor chords back and forth in your sleep, then we'll start learning your 'Summertime'."

Rmi-lam fought back in vain, her face wrinkled, her eyes almost touching her nose they were so close with concentration, her nose slowly merging with her pursed lips. "There's no way I'm starting from the beginning!"

"Oh, yes you are. This is completely different from the plastic toy. If you really want to learn to play the piano, it takes years and years of practice. Now, you're just putting on a well-practised acrobatics show. Even a parrot can learn to speak…"

– – –

Lu Cheng the butcher came running with the news. Aviel lay in the Jadhang Gad River with his head shattered. Dead. Time stopped. The circle of life stopped. His death touched everyone. Vitas wandered around the lamasery in disbelief, repeating: "Why? WHY?" Reminiscing about the final moments. What had happened? Vitas was with Rmilam, when Aviel went angrily running around the lamasery, looking for… He realised he was looking for Kromen. And what happened before that? Had he even been with the whole group when they went to fetch the piano? Yes, he had. He most certainly had been and then he'd disappeared… Where? Why? Kromen. Kromen again. No proof anywhere, but… Vitas had no explanation, but something was moving in the breeze; he felt it. Hunter-like as he wanted to be, his investigative feelings were muffled by the great pain of losing a friend. He felt another stage of his life coming to an end.

As Vitas entered the Lama's chamber, he saw Aviel laid out in the right corner with his knees slightly bent and his right palm under a wet wound. His right temple, partly covered by his palm, was heavily bruised – perhaps hit by a stone. The Lama spoke to him slowly and quietly, no more than a few inches away.

"Aviel, son of a noble family, the time has come, death!"

"But you are not alone in leaving this world, this must

come to all. Neither dwell on nor long for life. Even though you dwell on it and long for it, you cannot stay here. All you can do is wander through the samsara. Don't dwell on life! Don't long for it! Remember the Three Jewels!"

The Lama paused for a moment, casually looked at Vitas, disregarding his presence, leaned back towards Aviel and continued.

"Oh, son of a noble family, no matter how horrible or threatening the bardo's phenomena may appear to you, do not lose sight of the following words, remember their meaning and journey on! The core of these words is to understand through them."

> O now, when the *Bardo* of Reality upon me is dawning,
> Abandoning all awe, fear, and terror of all phenomena,
> May I recognise whatever appears as being my own thought-forms,
> May I know them to be apparitions in the Intermediate State;
> It has been said, 'There will arrive a time
> when the chief turning-point is reached;
> Fear not, the bands of the Peaceful and Wrathful,
> are thine own thought-forms!'[37]

Vitas alone refused a traditional Buddhist funeral and since he didn't know the exact Jewish ritual, he buried his Jewish friend on Buddhist soil, in a half-Jewish, half-Christian tradition. Well, he'd wanted it to be exclusively Jewish, but this was something about which he knew little. No Jew had ever been buried the Jadhang. So, he only followed what he had known about Judaism and filled in the gaps with his Christian beliefs. Once Aviel was cleansed, his naked body was wrapped in white cloth and, following the ancient Jewish tradition, his eyes and mouth were covered with shards of clay, leaving him to rest in peace.

---

37 *The Tibetan Book of the Dead*

Vitas stood at the bottom of the lamasery, where the soil was more aerated, making it possible to dig a grave. He gave his final speech to his friend, who lay on a plain, rough board, everything but his head wrapped in a white cloth.

He stood surrounded by dozens of monks. It was his task to ensure that everyone said their final farewell to Aviel. For a while, he rubbed his gau with the Jadhang verses engraved on the chorten in his hands. Then, he threw it into Aviel's grave at the foot of the mountain and cut his collar with a knife to express his grief. He had no idea what he was saying. Memories of his life were running through his head. He felt like the frozen, dead dog in the trash can in Cheb, with only his stiff legs, snout and a piece of his body sticking out.

He fell silent and looked around at all the faces of the monks and Rmi-lam. What was the meaning of his own words?

– – –

At the same time, just a few miles from the Jadhang, metal strips flattened the soil. Iron, oil, diesel, armour, all screeching in a resounding harmony. Steady, harsh, tremulous, causing an air of greasy dust and a stabbing pain in the lower abdomen. A menacing counterpoint to the final farewell with Aviel. Major Li C'cheng is preparing his squad for attack. He knows the basic terrain from Kromen. He doesn't want to waste too much time at the Jadhang. He just has to deal with his mission, then disappear and reap the benefits. What remains to be done? One massive attack with all the resources available to him. There was no sense is sparing anything now. All liquidating attacks in Tibet happened the same way, the finest strategy of the Chinese commander being to draw everything he had on hand to crush and crush again. And since human material is most abundant, the cheapest and easily replaceable, it's necessary to throw everything into the attack. Whether a well-trained enemy and armed Khampa, or a mother with her child. All crushed and crushed again.

– – –

"Man is able to destroy anything in the world, including the world itself, but not the life he lives. No one can touch your life anymore. You are immortal. Let your name be written in the Book of Life. Mazel tov," Vitas concluded the ceremony and stepped away from the grave, so that the monks could throw handfuls of stone clay into it one by one.

And that's when Rmi-lam started. At first she searched for the right tone in her voice, but after some time she located the right key for the famous Jewish song, 'Shalom Aleichem', orienting the sensitive environment of united souls. It was Aviel's last surprise. He had secretly practised this song, which had gripped his chest, robbed him of his breath and strangled his voice, for several weeks with Rmi-lam. The Hebrew words, though incomprehensible, spoke clearly to the Supreme King of the Kings, begging for his blessing. Lumps of soil rustle lightly as they hit the inside of the grave.

– – –

The long, mournful Hebrew words of 'Shalom Aleichem' cut through three rapidly exploding grenades, one following the other, accompanied by the clattering of machineguns and small-arms fire. This all happened at the lowest part of the Jadhang. In places, where the river flows, there are pastures, modest stables for cattle and a few industrial buildings for panning gold. The vast majority of Jadhang inhabitants were

474

at Aviel's funeral – in the middle and far sides of the pastures. Nevertheless, at this time, fifteen monks were fulfilling their duties in the agricultural and industrial areas. Yaks, horses, sheep and goats require care, despite human funerals.

The Chinese military shot everything in sight that moved. It didn't matter if it was a yak or a person. They even fired at anything that potentially smelled like a hotbed of reactionary resistance, so buildings, footbridges and anything built by human hands.

Butcher Lu Cheng was the first one to end up in the ruins of his home, the convoy of military vehicles, a tank leading the way, coming from his side. Whenever there was more space, the squad spread out as much as possible to show their strength, suggesting an entire invincible army following behind. But due to the terrain, the convoy receded back like a line of geese, one behind the other immediately afterwards, grateful it could even make its way through the difficult, rocky terrain.

The attendees of Aviel's funeral scattered like steam under a pot. The grave was left unfinished, a bouquet of Tibetan astras with a yellow pistil and beautiful white-purple petals that Rmi-lam had picked for Aviel's farewell, was hastily thrown down, an unfinished stone standing as a tombstone for the many unspoken words.

– – –

They all ran up to the lamasery in search of shelter. They had a significant head start in terms of distance, but more so thanks to the terrain, which was very complicated for the Chinese heavy machinery to navigate. Everything was hurried but calm, as if something like this had always been expected to happen. Sonam automatically took over governing the lamasery. He was the only experienced warrior, with the soul of a Chinese soldier, who knew how to fight against the invaders. The abbot opened the secret hiding places of the lamasery and together with Sonam, handed out weapons that no one in the lamasery even knew they had ever possessed. Earlier, back in the fifties, it was common for a lot of the weapons to be hidden in the lamasery during the revolt against the Chinese, causing havoc for the Chinese frontlines. There were around thirty rifles from the time China invaded Tibet. By now, most of them were near-obsolete, American Lee–Enfield .303 rifles with a loader for five bullets, supplied to Tibet with the help of the CIA, as contraband dropped by parachutes during the many covert missions conducted by the US Air Force. Unfortunately, they didn't have much ammunition, but they had several boxes of defensive grenades in the shape of traditional eggs, which could have been the most important aid. And then, bows and arrows, second nature to Tibetans, many of whom could use them brilliantly. Doubtless they would be less useful on this open field, but they could be a very dangerous enemy in a concealing terrain of rugged rocks, where every gap was known and every protrusion could be hidden behind. Fifty monks had this ancient weapon in their hands and about thirty of them were master archers. Vitas took a rifle, which he knew how to use quite well. The Lama handed it to him personally and his eyes seemed to tell Vitas that he didn't have to do this, that this wasn't his fight. But Vitas knew that this must be his battle, too. He didn't know if he was more Buddhist or Christian, but he knew he belonged here in the mountains and he had to protect the Jadhang.

"But your task isn't over," said the Lama. "You must be careful."

"I'm not going into battle recklessly," Vitas smiled with reassurance. "But my place is there," he nodded towards the rocks, where armed monks hid on their way up the Jadhang.

"I understand," the Lama said, a tinge of regret to his voice. "But realise that we have someone here who we must protect, no matter what happens to us."

Vitas stopped. He knew what or rather who, the Lama was referring to. "I understand and I will do everything in my power. But I can't just sit here and stare at the tanks coming towards us," concluded Vitas, preparing to leave. The Lama grabbed him by the shoulder with his left hand and glared intently into his eyes. Without saying a word, he pulled out a beautiful phurba from his cassock, a ritual dagger, richly decorated with shining stones. The phurba is one of the most powerful energy emitters. Its purpose is to dispel negation, but it's also associated with numerous myths and can possess immense power. At least that's how believers of certain Eastern religions see this tool.

Vitas slowly accepted it without a word and hid it under his chupa. As a token of his gratitude and as a farewell, he nodded his head and ran towards the only access road to the lamasery.

— — —

The Chinese forces did not stop firing. The loss of the water reservoir was shot down, too; a tragic loss for the lamasery. In an instant, the monastery was deprived of this most valuable liquid. After losing his piano and thus all his motivation, Private WanYung thoughtlessly shot at the surrounding rocks, at the meadows, at the yaks... He saw a footbridge high up above him and some outcrops here and there. Without actually killing anyone, he unknowingly succeeded in one meritorious deed. He had significantly damaged the mechanism of Kromen's execution bridge, which was a major source of the lamasery's protein balance. Now, the bridge seemed held together on a word of honour alone, which, as had been demonstrated so recently, couldn't always be trusted.

Once the squad came across the only zigzagging path, which was somewhat suitable in width for the tanks that passed between the rocks to the lamasery, Major Li C'cheng realised the scale of the risk he was taking. He knew the terrain approximately from Kromen's description, but he couldn't be sure of its precision. They had wasted the element of surprise with meaningless gunfire, and in any case, ascending steep mountainous paths posed a real threat. Failure in the form of an embarrassing defeat would mean the end of him. He was very well aware of that. Yet, he had power that no other lamasery could compete with. Therefore, he gave the command to a tactical retreat. He closed off and strictly guarded the paths from the top of the Jadhang and destroyed the camp below, the area of the destroyed pastures the pinnacle of his foresight. There was no shortage of food or water. There was an abundance of dead yaks, sheep and goats lying all around.

It was already late in the afternoon. Li C'cheng had decided that the attack would take place early the next morning, before dawn. The top priority was to explore the terrain, and accordingly scouts were to be deployed at night. Following this, he would ensure that the tanks had easy access to the lamasery, sending his infantrymen ahead, eliminating the monastery itself with mortar shells and tank fire. There would be no problem there. A simple operation, but no mistakes could be allowed. Losses wouldn't matter. However accomplished, the target must be achieved. And then: a hasty retreat. He knew he had to do his job quickly and then disappear. An international affair wouldn't be desirable. The territory on which he stood was under dispute, belonging more to India than China. According to law, the jurisdiction was Indian, at least for now.

There was peace at the bottom of the Jadhang. They threw the corpses of about fifteen monks into the river, farther from the camp. The soldiers made several campfires, using the remnants of local juniper bushes and timber taken primarily from ruined structures. They greedily devoured the grilled meat from the cattle that had been shot dead. WanYung piped a light melody on a flute, occasionally piercing the commander with an angry look for depriving him of a great darling. Finally, everyone could unwind, as if they were on a relaxing, military trip. One of the soldiers also stated with a loud burp, that for total perfection, he'd need booze and a woman. Everyone agreed that the latter could be upstairs, but the booze would be a long shot.

It was one of the most beautiful evenings on the Jadhang, illuminated by a vista of stars that seemed to be blessing the liberators of Tibet, which the Chinese armed forces had always pretended to be.

9.
The Counter-Attack

In the meantime, thirty monks were preparing for defence on the only access road to the lamasery. If it's possible to speak of peace, the situation was even calmer, once the information came through concerning the Chinese army withdrawing at the lower part of the Jadhang. The kashag was held quickly, immediately changing its function to a military crew. Repeating chords and practicing were stubbornly heard resounding, Vitas having told Rmi-lam that this was the only way to achieve virtuosity on a musical instrument with Chinese sovereign symbols. Although everyone respected the Lama as the abbot, not only as the highest spiritual leader, but also as the secular ruler of the monastery, Sonam, the military general became the central figure.

"It has to be clear to all of us that the only target of the Chinese army is to destroy us. We are in a situation in which we have nothing to lose," said Sonam, scanning those gathered before him. "And if the Chinese retreated down to the river, it's only because they plan to launch a far more violent attack in the morning. I know them. I know their fear of the road leading to the monastery. It's too dangerous for their machinery, so their decision cannot be ad hoc. That's why we have to be the first to attack."

"We? Attack?" Lao PuWei, who had once so strongly opposed Rmi-lam's stay at the lamasery, stood up indignantly, almost bending at the waist, addressing his objection towards Sonam. "But we're not built for this!" Lao suddenly waved his arms, as if in some tantrum. "For the sake of the highest Lord, can't someone tell the crazy girl to stop pounding those keys? I can't listen to it anymore!"

Everyone's eyes widened, shocked that Lao had lost his nerves, but no one said a word. They could only wait in anticipation of what he would say or do next. But Lao no doubt realised he had gone too far, and continued as if nothing had been said. "Other than you, none of us have ever gone into battle. And since when are you such a fortune-teller, Sonam? How do you know the central priority of the Chinese military is to destroy us? Perhaps they want something else."

"Aha," Sonam called out indignantly, loud with melodramatic astonishment, gazing around at the others, as if considering them witnesses to the injustice just pronounced. His eyes narrowed as he tried to sharpen his vision, perhaps so that he could examine the gestures and reactions of those present. "They will kill many of our people, almost all of the cattle, they will destroy all our home and we're now going to ask them, 'What would you like, little dears? Would you perhaps like Rmi-lam, too? Let's say we give you your own Empress, whom we have brought up here, took care of and protected from you? All in our own country that you dared to invade? Well, I see, you plan to behead her instead of placing her on the throne, but that's your decision now, after all, she is YOUR Empress and what should we care, yes? Especially when you leave your own homeland rock untouched, for this immense, immobile, unspeaking rock.'"

After his performance, Sonam looked around his audience, who gawped at him in astonishment. Only a few of those present stared at the ground – clear proof that they knew of Rmi-lam's origin.

"We have to fight!" burst the red-faced Mhosai Mangcug, standing in the warrior pose. "By the king of all gods, Indra, just like Rama fought to save his wife, Sita against the demons, the king of the Rakshasas Ravana. With the help of the monkey kingdom, with the help of the bears and all Gods. Neither he nor we knew that He, standing here before us, is the great God Vishnu. There is no other way than to fight and protect Rmi-lam and to place our trust in you, commander."

Sonam smiled falsely, an expression of gratitude, and continued silently but with further emphasis. "Anyone here can die, but Rmi-lam must survive. If she survives, then Tibet has a chance of surviving. You know we only have a few decades left before the culture of Tibet goes extinct. No one will then be able to lift it from the dust and ashes. The shoes of the Chinese, the boots of the Communist soldiers have already trampled over everything. If you believe in the mythical Phoenix, then Rmi-lam is our Phoenix. She is our last hope."

Vitas quite undiplomatically interrupted the long silence with something seemingly unrelated. "Has anybody seen Kromen?"

A sea of vacant stares. The abbot interrupted the monologue impatiently. "Enough. I know exactly where you're heading with that question, Kushok Vitas, but we can't mitigate this meeting with questions and opinions, which hinder us from the heart of the matter. We can't even be distracted by examining the causes of the situation you're no doubt heading towards with your question. Kushok Vitas, I appreciate your democracy, but I don't like it. If we follow it, we'll fall only into a meaningless circle, with all present piping in to have their say. Ordinary people can never be so wise to know all pitfalls. You cannot bestow it with power that grants them democracy. Sometimes, it's necessary to make a clear and quick decision. It may not be the best decision, but it's a decision! And not meditate over the injustice in the world all day long."

"I propose," the elder librarian, Akhum said, "we confirm that which is already the case – the fact that Sonam is our commander – by means of a vote. We need a unanimous vote, saying he has an undoubted mandate to lead the defence. Then, there will no longer be a discussion over what is and isn't to be done, or any such similar nonsense," he glared intently at Lao. "Well, although the honourable Lama Rinpoche doesn't like democracy, I want to ask you all democratically, whether anyone objects to Sonam being commander? And if so, why?"

No one raised their hand, no one had any objection. "You have our complete and utter trust," librarian Akhum nodded.

"Ok, then, let's get to work," Sonam concluded the meeting.

And the kashag adjourned on the spot.

– – –

"I understand you, Kushok Vitas," the Lama took Vitas to the side. "Kromen is not a pure soul, but we don't have to deal with that now."

"I have no proof, but I have a feeling that he's involved with everything happening here now. He could be the one who betrayed the whole lamasery. We've known each other for a long time and…"

"I know, I know, Kushok Vitas. He did what he did, but how should we know if it was right or wrong? The level of good can only be measured by the same level of evil. Let

Buddha or your Jesus decide the guilt and punishment. Did you not say that the ways of the Lord are unpredictable?"

Vitas' indignation was dulled, but the same couldn't have been said for his curiosity. He wanted to get to the root of the problem, and for this reason he continued searching for Kromen all around the lamasery. In vain.

Sonam gathered his entire militia. Akhum informed everyone of the unanimous mandate, which made Sonam the supreme commander of the lamasery. "No one shall dispute his commands," he warned everyone and handed over more work to him.

Sonam assigned guards both for the only access route from which the tanks could arrive, as well as for all other routes, though they crossed tougher and rockier terrain, fit no less for infantrymen to traverse. A bushel of grenades had been prepared at his hand before the entry to the top floor of the lamasery, their potential detonation causing the rocks from the surrounding mountains to fall and block the access road, preventing tanks from getting in. He declared peace until three o'clock in the morning. The counter-attack was to commence one hour later.

– – –

Major Li C'cheng sent four groups of two scouts out at midnight for reconnaissance of the lamasery and to explore all routes of access, all but for the only wide road, the one most suitable for tanks, anticipating that this road would be well guarded.

Eight Chinese scouts ascended the rocky cliffs. Two groups of scouts had to secure themselves with ropes in order to overcome the steep slopes and overhangs. One group of scouts even gave up soon afterwards. The cliff in front of them was beyond their abilities.

"Did you not think of trying another route? Or joining another group? The order was clear," Li sobbed with anger, clutching the stock of his rifle. He had an urge to pull it out and shoot both the culprits. He certainly would have done, if not for the noise it would have caused. He didn't want to warn the inhabitants of the lamasery that something is going on. "You'll be on the frontlines," he said, grinding his teeth, unconcerned with them any further. The rest of the battalion were resting. The command was: Rest until five o'clock in the morning. Then, the attack would commence. Li wanted to ensure that the tanks had safe access along the main road beforehand – to guard it with his soldiers, but not until his scouts returned and clarified the opponent's position and the accessibility of the terrain.

– – –

The lamasery was awakened by a silent alarm that was tripped early, right before two o'clock in the morning. The commotion of the monks running around the lamasery was as calm as any other evening on the Jadhang, reminiscent of the hustle and bustle of a big city. The guards had captured one group of Chinese scouts. They were harsh on them by most standards, puncturing one's throat with an arrow and seriously injuring the other – the arrow had hit him just below the right collar bone. He was dragged in front of the chorten, where the entire Jadhang army gathered in a second.

"How many of you are there, what technology do you have, what's your strategy…?" Sonam bombarded the prisoner with questions, throwing him around mercilessly back and forth until the Chinese soldier sobbed in pain.

"Six tanks, mortars, about fifty soldiers, but I don't know anything. Nothing. The Major doesn't tell us anything, he only gives us orders. Please don't kill me…"

"And why should we spare you? Is there any reason?"

"Because I want to live!"

"Right you are man, but so do we. So, tell us one more thing, if you deserve to live."

"There are three more groups of scouts coming to explore the terrain here," the soldier spat.

"Explore the terrain, you say," Sonam glared into his eyes inquisitively. "Six more soldiers. Well, fine then, let's see. Lock him in the lamasery," he ordered two monks, soon commanding a slow descent to the enemy camp.

It was a clear, starry night. So much starlight fell on the Jadhang, it was possible to read by the glow. This dampened Sonam's plans somewhat. He knew that their biggest strength was their knowledge of the terrain and that darkness was their ally.

They descended carefully. Sonam ordered no rifle fire, with which in any case, only a few of their number were properly trained. His main concern was not to alarm the enemy below. Over seventy Buddhist warriors advanced from five locations, where it was possible to descend. But the terrain had to be crossed among stones and descended using guide-ropes. It didn't take long before they ran into another group of Chinese soldiers. One was just helping the other, hanging onto a rope, to get up onto the rock overhang, so he wasn't paying attention to his surroundings. Several lightning-fast arrows ended their attempt in an instant.

There were – as they had mistakenly thought – two more groups of scouts left. They had no idea that one group had already given up. They continued in their descent.

What followed was probably inevitable. Perhaps the slackest duo, and the slowest in their descent, rested behind the rock ledge on the overhang that they had scrambled so hard to get on at first. Since both soldiers were resting in silence, motionless, they slipped the eyes of the descending warriors. They clutched their unsecured machineguns tightly in their hands, their eyes round with fear, glowering up at the stars. They hardly moved as the shadows shot by them. It didn't take long before one of the descending warriors made way for the faster descending warrior that was above him. He went over to the overhang and before he realised who was standing in front of him, around forty shots fired from two submachine-guns pierced his body. Both of the Chinese soldiers held their fingers over the trigger so firmly that their index fingers hurt. Still staring in horror at the pierced corpse in front of them, still aiming their weapons in its direction. Shots went off far and wide with incredible penetration, given the local altitude. The group were now expecting a huge uproar, but everything remained silent. The blunt thuds of stones, of axes and of knives jabbed the bodies of the helpless scouts, who were in such a trance that they couldn't even reload their magazines. No one from the camps had heard them. There was silence again and all assumed that, this time, it would be unbroken.

Major Li looked suspiciously at the flesh of wrinkled stone before him. The rock overhangs formed so many shadows that not even the stars could help the eyes perceive the multitude of surfaces. Li felt there were hundreds of enemies swarming around him. He ordered a state of alert. Tank drivers clambered into their tanks, mortar-men primed to their mortars, infantrymen first hiding behind the heavy weapons, or behind any other ridges in the field. There was silence. Tense, emotion-filled silence. The Chinese soldiers, led by Major Li C'cheng, expected the Buddhist warriors to be sitting on the vertical rocks, scattered like birds, prepared to spare no one. The monks knew that the large-headed shadows were prepared to wreak destruction. In the monastery, no one was sleeping. Everyone was waiting to see who would begin… Silence. Even the breathing of the enemy could be heard. Every stone that fell unprovoked or was knocked by the foot of a monk moved its centre of gravity elsewhere. Everything remained that way for a long time. Endless absence of noise whipped at the nerves.

And then without hesitation it sounded. From fortissimo to mezzo-piano. Sliding tones that skipped, swept, trembled and soared as if someone in front of the soldiers had been skipping stones on the monstrous rock amid the swirling shadows. Free – perhaps improvised – play by Rmi-lam above. The tones evaded, moving quickly from rock to rock, abruptly slowing down, swaying like a branch from side to side, vibrating across the rocks, clapping like thousands of drunken, dancing birds. The rain of moist dew sprinkled the eyes of helpless soldiers running across the rock, perhaps in an attempt to catch the sounds.

Li stared vacantly in disbelief. He couldn't understand. It was beyond his comprehension. He had to cover his ears with his hands, as if it were unbearable, an inaudible scream, close to ultrasound. It rang dark blows with the whole accompanying army of glittering beads penetrating his hands, forcing him to kneel and bow his head to the ground. The soldiers continued to watch the stationary rock as if hypnotised, peeping out of their tanks and listening…

WanYung scrambled out of the tank. He left his machine-gun and wandered towards the rock, stunned. Up towards the lamasery. Despite the occasional slip of the fingers and still a bit off key, he understood that he had met his duet partner. The technique wasn't exceptional, but the mentality was far beyond his imagination. He called out as if in a fit of rage: "Schubert's *F-Minor* is waiting! She is here for us!"

He had forgotten he was a soldier. A machine-gunner. That his duty was to exterminate all the revanchists. He stepped out onto the path with the final sliding tone of the piano. But these final tones woke Major Li, too. Overcoming this unknown force that had deprived him of his abilities, he got to his feet. Full of resentment, as if wanting to exact his anger on an innocent worm, blaming it for all human sin, as well as for his newly acknowledged weakness. He raised his hand, straightened his index finger at WanYung, who was disappearing out of sight towards the lamasery and bellowed: "A deserter! Fire!"

Fire and thunder. WanYung was dead even before he hit the ground. At the same time, however, the Chinese soldiers had revealed their positions by shooting him down. The monks opened fire on the rock upon Sonam's command. At this point, a lack of firearms seemed rather advantageous. Shots always reveal the place where the trigger was pressed. A bow and arrow shot, then, is more effective, triggering no reaction. But in darkness not all arrows find their target. The Chinese forces fired, recklessly shooting at the rocks before them. The mortars were virtually useless, the almost vertical cliff-face making it very difficult to aim. The tanks fired one cannon after another. Despite the poor visibility, many monks were killed. Sonam ordered five monks to attack as soon as the firing began. Every man carried a wreath of interconnected grenades. Half-crouched, they ran towards the tanks. Three of them managed to dodge the shots to get close enough. Three tremendous explosions lit up the sky. Two tanks burned like torches. The mass of rising smoke could only be sensed, hardly seen. The third tank survived the attack unscathed. The wreath of grenades slid helplessly across the armour and the blast bent it slightly, leaving a mark on its surface, dark as tar.

Maddened with rage, the Major ordered a retreat. He knew he had to withdraw if he didn't want to incur serious losses. But he didn't care how many men he'd lose. He cared that he had to win.

The battalion retreated some 300 metres, no more. It was enough to make both sides cease fire. Li allowed the troops to quickly recuperate and update themselves to the situation. In addition to two tanks, he had lost one mortar and fifteen soldiers. And the gains? None. He felt helpless. What hurt him the most, however, wasn't the loss of firepower, or of his unit, but the strange force that seemed to radiate far overhead. It was something indescribable. It couldn't be analysed, it couldn't be answered, and no handbook could offer an explanation. And then, there was the fear of the unknown. An inconspicuous but creeping, intrusive, but intoxicating, crippling but enveloping, suffocating but cold and greedy fear. A single blast. It arrives.

Where is this damned Kromen? He'd helped him, guided him and then disappeared from all knowledge. Perhaps the battery of his walkie-talkie had died. But they had never agreed on any further cooperation. It was somehow a given fact that there would be nothing left to deal with. The Jadhang would simply be wiped out, and Kromen would take a share of the gold – this was not Li's worry. With no intentions of leaving Kromen alive either, he hardly let this thought bother him. Why should he care about some European, concerned with cash? Even his opponents were more valuable, caring at least about something, obvious nonsense it may or may not be. But now he needed him here. He needed information. Where is this damned Kromen?

– – –

The warriors from the lamasery retreated. The Chinese were out of range and they couldn't go out into the open terrain. That would mean suicide. Once Sonam positioned his guards, he made a headcount. Nine dead and twelve wounded but combat-ready. He had to add the losses during the first attack to this, however, when the Chinese had first entered the Jadhang territory. Moreover, he could hardly leave out the material damage, which was considerable. Water and food supplies were low. And they were surrounded. Cut off from all resources. Although the enemy were perhaps demoralised, they were still strong and ready to fight. But the first round could be deemed a victory. The inhabitants of the Jadhang could smile, their eyes aglow… Moments of great revolution, great emotion, calling people to touch one another, to treat each other politely, to do favours for one another, to respect one another. They knew they were a part of an important moment that transcended their own lives.

Sonam decided when the guards would change and ordered everyone off-duty to sleep. Rest is necessary. Dawn would break in a few hours and this would decide the future of the Jadhang. Nonetheless, Sonam, the Lama, and several others felt the future of the Jadhang had already been decided, defeat or victory left aside.

10.
Day Break

An explosion. Followed by gunfire. Not even half an hour after both sides withdrew from the battlefield. This was something of a shock. No one had expected such a fast reaction. But Li C'cheng had to make such quick decisions. A mixture of fury, helplessness and incredible ambition heated him to such a degree he had no choice but to conclude: victory or death. There would be nothing in between. And at this moment, when no one could expect it. Like a bull determined to charge against a mountain. And then, he ran full speed ahead, his whole body clenched, eyes partly closed. There would be no turning back. The only way ahead was straight. A red-eyed bull has to be able to break through a rock, take off, soar above the surface and dart his horns into his enemy. This is how Major Li C'cheng chose to proceed.

And strangely enough, he began quite well. At first, he capitalised on the element of surprise. The infantrymen moved hastily forward and it wasn't until they heard the first shot that it became clear to everyone far and wide, that he was clearing the access road for the tanks. The groups armed with mortars always advanced about sixty-five feet, laid out their weapons, then lobbed several shells at the road ahead, thereby clearing the way before advancing forward. The armoured cannibals moved on further and further, step by step, the iron rumbling, and the sounds of moans, howling and screeching audible all around. Intractable. Stubborn. Using a few shells, the artillerymen successfully eliminated the guardian monks, whose duty it had been to detonate the rock, thereby disabling access for the tanks into the lamasery. The attack caught them by such surprise, that they had no chance to trigger the device. The tanks roared and crept. Before the warriors could vacate the lamasery, the barrel of the first tank was already visible from around the bend, behind which the courtyard with the chorten opened up and the drilled rock stood there in all its grandeur and inconspicuous modesty – the monastery. It was just before five o'clock in the morning. The first stars were just falling asleep.

– – –

Kromen was utterly undisturbed by the shots and explosions. He was already certain of the result. He had no illusions regarding Major Li C'cheng. As such, he maintained his guard, not allowing the Major into his personal space. Yes, he had assisted him, but he would go no further. While they were there fighting like roosters over one useless frog, he tossed away his two-way radio and calmly began moving his valuable possessions into his secret cave in a rock under the lamasery, right above the pastures. A place reachable along a narrow path, the location of his infamous execution footbridge. This was the site of his own relocation and that of all the treasure he had acquired. Bars of gold and a few pieces of the lamasery fortune that he had managed to obtain from Lama Thorpe Tenzin. The key thing was not to deposit his reclamations anywhere near the peak of the lamasery, the battalion of invading troops likely to forcibly appropriate them, or otherwise dispose of what remained.

Chinese soldiers would soon enough be seizing control. Therefore, he was grateful for the moonlight. After all, he knew the route with his eyes closed. He lay prone in his hiding spot like an exhausted dog, as if he had been the one in combat, instead of those deluded monks or illiterate Chinese troops. But he was satisfied. He was ecstatic in the midst of his winnings. He had to laugh. The best-case scenario would be that each brutal side exterminated the other. Well, when any two fight, the onlooker can only watch in amusement. After that, only the means of transportation would remain to be dealt with. This would clearly be quite the technical and organisational matter, and accordingly joyful. As the conclusion and confirmation of his success, this final step was always the most enjoyable.

He was exhausted, but there were only two or three batches of valuable cargo left that he had temporarily stored down by the foot of the mountain, forming a boundary wall to the sweeping pastures. Neither the Chinese soldiers nor the monks could see him here. Now, only the dead animals and the corpses of a few monks could observe him out in the pastures. But soon, dawn will break. He must hurry, get to it!

Kromen got to his feet, seized the sack from which he had previously emptied several of his acquisitions and descended along the narrow execution footbridge. Though he felt the way ahead should've been safe, he scanned around attentively. One can *never* be careful enough. There were still a few gold statues, a gilded Buddha, several Bodhisattva Avalokiteshvara statuettes, some painted thangka canvases displaying deities of joy and fury, as well as other tableaus, candleholders and many other objects lying hidden behind a rock. With great impetuosity he shoved everything and anything that he could into the sack and set off ahead. He knew that no one would find this place without him. He could come back here whenever he liked. It would be his fortune alone. The sack was heavy, weighing a good thirty-five pounds. Step by step by step. No choice of surrender. He would reach safety, soon enough. He trod stubbornly, hardly noticing the infamous execution footbridge beneath his feet. Gunfire had damaged its mechanism. After two more steps, it came loose.

The world turned under Kromen's feet. He released the sack, which rolled and crashed down at the foot of the mountain with a sonorous roar. Helplessly, Kromen waved his hands. A knifing pain shot up his leg as he grasped hold at the final moment. But he hung powerlessly, his ankle aching. The end? Here? Like this? Kromen was exhausted and injured. He had no idea how to get over the overhang that he clung onto with his last ounce of strength. His fingers were weak. He started laughing. He giggled like a madman, until his laughter echoed all around. He had realised the monstrosity of the fact that he was dying in the same spot where he had formerly killed so many goats and sheep. Manic, he bellowed out into the countryside: "Whoever digs another man's grave, the pitcher goes so often to the well…" His fearful and penetrating laughter had to arouse a feeling of terror in every living thing. Fortunately for them, no one heard him. Neither the dead monks nor the living Chinese soldiers down in the fields below could hear him, having long abandoned the lower part of the pastures, ascending up to the epicentre of the battlefield. Kromen's chuckling, accompanied by the gunfire and the gasping explosions, was his final blessing over a landscape of the dead at the foot of Mount Jadhang.

– – –

The first tank made its way into the courtyard, making room on the narrow path for the other tank, which drove in alongside the first one. And others followed. The Chinese troops intensified their firepower. The circle of life on the upper left-hand side of the mountain shattered like a lit match. The other one trembled under a less precise impact and slid off its handle. It began rolling slowly down, as if deciding what to do. It rattled and hit the rocks until it landed on the hard ground of the courtyard. It sunk a little in the stone, then, bounced back trampoline-like and cracked, falling apart into individual boards. Brick and concrete structures, mounted to the openings in the rock, were scattered all around like the multicoloured prayer flags that withered and smouldered and burned... Smoke billowed from several openings into the lamasery. The library was burning down. In the distance of the dawn, that fiery spherical witness rose, allowing no one the liberty of looking away, or of avoiding the reality of their deeds, of their intentions, and the reality of the crumbling legacy on Mount Jadhang.

Anyone who could and had able hands, fired at the Chinese soldiers. With rifles, with bows. The Chinese troops had ceased fire. All of them were dead or injured, incapable of battle. In cover behind a rock wall, the final mortar fired a crescent-bound shell that burst and showered the lamasery with deadly shards from above. But it was the four tanks that caused the greatest damage. They sowed death itself. The lamasery no longer resembled its former self. Denotations and blast-waves shuddered within, an annihilation of all in sight.

Vitas hid behind a raised rock, where the trail led to Sonam's former hermitage. He made sure to always load his rifle behind the large rock, then only the barrel and a bit of his head peered out, before aiming and taking fire. Eight of the ten shots hit the bull's eye. But now there were only tanks left and no rifle powerful enough to stop them. No more grenades remained. He tried hitting the holes in the tanks, but he didn't even know if he had ever hit it. No effect.

The shadow of the distant peak still prevented the fiery witness of the sun from seeing the full force of hell raised by human hands. Rumbling everywhere was gunfire and the crushing of stones.

But the dawn broke and the peak allowed the sun to bear witness on the carnage below. The first rays touched the barrel of the Lee–Enfield rifle Vitas held in his hands, then drumming into the armour, slowly dispersing further, as if someone were taking a large tarpaulin from over the whole lamasery. Everything was flooded with noise, the rising sun radiating above, as if all present, the living and the dead, were to ascend into higher, divine spheres.

Silence. Everything abruptly fell silent. It was like a blow to the head, stunning anyone left alive. What had happened? What greater tragedy could come? Wide-eyed and open-mouthed tank drivers peeked out of the cabins of their armoured destroyers; mortars, concealed by the rocks, clambered out to see it all. Vitas left his hiding place and dropped his rifle.

A grown woman stood on a small platform that used to be a short path onto individual floors among the different openings of the monastery's corridors, but amid the ruins of the lamasery, it was now no more than a rock, gnawed by artillery fire, with smoke surging from the holes like a chimney. Rmi-lam. The long and variegated blue sari she wore billowed in the wind. Its colour lay somewhere between moonlight and ocean blue, though patterned – variously overlapping according to the sunrays, almost dissolving into brownish and off-green shades. Large, sparkling hoops dangled in her ears, intertwined like snakes. From the distance, it was only possible to assume they were glistening stones at the end of the intertwined snake bodies. It was difficult to determine the colour. Perhaps dark blue turning green. Her hair was as shiny as obsidian and pulled back, where it flowed freely above her shoulder blades. Her hands were outstretched as if appealing to some unknown God.

Rmi-lam took a deep breath. She seemed to expand. Vitas watched her helplessly, in complete awe. Rmi-lam was well aware of every piece of her body, of her own axis and had become unconquerable, her eyes fixed on something very specific but very far away... "I am in your hands," she said slowly into the silence. "We are all in your hands. Please, I beg you. Shield us from our mistakes. Have mercy on us." Then her eyes narrowed from the infinite distance and gazed down at the monastery courtyard. Her arms dropped to the sides of her body. Her right hand rose in a fleeting gesture with the blowing sari sleeve. "Please, come in, you are welcome. I am your Empress. I am your Rmi-lam. I am your dream." Then her arm descended again. Her wide eyes searched into the distance, gradually, as if reaching out to any living soul.

Major Li C'cheng stared at her in astonishment for some time, dividing one half of the formation of tanks and the other half covering the opening, as if Rmi-lam's words were gunshots and he had to take cover. He glared at her with rage in his eyes. Then he looked around at all his soldiers, who were looking at Rmi-lam as if she were a god. He quickly exited the tank and started running in between the tanks that were spread out in front of the lamasery, around the half-destroyed chorten. "Shoot! Fuck, why aren't you shooting? What are you afraid of? Shoot, you bastards!" Li was furious, spitting with rage. Helpless, he pulled out a pistol and aimed it at one of the tank commanders, who could only stare at Rmi-lam in awe.

"Shoot! Shoot!" Li aimed at him and pulled the trigger. The commander of the vehicle lifelessly slid down into the tank. Li turned to another soldier. "Shoot!" He took aim with his pistol but was afraid to fire. There'd barely be anyone left to fight. Li turned to Rmi-lam with hatred, aimed and emptied the pistol in her direction. The projectiles landed at a safe distance around her. He wasn't able to hit anything at such a distance and with such an anger-trembling hand.

Li scurried onto one of the tanks, dragged one of the soldiers from the tower opening, seated himself by the range-finder and fired quickly. The shell darted by Rmi-lam into one of the openings, the entrance to the lamasery, exploding within and leaving Rmi-lam unharmed by the shrapnel. But the pressure wave knocked her off her feet. Li wanted to load the cannon again, but there was no automatic loading system. So, the only choice was to insert a new shell into it himself. This delay gave Vitas enough time to grab Rmi-lam by the waist from behind his hiding place, his hands clasped around her like a clothespin – she was as light as a feather – and to hide with her up on a cliff above the lamasery. He dragged her as far away as possible.

Li shot blindly into any place he thought they might be hidden. But the long interval between loading and shooting, not to mention the expansive terrain where Vitas and Rmi-lam could take cover, partially protected her. It was clear, however, that this wouldn't last for long. They were both holding on to one another, shaking. One way or another, it must all come to an end! The other tank-drivers, gradually recovering from the shock, continued to fire at the lamasery to Li's delight. They aimed into its corridors, so the surrounding rocks shook following each detonation heard within.

Vitas didn't know where to hide anymore. All around him flew shrapnel as he held Rmi-lam beneath him, protecting her on the ground. He was running out of options and soon it would be too late. There was no sense in running, the average range of a tank-cannon being more than two miles. And with precision. The only thing they could do was hide behind rocky protrusions, in the rugged terrain...

The air crackled and wheezed. The tank-tower jumped from its fixture. Of Li's body, nothing remained. The whizzing sound was heard three more times simultaneously and all at once no functional tanks remained. Several machine-gun salvos took care of the remaining living Chinese soldiers, including the mortar-operators. Only then, in silence, without explosions or gunfire, was an unpleasant and rhythmic knocking heard; for Vitas and Rmi-lam, this was the sound of paradise. Three British military helicopters, SAS airborne units, swept over the courtyard of the lamasery, littered with the dead and dying soldiers and monks. They briefly scanned the terrain, then, they flew in a larger radius farther away from the courtyard and disappeared around the crook of the rock. From below, from the places of the lower Jadhang, where spare transporters and tankers remained, massive detonations and machine gun salvos were heard.

"So let's continue in our studies," Vitas said, a healthy dose of irony in his voice; astonished, he was still tense with fear, but finally broke into a smile. "In ancient Greek theatre this was referred to as: deus ex machina, meaning *God from the machine.*"

"Yes, deus ex machina," Rmi-lam exhaled with a faint smirk, still firmly gripping Vitas' hand. Emotion and tension ran taut. It was hardly possible that it was all over. They precariously got to their feet and hobbled towards the ruins of the lamasery in fumbling strides.

They had made only a few steps before all three attack-helicopters circled back around towards the courtyard of the lamasery, slowly descending to the ground. The multicoloured prayer flags fluttered furiously all around. And the rumbling of the rotors drowned out the once-heard gasps of the armoured destroyers, now smouldering from their jagged insides.

At that moment, some ten British SAS paratroopers jumped dismounted from the helicopters. Six of them assumed a defensive stance, wary of any surviving targets and any potential assailants, two soldiers inspecting the corpses scattered about, while two others entered the smoking lamasery. One soldier, apparently an officer, scanned ahead thoroughly, wandering quite certainly towards Vitas and Rmi-lam. He stopped some fifteen feet away.

The soldier saluted. "Captain James Laver. It's an honour to make the acquaintance of Your Highness, Rmi-lam."

"Yes, soldier," Rmi-lam said quietly but confidently, looking intently into his eyes. Vitas suddenly realised that her facial features were different, harder and more resistant. Here stood an unassailable Empress, changed unbelievably from a once delicate and temperamental little girl.

"I've got a message here for you from Her Royal Majesty Queen Elizabeth the Second."

"Yes, soldier."

"Primarily, she begs your forgiveness for her most belated response. It took quite some time for your letter to reach Her Majesty and before it – if you'll please excuse me the indiscretion, Your Highness – well it took some time before it could be verified. That is, before it could be quite – comprehended – that you truly are the legitimate successor to the most high and glorious Imperial Chinese throne."

The Captain paused for a moment, searching inquisitively into Rmi-lam's eyes, wanting to continue. He had even taken a breath, when one of the soldiers who had been inspecting the corpses in the courtyard of the lamasery, rapidly approached.

"'Scuse me, Sir, we 'ave a report."

"Go ahead," the Captain agreed with cold impatience, still looking intently into Rmi-lam's eyes.

"There're no survivors down in the courtyard. Of either designation."

"At ease!" commanded the Captain sharply and continued with Rmi-lam, who could only gulp lightly after hearing the harsh news. "Her Royal Majesty expresses her deepest possible regret and sympathy for the massacre facilitated by her sovereign British Armed Forces in Tibet at the beginning of the twentieth century."

Rmi-lam frowned and wanted to interrupt the Captain's speech. But he raised his hand to avoid being interrupted, immediately seeming to apologise with a light bow. "I do beg your pardon, your Most Illustrious Highness, but please, do allow me the privilege of delivering the entire message." But this would not be the case. Another soldier, formerly patrolling the inner remains of the lamasery, bounded towards him.

"Sir, area status report."

"Make it quick," growled the Captain.

"Counts confirmed, no survivors within the structure."

"At ease," the Captain growled again. There was a silence in which he plainly glared into Rmi-lam's eyes, nothing interrupting their contact, her eyes only reddening, glazed with tears.

"Her Royal Majesty the Queen would like to take the opportunity to beg forgiveness for the indifference of the British Empire during the invasion of Tibet in the latter part of the last century. At the same time, she implores your understanding. She wouldn't want you – Your Illustrious Highness – she wouldn't want you to think that the question of her indifference was the result of any international treaty, what with India's God-given independence and the then-prevailing national aversion towards British involvement in East Asian matters. Nevertheless, Her Royal Majesty certainly admits that a more than significant part of the blame rests on the shoulders of the British Empire in failing to halt the proceeding massacres, or to intervene in the dreadful bloodshed committed in Tibet – and she might add, that is still being committed to this day – by the People's Republic of China in the years that have followed. Her Majesty also apologises for Britain's total failure to collaborate with the United Nations towards the peaceful resolution of Tibetan issues."

The Captain paused for a moment once again, but soon continued slowly. "Her Royal Majesty Queen Elizabeth the Second hereby declares – in the most solemn sympathy – to you – Your Most Illustrious Highness – that as of this moment forth, the United Kingdom of Great Britain and all her sovereign commonwealth shall respect the independence of the Tibetan…"

"But why are you telling me all this, soldier? Why don't you tell His Holiness the Dalai Lama? The Panchen Lamas? The Lamas, the Buddhists, the Tibetans?" Rmi-lam could no longer hold back. "You know who I am. The Empress of China, but I have almost nothing to do with Tibet. Almost…" repeated Rmi-lam, glancing around sadly, "so why are you telling me this?"

It was impossible to avert the eyes from the Captain's nervous fidgeting. "Yes, but of course, I am aware…" he looked back at the lamasery uncertainly. "I – in essence, well I – I don't know who to tell. It's quite absurd, as I understand, to express my – I mean Her Majesty's – apologies to the Chinese Empress for not preventing the Chinese from decimating Tibet… But what's important," the Captain grabbed on to the safety-ring of his flight-jacket, "is that the British Sovereign now recognises Her Illustrious Highness

Rmi-lam as the Chinese Empress, which must certainly speak for itself."

Each glared into the other's eyes. Rmi-lam slightly raised her eyebrows, unable to accept the words she received.

"Tip-top, everything is A-OK, it's just a pity as ever there was that you didn't arrive a few hours earlier. What now, soldier?"

"Captain," an SAS soldier enjoined the Captain again, yelling from a distance. "There's one survivor here. He's injured but he'll make it."

"Who is it? A Chinese or a Tibetan?"

"Neither. European." A moment's pause. The soldier bent over the wounded figure, calling out: "Some Kromen or other. Says his name's Kromen," he bellowed across the distance.

Rmi-lam and Vitas looked at each other quickly in horror. What did he want here? And what should they tell the Captain? That he's a traitor? They flew here on a supposed rescue-mission and now they discover there are hyenas amongst them?

"Bring him here!" the Captain snapped to the soldiers. "Look sharp!" Then he turned to Vitas. "I have to explain one more thing to you," he seemed embarrassed, as if not knowing what to say. "It's a bit – difficult – but as I'm sure you're no doubt aware, I stand on disputed land here, officially belonging to the state of India, although sought for claim by China. We officially consider it Indian Territory, but I have strict orders not to provoke the Chinese authorities. For this reason, we must vacate this territory as soon as possible." James Laver stared questioningly into the eyes of Vitas and Rmi-lam, who patiently awaited his next announcement.

"That's probably not a major problem, is it?" inquired Vitas.

"Certainly not…"

"Welcome, you got here just in time." Although tired, Kromen's voice was cheerful, the soldiers dragged him towards them. He was rugged, dirty, and clearly exhausted, his ankle was swollen and a machine-gun he had seized from a Chinese soldier was swung loosely over his shoulder. He knelt on the ground, giving the impression of an experienced partisan, a veteran who had spent his life fighting for justice. "Just in time, no doubt. We fought as hard as we could. But if it weren't for you, they would have got us. We owe you one."

The Captain smiled; Kromen was offering him a simple topic, black and white. A topic that made it clear who was the villain, what was the right thing to do and that nothing was complicated by confusing ethical questions. He was a soldier. For that reason, he too, was accustomed to dealing with matters in black and white. "Well, just let me finish," turning to Rmi-lam and Vitas, the Captain laid the whole problem out, seeming to want nothing more than to be done with the issue as a whole. "We're incognito here. That means that – according to official reports – there were no helicopters present. We're glad that we helped you, but that's the end of that. We cannot load you aboard a helicopter and transport you to India – this is conflicted soil. Perhaps just you," he pointed his finger at Vitas and then turned to Kromen, "or you! Especially you, what with the injuries you've sustained. But since you – Your Highness – you're Empress of Imperial China, we cannot assist you further without possible incidents on this soil. However, I am aware that the border isn't far from here – about a day long trip. You will be accepted there on Indian soil with all the respect and honour you deserve."

"I appreciate your nobility," exclaimed Kromen. "I will gladly accept your offer. I really wouldn't know how to get

out of here with my injuries. I'd be completely helpless..." he
winked at Vitas the moment the Captain stopped listening.

"There's no way I'm abandoning her," said Vitas abruptly.

"Of course, I'd assumed so," nodded the Captain, not at
all surprised. "We must vacate the area as soon as possible.
But rest assured, we will be waiting for you at the border.
Your only choice is to travel along the Jadhang, past the last,
nameless village. Everything that lies beyond that point is
one-hundred-percent Indian land..."

"I see, so this must be fifty-percent Indian," Vitas commented sarcastically.

"Please, do try to understand. I have orders to fulfil.
There's no more I can do in the given circumstances. It's
only about twenty-five miles..."

"Don't worry about it," Kromen relieved the Captain of
his humiliating position as the soldiers lifted him into the
helicopter. "We're grateful to you for saving our lives. And
every SENSIBLE PERSON," Kromen emphasised "must
understand that no international incident is desirable.
After all, once the intel leaks regarding our harbouring an
Empress here, some situation is sure to escalate, but at that
point the cards won't be in our hands, right?"

"I'm pleased to hear the matter resolved," the Captain
concluded the discussion in typically terse military style,
and with the gesture of his upturned hand, index finger outstretched, he instructed his troops to embark the helicopter.

"When are you leaving the Jadhang?" Kromen howled
at Rmi-lam and Vitas, as they packed him into the aircraft.

"Tomorrow morning. There's no use today. We have to
get ready for the trip..."

"Great, we'll prepare such a welcome-party at the border
tomorrow evening that the whole world will be in awe.
Look forward to it. We'll make headline news worldwide.
We'll be the last of the Mohicans, the ones that..." no more

could be heard through the thunder of the propeller-blades, which drummed to a tune of their own.

The helicopters took off in an instant. Vitas and Rmi-lam were alone. They sat down, holding each other's hands and Rmi-lam rested her head on his shoulders. Everything was razed to the ground; corpses, blackness, the dead armoured destroyers raising their heads somewhere out towards the unknown… and silence. Falcons and vultures soon broke in, as if they had sensed an unprecedented feast awaiting them. They sat like this for a long time, gazing out thoughtfully into space, until the first vultures descended upon the corpse.

They got up and went to finish Aviel's grave. They covered it with coarse and stony soil and laid heavy stones on top. Vitas even rolled over a large boulder fit for a tombstone. Everything took place without a word. Neither Vitas nor Rmi-lam needed to speak. They only felt the need to be close to one another. Vitas tried engraving some words into the tombstone. But once he realised how difficult it was to carve a single letter, he shortened it significantly.

Aviel – * 5722, † 5774.

Then they set off for the pastures, where they found five yaks and three horses. The only animals that had survived. They fenced them off and headed out to the lower, industrial part of the lamasery, where they prepared a sack of dried meat, vegetables, a tent and some tools for their trip.

After much hesitation, Vitas mustered up the courage to enter the lamasery. Rmi-lam, however, remained waiting outside. An argument broke out between them, as she wanted to bid farewell to her chamber. He reconciled with her only after promising to bring her all her mezuzahs and her other personal belongings. He knew he also had to pack extra clothes. He climbed through the bombarded corridors, stepping around his dead friends, scrambling over the charred remains of a once-refined piano, from which the strings contorted in all directions like a fence of barbed-wire come alive, stretching its existence into new dimensions. The library had completely burned down. Some of the corridors were no longer accessible. But he grabbed the prayer wheel that rolled around the dusty floor, still completely functional. He even found the armless clown, which had long been absent of its valuable content. And he was able to take the Bible and the rosary from his former shrine, or rather the torso that remained. This probably means something too, Vitas thought sadly.

They gathered their belongings on their way down to the animals so that they wouldn't have to do much in the morning. It was a huge pile, as if they were preparing for a life-long pilgrimage, not a one-day trip, with luxurious hotels awaiting them afterwards. But not a word was spoken.

They wandered the lamasery long into the night. According to Buddhist tradition, they circled the ruins of the chorten several times, the last time in a clockwise direction, then they walked up the rock, where they called out together: "I am in your hands…" for a final word.

They slept outside, under a blanket, next to each other, looking up at the stars. They both knew they would never return again. Never. Not in Cheb, he grinned, in the old spirit of Vitas. There, they have no idea what Chebness is. This is the real, dense Chebness. The kind that makes your stomach clench. Our eyes must be closed, or the strength we need may never be mustered to step into the emptiness and the night, just to exist.

11.

Indian Chapati Pancakes and Confetti

Kromen had a severe ankle sprain. Although a very painful matter that required an ankle cast, it didn't stop him from arranging a grand affair on the real, one hundred percent Indian side of the border with Tibet. Right beside the Jadhang River.

Kromen smelled of fame and fortune. He knew he could make the best of any situation, no matter how twisted. He really had managed to contact the most important media and press agencies – BBC, CNN, Reuters and so on. Once her Majesty's Press Office verified at least the general information, this quickly became report Number One. But everyone respected the clear request for confidentiality. No announcement could be forwarded until everything was complete. The most important thing was to wait until the Chinese Empress was safely and entirely on one hundred percent Indian soil. Otherwise, the reaction of the Chinese government could be expected, making it difficult for the media to defend the moral aspect. There was even a relatively non-traditional agreement amongst competitive media stations.

Seven helicopters hovered over a desert, right before the unnamed village on the Jadhang River, in the afternoon the following day. The filmmakers even put together two camera cranes to keep an eye out for the Empress' arrival with absolutely perfect visuals. They obviously couldn't do without the appropriate catering. There were several vehicles with fast food on location. Kromen, himself an agile businessman, initiated several kiosks selling the infamous Indian chapati pancakes, and even sourced hamburgers and chicken delicacies for the film carnivores of Western civilisation. In addition to Indian government officials, the British Ambassador was also an important figure in attendance.

Despite being in great pain, Kromen was the centre of attention. As the first martyr wounded in a fight against the Chinese aggressors, he relayed into a microphone and on camera his heroic tale of perilous conflict, as well as happier tales of the Empress's childhood. With his own modesty, he revealed her hidden wisdom, which had been manifest in her from an early age. He described the strength of her spirit, how she had had every monk in the lamasery eating out of the palms of her hands, while never even knowing who they were raising. Kromen soon realised that it didn't all happen on its own. The wisdom, the magical strength in her eyes, her foresight… He knew this had to be a person who, in her very genes, possessed special abilities, drawing from the wisdom of ancient generations, through to the present. He figured that everything he had gone through in his life, all the adventures he had undergone, were all merely an embarrassing prelude, preparation for what was to come in the form of the spirit of Empress Rmi-lam. "You must experience it for yourself, it's inexplicable. This experience cannot be transferred. Wait until you meet her face to face. Only then will you witness her strength and understand what a real mandate from the Heavens means."

The assistants to the British Ambassador had prepared a red ribbon over the imaginary line of the border to make the arrival of the Empress even more spectacular and more interesting for the camera and for the viewers. For some time this became a matter of controversy after one of the American producers, casually rocking back and forth on a crane-seat by the camera, asked jovially through a chewing jaw, whether they were expecting an Empress, or a racehorse. There was a moment when everyone argued over what was and wasn't tacky, what is and isn't a bit over the top, and where to draw the line of tolerance, until the discussion gradually subsided into total disagreement. Everyone parted ways angrily, but it was an important dilemma nonetheless. Suddenly and inconspicuously, the ribbon disappeared.

Another active filmmaker then came up with the idea that they could put large boulders along the sides of the road, representing the border. Since there was an abundance of rocks all around, they rolled over two large rocks and painted them lime white. Then, one of the filmmaker's technicians wrote the letter I in black, on the white background, signifying India, and T on the other side, representing Tibet. However, he then quickly scratched it out and wrote CN, meaning China, because it had to be clear in the film that China was the true hell from which the Chinese Empress was being rescued.

Even so, this was the subject of immediate protest by representatives of the Indian government. It was impossible to come to terms with the fact that India would acknowledge this territory as the border with China. There was a greater distance. If this is disputed land, then it was certainly not under dispute for India, it being sovereign Indian territory without question, and in those days even somehow acknowledged, or at least neglected by China. So, the technicians rolled the boulders away again with indignant grunts. The chewing film producer, sitting on the crane, only casually stated: "So, why don't we go over there, where the real border is…?" Fortunately, no one heard his remark. Maybe, it didn't even want to be heard.

No one wanted to deal with anything anymore. It was late afternoon and the arrival of the Empress was expected at any moment. The spotlights were being prepared, the reporters were powdering their faces, the cameramen were in position behind their cameras, and Kromen held a VIP spot near the imaginary border, ensuring that he, the hero of the partisan resistance of Tibet, would be the first to greet the Chinese Empress, before even the Indian and British government representatives. The champagne was ready on ice and the confetti was prepared to make its minor explosion.

12.
The Departure

A meagre caravan of five yaks and three horses slowly descended down the narrow path along the river, bearing heavy loads on their backs. There were still many things that Vitas had had to leave behind in the lamasery. Rmi-lam and Vitas didn't say a thing. They had no reason. Both of their worlds ran freely through their minds.

In the morning, Rmi-lam ran over to her place up on the cliffs. Vitas observed her from afar. There stood a young woman with her eyes closed. She wore the clothes for her trip – trousers with a partially exposed cassock, so she looked more like a tomboy. She slowly spread her arms and called out: "I was here! I am in your hands!" Vitas couldn't resist and had to take a mental picture.

– – –

It was already afternoon when the caravan approached the confluence of the Jadhang Gad and Jadhang Rivers. All they had to do was turn right along the Jadhang and arrive in one hundred percent India, some seven miles ahead, where they sensed that the representatives of India, of Great Britain, as well as Kromen, the media and God-only-knew who else, would await them.

They had enough time, so they took a break. Not so much out of fatigue, but rather out of nostalgia. They looked around, as if bidding farewell to the distant mountains out East, deeply inhaling the brisk air... Vitas brewed a cup of tea and Rmi-lam perched on a rock by the small, but clearly wild, Jadhang Gad. She watched the outstretched fingers of her right hand thoughtfully, as they rippled through the freezing water. The water's strong current played with them, making them vibrate as they would when sweeping over the keys of a piano. She heard the off tones and sliding tones of Gershwin's 'Summertime' in the water's strong murmuring. Vitas watched her attentively as he stirred the cup of tea with a spoon.

Rmi-lam was thinking of how fast the water flowing between her fingers, the icy water of the Jadhang Gad, reaches the Jadhang, before her thoughts meandered onto a freer path. And how quickly it would reach holy Bhagirathi, only to be greeted at last by the holiest of the holies, the Ganges River.

The crystal clear, blue-green water, lightly foaming around the stones, formed a glaze of melted wax on the rocks itself. It turned sharply black in her eyes. Dark black, lined with dull, grey-brown foam. She smelled her hands in awe, as the dark liquid dripped from her outstretched fingers. She needed to make the discovery alone. She quickly rose with an expression of understanding and realisation. She turned to Vitas, who was only waiting to see what was to come.

She walked over to him, took a sip of the tea, gesturing to Vitas to hurry up. They poured the valuable tea into a travel kettle and set off. Vitas let Rmi-lam take the lead, leaving all decisions to her. After a steady ride of some several hours, they came to a crossroads. Turning right at this crossroad and strolling for another two hours would bring them to the border with India, where all the pompous preparations awaited them. Rmi-lam looked in that direction, and hardly noticed, her eyes glistened as she smiled and said, more to herself than to Vitas: "Coca-Cola cannot reverse the flow of the holy river."

She turned her horse to the left. To the East. Towards the high Tibetan mountains, towards the winter, the frost and the difficult terrain. Not far from the sacred Mount Kailash, with Lhasa somewhere in the distance and the Forbidden City, the residence of the Chinese emperors, even farther, much, much farther beyond.

Vitas followed her without a word. His dream. Had it been a dream, or a reality? Was it still reality, or had it all become no more than a dream? The feeling of an ending came over him, a moment of indescribable beauty glimpsed within his life. Yet, he was satisfied, now he was content, though he knew that difficult days lay ahead. Where Rmi-lam's mission would lead them and what trials they'd have to suffer before arriving home, were left unasked. He felt only an obligation to make it easier for her. But this called for thinking only minutes and hours ahead, and beyond that, nothing. After wandering for so long, he realised that no matter the wrong he had committed, he was forgiven, that forgiveness from his Eva could now be granted, forgiveness from the butterflies stepped on by accident or design; everyone might forgive him. Free. No longer burdened by metaphysical questions of life's meaning, passing on all responsibility for these questions, for all the actions related to Rmi-lam and to the many other people who should encounter her and who she would raise from the ashes, from the decadence of human slavery. He would save Rmi-lam and therefore a piece of humanity from Kromen, who would never die, though all things must have their counterweights. He passed on the responsibility for the mysterious meaning, the essence of life and the future, to those he had saved. He no longer had to search. Free. "God, thank you for giving me one more chance. I know this is probably my last one…" filled with gratitude, he looked at Rmi-lam.

The dream becomes reality for Vitas, while somewhere behind them, on the borders with India, Kromen and the representatives of the British and Indian governments are asking what it is that they are really waiting for, whether it isn't merely a dream… Whether they're waiting for some Godot of Beckett, some shining star that changed its course, and whether anyone had informed them of what it is they might be waiting for. Had someone tricked them? Who? Kromen? Or were they tricked by their own false imaginations? The hard and tired features of Kormen and the others waiting expresses a misunderstanding over why they had danced around like jesters. The evening wind plays with the napkins and the papers, confirming the past of some unrealised event, an embarrassment, consigned to oblivion. No one would ever boast of this, ever. They had quite simply been tricked.

In the meantime, Vitas, content with his lot, began to gradually vanish, first with Rmi-lam, then their furry yaks until, in a line of dark and insignificant spots, they dispersed somewhere out Far East.

THE END